A Matter Of Privacy

A Matter Of Privacy

❖

H.R. Silvastorm

For Helen
Every once in a rare while,
the world produces two people
who were made for each other
and destined to share a life together.
Such was the case with my dear wife,
Helen Sue, and myself. Tragically,
I lost her to cancer, and it happened
at a time when she was, once again,
transforming into a neoteric butterfly.
Her love, devotion, inspiration
and support moved me to write this novel.
Helen chose not to have a gravestone
or any monument to denote her passing.
As a result, the children opted to get her
a star in the sky. My wish is to dedicate
this book to her memory and to the
unbounded love we shared.
May it always reflect her light.
May it be her eternal marker.

H.R. Silvastorm

" . . . and by doing so, we must realize that we are unleashing a most insidious device upon our citizenry; a device that will forever jeopardize anyone's right to privacy."

Supreme Court Justice, Fred M. Vinson, 1952, Baldwin vs. United States, in his brief referring to the use of wire-taps.

CHAPTER ONE

1969, Altos de España, Spain

Claude Mendosa had a secret spot. A place he went to hide and to be alone. It was located almost fifteen hundred feet up the side Mont Valier, a mountain that overlooked his village. He hurried up the trail muttering to himself and cursing his father for having given him such a painful bruise. It was a very warm day at the end of September and Claude's heart was racing from the heat and the exertion from running up such a steep mountain path. His anger and frustration were causing his temples to throb to the beat of his heart. Soon, he would be in his private place and would take the time to nurse the welt on his cheek.

It seemed to Claude Mendosa that his special place was on the edge of the world. It was merely a ledge, but very special indeed. Jutting out of the southeast side of the mountain, it overlooked a magnificent landscape. Although the ledge was almost fifteen feet long, its width was only two long strides to the outer edge. From there, it was eight hundred feet of swirling air, cool updrafts and an occasional mountain swallow that swooped by in search of an insect on the wing.

The strain that Claude used to run up the mountain had a calming effect. However, his real inner peace came from knowing that this place was all his. Only his. No one knew about it, and he had no intention of ever telling anyone. An aura surrounded it, giving him solace and solitude as one. It was his salvation.

It wasn't long before Claude was off the trail, picking his way through some thick foliage. He was only twenty yards from his goal when he was stung. It was a ring-tailed hornet that got him on the left side of his neck just below his earlobe. Slapping viciously at the area, he saw the hornet as it fell to the ground. Claude stomped his foot on the writhing insect, over and over, grinding it into oblivion.

The swelling and pain were immediate. Worse yet, the sting reinforced the ache on his face where his father had punched him. With renewed frustration and clenched teeth, Claude hurried to get to the ledge. He wanted to sit down, close his eyes and feel the winds from the valley sweep over him.

Breaking through the underbrush and into the clearing, Claude was startled to see another person standing on his ledge and looking over his valley! He screamed at this intruder, "Hey! What are you doing here? You don't belong here!"

The intruder spun around at the sound of Claude's voice. It was Hector Montoya. Even though Claude had grown up with Hector, they never got along. Hector had always been big for his age and loved to bully anyone smaller than himself. Claude was four years younger and continually on the losing end of Hector's taunts as well as his fists. Today however, there was parity. Claude Mendosa did not care about the difference in size or strength. He only wanted this trespasser to be gone.

Hector instantly recognized Claude and saw the condition of his swollen face. Putting his hands on his hips, Hector struck a defiant pose. His lips curled into a sneer and he mockingly whined, "Claude, Claude. Have you been crying? Did your poppa beat you up again?"

Claude charged at him. With no regard for his own safety, he ran at Hector full force. It was too late. Claude saw the fist at the last instant. Unable to escape its force, it caught him on the side of his head. Claude went down and saw odd flashes of light from his left eye.

Claude recovered in time to see Hector getting ready to wield a kick and hear him shout, "You fight like a girl! I'll beat you until you cry!"

Claude saw the booted foot swing toward him but was able to roll out of the way just in time. The dark leather boot missed its mark and only managed to graze his thigh. Claude suddenly became aware that he had rolled dangerously close to the edge of the precipice. Hector was again winding up his foot for another kick. In desperation, Claude rolled hard and fast toward Hector. Claude's momentum rolled him onto the bully's foot. Losing his balance, Hector fell backwards. Although he was able to quickly flip over onto his stomach and get up onto his hands and knees, Claude was first to scramble up to his feet. Sensing the opportunity, he jumped onto Hector's back.

Hector was a head taller and much stronger. Even with Claude hanging on to his neck and shoulders, Hector was able to get to his feet. Disregarding the pummeling from his opponent's one free fist, Hector gave a mighty roll of his shoulders and dislodged Claude from his back.

Claude lost his grip and slid down. As he did so, his hands slipped into Hector's belt. Hector started to turn to face him, but Claude held onto the back of his rival's belt, preventing him from doing so. Gripping the leather strap and using all his strength, Claude began to spin him around. The ledge was narrow, and Hector flailed his arms trying to get a grip on anything substantial. Claude was determined to hold fast to the backside of the belt and continued to spin. Hector was out of position and helpless. His only focus was trying to maintain his balance so as not to be thrown to the ground.

Using his weight as leverage, Claude leaned back, straining to keep his advantage. From the corner of his eye, he saw the valley coming into view. Like an athlete competing in a hammer-throw, Claude let go of the belt as maximum momentum and inertia gripped Hector and catapulted him off the ledge and into space.

Claude stumbled once, but never lost his balance. He stood on the edge of the precipice with his knees bent and his fists curled into white-knuckled balls. Suddenly, Claude screamed. It was an incoherent, primitive, animal sound that he directed at the falling body. He watched as Hector's body hit against a jagged outcrop of rocks, some four hundred feet below, and bounced like a rag-doll, twice, before almost disappearing in the mist of the valley.

Squinting his eyes, Claude gazed at what little of the body he could see while his breathing returned to normal. Finally, he lay back on the ground and stared up at the sky. With pronounced determination in his voice, he hissed, "This is *my* secret place."

The next day, when Hector failed to return home, a commotion filled the village. The elders organized search parties, but Hector was never found. Claude, along with others in the village, was questioned for any information that might prove helpful in the search. Claude casually lied that he did not know anything that might be useful.

Two weeks after that incident, Claude Mendosa celebrated his thirteenth birthday.

CHAPTER TWO

1981, Fort Lauderdale, Florida

When you are a high school senior, life can be perfect. That was especially true for Lincoln Donald Bradshaw. As a popular standout on the varsity football team, he had an overabundance of exuberant friends. He was tall, good looking and envied by more than just a few of his peers. "Linc," as everyone called him, and his girlfriend, Malissa, were voted "most-popular" by their classmates and had that title indelibly imprinted under their photographs in the senior class yearbook.

A favorite among the teachers, Linc also excelled in academics. The air of confidence he exuded was born out of years of success in academics and athletic competition. The constant backslapping and "atta-boys" made him relish his time in high school.

Now, that was over. Graduation had come and gone.

It was Sunday, August 27th, and the next day would be his eighteenth birthday. The summer, now almost over, had passed in a surreal sort of way. Things were so different. For the first time in his memory, he wasn't surrounded by throngs of other laughing teenagers or listening to the stirring sounds of the drum and bugle corps heralding the successes of his triumphs. Instead, Linc spent that summer working at a local convenience store. It was menial work and only added to the realization that life was going to be very different. Linc questioned how he would manage to cope now that the bonds and security of high school were gone.

After giving notice at his job and spending the rest of the day celebrating his birthday, Linc intended to use the final week preparing for his trip to college. It was going to be a new experience. Memphis, Tennessee was so far from Fort Lauderdale, Florida. None of his classmates had opted to go to Memphis University, and that further added to the emptiness he was feeling. He would have to start all over again. Linc knew he would not have any trouble making new friends but wondered if he would ever achieve the glory and status that had been heaped upon him during the last few years.

Linc's mother, Margaret, had planned a surprise birthday party for her son. Unfortunately, Linc had spotted one of the invitations that his mother had accidentally dropped under the dining room table. Linc thought about not spoiling her surprise but decided to let the cat out of the bag. He wanted to be sure that his girlfriend, Malissa, had been included on the invitation list. After all, Malissa was leaving for college as well, and the two would not see each other until winter recess. The birthday party was intended for family only, but Margaret had no objections to Linc inviting Malissa.

The party was to be held at *Gibby's*, a big, popular restaurant located off Andrews Avenue in Fort Lauderdale. The fifteen family members were scheduled to meet there at one p.m. The plan called for Linc to pick up his mother at her office at half past eleven and to drive them both to *Gibby's*.

Linc's mother, Margaret Bradshaw, was a licensed real estate broker. Her business, "Lincoln's Real Estate," boasted her maiden name. She often said, "It gives my customers a good feeling of honesty, trust and Americana."

Linc had always been told that his mother was a direct descendant of President Abraham himself, even though neither Linc nor his mother was ever able to trace that particular lineage. Nevertheless, she was immensely proud of her maiden name, and not only used it to title her business, but also gave it to her son as his first name.

Her office was located on the tenth floor of the Talmadge Building on Andrews Avenue in downtown Fort Lauderdale. The building, one of the oldest office buildings in the city, was in desperate need of refurbishing. Unlike the lobby, which was kept clean and bright, the elevator was a dimly lit relic of the past. The ride up to the tenth floor was always an adventure. The elevator jerked, creaked and constantly moaned. People nervously joked that it was being suspended only by ancient, dusty cobwebs. For fear of the elevator becoming stuck between floors, many of the business people on the lower levels took the stairs. The building's management company promised to replace it and had actually contracted with *Miami Elevator Company* to start work on the project the following week.

It was Sunday morning, and Linc's mother had gone to her office to clear away some paperwork on a property that she had sold the week before. There never was any traffic in this part of Fort Lauderdale on weekend mornings. As a result, Linc had no trouble finding a parking spot right in front of the building. He knew that almost all the offices would be empty and that the lobby would be deserted. He was sure he would be riding up the elevator by himself. On those rare occasions, his teenage exuberance would take over. As the elevator ascended, he would get a thrill out of violently shifting his weight from side to side, causing the elevator to bang loudly against the walls of the shaft. Sometimes, he would jump up and down, giving the elevator car a yo-yo motion. The last time he did that, there was an odd metallic pop, followed by an eerie hissing noise like cables unwinding. It was kind of exciting.

Bounding up the front steps, Linc hesitated a moment to admire a new red Corvette that cruised by. Still appreciating the design of the automobile, he entered the lobby and was immediately disappointed to find four people waiting for the elevator.

'Unbelievable.' he thought to himself. 'Don't these people know that it's Sunday morning and they shouldn't be here?' He was slightly annoyed at the prospect of not being able to give that old elevator one last dance.

The group consisted of a man and woman in their seventies, plus a young mother and her son. The old man was frail and was being held by his wife who had a good grip on his arm. Both of them were dressed in their Sunday-best and looked as though they had just come from a religious service.

Linc looked at the mother and her son. A fine looking young woman in her late twenties, she wore a very short, sleeveless summer dress. It had a pale green and coral print and fake buttons down the front. Pale green shoes with small heels adorned her feet. Linc took notice of the skimpiness of her dress, her exposed thighs, and the fact that there were no signs of a brassiere peeking through the armhole of her dress. She smiled at Linc just before taking her son's hand.

Watching her out of the corner of his eye, Linc felt disappointment. During the workweek, the lobby's air conditioner pumped away at full blast keeping the area quite cool. Sundays, however, was the time it was shut down. If the lobby had maintained its normal chill, the young woman's nipples would have been pushing at her fabric. Instead, raised temperatures and deflated nipples produced the teenager's disappointment.

The young woman's son was a cute little guy, perhaps six or seven years old, with a bowl cut on a thick crop of blonde hair. Linc wondered if the four of them were related. He hoped they were not going up to see his mother. That would certainly delay his party.

The elevator started it's descent to the lobby and announced it with a series of groans, followed by a very loud grinding noise. All eyes, except Linc's, looked up at the floor indicator arm, hoping to see the source of the cacophony.

The little boy moved close to his mother. Scrunching his face, he held his ears and said, "What's that noise?"

She tousled his hair and laughed nervously as she said, "That's the elevator, Tommy . . . I think."

"Don't worry," said Linc. "I've been riding this elevator for years. It sounds like that all the time."

Little Tommy lifted his eyes up to Linc, "What's your name?" he asked.

"My name is Lincoln."

"Like Abraham Lincoln?"

"Exactly," said Linc.

"What's your first name?" asked Tommy.

"That is my first name," said Linc. "Are you going to be brave and ride the elevator with us?"

Tommy looked up at his mommy, seemingly for an answer. The elevator became louder as it approached. When the indicator arm swung past the fifth floor, the old box made a deep clanging sound that reverberated for a second or two like a tuning fork. That one made Linc glance up along with the others. He had never heard that particular noise before. 'Should be interesting,' he thought, 'with the weight of all five of us in there.'

The young woman said, "I'm not sure whether I'm brave enough to try this."

Speaking in a heavy Jewish accent, the old woman looked at Linc and spoke for the first time. "Young man, vud you say dis elevator is safe? Haff you been on dis elevator before?"

"Yes, Ma'am," said Linc. "Quite a number of times. My mother works on the tenth floor."

The old woman tugged at her husband's arm and said, "Don't vorry, Izzy. It's going to be jus like Coney Island."

"Coney Island," Izzy repeated.

When the elevator arrived, Linc pulled open the pocket doors and slid back the brass, accordion grating and allowed everyone to enter before him. As he slid the doors closed, he asked everyone what floor they wanted. The older couple was going to nine. The young mother and Tommy were going to the eighth floor. Linc pushed the appropriate buttons before pushing number ten for himself.

With the five of them inside, the tiny car became a rather cramped space. They were all facing the front of the elevator. As it approached the fourth floor, an intermittent grinding was followed by a very loud scraping noise that came from the left wall of the car. It was another new sound that Linc had not heard before.

Just as the indicator light proclaimed the approach of the seventh floor, there was a bright flash of light from above the elevator. It reflected off the blank wall, visible through the open accordion door. Next, came a clamor of sharp crackling and pops that sounded like small exploding firecrackers. That was immediately followed by a shower of sparks that cascaded down the shaft in front of their eyes.

The old lady cried out in alarm, and Linc heard old Izzy *saying,* *"Oy vey"* over and over. The plume of burning embers made everyone instinctively duck back towards the rear of the car. The sudden shift in weight was all that was needed.

There was an earsplitting, metallic twang, and the whole right side of the elevator dropped a foot. Linc's right shoulder slammed into the wall. He turned to try and stop the same thing from happening to the others, but he was not in time. The older couple was already pinned against the wall, as Tommy and his mother came flying across the small space into Izzy and his wife. She began chanting *"Oy, Goht. Oy, vey is meer!"*

Little Tommy went down. It looked as though he might be in danger of having someone fall on top of him. Reaching for the boy, Linc turned and stepped away from the control panel and pulled Tommy to his feet. It was at that moment that Izzy's wife had the presence of mind to hit the emergency stop button. The idea was good, but the results were not. The elevator began bucking violently. Severely tilted, it was scraping the outer walls. With everyone's weight shifted to one side and one cable already broken, it was too much for the remaining one. The elevator jerked upward and, on its downward motion, broke loose and began falling at a terrifying rate of speed.

The elevator dropped three floors making a deafening screeching sound, sandpapering its way down the shaft. Suddenly, the car came to a jolting stop. A large piece of metal had pierced its way into the elevator car by breaking up through the floor on the left side. The impact of the elevator onto that protruding metal arm caused bits of paneling and embossed wood chips to go flying through the small crowded space. Everyone, still sandwiched on the right side of the car, got pelted with ricocheting debris.

The tilt of the elevator worsened, and everyone was further jammed together into a pile of people. Small cries of nervousness and fear were coming from the two women. Little Tommy began to cry softly.

Linc regained his balance quickly and pulled Tommy and his mother off the elderly couple. They were both sitting on the floor, and Izzy's wife was whimpering quietly. "Izzy?" she called. "Izzy?"

Izzy seemed to be unconscious. Linc moved next to him and tried to feel for a pulse. Despite the warm temperature in the elevator, the old man's hands and fingers were very cold. Linc could not feel a pulse. Still holding Izzy's wrist, Linc looked questioningly at the old woman. She said tearfully, "He had a 'quadruple' about six months ago."

Tommy, sniffling back his tears said, "Is he dead, Mommy?"

When Linc moved Izzy from a sitting position to flat on his back, he started to cough. Linc breathed a sigh of relief and propped the old man up so that he was cradled in his wife's arms. As Linc stood and tried the emergency alarm, he immediately became disappointed. The only result was the onset of erratic blinking from the single overhead light bulb.

"Come on, Tommy," coaxed Linc. "Let's you and me yell for help,"

"I can do that, too," said Tommy's mom.

Before the three of them could begin calling out, the piece of metal jutting up through the floor began to bend under their shifted weight. Linc got a sinking feeling in the pit of his stomach, as he realized the metallic bar was the only thing holding them from plummeting to their death.

Linc looked up and spotted an escape door on the ceiling of the elevator car. Although it was narrow, Linc felt that he could fit through it. Not wanting to take the chance of jumping up and down in an attempt to open it, he looked around for something to stand on.

His gaze locked on Tommy's mother. "I need to get up there," Linc pointed, "to try and unlatch that door."

She stared up at the opening before looking at Linc and his broad shoulders. "No way I can hold you. But you can lift me up there."

The light bulb on the ceiling was blinking intermittently. It would stay on for fifteen or twenty seconds and then blink off for three or four. When it blinked off, it became very dark.

"Okay. Come on," said Linc as he interlaced his fingers, creating a foothold for her. "Put your foot here. I'll lift you right up."

She slipped off her shoes and put her bare foot into Linc's handhold. Grabbing on to his neck, she felt herself being lifted with ease.

The hem of her short dress came to Linc's eye level, and he became entranced with the sight of her bare thighs so close to him.

She pushed and pulled and tugged at the trap door until, with a clack, it came partially loose. It lifted up only about ten inches, before becoming stuck again. Balancing on her one foot, she stretched herself and reached her arm through the opening to feel what was blocking it. Whatever it was, she couldn't quite reach it.

"Lincoln. Lift me higher!" she called.

Linc raised her up. She was standing with one foot in his handhold and the other leg spread wide for balance. He glanced up and held his breath. Astonished to see that she was not wearing any panties, Linc's cheeks flushed crimson.

The young woman reached her arm through the opening and felt a piece of wood lying across the little doorway. Straining to move it, the trap door suddenly opened all the way. Sticking her head out into the empty shaft, she saw a shadowy movement of something scurrying across the top of the elevator. It looked like a rat. Then, the light blinked off.

Linc's heart was beating a little fast, and not from the exertion. When the light went out, she panicked and screamed, dropping back into the elevator car and into Linc's arms. Uncomfortably cognizant of where his hands were planted, Linc stammered, "Are . . . are you okay?"

She held onto him for just a moment until the light came back on. At the sound of his mother's panic, Tommy started crying again. "Don't cry, Tommy," she said as she came out of Linc's arms. "It'll be all right."

The protruding piece of metal that was holding the car from falling was still creaking, and slowly bending.

Linc said, "I'm going to see if I can find us a way out of here. You keep an eye on Izzy."

Linc looked up and judged the height of his jump in order to grab the lip of the trap door. As he leaped, the force of his motion caused the metal arm to bend even more. 'Oh, shit!' thought Linc as he caught the edges of the opening with his fingertips. Using the strength in his hands and arms, he was able to hook his elbows and shimmy through the opening.

Standing on top of the elevator car, he looked in all directions. The cables were all busted and laying on and around the car. It was only God and that metal bar that were keeping them from rocketing downward into the basement. And that metal bar was giving way fast.

Linc looked up. The door to the fifth floor was less than three feet above his head. He could easily raise his arms and jump to reach the lip of the doorway. Just as he crouched into position for the jump, the elevator jerked downward again and he lost another three inches. Realizing that the force of his jump could be disastrous, he decided to ask for help.

Linc hollered into the car, "Hey, um, you . . . Tommy's mom?"

She looked up. "Claire. My name is Claire."

"Claire. I need your help up here." Linc bent over and put his hand down into the car. "Come on. Grab my hand."

Claire gave Tommy a quick hug and said, "It'll be all right, Tommy. I'll only be gone a few moments."

Claire reached up and grabbed Linc's outstretched hand. Effortlessly, he pulled her up in one smooth, swift motion. She was shocked at how easily he did that.

Once on top of the elevator, Linc wasted no time. He got down on one knee in front of Claire, as though he were proposing and said, "I want you to get into this position. I'm going to stand on your bent knee, so I can reach that doorway without jumping."

"Are you sure about this?" asked Claire.

"Don't worry," assured Linc. "In that position, you'll definitely be able to hold my weight."

Claire bent down on one knee, while Linc gently placed the ball of his foot so as not to create any undo pressure on her leg. He stood up straight in a fluid motion.

Linc was able to grab the two pocket sliding doors to the fifth floor and with a mighty heave, he pulled them open. They came flying apart much easier than Linc had anticipated. Luckily, they stayed in the open position. He heard voices that sounded as though they were coming from the upper floors.

As he dropped back down and took his foot off Claire's leg, she stood up to face him. She moved close to Linc and said, "Please, Lincoln. Get Tommy out of here first. Please."

The exploding hormones of an eighteen year old tend to make

all rational thought evaporate. Linc was no exception, and he totally misunderstood her. He thought her words meant that she wanted to be alone with him. Then, the moment passed, and Linc recognized it as a natural plea from a mother for the safety of her child. He was thankful for not blurting out anything stupid.

Linc lowered Claire back into the car. She lifted Tommy up and told him to grab Linc's hand. In less than thirty seconds, Linc had Tommy up and out and sitting safely on the fifth floor. Linc bent down and called to Claire, "Get me the lady, next."

First helping Izzy's wife to her feet, Claire positioned herself into the kneeling position that Linc had shown her. "Stand up here on my knee," she ordered, "and Lincoln will grab you."

"Are you '*mishoogeh*? I'll fall and break my neck.".

Linc shouted down, "Just reach your hand up so I can grab it."

The old lady did as she was directed. Taking a tight grip on her outstretched hand, Linc began to pull.

The old woman weighed a lot more than Claire and the action exerted a lot of drag on her arm. She began yelling, "*Oy*! It hoits! You're hoiting me!"

Ignoring the complaints, Linc hauled her to the top of the elevator. Her face was contorted in pain. She rubbed her shoulder and muttered something in Yiddish. Then, in a whining voice, she complained, "Someting hoits me bad. I vant you should know, you're going to pay for dis, big shot!"

Holding her around her hips, Linc hoisted the woman up, allowing her to get a grip on the door threshold above them. Once she grasped it, he gave her a boost by pushing up on her legs. Managing to get one knee on to the fifth floor, she scampered to safety.

Linc was about to bend the top half of his body back into the elevator when he heard the voices in the hallway. They were getting louder, and Izzy's wife and Tommy began shouting for help. The elevator creaked lower as its weight punished the metal arm that was holding it.

Claire was lifting Izzy to his feet and trying to motivate him into standing straight. "You can do it! Come on, Izzy. That's it!"

Izzy was too weak and couldn't hold his arm up high enough for Linc to grab. "Claire?" called Linc. "Can you lift him? Even a little?"

"I'll try!" she yelled back. Positioning herself in front of Izzy, she wrapped her arms around his buttocks. With a determined grunt, she lifted him a foot off the floor.

Linc had lowered himself so that the upper part of his body protruded deeply into the car. Grabbing Izzy by the back of his suit jacket, Linc pulled him up, as the elevator vibrated and dropped another couple of inches. Izzy was in bad shape. Moaning softly, he lay there, almost motionless, in a fetal position. After reaching down again and quickly lifting Claire, Linc looked up at his escape route.

Disregarding the commotion coming from the fifth floor, Linc and Claire tried to prop Izzy up. In the middle of doing so, two women poked their heads through the doorway. In spite of all the yelling and confusion, the two women acted promptly by laying on their stomachs and reaching down to help hoist Izzy to safety.

Now, it was Claire's turn. Linc had so much adrenaline pumping that he practically threw Claire up to the safety of the landing in a single motion. Fascinated, he stood there looking up at Claire's bare bottom as she scrambled over the edge and out of Linc's line of sight.

Once again, the elevator lurched downward, but, this time, with an ear-splitting screech. Linc came out of his trance and jumped as high as he could. Fully extended, he was only able to get his fingertips onto the ledge. As the metal arm broke loose, there was an extraordinarily loud bang, and the would-be coffin spewed sparks and smoke as it raced downward into hell.

The sounds of the runaway elevator were suddenly mixed with screams from Izzy's wife and Claire. Both of them had been sitting on the floor, anxiously waiting for Linc to crawl out of the elevator shaft. When the roar of destruction filled the hallway, they each assumed that Linc had been unable to rescue himself. With a deafening shriek, Claire called out, "Lincoln!" while Izzy's wife wailed, *"Oy, Goht, nain!"*

Linc held there for a moment suspended on the inside of the shaft by his fingertips. He gathered his strength while a huge dust cloud caused by the elevator crumpling into the basement, billowed up and swirled around him. He began to lift himself up to the solid safety of the fifth floor while Claire and the two women bystanders pulled and tugged at him to aid his ascent.

Once on top, he lay on his back, eyes closed, suddenly weak from fatigue, and listened as the sound of sirens came closer. Through everyone's chatter, he heard someone say that the paramedics, the police and firemen were on their way. Despite being totally exhausted, his mind kept flitting back and forth between Claire, Izzy and his wife. Those thoughts were interrupted when he heard Izzy's wife exclaim to one of the bystanders, "*Oy, danken Goht.* He's such a good boy."

Linc became aware of someone holding his hand. Opening his eyes, he saw that it was Claire. She was talking to someone else when she said, "He saved us. He saved us all." Then, he heard Tommy say, "Yeah! His name is Lincoln. He's great!"

CHAPTER THREE

Present Day

F riday evening in the girl's dormitory was an exciting time. An air of electricity and anticipation simmered just below the surface. Most of the coeds were getting ready to go out for the night. Telephones were ringing and effervescent chatter was adding to the frolicsome mood, while they made their last minute preparations. The animation was palpable.

Although the hour was approaching eight p.m. and the showering and blow-drying were, for the most part, complete, only some of the girls were dressed and ready. To a casual observer, it would have seemed like the dress code had been arranged by *Victoria's Secret* and called for the latest fashions in bras and panties.

Most of the doors to the various dorm rooms were open, allowing for a lot of good-natured prattle to go back and forth. A girl named Lucy called to a friend across the hall, asking to "borrow" her new eyeliner. The friend yelled back, "I saw that yellow crud in your eyes, Lucy. Get your own eyeliner." Lucy hollered back, "That's just from my contacts. My eyes aren't infected or anything!"

Lucy's friend retorted, "I know. You're just oversexed. Your eyes get that way every time you look at your vibrator!" Someone else added,

"Or think about Brad Pitt!" A third girl shouted, "Or the school's soccer team!" This exchange created more laughter from the nearby rooms, and some of the coeds chimed in with their own wisecracks.

Lucy was a buxom girl who never wore a bra. The stir she created around the campus was incessant, and she now owned a reputation for being the queen of the partygoers. Nevertheless, she had a good sense of humor and, despite the ribbing, was liked by most of her peers.

Jennifer Morano and Crystal Richards were giggling over the party-like banter that was coming from the dormitory residents. It was the second year the two young women had been roommates at Southeast Florida State University. They were very compatible. Not only did they like the same music and wear the same size clothes, but Crystal was the kind of girl who needed a role model, and Jennifer obliged by mothering her. The girls attended a couple of the same classes, shared a common study schedule and, together, spent some of their spare time shopping at their favorite malls. For the past few months, they had even been double dating.

Jennifer had just hung up the telephone and was looking in her closet when it rang again. Grabbing the phone, Crystal listened for a second before hanging up. Jennifer called over her shoulder, "Who was it?"

"Nobody," answered Crystal. "Just a dial tone." Then, arching her eyebrows, she returned to the subject of Lucy, "That Lucy is really wild about Brad Pitt. Did she, like, show you that naked poster she has of him?"

Jennifer said, "You mean the one on which she hangs her only bra?"

"Yeah," giggled Crystal. "That humungous 38-D!"

"I saw it," said Jennifer, "but I don't really think it's a picture of Brad Pitt."

Crystal was aghast. "What do you mean? Of course it's Brad Pitt. Besides, it says 'Brad Pitt' right on the bottom."

"Crystal," said Jennifer patiently, "you can't believe everything you see. To me, it looks like one of those doctored-up photographs where they superimpose someone's head onto someone else's body." Jennifer smiled and continued, "Besides, you ought to spend more time studying his face and less time studying his genitals."

Crystal attempted to talk through a snigger. "At least I'm studying," she said.

Feigning horror, Jennifer said, "You call that studying? It's more like drooling than studying. Besides, I don't think the real Brad Pitt would ever allow himself to be photographed while being totally exposed."

The look of mock shock on Jennifer's face coupled with her comment, struck Crystal funny, and she started to laugh uncontrollably. "That exposed," she repeated. "That's like, really exposed!" She was holding her stomach and said, "Exposed! That's like a whole exposition. An exposed exposition." Crystal's laughter was infectious.

Jennifer was giggling as she said, "Did you see the size of his exposition?"

Crystal could hardly speak as she stammered, "The size of his exposition. No wonder Lucy has yellow crud in her eyes."

That did it. The two of them convulsed with laughter.

Marti and Amy, two girls from across the hall, came in to share in the hullabaloo. Crystal and Jennifer could barely make themselves understood, but their laughter spoke for itself. Marti and Amy caught the gist of the moment and came up with their own good heckles about Lucy's breasts and her hormones. Laughter was floating up and down the hall and Lucy was being a good sport.

When the tumult subsided, Jennifer, who was only wearing a terry robe, asked, "Crystal, can I borrow your white slip dress with the polka dots? Y'know, the one with the big yellow polka dots?"

Jennifer Morano was a native New Yorker. As a child, Jennifer would often come down to Florida to visit with her grandparents. She grew to love the region, the palm trees and the warm winters. When the time came for selecting a college, the choice was easy.

Jennifer was tall and slender, and her Italian heritage gave her an olive complexion that tanned dark in the Florida sun. Even though her face had the beauty of an oval, Victorian cameo, her most striking feature was her shoulder length auburn hair. Thick and wavy, it framed her like a portrait. She was aware of the effect and emphasized it by wearing light colors or exposing a lot of skin around her neck and shoulders.

Crystal replied, "Sure. Which shoes are you going to wear?"

"My yellow ones," Jennifer replied dreamily. "I'm in a yellow mood. I'm even going to wear my panties with the little yellow flowers. I think Peter will like the outfit. What do you think?"

Crystal said, "I think he'll like all that skin showing." Then added with a giggle, "I think he'll also like all the little yellow flowers on your panties."

Before Jennifer could think of an appropriate response, Crystal changed the subject and asked, "Why don't you call him 'Pitch?' I think it's a great nickname."

Jennifer replied, "I much prefer to call him Peter. Nicknames are so juvenile."

"Well, I like nicknames, *Jenn*," said Crystal, pretending to be insulted.

"All right," agreed Jennifer. "From now on I'll call you 'Crys!'"

Crystal giggled.

February in Southeast Florida was perfect. The days were deliciously warm and the nights were balmy. The humidity, which would become oppressive in a few months, was now comfortable.

The location of the university was ideal. Just across the Intercoastal waterway from the world famous "Palm Beachers" with their glorious mansions, luxurious cars and extravagant lifestyles.

On Friday and Saturday nights, many of the coeds would go out in groups of two or three to some of the local nightclubs hoping to meet their prince charmings. Although Jennifer and Crystal had done that same thing, tonight they were double dating with Scott Aarons and Peter "Pitch" Pechowski.

Crystal was very excited and nervous about going out with Scott on this particular evening. Jennifer was just as excited about dating Pitch but showed an outward calm. The boys had not been specific about the arrangements but left an air of anticipation by saying that they had a special evening planned. Scott was a legitimate Palm Beacher. While he spent a lot of time at Pitch's apartment, he actually lived with his parents in a very big mansion on the beach. He was a handsome young man with thick eyebrows and high cheekbones, which Crystal said made his eyes look very sexy. Scott's lifestyle made Crystal giddy. That, coupled with the growing feeling of falling in love, had a tendency to occasionally make Crystal incoherent.

Crystal said, "I'm hoping we can spend some time alone."

"We are alone." Jennifer replied.

"Not you and me, Jenn. I meant Scott and me."

"Oh?" Jennifer questioned like a mother hen. "What have you got in mind?"

"Well, my panties are blue and that's Scott's favorite color."

Jennifer's mouth dropped open in shock.

Crystal was well tanned with platinum blonde hair that she styled with bangs. She had long, shapely legs and almost always wore shorts. She loved wearing sandals and at one time or another, everyone on campus saw her giving herself a pedicure. This evening, she wore a pair of light blue shorts that were blowsy on her thighs and a short-sleeved blue knit top with a scoop neck that showed a considerable amount of cleavage. A gold chained necklace that held a small cross was her only jewelry.

"Well," Jennifer said, "Let's see how the evening goes. If it doesn't go well, we'll come back here and study for our history exam."

Crystal said, "You ended up with a ninety-five on that last test and I got a lousy sixty-six. Coming back here and studying would be the smart thing to do, but nobody ever accused me of being smart."

Jennifer said, "We'll keep on studying together Crystal. You'll do just fine."

The girls kept up with some small talk between them and occasionally joined the razzing that poor Lucy was still enduring. The telephone rang again. It was Pitch saying that he and Scott would pick them up in the parking lot at eight-thirty.

Their lives were about to change.

CHAPTER
FOUR

C laude Mendosa sat perfectly still in the darkness. He was waiting for Roger and Sandi Blanchard to come home. Despite the one a.m. hour and the fact that Mendosa had not slept in more than twenty-six hours, he was still wide-awake. He had found a small upholstered chair in the upstairs guest bedroom and moved it to a window which overlooked the approach to the house. Having completed his preparations, he was now comfortably seated and waiting. Claude Mendosa had extraordinary patience. A successful assassin had to have many uncommon qualities, with patience being very high on the list.

He allowed his mind to drift, but never stopped scanning the driveway and the street beyond. He thought about his youth.

*   *   *

Claude Mendosa was born in 1956 in the small mountain village of Altos de España, Spain. Located high in the Cantabrian region of the Pyrenees Mountains bordering France and Spain, the village lay in the southern shadow of *Mont Valier,* one of the landmark peaks of the Basque Separatists. Mendosa was raised during the turbulent years of Francisco Franco and the political unrest of the time. Both of his parents were ardent Basque Separatists, zealots who passionately fought for their freedom and spent all their time making bombs and planning destruction. Despite his youth, Claude Mendosa's parents demanded his participation in their affairs. From his mother, he learned how to put together bombs from plastique, TNT or, when nothing else was available, plain black powder. Having been a nurse, she also taught him first-aid and pharmacology. His mother was a hardened taskmaster who constantly pulled small tufts of his hair as punishment for his not paying attention to her lessons. Whenever he failed to get the wiring right on a timing device of a booby trap, his scalp would sting for hours from her hair pulling.

Mendosa's father taught him the chemistry of explosives, including how to combine the right amount of simple potassium nitrate, water and toluene to create tri-nitro-toluene or TNT. The man also taught his son all about hunting and firearms, including their care and maintenance. Claude learned the craft by firing off thousands of rounds of ammunition. By the time he was twelve years old, he was a crack shot with both a rifle and a handgun. Despite his son's prowess, Claude's father was very demanding and, to the dismay of others, quite abusive. His violence manifested itself by constantly yelling at Claude, hitting him about his face and head, each time the boy neglected to do exactly what he was told. The father's anger would flare and he would shout the words that became the young man's mantra, "If you are careless or stupid, they will kill you."

Claude Mendosa's parents were active members of *Euskadi ta Askatasuna*, also known as the ETA, the terrorist regime that was constantly doing battle with government police and militia.

Claude was brought into the organization when he first became a teenager. They taught him how to lay down covering fire with his rifle in order to protect his comrades while they committed atrocities. This act of protecting the troops was usually carried out from nearby rooftops. In that way, Claude, along with a few other exceptional youngsters, could have a clear view of the action and still be safely protected.

During one such bloody incident that occurred three months past his fourteenth birthday, Claude was on a rooftop with two other teenagers from his village. While other ETA members were across the street murdering the mayor of the town, two police cars pulled up, sirens wailing. Five policemen jumped out with their guns drawn and began making their way towards the mayor's villa. Claude and his fellow ETA militiamen began firing at the advancing patrol. All the police ran for cover except one. He was either brave or foolhardy, for he kept inching his way towards the mayor's residence. The elders in the ETA would use an opportunity such as this to teach the teens how to be effective rather than lethal with their covering fire. Those lessons involving murder would come much later. Claude and the others fired their bullets close to the advancing policeman, trying to frighten him into retreat, but still the patrolman moved closer to his target. Turning to the boy next to him, Claude whispered, "Enough of this. It's time to take some real action." He took aim at the side of the policeman's head and calmly squeezed off a single round. The bullet hit the officer square in the temple. For a brief moment, his eyes went wide and his mouth opened, but no sound came out. Then, the young policeman slumped up against the stucco wall and died in the street. Working the rifle bolt smoothly, Claude Mendosa eased another round into the chamber before taking aim at one of the other policemen cowering behind the patrol car. Claude could only see the top of the policeman's cap, but that would be enough of a target. Firing off one more round, Claude watched as his second victim died instantly under the glare of the Spanish sun.

Claude Mendosa felt a calm wash over him. It was confidence. It was knowing all that had to be known, seeing all that had to be seen, being able to calculate the variables and, most of all, doing what needed to be done. Feeling a surge of power course through his body, Claude exalted in the euphoria. From that day forward, he stood straighter and never shifted his gaze.

The story of Claude's killings was told again and again, and his reputation grew. He never felt remorse for what he had done. That was clearly evident in the way he handled himself on a day-to-day basis. Young Claude rarely showed emotion. An occasional smile over a joke or funny story was rare. When Claude turned fifteen, he received word that his father and several of his party members had been conducting a raid on a municipal building when they all were killed in a hail of bullets from a military ambush. Upon hearing the news, Claude never shed a tear and never spoke a word about it. Not even to his mother. The members of the ETA had several nicknames for the teenager, including *"Tueur au sang-froid"* which translated into "cold-blooded killer." But the one he liked best was *"L'assassin du Mont Valier,"* the Assassin of Mount Valier," named for his deeds and the mountain that protected his home.

Claude proved to be very adept at many things. Besides being fluent in Spanish, French and English, he had a good ear for dialects. He was tall, handsome and, despite his youth, had become very bold in his nature. Instinctively knowing the right things to say in tense situations, he could easily pull people off their guard, making them feel at ease. As such, he was an excellent candidate for the ETA's spy network, able to infiltrate a city, win the confidence of the locals and learn the current news by speaking like one of the townsfolk. He excelled at sports such as soccer and running, and due to his agility and quick reflexes, none of his peers could best him in racing or wrestling. More than once, he displayed his deadly ability at hand-to-hand combat. Claude was a good student and an avid reader. He taught himself history and science, while his Separatist friends taught him things like how to read blueprints and the science of police forensics. They showed him how carelessly left fingerprints could spell his doom. They drilled the boy on how to "clean" a scene of mayhem, leaving only the signs he wanted to leave. Claude Mendosa understood the importance of pre-planning.

In 1973, just before his seventeenth birthday, Claude and three other ETA freedom fighters were dispatched to the capitol city of Madrid to do "some real damage." Each of them spent a couple of days scouting out the presidential palace and other seats of power, looking for a fairly high-ranking bureaucrat who would make a good target. When the team got together to discuss their findings, Claude suggested assassinating the Spanish Premier, Luis Carrero Blanco. Claude's grandiose plan was scoffed at by the others. They blamed his youth for being so impetuous and foolhardy as to think that he could kill a head of state. Nevertheless, Claude insisted, saying that he had watched the Premier come and go with a minimum number of bodyguards. Claude designed and laid out a simple, yet elegant plan for murder and escape and accomplished it almost single handedly.

He first built, and then hid, three radio controlled explosive devices along the top of a broad stone fence that ran the length of the east side of the palace. The charges were placed about forty feet apart. Next, he planted himself and his sniper rifle, with silencer, on the roof of a five-story building that was on the west side of the palace and offered him a shot of between 475 and 500 yards. Claude crouched in ambush. The radio controlled triggering device for the bombs sat on a small ledge, just inches away from his hand.

The ETA was a rag-tag organization, and their weapons reflected that status. Money was hard to come by causing the leaders of the movement to buy whatever they could afford or whatever was available. As a result, there were many different firearms in use at any one time. Rifles and pistols manufactured in Spain and France were most common, but many of the weapons came from Germany, Czechoslovakia and Russia. There were even quite a number of old M-1 carbines from the U.S. Military's involvement in World War II.

Normally, weapons were issued on a willy-nilly basis. However, if any of the Separatists showed an aptitude for handling a firearm, the people in charge of distributing the ordinance would make an effort to furnish those few with an exceptional rifle. That was the case with Claude Mendosa. Despite being a teenager, he had proven his skill as a marksman and, as such, was given one of the world's best sniper rifles. It was an Israeli model known as the "Galil." Weighing a mere 2 pounds, 14 ounces, it had a short 20" barrel. Although firing a .308 caliber bullet, it still had an excellent silencer with a very low decibel rating. The weapon boasted an accurate range of 2240 feet.

The problem with silencers was in how they tended to reduce the accuracy of a rifle, especially at that distance. But this rifle was different. In the past, Claude had fashioned his own silencers, a craft he learned from old Miguel Sancho-Bonez, the master gunsmith. With the "Galil," there would be no need. The muffled "pop" produced by the rifle would be covered by the diversionary tumult of the explosions he intended to set off.

At three o'clock in the afternoon, the Premier of Spain, Luis Carrero Blanco, emerged from the palace with four of his bodyguards. He was on his way to the Procession of Corpus Christi, and throngs of citizens were everywhere. Claude Mendosa was as calm, cool and still as a mountain lake. He watched as Premier Blanco hesitated on the broad steps, while he said something to one of his bodyguards. Then, he waved to the crowd. With the sun fairly low on the horizon, the afternoon light, which was coming over Claude's shoulder, illuminated the Premier. Claude steadied the rifle and squeezed off the nearly silent round. Even before the Premier reacted to the impact of the bullet, Claude hit the switch that ignited the first bomb. Luis Carrero Blanco was dead instantly, and the three sequential explosions did exactly what they were supposed to do. They caused chaos and diverted everyone's attention to the opposite side of the square and away from what really happened.

Claude's reaction was dispassionate. He ignored the screams from the crowd and the headlong confusion of the guards. Instead, he concentrated fully on the details at hand, such as breaking down the rifle and cleaning up the area of any trace evidence. Certain that the bullet he fired was a killing shot, he did not even bother to peek over the wall at the aftermath of his act. Mendosa was fast becoming the best at what he did.

*   *   *

Two hours earlier and with the casualness of a family member, Mendosa had let himself in through the front door of the Blanchard residence. The home was located in a suburb of Memphis called Germantown, an affluent neighborhood of stately homes and wealthy individuals. He had done his homework for this job. First discovering that the nanny would be off duty for the night, Claude also mastered the layout of the house, including the location of the children's' bedrooms. Most importantly, he learned that the computer was in the study. It had taken Mendosa only a few moments to disarm the alarm system.

Mary Franzheimer, the 15-year-old babysitter was startled out of her TV trance as Mendosa appeared in the doorway of the family room carrying what looked like a small overnight bag. "Oh! Oh my God! Who are . . . who . . . ?" Mary stammered.

Claude Mendosa interrupted, "Hi. You must be Mary," he said

with a slight Tennessee drawl and pleasant smile. "I'm Skip. Skip Nelson, Sandi's cousin. Sorry I gave you such a start. Didn't Sandi tell you I'd be coming in tonight?"

Mary's heart was still racing, but she was fast feeling at ease. The man standing in front of her was forty-five years old, but Mary guessed his age to be in the early thirties. Maybe as old as thirty-five, not more. She took notice of how nice he looked; six-foot tall, lithe build with dark curly hair that framed a handsome face with a ruddy complexion. Mary thought he was very good looking and noticed the way his lips curled into dimples at the sides. A dark blue turtleneck accentuated the fine proportions of his slim body. Designer blue jeans and a quality leather jacket finished off the ensemble.

Mary was thinking of the long list of verbal instructions Sandi Blanchard had given her and said, "No. I don't think . . . um . . . she might have. I don't remember."

Smiling pleasantly, Mendosa perceiving that the baby-sitter would pose no problem at all. "It's so nice to be home," Mendosa said conversationally. "Are the children getting big? Are they still up? Can I see them?" He said all that as he grabbed his satchel and started towards the kitchen. "Boy, am I thirsty. What do you have that's cold? Juice? Soda? Ice tea?"

Hurrying after him, Mary took out the hair tie that held up her ponytail. She was combing out her hair with her fingers and shaking it loose as she walked. 'Ponytails are so adolescent,' she thought. Coming back to the moment, Mary said, "Well, the children are sleeping, but . . . um . . . let me see what we have in the refrigerator that's cold." She was bent over in front of the refrigerator, thinking about what a man like Skip Nelson would want to drink, when, strangely, her feet began to slip backwards.

Claude Mendosa had moved in behind Mary, grabbed both of her ankles and yanked viciously. The movement was so quick that she did not have time to break her fall. Going down face first onto the hard tile floor, she broke her nose and split open her bottom lip. Her right hand grabbed at the inside of the refrigerator door, twisting off a metal shelf and rattling some jars and containers. Mendosa was on her in a flash. Removing a roll of duct tape from his satchel, he quickly applied it to her mouth. Disregarding the blood that was oozing out from under her taped lip, he spun another length of tape around her wrists and ankles. Mendosa moved with the speed and agility of a spider.

Attempting to break her bonds, Mary began writhing, which caused Mendosa to halt his taping actions. Sitting on the back of her legs, he grabbed a handful of her hair before slamming the side of her head onto the tile floor. In doing so, the jagged metal shelf in the refrigerator door scraped Mendosa's arm, and it started to bleed. Mary let out a single grunt and lay still. Mendosa resumed applying the duct tape restraints. His movements were fluid, and he never broke a sweat.

Satisfied that Mary was secured, Mendosa removed the initial layer of tape that had kept her from crying out. Stuffing a wad of foam rubber into her mouth, he re-taped over it before carrying her dazed body into the study. Snatching up his black bag, he went upstairs to where the children were sleeping. He moved swiftly and silently, taking the steps two at a time and never touching the banister.

Adam and Sarah, ages 10 and 8 respectively, had bedrooms directly across the hall from one another. Mendosa opened his satchel and removed a small cylinder with an attached mask. In the canister was halothane gas. Sarah was sleeping face up allowing Mendosa to hold the mask over her mouth and nose while barely touching her skin. A slight hissing noise ensued as he turned the valve. Within twenty seconds, Sarah was no longer in a natural sleep. Rather, she was in a gas-induced state of cataplexy. When Mendosa went into Adam's room, he saw that the boy was lying on his stomach. Realizing that the administering of the halothane would be impossible, Mendosa tried to gently turn the youngster over. Still sleeping, Adam called out softly and began to say something unintelligible. Changing tactics, Mendosa quickly wrapped the boy in his own blanket making his arms and legs immobile. Then, grabbing the gas canister the intruder forcibly held it onto the boy's face. The hissing sound of the escaping gas grew louder. Young Adam began struggling, but once again, less than a minute was all that was needed for his small body to go limp. One by one, Mendosa carried the children down to the study and plopped them unceremoniously onto the carpeted floor next to Mary. He needed these children alive . . . for the moment.

CHAPTER FIVE

Peter "Pitch" Pechowski was stretched out on a chaise lounge in Scott Aaron's bedroom. He was mulling over the phone call he had placed to Jennifer and Crystal just a half-hour earlier. Pitch had promised that he and Scott would pick the girls up at eight-thirty, and now, he was worried about being late. Pitch was normally a free spirited sort of guy who rarely concerned himself with being late for a date. Tonight, however, he was faced with two dilemmas and that made things different. First, since it was Jennifer Morano he was dating, he did not want to be late. Secondly . . . well, he was having second thoughts about the venue for the experiment of his prototype. He was worried about the possibility of Jennifer becoming upset.

Pitch and Scott had been friends since childhood. They met while attending the exclusive Clairmont-Pas School, a private school in the Palm Beaches of Florida that was reserved for gifted children. Wealthy parents, who deemed their offspring to be gifted, tended to send their children there as well. The two boys had been friends since fourth grade. Pitch was the gifted one. Scott was the only child of well-to-do parents. Scott's father, Sidney Aarons, was a powerful and respected member of the Palm Beach community. The senior Mr. Aarons owned the *Sun-Coast Ledger*, South Florida's second-largest circulation newspaper. Scott's mother, Lenore, spent all of her time trying to be the perfect socialite. She worked hard at befriending the right people, belonging to the right clubs, aiding the right charities and throwing wonderful dinner parties while inviting all the right guests.

Scott lived with his parents in grand style. The Aarons' home was a mansion on the ocean, and Scott was raised with the opulence of his surroundings. Besides the ever-present servants and chauffeurs, limousines and yachts, he was always supplied with the sportiest of automobiles, the latest in fashion and the best education.

"I'm almost ready," said Scott, his voice sounding muffled, as he rummaged through his walk-in closet. "I just need to change my shoes and splash on some cologne."

Pitch didn't bother sitting up. Instead, he craned his neck in Scott's direction and replied, "I've been watching you, 'Mr. Smooth.' This will be your third attempt at a pair of shoes. I could have fashioned a pair out of tree bark in less time."

Scott jammed his bare feet into a pair of well worn *Docksiders* and asked, "How much time before we have to leave?"

"Does it make a difference?" asked Pitch with a patient smile. "Even if you moved faster than a sidewinder missile, we'd still be late."

"I'm hurrying. I'm hurrying," Scott said.

"I told the girls we would arrive at precisely eight-thirty," Pitch added.

"Eight-thirty? Are you nuts? You know it takes us a while to get ready,"

"Us?" repeated Pitch, wide-eyed. "What do you mean 'us'? I get ready in a 'quark-flash' and you move like a glacier during the ice age."

Scott countered, "It sounds to me like you're describing your love-making techniques when you mention that quark-flash business."

Pitch chuckled. He appreciated Scott's quick wit. This kind of banter had been going on a long time. While Scott busied himself with re-tying one of the leather thongs on his shoe and splashing on just the right amount of Giorgio Armani, Pitch wandered over to the window that overlooked the Atlantic Ocean. The moon was three-quarters full and fairly low on the horizon. He was thinking how perfect the night air would be for a walk on the beach with Jennifer. They had only been seeing each other for a little over a month, but he felt the relationship was becoming special.

For the most part, Pitch had a unique ability to stay very focused on tasks at hand. Although he was proud of his powers of concentration, thoughts of Jennifer had intruded into his mind over the past two weeks. He found it disconcerting. His work at the laboratory on campus involved the latest generation of robotics and, by its nature, was therefore very detailed and exacting. Having Jennifer on his mind made him frown and smile simultaneously.

With one last scrutinizing glance in the mirror, Scott Aarons finally finished readying himself for the evening. He and Pitch went downstairs, said goodnight to the senior Mr. and Mrs. Aarons and took off in Scott's Silver Cloud convertible. The Rolls Royce had been a gift from Scott's mom and dad. Scott had received it the previous year when he completed the requirements for his Master's Degree in journalism.

As they drove with the top down, Pitch enjoyed the balmy comfort of the seventy-degree temperature and the wind as it whipped at his hair. Despite his relaxed look, his mind was racing around several scenarios that might occur among the four of them tonight. Pitch's initial thought was that this little device of his would bring good spirited laughter from Jennifer and Crystal. Now, he was not so sure. Even though he was looking forward to Jennifer expressing her pride in his inventiveness, a nagging doubt was growing over whether or not that particular scenario would actually play out.

Glancing over at Scott who was concentrating on weaving in and out of traffic, Pitch asked, "Do you think we just did something that will bring us accolades, or did we just commit a sophomoric stunt?"

Scott flashed a peek at his friend. "Pitch, would you please stop agonizing about it? This is going to be great!"

"I hope so," Pitch said, "I'm just wondering if we couldn't have come up with a better first trial."

"What could be better," Scott asked rhetorically, "than trying it out on Crystal and Jennifer? They know us. They trust us. They know we wouldn't do anything to deliberately embarrass them. They'll love it. Guaranteed. You'll see."

"Your presumptions could be wrong, you know!" moaned Pitch. "You're just hoping they trust us. And I'm hoping you're right. Besides, you allowed your hormones to inspire you when you came up with this cockamamie idea to test my device."

Scott began vigorously nodding his head. "You bet!" he said. "My hormones guide most of my actions. I mean, have you been paying any attention to Crystal's body? She is *awe-some*! And you know what, Pitch? You gotta start getting with the program, too. Loosen up, let yourself go."

"I'm working on it," said Pitch sullenly.

Scott continued, "Jennifer will be so ecstatic over what you invented, she'll ravish you!"

Pitch turned his head to look at Scott. "'Ravish' would be good," he said.

"I'm dying to see their reactions," said Scott. "Now, remember, Pitch. Don't say anything until we get on board. Let's work the conversation slowly. We'll take our time bringing out the intimate details of their private chatter. Slowly, my friend. Let's not rush it. Okay? And let's leave the panties stuff for last."

Pitch exhaled a sigh before saying, "The prospect of my world collapsing is looming larger. However, I'm just the inventor of this gizmo. You can be in charge of public relations."

"Deal!" agreed Scott.

CHAPTER SIX

Watching from the darkness of the upstairs bedroom, Claude Mendosa saw the Blanchard car approaching the long curving driveway. His vantage point allowed him plenty of time to prepare. Moving silently down the stairs, he glanced into the study to check on the stillness of the children and Mary, the babysitter. Adam and Sarah were quiet and breathing deeply. Mary was whimpering softly. Listening a moment, Mendosa decided that although her moans were probably not loud enough to be of any concern to what he was about to do, he went into the family room and increased the volume on the television set just in case.

Claude Mendosa had long ago left the world of the Basque Separatists. His reputation and notoriety in Europe and North Africa had grown to the point of being hunted. Years before, Mendosa had arranged to smuggle himself into the United States. Once in America, he constructed several new identities and went looking for work. He no longer killed for freedom, human rights or even revenge. These days he plied his trade for money, and this particular job was a high paying contract.

Mendosa's primary contact was a man named Vincent Parlotti, a powerful and ruthless man with very little patience and zero tolerance for error. His name alone could strike fear. Parlotti headed up some sort of clandestine agency known as "T.C.H. International," and Mendosa's orders originated from there. Mendosa was not sure whether T.C.H. International was an agency of the U.S. Government or an arm of the Sicilian Mafia. It did not make a difference.

Mendosa had seen Parlotti on several occasions, even met him twice before. However, because Mendosa was disguised and using an alias at the time, Parlotti never realized, or got to know, the assassin's true identity. Treasuring his anonymity, Mendosa had, over the years, mastered several separate identities, each with its own driver's license, passport and persona. Mendosa could be as elusive as a chameleon in a forest of shadows.

Parlotti had many informants at various levels of society, but especially throughout the hierarchy of government. As a result, Mendosa often carried out his assassin's role on an eclectic array of victims, and he sometimes wondered which of his murders aided the government of the United States and which ones aided Vincent Parlotti himself. Over the years, a system of contact had been developed. Whenever Parlotti had an assignment to hand out, he contacted Mendosa by placing a personal ad in *The Washington Post* or in *Le Monde* in Paris. The ad would be ambiguous and short but would always contain the heading, "The Lass of Mount Valier." It was a shortened and Americanized version of his old nickname, *L'assassin du Mont Valier*. Even though it contained a feminine reference with the word "Lass," it worked to divert any connection.

Mendosa was being well paid for this job, but there was a major bonus if he were completely successful. Roger Blanchard had ten million dollars squirreled away at a bank in Zurich, Switzerland. Even though the prime directive called for Mendosa to kill Mr. Blanchard, Parlotti had sweetened the pie. If Mendosa could convince Roger to divulge the passwords to his Swiss account, the money could be recovered and transferred to Parlotti's control. The completion of such a transaction would net Mendosa an additional one-half of one percent of the total.

Even though an extra fifty thousand dollars was an incentive to promote honesty, Mendosa was always aware of the inherent temptations in his line of work. He had a reputation for getting the job done, and this job would not be an exception. However, in the back of his mind was the allure of the big score. Mendosa knew that someday he would be seduced by its attraction.

Roger and Sandi Blanchard came up the walk as Mendosa was putting the finishing touches on his trap. He made sure that the front door was locked and that the alarm was reactivated. In this way, the Blanchards would not become suspicious upon entering. Next, he jury-rigged the toilet in the guest bathroom to make it sound as if the babysitter was inside. It would buy him the needed seconds to overpower the couple. Moving silently, Mendosa made his way to the darkened study and waited.

Roger Blanchard was a paunchy forty-five-year-old. He was badly out of shape from too many years behind a desk and too many high calorie meals. Round faced and balding, the man had a small tuft of hair directly on top of his head. The Blanchards were returning from an important social gathering, for they were both dressed in formal attire.

As they entered the house, Mendosa heard Sandi Blanchard bark, "Roger, I'm going upstairs to get out of this stupid bra and check on the children. You take Mary home and, for Christ's sake, don't dawdle." Sandi started up the stairs and added, "And, for Christ's sake, don't over-pay her!"

Walking towards the sound of the TV in the family room, Roger called out, "Mary. We're home." Passing the guest bathroom, Roger noticed the door just slightly ajar and heard the flushing of the toilet. He took two steps backwards and said to the door, "Take your time, Mary. I'll be in the study."

In the interim, Mendosa had silently crept up behind his victim. Turning, Roger was startled to find Mendosa less than two feet from his face. Roger saw only the blur of the intruder's open hand as it shot forward and caught him full in the throat. An explosion of pain filled Roger's face and eyes. His hands went to his neck, while an odd gurgling sound came out. His legs buckled, and he fell to his knees.

In less than a split second, Mendosa was on him. The roll of duct tape was at the ready and strips of the metallic tape were hissing, as he pulled them off the roll. First, Roger's wrists were bound, and that was followed by his ankles. Then, Mendosa secured Roger just above his knees.

Preparing to apply a layer of tape to Roger's mouth before dragging him into the study, Mendosa hesitated when Sandi hollered from the top of the stairs, "Roger! Are the children watching that goddamned television?"

Mendosa did not answer. Instead, he quickly taped Roger's mouth before the man could call out. Grabbing his ankles, Mendosa dragged Roger behind a small love seat, concealing his trussed body from view. Moving into the family room, Mendosa increased the TV's volume and waited for Sandi Blanchard to enter.

Sandi screeched as she started down the stairs, "Roger! I can't believe that girl allowed the children to stay up and watch television!" Her voice was shrill, as she moved towards the sound of the TV. "Mary, what the hell is the matter with you?" she demanded, as she crossed the tiled foyer to the family room. "Were the kids sick or something?"

Sandi stood in the doorway of the family room looking at its emptiness and feeling momentarily confused. She was about to holler out Roger's name when a hard blow to the side of her head made her crumple to the floor in a heap.

Mendosa knew he had to act quickly. An unknown time constraint loomed because the babysitter would probably be expected home at a certain hour. Mendosa had no idea if Mary's parents would be up and waiting, but he could not take any chances. Precious little time existed to convince Roger to give up the codes. Mendosa's method of torture needed to be immediate, yet dramatic enough to terrorize Roger into cooperating. Mendosa's stone cold demeanor was at its peak.

Roger became aware of his name being called over and over again. As he tried to open his eyes, he realized, oddly enough, that he had them squeezed shut and had to make a concerted effort to open them.

Mendosa gave him a moment to focus on the scene in the study. Roger was sitting on the carpeted floor and leaning up against a settee. His wife, Sandi, was on his left and Mary, the babysitter, on his right. Both women were tied with duct tape, semi-conscious and in obvious pain. There was dried blood on Mary's chin as well as the front of her blouse. Fresh blood was running down the side of Sandi's face. His children, Adam and Sarah lay in the middle of the floor and looked dead. Roger looked into Mendosa's face and gasped, "My God! What have you done?"

Mendosa shocked Roger by abruptly slapping his face very hard and causing his head to snap to the side. In a low stern voice, Mendosa said, "You will only speak when I command you."

Roger had an innate fear of being hurt and now, suddenly, the prospect of being tortured was causing panic to well up inside of him. His lips contorted and he began to whimper, "Please. Oh, please don't . . ."

Mendosa interrupted. "Parlotti sent me," he said, enunciating the name. "Do you know what he wants me to do?"

Roger's eyes went wide at the mention of Parlotti's name, and he violently shook his head from side to side.

"He wants access to your Swiss bank account. The one with the ten million dollars. You and I, together, are going to access those accounts through your computer. What are the passwords and the codes?"

Roger blubbered, "I don't know the codes. I don't remember."

Mendosa was methodical. He had prepared a small tape recorder which was now running. He had also laid out a note pad and a pen to write down the codes as Roger would speak them. In his little black bag Mendosa had several pairs of fine latex gloves, an additional roll of duct tape and a chamois cloth for wiping fingerprints. Besides the anesthetic gas canister, he had a scissors, his favorite stiletto and a Waltham PK nine-millimeter pistol with a silencer. Having predetermined the upcoming order of his killings, Mendosa first chose the babysitter. Not only could she identify him, but taking her out in a dramatic fashion might make Roger break early. His wife, Sandi, would be next. Mendosa didn't know whether her shrewish behavior was the result of an earlier argument, or whether she genuinely did not like Roger. It was possible that killing Sandi might actually have a satisfying effect for Roger. Either way, the next one to die would be the little girl. The ten-year-old boy needed to be last because, in Mendosa's mind, a man would do more to protect his son than anyone else. Roger's demise, of course, was a foregone conclusion.

Mendosa spoke in a soft monotone, "Pay attention, Roger. Let us see if this will help you to remember." Mendosa grabbed the front of Mary's shirt and jerked his hands apart. The fabric tore and her buttons went flying in all directions. Mary lay there moaning with her breasts exposed. The act was not sexual. Rather, Mendosa wanted Roger to witness the full extent of the upcoming bloodbath. The assassin removed his knife from the black bag. Almost nine inches long, the stiletto housed a deadly blade. Mendosa held the weapon in front of Roger's eyes for a moment before pushing the release button. Focusing intently on the knife, Roger involuntarily sucked in a big gasp as the gleaming blade flashed upright. Mendosa placed the point just above Mary's left breast and plunged it in.

Sandi Blanchard had become fully conscious and had been watching the events in silent fear. When Mary convulsed with the pain of the stabbing and blood began to spurt, Sandi became hysterical. Although her mouth was taped, her muffled screams were surprisingly loud, and she began thrashing about.

Mendosa turned to Roger, "Tell me the code and password to your account."

Roger became distracted by Sandi's screams and her violent movements. Mendosa was slightly annoyed that Roger was not paying full attention. Roger was experiencing panic and hysteria was about to erupt. Mendosa had to shut Sandi up and get Roger to re-focus. Time for step two. Grabbing a handful of Sandi's hair, Mendosa brandished the lethal stiletto in front of her face. He turned to Roger. "This blade will go right into her eye, unless you tell me the codes."

Roger felt like his heart would pound out of his chest but still, he could only bring himself to say, "Please don't . . . oh, God. Please don't."

Mendosa had his knee and leg on Sandi's chest, preventing her from moving. His left hand had a vise like grip on her hair, which kept her head still. With his right hand he moved the blade tip a half-inch from her eye and glanced at Roger. Mendosa slowly pushed the shiny blade into her eye. She jerked spastically a few times while an abbreviated coughing sound came from her throat. Then, she was still.

What Mendosa did next caused Roger to vomit. Mendosa released his grip on Sandi's hair as well as the knife and stepped away from the body. Sandi lay face up at Roger's feet with a long, steel knife blade sticking out of her eye.

Mendosa waited for Roger to catch his breath. Then, he said, "I can make this all stop if you will tell me the codes."

Roger was sick. He was furtively looking back and forth at each of the bodies in the room when he heard Mendosa say, "Do you want your children to be next?"

Roger could only shake his head from side to side.

"Then, tell me the codes," Mendosa demanded.

Blubbering almost incoherently, Roger told him the codes.

Mendosa used the computer in the study to verify the authenticity of the codes. Satisfied that Roger had given him the correct information, Mendosa dispassionately fired one shot into Roger's forehead.

Mendosa made sure that all his victims were, in fact, dead. He went through the house checking all the little details of his actions, studying each scene as if he were a forensic specialist. He went through the house, going over each of his previous movements, looking for a telltale sign that might leave a clue or give away his identity. All the while, he silently recited the mantra he knew so well: "If you are careless or stupid, they will kill you."

Mendosa finished and disappeared into the night, leaving behind three dead bodies and two children. One of the children was sleeping. The other was not.

CHAPTER SEVEN

T he four of them were cruising south on Interstate 95 and enjoy ing the balmy winter air of South Florida. With the convertible top down, the rush of air was exhilarating. They passed the exit for Riviera Beach and traffic began to build. Scott exited at the next interchange and headed east toward Flagler Drive.

Crystal, sitting up front with Scott, was very animated and kept bouncing around in her seat attempting to talk with Pitch and Jennifer who were sitting close together in the back. "I'm so excited!" Crystal said. "I've never been on a big boat before. They look so cool! Is it called a 'yacht'? What's the difference between a yacht and a regular boat?"

Pitch was enjoying her adolescent exuberance and said with good-natured sarcasm, "One is larger than the other."

Scott added, "A boat is for holding a bucket of bait, while a yacht is for holding a bucket of champagne."

Jennifer spoke above the roar of rushing air. "Scott, I think it's wonderful of your parents to let us use their yacht this evening."

Pitch agreed, "It was nice, but we won't be seeing much of Scott tonight. In return for using the vessel, he had to promise to scour all the barnacles off the hull."

Scott, Pitch and Jennifer were all laughing as Crystal asked, "What *are* barnacles, anyway?"

Jennifer took a moment to focus her attention on Pitch. He was handsome in a studious sort of way. Although he wore his contacts most of the time, Jennifer felt he had the kind of face that would look good in glasses. His dark blonde, curly hair was piled heavily around his head and down his neck. He was almost six feet tall, which allowed her to wear heels and not worry about towering over him. A dry sense of humor seemed to be Pitch's hallmark, and she liked that quality. He also had a dazzling smile and she loved that. Most of all, Jennifer admired his intellect. It seemed that everyone had a story to tell about Pitch's sharp mind and clever inventiveness. She smiled at the recollection of Scott's story about the time Pitch was fourteen and built a series of motion detectors, each with a high decibel siren. Two nights after installing them around his parent's home, all the alarms sounded when a burglar broke in. Besides waking the entire neighborhood, the earsplitting wails of the multiple sirens disoriented the intruder. The police were called, the burglar was arrested and Pitch achieved notoriety when his picture was plastered all over the local news.

Pulling up to the gate of the yacht club, Scott was recognized by the guard on duty and waved through. Chattering brightly, the two couples walked down the long dock to where the biggest of the boats were moored. As they walked, Jennifer slipped her hand into Pitch's, giving him a tingle that shot up his arm. Approaching the yacht, Jennifer asked, "Peter, have you ever been on board?"

Pitch nodded. "Yes, quite a number of times. I even lived on board for about three weeks while I was apartment hunting."

Scott and Crystal had gone up ahead, boarded and turned on all the lights. The luminescent beauty of the scene made Jennifer catch her breath. With the lights reflecting against the sleek lines of the yacht and shimmering off the blackness of the water, it took on the look of a fairy tale, a picture postcard that wasn't quite real. Jennifer whispered, "Oh, Peter. This is beautiful!"

Pitch was warming to the moment. It began when he picked her up earlier and was awestruck by how beautiful she looked in her outfit. Big yellow polka dots painted against a white linen background, enhanced the deep olive tones of her skin. Pitch would have liked to say something complimentary such as, 'Not as beautiful as you.'

Instead, he weakly said, "Larger than the house I grew up in." Then, he bit his lip at the stupidity of his remark.

In a few minutes, the four of them were sitting out on deck chatting about the pros and cons of owning your own yacht. Scott suddenly changed the subject and asked, "Say, did either of you girls see the movie, 'Meet Joe Black?'"

Crystal became excited. "Ooo. Ooo," she bubbled. "That's the one with Brad Pitt."

Jennifer said apologetically, "Forgive Crystal. She gets tongue-tied whenever anyone mentions Brad Pitt. And, yes, we did. We rented the video just last week."

Pitch instantly recognized that Scott was moving the conversation towards their preplanned strategy. The thought of how this dialogue was going to proceed was making Pitch nervous. However, he kept recalling that they both agreed that Scott would broach the subject and do most of the talking.

Scott said, "How about 'Oceans Eleven?'"

Crystal stood up and walked to the railing. Her eyes closed as she rolled her neck and said, "He was so dreamy in that picture."

Scott said, "I heard he's going to make a movie with Jennifer Aniston."

Jennifer said, "Uh-oh, you just brought up a sore subject."

Crystal spun around. "Jennifer Aniston? That slut! She can't act her way out of a paper bag. And she definitely doesn't deserve Brad Pitt!"

Pitch nervously entered the conversation. "I disagree. I've seen her act on a number of occasions and think she's very accomplished."

Jennifer said, "Crystal, you don't like the woman because she's married to Brad Pitt, not because she's a bad actress."

Scott deliberately directed his next question to Crystal. "Do you have a poster of Brad Pitt?" he asked innocently.

Glancing at Jennifer, Crystal flushed just a bit and said with a big grin, "No. But I know where there is one."

Scott said, "Wait now. Don't tell me. Let me guess. It's probably someone like Lucy who has it hanging in her room."

Nervously, Pitch put his drink down on a stack tray. His hand trembled slightly.

Crystal said excitedly, "Yes. Exactly. She's got this humungous poster of him. And he's naked!"

Pitch felt the tips of his ears getting hot.

Jennifer turned to Scott and asked, "How is it that you know about Lucy?"

Pitch's mouth went dry as he wondered how Scott intended to answer that unanticipated query.

A blank look formed on Scott's face as his mind raced for a plausible reply. Jennifer's tone was one of curiosity as she continued, "I mean, you don't go to our school. I'm just surprised you would know her." As soon as the words came out of Jennifer's mouth, she was sorry she had spoken them. After all, Scott was a red-blooded American boy, and Lucy was a hot-blooded girl. It was possible that they might have had some kind of past relationship or something. More importantly, Jennifer did not want to upset the evening. She didn't want to open a can of worms that might hurt Crystal's feelings. Consequently, she decided to quickly change the subject.

Before she had a chance to do so, Scott said, "Pitch told me all about her!"

Pitch was stunned. Closing his eyes, he slumped down in the seat until his chin rested on his chest. Silently, he repeated the word, 'disaster.'

Turning her attention to Pitch, Jennifer said, "Really, Peter."

His brain ricocheting between a reasonable explanation and thoughts of murdering his pal, Pitch slowly sat up. He felt a coldness in the pit of his stomach, as he looked into Jennifer's eyes.

Before Pitch could answer, Scott said, "Are you kidding? Lucy's reputation extends much farther than your campus. I think Pitch was one of the first people to tell me about her but, believe me, everyone knows about Lucy."

Oblivious to the nuances that just swept past, Crystal saved the moment by saying, "Me and Jennifer were hysterical over that poster." Laughing over the memory, Crystal said, "Jennifer was pointing out the size of his 'exposition!' Weren't you Jenn?"

As Scott and Crystal chuckled over the remark, Pitch turned to

Jennifer and said with mock disappointment, "Really, Jennifer. 'The size of his exposition?' You surprise me."

There was a very brief moment of uncomfortable silence that was followed by the four of them breaking into gales of laughter.

When the hilarity subsided, Scott asked, "So, how is school going? Are you managing to keep the grades up?"

Jennifer was hoping the conversation would not be about her daily academic life. She had been looking forward to Pitch talking about something deeper, or perhaps more romantic.

Crystal said, "School is going okay. You know, some good, some not so good." She looked at Jennifer and said, "Miss suma-cum-laude here, is sailing right through all her classes. I don't know whether it's because she's so smart or because she gets all the good teachers."

Jennifer scoffed, "Oh, please! Professor Lunderman is positively disgusting. Such a slovenly man. How do you continue to work for him, Peter?"

Professor George Lunderman had the dual role of not only being one of Jennifer's instructors, but also Pitch's employer. Pitch had received his masters degree three years earlier and presently had a job working for Lunderman. The Professor had acquired a grant to study robotics and Pitch was the number one man on his staff.

Pitch said, "He leaves me alone and lets me do my own thing. I can be creative and even move off the parameters of the study. The Professor runs a very loose ship."

Scott said, "How about you, Crystal? Weren't you telling me about problems in your history class?"

Crystal said, "Yeah. Eastern Studies. It's okay, I guess. Jennifer has been helping me."

Pitch said, "Eastern Studies? What specific area are you studying?"

Jennifer replied, "We just got finished with Genghis Khan and the Mongols."

Crystal wrinkled her nose and said, "Doesn't that sound like a rock group?"

Scott put his hand to his forehead, posing like a man about to receive a vision from above and said to Crystal, "Let me see if I can guess your last exam score."

Crystal was not proud of her test score. "No," she said folding her arms and pouting. "I don't want to play this game."

Pitch was paying close attention to how Scott was maneuvering the conversation.

"Come on," urged Scott. "It'll be fun."

Crystal gave a little ground. "Well," she said, "I'm not going to tell you if you're right or wrong."

"Why not?" asked Scott.

"Because I'm not real proud of how I did on that that particular test."

"Did you pass?" asked Scott.

"Yes, I passed!" said Crystal indignantly.

Scott said, "Then, you must have gotten a sixty-six!"

Crystal went wide-eyed with gleeful surprise. Skipping over and sitting on Scott's lap, she said, "Oh, my God. You are just amazing!"

Scott turned to Pitch and said, "Pitch, old buddy, why don't you try and guess what Jennifer got on that exam?"

Pitch blanched. He assumed that 'guessing' Jennifer's score would not elicit quite the same reaction.

Although mildly surprised at Scott's revelation, Jennifer became much more interested in what Pitch was about to proclaim. She knew Pitch was super intelligent, a true prodigy in math and science, but doubted that he was also clairvoyant.

Hoping that Jennifer would not throw him overboard, Pitch drew a big breath and said, "Let's see. Wonder-woman that you are, I venture to guess . . . ninety-five."

"How close was he?" asked Scott.

Jennifer had a quizzical smile on her face as she looked back and forth between Pitch and Scott. She had a recollection of Crystal and herself talking about their grades while they were getting themselves ready for the evening. Then, she remembered that Marti and Amy, the two girls from across the hall, had come into their dorm room. "Have you fellas been talking to Marti or Amy?"

"Nope," said Pitch. "It is merely a manifestation of my psychic powers."

Crystal was becoming more and more excited with what was going on and began squirming around on Scott's lap. He was definitely enjoying the way things were going.

Continuing to glance back and forth between the two young men, Jennifer said dubiously, "Well, aren't the two of you the clever ones."

Crystal said, "You guys are great! What else can you tell us?"

Scott said, "Lucy is a size 38-D."

Jennifer said, "Well, if you knew Lucy had a poster of Brad Pitt in the buff, then knowing the size of her bra is no big deal."

"Yes it is," Crystal said defending Scott's pronouncement. "I didn't know that until earlier."

Pitch, who was now emboldened by how well this was all going, looked at Crystal and declared, "I know what color panties you're wearing."

Crystal jumped off Scott's lap and began smoothing down the fabric on her shorts. "Hey!" she declared aghast. "You've been looking up my leg, Pitch!"

Scott reached for Crystal's hand and said, "Don't worry about it, Crystal. Blue is my favorite color."

Crystal spun around to look at Scott. A coy smile crept to the corners of her mouth.

Jennifer turned to Pitch and said with a cynical smile, "Tell me, Mr. Pechowski. Which panties am I wearing?"

Her look was riveting, and Pitch watched her smile fade. He swallowed before answering. "White with yellow flowers?" he said, like a man waiting to be executed.

A sudden flash of insight came to Crystal as she exclaimed delightedly, "Hey! You fellas were watching us get dressed!"

"It would certainly seem so," agreed Jennifer.

"No. No." said Pitch sensing that Jennifer was becoming perturbed. "That's not it at all."

Scott quickly added, "We wanted to make you girls a part of this great experiment."

Crystal was bubbling over with enthusiasm as she said, "This is so cool. So . . . excellent!"

Jennifer cocked one eyebrow and asked suspiciously, "What great experiment?"

Pitch said, "A kind of a test run for my prototype device. I've been working on this gizmo that allows me to activate someone's telephone, without them picking it up."

Scott chimed in. "Pitch is going to become a multi-millionaire. As soon as it's complete, every guy on every campus in the world will want one. Tell them what you call it, Pitch."

Pitch said, "I call it 'The Ultimate Bug.'"

Jennifer said, "So, you had it hooked up to the phone in our room."

"Yes," said Pitch watching her face for any signs of consternation.

Crystal asked, "How did you guys get in there without us knowing?"

Scott said, "That's the beauty of this thing. You don't have to be there to hook anything up. Pitch figured a way to do it through electronics and computers and . . . I don't know. Tell 'em, Pitch."

Pitch began describing his invention and was soon directing all his explanations toward Jennifer. He told her everything from the beginning. The seeds that germinated the idea came from that silly device known as "The Clapper." If The Clapper could turn lights on and off just by clapping your hands, then there must be a way to activate all sorts of electronic devices through sound or vibration. Listing his experiments with a toaster, a can opener, and a microwave, he explained how each appliance required a slightly different signal to turn it on or off. He described how he was able to manipulate different electronic signals with the aid of a computer program he developed and how easy it was to control. In addition, technology was already in place whereby a person, dialing his own telephone from a remote location and punching in a few numbers on the keypad, could make his answering machine perform a variety of different functions. That was the signpost that led him down the right path.

Pitch said excitedly, "So, if a person wants to listen to you and Crystal talking in the privacy of your dorm room, all he has to do is plant a microphone in your room. Right?"

"Yes," said Jennifer, somewhat dubious, but nevertheless mesmerized. "Go on."

"Well, the microphone is already there!" Pitch said enthusiastically. He paused a moment waiting for Jennifer to acknowledge his statement.

Jennifer just stared at him.

Pitch continued, "It's been there even before you girls moved in."

Crystal sat on the edge of her seat, wide-eyed, hoping that clarity would set in and give her even a hint of understanding. Jennifer narrowed her gaze, as the significance of his words began to make sense.

Pitch tried again. "The microphone . . . it's in your telephone receiver!" he said excitedly. "Every telephone has one. All I had to do . . . was turn it on."

"So, this is like . . ." Jennifer paused, trying to think of a particular term, "a wire-tap?"

"No. Not at all," answered Pitch shaking his head. "A wire-tap is designed to listen in on your telephone conversations. My device works more like a 'speaker-phone' that's been set up in your room."

"A speaker phone?" repeated Jennifer.

"Right," agreed Pitch. "Just picture a big invisible microphone sitting in the middle of your room. When I turn it on, I can listen to any conversation that's taking place within forty feet of it."

"Really?" exclaimed Jennifer. "Not just phone conversations?"

"Right," said Pitch nodding his head. "I can hear everything."

Scott piped in. "Pitch figured a way to enhance the voices and clean up any extraneous sounds. He can hear you, even if you and Crystal are whispering in the corner."

"Oh, my God," said Jennifer softly.

As Pitch continued his dissertation, Jennifer was experiencing several emotions simultaneously. She was fascinated with what Pitch had done, but she had a nagging feeling about it as well.

Crystal was becoming bored with the technical details. "I have to go to the bathroom," she declared. "Come show me where it is, Scott."

Scott stood and took her hand. "I'm not sure I remember where it is," he said, "but let's see if we can find it. Then, we'll see what other trouble we can get into."

Crystal giggled and the two of them disappeared into the main stateroom.

Jennifer listened as Pitch explained the details of the computer program he had created. It was a program that allowed him to initiate the signal and activate the microphone. "What happens," asked Jennifer, "if while you're listening in on the conversation between me and Crystal, one of us picks up the phone in order to make a call?"

"Nothing," answered Pitch. "Once I have the microphone turned on, it stays on. I can still listen in on everything, including your phone conversation. But the really cool thing is that it doesn't disconnect even when you hang up. The microphone stays activated and I can still listen to you and Crystal when you resume your private little chat."

"Does it work on business phones as well as residential phones?"

"Oh, yes," answered Pitch. "It works just fine. Let me give you an example. I have it programmed so that I can call the main switchboard at the university. Once they answer, I use that connection to link up with any extension within the building's telephone system."

Jennifer wrinkled her brow. "So, let's say you wanted to listen in on a private conversation that the Dean of our university was having in his office . . ."

Pitch interjected. "Dean Albert Chase? Simple. All I need to know is his extension. After I'm connected with the main switchboard, I just enter his extension number into my program, and . . ." Pitch snapped his fingers making a loud pop. "I can hear everything that's going on in his office."

"So, you could do the same thing at say . . . IBM, or General Motors, or any other corporation, right?"

"Uh . . . yes," said Pitch. "I suppose so."

Jennifer had a few more questions, but soon was discussing the moral implications of listening in on someone's private life. "Peter," she said cautiously, "I'm not so sure this is a good idea."

Pitch was silent.

Looking at him, Jennifer realized that, instead of being complimented for his ingenuity, he was being chided for it. Jennifer tried again. "It doesn't mean your invention is no good," she explained. "I mean, it took somebody with unquestioned brilliance to invent napalm, for God's sake, but that doesn't mean it was a good idea."

"Napalm?" cried Pitch. "Isn't that a little heavy handed for an analogy? This is just a listening device. Nobody dies."

Jennifer was biting her lip. She was immediately sorry for the words she had spoken and hoped it would not start an argument. However, she was concerned about just how invasive a device like this could be. "It's just that . . . I don't know," Jennifer hesitated. "It's just that, now that I know you were listening to us earlier, it feels a little creepy. It's like having somebody say, 'Hey Jennifer, while you were in the shower, there was some man looking in your bathroom window.' Do you know what I mean?"

Pitch lowered his head and nodded, now understanding her feelings. As they talked, Pitch was becoming aware of her deeper nature. She had an ability to think beyond the moment and a willingness to prod him into thinking about the wider scope of things. She seemed to be enveloping him, and he was feeling himself being drawn inside. It felt very good.

For Jennifer's part, she began to understand the range of his intellect. She was impressed with how he could pull knowledge from a variety of sources to focus on one point. He was like a chess player constantly having hundreds of simultaneous games and still able to remember the details of each one, even though the boards were not in front of him. He was a genius. All he needed was a little humanity, and it seemed to her that he was craving it. It also seemed to Jennifer that he wanted it from her.

Pitch and Jennifer continued to sit on the aft deck and spoke softly about many things. After a time, they, too, went inside the sleek-hulled vessel.

CHAPTER
EIGHT

Lincoln Donald Bradshaw was sitting on the poolside patio at the home of his friend and mentor, Preston Collingsworth. The patio had a textured, multi-colored stone decking surrounding the pool. Both sides of the expansive patio had rich foliage consisting of Empress palms, Queen palms and other broadleaf plants. The home was in Palm Beach and, as usual, the sea breezes were causing the palm fronds to whisper hisses as they danced in the wind.

Located in the southeast region of Florida, Palm Beach is a barrier island that sparkles diamond-like in a bed of precious stones. It is bordered on the west by Lake Worth, a beautiful body of water almost thirty miles long north to south, but a little less than one-half mile wide at its widest point. The east side of Palm Beach hugs the wave-swept and sandy beaches of the Atlantic Ocean.

Alone for the moment, Lincoln moved over to a softly padded chaise lounge, closed his eyes and cleared his mind. He took a few moments to inhale the ocean breezes and, since the sun had not yet broken over the top of the three-story mansion, enjoy the coolness of the shade.

"Linc," as his friends liked to call him, was a tall man, six-foot-four, with rugged good looks and sandy hair that tended to streak blonde from the sun. He was in his middle thirties and although he was very athletic, he still worked hard at keeping himself in shape. For five days a week, he found two hours each day to go to the gym and work out. Even though his days as a professional athlete were over, three knee operations had taken care of that, he still split his gym time between judiciously lifting weights and running on a steeply inclined treadmill. His knee, on the other hand, was like a barometer, twinging when it signaled a drastic weather change. Sometimes, when he was extremely tired, it would get sore enough to cause a slight limp. Today, however, was a good day.

Preston Collingsworth came striding out of the house and across the patio. Slim, well-groomed, and properly postured, Preston was a man in his late fifties who always looked a decade younger. Preston had been blessed at birth with good fortune. His father, an Englishman, had made a great deal of money as a munitions dealer during World War II. Preston however, had been skillful enough to take the money his father left him and parlay it into a veritable fortune. Over the years, he was able to amass more than a billion dollars through a series of insightful and serendipitous investments. Besides living well, he was a compassionate and generous man.

Seeing Linc stretched out on the chaise lounge, Preston smiled inwardly. He was pleased to see how well Linc had grown as a man. Preston was proud of his friend. Linc had strong character traits. He had integrity. He was honest, intrepid and smart, and Preston loved him like a son. Their relationship had come a long way over the years.

Although their personalities were very different, they got along famously. Like a father, Preston would boast to his friends about Linc's accomplishments. Linc, in turn, viewed Preston as his role model. Preston had some quirks to his nature but just like a son, Linc overlooked them. Instead, Linc chose to respect and admire the man's good qualities. Whenever there were times when Linc needed advice or help in financial situations, Preston was always there to offer whatever he could. Likewise, circumstances arose when Preston needed Linc's help and, of course, Linc would always come to the rescue.

One such literal incident happened six years prior. Preston was in the middle of trying to convince Linc to go into business for himself. Preston wanted Linc to become a private investigator and offered to fully finance the venture. Both men were in Miami and stopped to have a quick lunch at a fast food spot called "Jeremy's Flame-Pit Burgers." Preston went up to the counter to place the order.

As Linc headed to the bathroom, he called over his shoulder, "Order me two Bomber-Burgers, loaded. Oh yeah, and a diet . . . whatever."

It was about two-thirty in the afternoon on that fateful day and the lunch crowd had thinned. Besides Preston and Linc, there were only five other customers in the restaurant. Preston was in the middle of placing his order when the front doors burst open. Two men came in holding guns in their outstretched arms and yelling. "Okay all y'muthafuckas! Everybody be cool. Dis here's a stick-up!" Flashing their guns and threatening death, they moved very quickly while yelling their obscenities.

The taller of the two young gunmen herded everyone up to the front counter while the shorter, skinny one jumped over the counter and gathered the employees together. The robbers began screaming at the manager to open the registers and hand over the money.

While the manager nervously tried to comply, Preston made a mistake. He made eye contact with the gunman standing nearby.

"What the fuck are you looking at?" hollered the tall one, menacingly. He held the gun just inches from Preston's nose. "You trying to Eye-dentify me, motherfucker?"

Preston broke eye contact and looked away, but it was too late. The gunman swung the pistol at Preston and caught him on the side of his head. Preston wasn't prepared for the violent act, and the blow opened up a gash just above his ear. It started to bleed profusely.

The armed robber screamed at the customers. "Empty your pockets! Put your fuckin' money on the counter! Do it! Now!"

Everyone looked at Preston. Bent over the counter, he had blood pouring from his head and down his face. He was trying to keep his knees from buckling. There was a momentary silence broken by the sound of a toilet flushing. Everyone glanced toward the bathroom.

The taller of the two thieves yelled, "Sonofabitch! Cootie, there's someone in the bathroom. Go check it out."

Cootie, the short, skinny one, slid back over the stainless steel counter, and moved quickly to the bathroom door. Using his foot,

Cootie snapped the door open hard and fast. The door stayed open. Fearing for Linc's life, Preston stole a glance inside, but could only see a partially concealed sink and mirror. Nothing else. Moving forward cautiously, Cootie kept his knees slightly bent, and his gun-hand fully extended. He disappeared inside the bathroom.

Everyone was startled by a muffled yell and a shot that rang out. It was followed by the sounds of a brief, violent struggle. Then, silence.

The man holding the gun on Preston panicked. "Oh, shit," he uttered, staring toward the bathroom. "Cootie?" he called. "Cootie, goddamnit! Come on, man. Quit fuckin' around!" He began a nervous two-step, first taking two steps toward the bathroom, then two steps toward the front door followed by a couple of steps toward his hostages. All the while, holding a trembling pistol straight out at arm's length.

Linc had heard the commotion from the beginning. Concealed in the bathroom, he had hoisted himself up to peer through a transom window above the door. When he saw Preston get pistol-whipped, Linc knew he had to do something to draw the gunmen to him. Flushing both toilets worked.

Cootie had nervously tip-toed into the bathroom with his gun arm extended. Linc flashed out from behind a short vanity wall, grabbed Cootie's arm at the wrist and pulled him forward. The gun went off just as Cootie came into contact with Linc's left hook. His fist had the force of a jackhammer, and it caught Cootie fully in his right ear. Linc smashed Cootie's forearm. It made a sickening sound as it broke into a compound fracture. Then, Linc grabbed the man by his collar and the seat of his pants. With the motion of a battering ram, Linc threw Cootie headfirst into the tile wall. Unconscious, Cootie slumped to the floor. Linc grabbed the gun and checked to see how many shots were left. The gun was empty.

Linc shook his head realizing that the thief had come to rob this place with only one bullet. "Dumb piece of shit," he whispered.

Linc turned his attention to the ranting of the remaining gunman who was yelling for his buddy. Hearing him call, 'Cootie! You get the fuck out here,' Linc gathered up Cootie's limp body and literally threw him out of the bathroom door.

Linc was big and strong. Cootie was small and light. From inside the bathroom doorway, Cootie came flying out like Superman. All eyes were on Cootie as he arced to a height of about five feet and landed a dozen feet away, crashing into a table and two chairs. What happened next was just a blur.

Linc charged out of the bathroom at full tilt. He covered the distance so quickly that the robber didn't even have time to turn. With the power of a wrecking-ball, Linc drove the man into the hard tile floor. The pistol that the gangster had been holding was jarred loose and skittered across the floor out of harms way. Linc lifted the man to his feet. Holding him up with his left hand, he was about to punch him directly in the face with his right. Instead, Linc hesitated. The man's eyes were glazed over and the fight had gone out of him. Linc plopped him into a chair as the manager of Jeremy's called 911.

Although that incident happened more than six years ago, Preston would be forever grateful.

"Sorry about that," said Preston, apologizing for leaving his guest alone at the pool. "But that was one phone call I had to take."

"No problem," said Linc. "It gave me a moment to relax."

Linc had spent many hours in the company of Preston Collingsworth and was used to the occasional interruptions that were a result of his business dealings. Linc enjoyed the time he spent with Preston. There always seemed to be something interesting to talk about or something new to learn. It might be a fresh twist on an old subject, an opportunity for a profitable investment or a new case into which Linc could sink his teeth. Sometimes, they would trade tales of their past. Stories of interesting characters who had come in and out of their lives. Even though they were both unattached, with Linc having never been married and Preston having been a widower for more than twenty years, they rarely talked about their escapades with women. Purposely, they chose to keep their love life and any past indiscretions to themselves. Their friendship included a healthy respect for one another.

Linc was a private investigator. After a stint with the Palm Beach County Sheriff's Department and a few years with the U.S. Marshall's Service, he opened his agency. It was the best thing he ever did. Despite almost no advertising, business remained brisk. Clients came to him by word of mouth and very often with the recommendation of Preston Collingsworth. Preston seemed to have a vast network of contacts, including Palm Beach residents and Capitol Hill VIPs.

One such VIP was Senator Boyd Williamson, a high-ranking member of the powerful Senate Appropriations Committee. Preston and the Senator were well acquainted with a sleazy Congressman by the name of Jack Higgins.

"What's the latest news about Congressman Jack?" asked Preston.

"Nothing that his momma's going to be proud of," replied Linc. "I've gathered enough dirt to start the ball rolling. The Ethics Committee has all the evidence and will be starting proceedings next week."

"Did you have any trouble getting witnesses?"

"No," said Linc. "Once Betsy started talking, three other female interns came forward. Then, surprise-surprise, one innocent-looking young man, who does odd jobs for the Congressman, also claimed that he was being fondled."

Preston mulled over Linc's reply before saying, "I trust the evidence is strong enough to get him removed from the Oversight Committee, or at least to get him censured?"

Linc smiled wryly. "Preston, I think there's enough evidence to send him to the slammer. Of course, that won't happen. When you had Senator Boyd Williamson get in touch with me, he clued me in to the things that his niece, Betsy, had been intimating."

"So, Boyd introduced you to Betsy," said Preston, getting it straight in his mind, "and she spilled the beans."

"It wasn't quite that simple," said Linc. "First, I had to dig up some dirt on Congressman Jack. Something that I could use to convince Betsy to talk."

"How'd you do that?" asked Preston.

Linc smiled and slowly shook his head. "Let's just say that some work was done around two a.m. on a moonless night. And everyone was wearing black camouflage."

"Did anybody break the law?" asked Preston with a frown on his face.

"Preston," began Linc, "I don't want to give you a lot of details about how the information was gathered, but suffice it to say, that Senator Williamson has a lot of connections. Covert connections. And those guys have all the latest in electronic toys."

Preston smiled. "So, poor old Jack Higgins never had a chance, did he?"

Linc shook his head. "Nope. No chance at all. There was a whole lot of sneakin' around, after which Congressman Jack ended up being wired every which way from Sunday. There was no way he could keep any secrets from us."

"What kind of information did you extract from Higgins?" asked Preston.

"Unfortunately for Jack Higgins, he's got a big mouth. He said some things about Betsy that weren't nice at all. When we played the tapes for her . . ." Linc chuckled at the memory. "Boy, was she mad."

Preston sat forward in his chair. "Really? What did she hear him say on the tapes?"

Linc turned with a raised eyebrow. "Preston, you're too much of a gossip," he said with a snort. "All I'm going to tell you is that Betsy was very forthcoming about all the sexual advances Congressman Jack was making."

"Sexual advances," repeated Preston shaking his head in disbelief.

"Wait. It gets better," said Linc hinting at a carnal tale that was even more provocative. "Guess what? A diary showed up. It turns out sweet, innocent Betsy had been keeping a diary with precise data. Dates, times, witnesses, you know, that sort of thing. That's where I got the names of the three other female interns and the young man."

"Then, why won't he be prosecuted?" asked Preston.

"Well, the 'put-him-away' evidence comes from Betsy and her friend, Holly. That idiot Congressman arranged to bring both of the girls to the Excelsior Hotel at the same time under the pretext of meeting some Middle Eastern potentate. Once he got them there, he actually jumped on the bed and dropped his drawers."

"Is that so?" said Preston suppressing a chuckle.

"Despite all of that," continued Linc, "Senator Williamson has convinced Betsy and Holly that it would be in their best interests not to have their names dragged through the Capitol Hill mud. As a result, they're not going to testify. Both girls remember what happened to Bill Clinton's favorite intern, Monica Lewinsky, and how the press turned her into an international slut. The damage to Congressman Jack from the Ethics Committee and the press is all going to happen because of the confessions of that young gay man who's accusing Jack of some very kinky things. Since Betsy and Holly aren't going to testify, the case for sending him to jail is considerably weaker."

"Then, Jack Higgins could fight this thing and conceivably retain his post on the committee. Correct?"

"No," said Linc with a big smile. "Boyd Williamson is too smart of a politician to let the man get away with that. Boyd had a meeting with Jack and showed him the evidence that the two girls put together. Boyd said that Jack was so scared, he almost crapped his pants. Boyd also said it'll be a long time before the good congressman even gets another erection. Fact is, Jack Higgins is going to step down and consider another line of work."

Preston smiled. "Monica Lewinsky and ultimately Bill Clinton both got trapped by a secret tape recording, didn't they?"

"That's true. But whereas that Linda Tripp woman had only used a little micro-cassette recorder that she probably got at Wal-Mart for twenty bucks, the equipment that the feds used was so sophisticated it put a whole new meaning on the word, 'eavesdropping.' Those boys really skirt the edge of what's legal and what's not."

Preston leaned back in his chair and half-closed his eyes. "I would love to be able to listen to those tapes," he said softly.

Linc continued, "By the way, Boyd Williamson said he would call you with the details sometime today. When he calls, act surprised."

Louise, Preston's administrator, came out to the pool deck. "Good morning, Mr. Bradshaw," she said to Linc. Turning to Preston, she said, "I hope I'm not disturbing you Mr. Collingsworth, but the people bringing the tables and chairs for the party have brought them early. I've made prior arrangements to have the floors polished today, and there is no place to store the tables and chairs. I plan to send them back and have them re-delivered tomorrow. Unfortunately, it'll incur an extra expense."

"That's fine, Louise," said Preston. "I trust your judgment implicitly."

Louise had been Preston's administrator for years. She took care of all the details of running a large estate, including managing the staff and paying the bills. She was in her early fifties, polite and gracious, but maintained a distinct air of formality. Preston relied on her expertise and, in turn, she was caring, diligent, and trustworthy.

Preston said, "Louise, could you have Manfred bring breakfast out here to the pool deck?"

"Certainly, Mr. Collingsworth," she replied. Then, added with a slight smile and nod, "Good day, Mr. Bradshaw."

Preston adjusted his position in the lounge chair and said, "Linc, I want you to come early to the party tomorrow night. There's someone very special I'd like you to meet."

Preston would have large social gatherings on a fairly regular basis. Often, he would use those occasions to extol the virtues or good deeds of people he knew. Other times, the parties would be veiled fundraisers for politicians or political action groups. Occasionally, they were his vehicle for introducing people in a social setting.

"Who's that?" asked Linc.

Speaking softly and with a warm smile, Preston said, "Emily."

Linc couldn't help but notice the twinkle in Preston's eye as he mentioned his daughter's name. Linc felt good for his friend and returned the smile as he said, "Wonderful news. How long has it been? Six years since she's been stateside?"

"More like seven," said Preston.

"Will she be staying long?"

For a moment, Preston turned quiet as his emotions got the better of him. Then, he smiled and spoke in a husky voice. "She's coming home to stay, Linc. Can you believe it?"

Manfred wheeled out a large rolling table filled with breakfast foods. Linc had been a guest in the house for numerous meals and Manfred knew exactly how Linc liked his eggs; over easy. The cart held a hot casserole consisting of chunks of Virginia ham, Colby cheese and roasted potatoes. There was also a selection of bagels, muffins, and breakfast pastries. Marmalade and warm blackberry jam took up one side of the tray along with fresh squeezed orange juice, slices of grapefruit and some fresh figs. Hot coffee completed the array. Manfred set one of the patio tables with colorful china in a contemporary geometric pattern of mustardy yellows and Wedgwood blues. Arranging the silverware and napkins, Manfred asked in his rich Austrian accent, "Vill zehr be any zing else, Mr. Collingsvort?"

Preston thanked him for such a fine presentation and Manfred departed.

"Well, I finally get to meet your Emily," said Linc, picking up the conversation from where it had left off and popping a piece of grapefruit into his mouth.

Preston sat up and became serious. "This introduction is very important to me, Linc. Over the years, you've become like a son to me, and I want so much for both of you to meet and like each other."

"From everything you've told me about Emily, a person couldn't help but admire her."

Preston sensed that he had not made his point. "Admiration be damned!" he exclaimed. "Sure she's intelligent. Genius, probably. But I'm talking about her personality, her character, her sense of humor. I'm hoping the two of you will mesh and become close."

"Now, Preston," said Linc shaking his head. "You can't rush people into friendships. It takes time and a natural course of events to develop a close friendship."

"I know that to be true," said Preston impatiently. "But I know people and what makes them tick. And I know the two of you were made for each other."

Linc almost choked on his orange juice. "Made for each other? What are you talking about? First, you make it sound like we should be brother and sister. Next, with a snap of your finger you have us set up as best friends, and in the next sentence," Linc spread his hands questioningly, "it sounds like you're trying to marry us off to each other!"

Preston's smile got bigger and broader as Linc was spouting off. "Lincoln, my boy . . . you've always been quick to grasp things."

CHAPTER NINE

Professor George Lunderman was upset. Exiting from a meeting with Albert Chase, the Dean of Southeast Florida State University, Lunderman realized that it had not gone well. George Lunderman was a slovenly man and the more upset he became, the more disheveled he looked. Wearing pants that were ill-fitted around his big belly, they kept slipping down, forcing him to constantly hike at them as he walked. In turn, that action caused his shirttail to ride up and out and to hang unevenly over his left hip and rump. The knot of his tie never seemed to be squared off at his shirt collar, and one collar point, like a rusted weather vane, always pointed in the wrong direction. The Professor's thinning hair was unruly at best, and when he didn't wash it for several days, an odd thing happened. The slightest breeze caused tufts of his hair to blow into an upright position and remain there.

Professor George Lunderman had been at the university long enough to have attained tenure and that was fortunate for him. Had it not been for the tenure, he probably would have been fired. Although he had adequate teaching skills, none of his students liked him, and he garnered almost no respect from his peers on the faculty. On the contrary, they were always making fun of him. Some years earlier, several faculty members had proposed a "Lunderman Day" during which everyone would dress like a slob, refrain from brushing his teeth, and wear their clothes to allow their "butt-crack" to show every time they bent over. Even though the proposition was strictly tongue-in-cheek, the Dean of the university got wind of the proposal and quickly had it quashed.

Two years prior, Lunderman had talked the school into funding a research project on robotics. It was his project. He had his name on the top of the research paper. It had taken him a long time to convince the Dean and the rest of the committee of the validity of such a project. The truth of the matter was, the study had very little merit. Lunderman had pushed to initiate the study to win the respect of the rest of the faculty, a validation he desperately craved.

Despite his efforts, things were floundering and going in the wrong direction. Dean Chase had just notified Lunderman that his funding was about to be cut off. He told Lunderman that he was sorry, but that his hands were tied and, that sometimes, these things didn't work out.

Dean Chase went on and complimented Lunderman on his ability to assemble a very good staff. "You know, George," said Chase, "you've been especially lucky to have had that Pechowski boy working with you. He was a real find, and it'll be a shame to lose a sharp mind like his."

The meeting had lasted a lot longer than the Dean had anticipated. Lunderman had pleaded, yelled, cajoled and cried, but Dean Chase stood his ground. Lunderman got angry, stamped his foot and inadvertently passed gas. Dean Chase was anxious for the meeting to end. Lunderman began nagging and whining until the Dean finally told him, "George, if you can come up with a better idea, I could reconsider this funding issue. Why don't you speak to that Pechowski boy? Do you realize he's a certifiable genius? See what ideas are floating around in his head. Maybe together you can come up with something worth while."

Mumbling to himself, Lunderman walked across the campus quad and into the school's cafeteria. He spotted Pitch Pechowski having lunch with Jennifer Morano and Crystal Richards.

Crystal was the first to see him coming and leaned across the table to whisper, "Oh no! Here comes the lecher." He was referred to as "the lecher," out of earshot of course, by some of his female students because of the way he stared lasciviously at their exposed legs and down the front of their blouses. If the view was titillating enough, a bead of sweat would quickly form over the man's upper lip.

The Professor shuffled over to their table, laid down his papers, books and shoulder bag and plopped into the remaining chair. Pitch and Jennifer were also unhappy with his intrusion. Had Lunderman paid attention, he would have seen it on their faces.

Lunderman, however, had something else on his mind and after a heavy sigh, came right to the point. "I've lost my funding for the project, Pitch."

Pitch looked back and forth between the girls and Lunderman. "What are you referring to, Professor?" he asked quizzically.

"The robotics study, Pitch. It's gone."

"Gone?" asked Pitch. "What do you mean, gone?"

"Dean Chase just cancelled all funding for my science project," Lunderman said with another sigh.

Pitch leaned back in his chair. He was not surprised. In fact, he had suspected that this sort of thing was inevitable. Lunderman was easily distracted. Pouncing on a good idea, he would set the ball in motion before quickly losing interest. Lacking leadership, Professor Lunderman was not a candidate to head up a scientific project, or any project for that matter.

"Why? What happened?" asked Pitch.

Jennifer and Crystal were fascinated with the conversation. Jennifer was concerned about Pitch's livelihood and the fact that his days on campus might be short-lived. Crystal was just tuned into the drama of the situation and with wide eyes said, "Yeah, What happened?"

Lunderman replied, "Dean Chase told me the project had lost its direction and wasn't accomplishing the goals I set for it."

Pitch knew that to be true. The Professor was more interested in accolades than accomplishments. Pitch said, "Professor, I'm sure you're aware of the lack of . . ."

Lunderman wasn't listening. He spoke over top of Pitch. "The Dean said the University could only afford limited funding and that I would need something really spectacular in order to get funded again."

"I understand, Professor," said Pitch, "but it isn't easy to come up with . . ."

Lunderman interrupted once more. "He actually suggested that I should speak to you about some fresh ideas. Pick your brain. That sort of thing."

Crystal had been snapping her head back and forth between the two men as if watching a tennis match and blurted out, "Pitch has this great invention! Don't you, Pitch? It's super! It can listen in on someone's private conversation without them ever knowing it."

Pitch was stunned. He had neither anticipated Crystal's exuberance for his invention, nor that she would blab about it.

Lunderman stared at Crystal. He was trying to absorb her words when Jennifer said, "Crystal, you shouldn't interrupt. This is between Professor Lunderman and Peter."

"I know," said Crystal excitedly. "But this might be what he's looking for."

Lunderman looked at Pitch, then Crystal and asked, "What is it, again?"

Pitch was recovering. "Nothing really. Just a silly prank thing I was working on."

"What kind of . . . prank thing?" Lunderman asked.

Crystal chimed in dramatically, "He calls it 'The Ultimate Bug!'"

Lunderman was a professor of engineering and had a modest understanding about such things. "A listening device?" he asked curiously. "A bug? What's special about a bug?"

Pitch stammered, "Really, Professor, it's insignificant. It's . . ."

Crystal was beginning to bounce up and down. "Don't let him fool you, Professor! He's so modest. That little bug is terrific! He got it to go inside our telephone without even being there."

Annoyed, Pitch said, "Crystal. Please . . ."

Jennifer said sternly, "Crystal, it isn't polite to jump into the middle of someone else's conversation when you haven't been invited."

Crystal said, "But Professor Lunderman said that Dean Chase said . . ."

Lunderman looked at Pitch, "Tell me about it, Pitch. How does it work? What does she mean when she said, 'without even being there?'"

Jennifer had many questions herself, but on a different plane. She wanted to know when the project was going to shut down. Would Pitch still be employed? What was he planning on doing now? She knew this was not the time to ask these questions. Pitch needed to have a private conversation with Professor Lunderman. Jennifer stood up. She had to get Crystal out of there. Poor Pitch was mortified with the things Crystal had divulged. "Crystal," she said, as she took her arm firmly, "We have to go. We're going to be late."

Crystal did not want to leave just yet, but Jennifer knew best, and she had a good grip on her roommate's arm. "Okay. So long," said Crystal as she quickly gathered her things.

Jennifer put a hand on Pitch's shoulder and said, "I'll talk to you later, Peter." Then, to Lunderman, "Nice to see you again, Professor. Bye for now."

As the girls walked away, Pitch could hear Crystal asking, "Late for what, Jenn?"

CHAPTER TEN

L underman was relentless. His understanding of engineering and electronics allowed for many of his technical questions to be dead-on. Pitch had very little room to maneuver. Although Pitch had no intention of giving up the secrets to his listening device, Lunderman had him squirming. Pitch tried his best to be vague and wished he were somewhere else. However, it was the middle of a work week, and Professor Lunderman was his boss. Pitch could not very well excuse himself by saying, 'Sorry, Professor, I have to be somewhere else.' Still and all, Pitch did have a slight edge. It was true that Lunderman knew a great deal about the theory of listening devices, but he was very weak in his knowledge of computers. Fortunately for Pitch, the use of a computer along with some specialized computer software that he had designed, played an integral part in the operation of the device. Pitch was able to dance around most of the key points that made his invention unique.

An hour into the interrogation, the path of their dialogue took a different turn.

Enthusiastic about what Pitch had created, Lunderman spoke at length about the uniqueness of the invention. The Professor realized that Dean Chase had been correct in his assessment of Pitch's genius. Lunderman was willing to partner up with Pitch in order to get funding for a brand new scientific study.

Speaking on a grandiose scale, Lunderman talked about how much money could be made from such an invention. The Professor suggested that this was not something to be sold, rather, it was something that should be licensed to various groups. That way, the inventor could control the distribution and ultimately, the profits. Even though Pitch had made it operational, Lunderman felt that the problems had not yet been worked out. He spoke to Pitch about a joint venture, one that would set them up as partners in a new scientific study and later as partners in business. When Lunderman told Pitch that this was the kind of program that would earn Pitch millions of dollars *and* his doctorate, Pitch began to pay more attention.

"My doctorate?" questioned Pitch.

"Oh, yes," answered Lunderman expansively. "This would make the perfect doctoral thesis. 'Professor Pitch Pechowski.' How does that sound?"

Pitch tried the title in a whisper. "Doctor Pitch Pechowski." He tried again. "Doctor Peter Pechowski." Aloud, he said, "Jennifer may be right. I think I may have to go back to using 'Peter' instead of 'Pitch.'"

Lunderman smiled. He went on to say that, together, they would chronicle the results of the study, and then publish an outstanding paper. It would receive worldwide acclaim. At one point in his spiel, Lunderman actually used the phrase, "Nobel Laureate."

Pitch was becoming intrigued. He liked the idea of being captain of his own ship. Always hoping to continue his education, Pitch dreamed about receiving his Ph.D. Making a truckload of money sounded pretty good, too. Pitch recognized that Lunderman was more worldly. After all, the Professor had been successful at getting funding once before.

Lunderman talked about contacts he had in Washington, D.C. who could get him huge government grants for serious research. As Lunderman continued to extol the benefits of a joint venture, he began to gain a broader view of what it would mean for himself. There would be no need to go back to Dean Chase and humiliate himself for the few paltry dollars the University could afford. Especially, not with something of this magnitude. He would talk directly to the power brokers at the National Science Foundation in the Nation's Capitol.

Pitch said he felt the idea of being partners was worth looking into. When he spoke those words, Lunderman became very excited. Tempering the Professor's joy, Pitch said that he was not yet willing to commit to it. There were three issues he would want resolved. First, Lunderman would have to demonstrate that he could actually get the funding. Next, Pitch would want his name listed as one of the two principal researchers. Then, Pitch sat forward in his chair. "Lastly," he stated, "if you could make arrangements with the faculty of the university to have this project be accepted as my doctoral thesis, I would be more interested."

Lunderman was ecstatic. He assured Pitch that none of his requests would pose a problem and that he had the wherewithal to make it happen. Following that, Lunderman asked to see a demonstration.

Pitch submitted to the request. "We'll have to go over to my place," he explained. "Everything I need is there."

"What all is involved?" asked Lunderman.

"Pretty simple, really. I have everything already set up. My computer is there along with some related equipment I use for sending and receiving."

When they arrived, Pitch went directly to his workstation. The apartment was a one-bedroom affair which forced Pitch to set up everything in the living room. Sitting in the swivel chair that faced the equipment, Pitch began flipping switches and setting dials.

"What's this thing?" asked Lunderman, gingerly touching one corner of the unfamiliar hardware.

"It's called a mixing board," replied Pitch. "It's made by *Audiovox,* and I use it to enhance the reception. I can tune out all extraneous noises, so the voices we hear will be loud and clear."

Lunderman was about to ask another question when the sound of the doorbell distracted him. It was Scott Aarons.

"Hey Pitch," greeted Scott. "Saw your car. Figured I'd stop in and say, 'hi.'"

"Come in. Come in," said Pitch hurriedly. "Your just in time for another demonstration." Entering the living room, Pitch added, "Scott, do you remember Professor Lunderman?"

Scott and Lunderman exchanged how-do-you-do's, while Pitch

went back to work saying, "Give me just a few more minutes to set up the program. Then, we'll see if we can make an intriguing phone call." Over his shoulder, he said to Scott, "I'm about to demonstrate The Ultimate Bug to Professor Lunderman." Pitch suddenly felt sheepish when he realized that Scott wasn't aware of what had transpired during the last couple of hours. Pitch explained. "He's considering presenting it to the National Science Foundation in Washington, D.C."

"Is that right?" said Scott plopping himself on to the sofa and unfolding the newspaper he had tucked under his arm.

A new thought process wormed its way into Lunderman's brain. Wondering just how deeply involved Scott Aarons was in this project, Lunderman thought about how many others might know about it as well.

Pitch logged onto the Internet and turned his attention to the big mixing-board. He flipped a series of four switches and set two additional dials.

Lunderman watched as Pitch took a single, three and a half-inch disc out of his shirt pocket. "What's on the floppy?" he asked, pointing.

Pitch answered off-handedly. "This is the disc that contains the program I wrote. It initiates the signal." He inserted it into the slot on the tower and clicked the mouse several times.

Folding his newspaper and laying it on the coffee table, Scott said, "That little disc is the key, Professor. He keeps it with him at all times because it contains everything you need to know about the system."

Watching the set up process, Lunderman asked, "Just how many people know about this thing you're doing?"

"Just Scott, here, Jennifer and Crystal," Pitch replied.

"And now you, Professor," said Scott.

Having met Scott a number of times in the past, Lunderman knew that Scott's father, Sidney Aarons was the publisher of the *Sun Coast Ledger*. "Doesn't your father know anything about this thing?"

"Not yet," answered Scott. "This is Pitch's pet, and he lets me know what, where, how and who . . ."

Spinning in his chair, Pitch interrupted. "This is all set to be activated. Whose telephone shall we dial into?"

Lunderman looked from one to the other before suddenly realizing that they were expecting him to make the decision. "Can we dial into any telephone?" he asked.

"As far as I know," Pitch said. "I know it works on business phones, residential phones and cell phones. I haven't attempted any long distance calls yet, but I don't see any reason they wouldn't work."

"Try calling my house," Lunderman said, sitting forward in his chair.

"Okay. What's your number?" asked Pitch.

Lunderman recited his number. As Pitch was inputting the information, Scott asked, "Who's home at your place?"

"Nobody," said Lunderman. "I live alone."

Pitch stopped what he was doing and looked at Scott for help. Scott thought to himself, 'For a Professor of Engineering, he's pretty dumb.' Then, he said, "I've got a better idea. Right about now there's supposed to be a big meeting going on in the law offices of Michael Sharpton. You know, he's the lawyer that's defending that rapist guy."

This particular story had been front-page news for the past several weeks. A convicted child molester, John Krum, had been arrested for raping an eleven year old girl as she walked home from her parochial school. Half of Florida's population wanted Krum in jail for the rest of his life, while the other half wanted him hung by his testicles, or worse. The sensational story was now swirling around the fact that Krum claimed he had vital information about a year-old murder of a wealthy Palm Beach family. The murder, known as the Blakely murders, was a gruesome affair involving the brutal slaying of a young philanthropic widow and her two teenage daughters. The police and D.A.'s office had no leads in that murder, and they were under a growing wave of pressure to crack the case. Michael Sharpton, an attorney with a sleazy reputation, had said publicly that his client, John Krum wanted to make a deal with the D.A. over the charge of rape and molestation. In return, Krum would pass on information that would allow the police to make an arrest in the year-old Blakely murder case. The highly publicized meeting was scheduled to take place in Sharpton's office. Nobody wanted to offer the accused, dirtbag rapist a deal, but if he had vital information about the year-old, multiple homicides, they might have very little choice.

"Yes. That's a good choice," said Lunderman sheepishly.

Pitch turned to Scott. "Beginning to think like a reporter, eh, Mr. Pulitzer?" he said as he cleared out Lunderman's home phone number. "If you will be good enough to tell me the number of Sharpton's office, I will fire this thing up again."

Scott used his cell phone to call his father's newspaper and get the phone number to Sharpton's office. "It's 565-5600," said Scott.

Pitch punched in the numbers to activate the system. It took less than fifteen seconds. The speakers on Pitch's desk came to life, but all they could hear was the sound of fingernails clicking on a keyboard.

"What's that?" asked Lunderman.

Pitch spun his chair to face Scott and said, "It sounds as though we tapped into the telephone in the reception area."

Scott suggested, "They're probably in Sharpton's office or maybe a conference room."

"I'm going to see if I can find an extension," said Pitch. Turning back to the computer screen, he clicked into a sub-routine of the program that allowed him to input an extension of the original number. Using the keyboard number-pad, Pitch redialed the last four digits, 5601. It was met by silence. Increasing the volume, Pitch tried 5602. Suddenly, there were voices. Hollow sounding, but clearly understandable. Obviously, the meeting was already in progress.

A woman was yelling, "This piece of shit has no rights!" Pause. "You are dead! Do you understand me? We're going to put you away forever. You're going to rot in some dark hole, you slimy piece of shit!"

A high-pitched, man's voice: "Laura! Settle down!"

A deep, gruff, man's voice: "You can't talk to me like that, bitch! You need me. You need what I got. And I ain't just talking about information."

Laura shouted, "Why are we doing this? Are you actually going to let him walk? After what he did?"

Another man, with a heavy New York accent: "This is turning into bullshit. Let's get back to basics here and get the bleeding heart liberals outta here."

A different man: "Ms. Parsons is right. My client is a rape victim. We need to focus on justice."

Heavy New York accent: "What we need to focus on is a deal. Are you interested or what?"

High-pitched man's voice: "Yes, I'm interested."

Laura, screaming: "I don't fucking believe this!"

High pitched man's voice, very angry: "Laura, get out of here! Go wait in the other room. You're no good to me in here."

Pitch, Scott and Lunderman were fascinated by the events coming through the speakers. They were silent as they listened to the receding sounds of high heels clacking, followed by the slamming of a door.

Pitch and Scott looked at each other and Scott said, "Laura Parsons."

Pitch nodded his agreement. "Yup," he added.

Lunderman, afraid of his voice being overheard by the people in the meeting, whispered, "You boys know her?"

"We went to school with her," Pitch said. "She's the Assistant District Attorney."

The three of them continued to listen to the drama unfold. Pitch and Scott were able to determine the players. The high-pitched voice was that of Warren Brock, the D.A. who was Laura's boss. The gruff voice belonged to John Krum, the rapist. The heavy New York accent came from Krum's attorney, Michael Sharpton. The remaining voice was that of Gary Gifford, the attorney for the eleven year old victim.

At the end of a loud and prolonged debate, the District Attorney and the victim's lawyer left the room for a private conversation. Afterwards, the adversaries managed to agree in principle. If the information supplied by John Krum led to the arrest of the murderer of the widow Blakely and her daughters, the charges against Krum would be reduced to assault. The meeting wrapped up with D.A. Brock reading the riot act about making certain that no one talked to the press. Brock got them all to agree that their only public comment would be, "Since this is an on-going investigation, we have no comment at this time."

Pitch broke off the connection.

Lunderman exhaled like a man who had been holding his breath.

Awed, he said, "You were actually able to activate the microphone in the telephone in that room, and they never even knew it!"

"Correct," Pitch said.

"And they couldn't hear us?" Lunderman asked incredulously.

"That is also correct," said Pitch.

"This is even better than I thought," said Lunderman. "You are good, Pitch. Real good."

Pitch was smiling.

Lunderman had some additional questions, but after a short while, he became eager to get started with his end of the project. "Let's not tell anyone else about this," said Lunderman as he stood up. "I need to talk with my contacts at the National Science Foundation. I'm going to have . . ." Lunderman corrected himself. "We are going to get ourselves a major research project, young man."

After bidding his goodbye, Lunderman seemed to be skipping as he made his way out the door. Pitch looked at Scott and asked, "Well, what do you think?"

Scott said, "I think he needs a bath."

"He always needs a bath," said Pitch, "but I'm referring to the device. It seemed to work well, don't you think?"

"Is that all you can say, 'it seemed to work well?'" asked Scott with a wry smile. "I would have expected you to be more impressed than that."

Pitch thought for just a moment and said, "Well, I certainly was impressed with Laura Parson's hot temper."

They sat in silence for a moment before Scott asked, "Does Lunderman really have high level contacts in Washington?"

"I think so," Pitch, said as he shut down the system and put the disc back into his shirt pocket. "He has mentioned them quite a number of times, and he *has* written some scientific papers in the past."

Scott thought a moment about his next words. "Pitch," he said tentatively, "I have a personal favor to ask."

"What is it?"

"I want to use the information we just heard to write a story for the newspaper."

"Oh," said Pitch dubiously. He hadn't thought about that possibility, and his mind began to churn over the ramifications of such an eventuality. It occurred to Pitch that, regardless of the focus of such an article, it would probably cause a sensation. Although it seemed that the public could not get enough of the story about the John Krum rape case, Pitch had concerns on a different level. He was worried about how Scott would handle the issue of his sources. "If you write about this incident, Scott, it could have a 'boiling-over' effect."

"You're right," concurred Scott. "I think it might."

"How do you think it will eventually play out?"

"I don't know," replied Scott. "But I'll tell you this much; this secret deal that we just overheard being hatched, really stinks. The public has a right to know what happened behind those closed doors."

Pitch had a troubled look, "Scott," he said, slowly shaking his head, "I don't think I want anybody to know about my invention prematurely. There are too many things that need . . ."

Scott interrupted. "No one will know, Pitch. I have no intention of writing anything about your gizmo. As for my sources, I simply write, 'an undisclosed source said . . . ' Nothing more. Besides, the law allows me to protect my sources. Why, the Constitution itself safeguards me from having to divulge where I got any part of this story."

Pitch mulled it over in his head. Then, as the beginnings of a smile creased the corners of his lips, he said, "If you say nobody will be aware of the existence of the bug, then it's okay with me."

"Trust me," said Scott with finality. "Your invention will be safe."

CHAPTER ELEVEN

L underman hurried back to his office. He wanted to call his friend Sean Reardon before he left for the day. Lunderman had exaggerated wildly about the number of contacts he had in Washington, D.C. The fact was, Sean Reardon, his old college chum, was the only person he knew who worked for the government. Before his transfer, Sean had toiled as a clerk at the NEA, the National Endowment for the Arts. These days, he worked for the State Department in the Office of Protocol. Lunderman was hoping Sean could steer him in the right direction for acquiring a grant. Perhaps, even introduce him to the right people. Lunderman called and was surprised to hear Sean himself, answer the phone. "This is Mr. Reardon speaking. May I help you?"

"Sean, this is George Lunderman."

Disregarding the usual pleasantries and only briefly catching up on the past, Lunderman went directly into the purpose of his call. Lunderman was careful not to divulge too much information about the listening device and spoke only in vague terms.

Without knowing exactly what Lunderman was looking for, Sean made a suggestion. "It sounds to me," he said, "like you might want to talk to the CIA or FBI. They're the ones that would most likely be interested in a listening device."

"No, no," Lunderman objected. "Too soon. I don't want to sell it yet. I'm looking for grant money so I can study the effects of it."

"Oh. I see," said Sean with renewed clarity. Understanding Lunderman's request, Sean came up with the name of the only person he knew in the Department of Grants and Allocations. "His name is Walter Mahler," said Sean. "He's a mousy kind of a guy, but he knows his stuff. If he can't help you, then at least he'll be able to steer you in the right direction." Sean made another suggestion. He offered to first call Walter Mahler and pre-introduce Lunderman. In this way, when Lunderman telephoned on his own, Mahler would at least be expecting the call.

Lunderman waited a half-hour before telephoning Walter Mahler. By the third unanswered ring, Lunderman became apprehensive.

Walter Mahler fancied himself a spy. The truth was, he was nothing more than a snitch, an informer who sold bits of information for money. He had a small network of people to whom he offered his information. Most of those people were in business and industry and were willing to pay money to know who was applying for grants and for what purpose. Mahler would make a big production out of setting up clandestine meetings in order to pass on the information. There, he would get paid for his services and usually wheedle a free meal with it. Sometimes, he could finagle an overnight stay in a hotel. He enjoyed that.

When Sean Reardon, who knew nothing about Mahler's secret life, called and told him about Professor Lunderman and the listening device, Mahler's curiosity became piqued. To him, this sounded as though it had a potential payoff.

Walter Mahler answered his phone. "Grants and Allocations. Mahler speaking."

"Mr. Mahler? My name is Dr. George Lunderman . . ."

"Oh, yes. Lunderman," said Mahler. "Sean Reardon told me you'd be calling."

Once the conversation began, Lunderman was very pleased with the reception and felt more at ease. 'Thank you, Sean,' thought Lunderman as he realized that this process would be easier than he originally thought.

As the two men talked, Lunderman knew that he had to be a little more forthcoming with Mahler than he was with Sean Reardon. Mahler was the man controlling the purse strings and therefore needed to know more about the details of the listening device.

For his part, Mahler was very intrigued by what Lunderman had to say. It sounded like a major hit, something that could make Walter much more money than he had asked for in the past. He decided that it was important enough to front some expense money if he had to. But only if he had to.

Mahler began reciting his standard presentation. He said that this project was the kind of thing that his department was eager to fund. He told Lunderman that the department had millions of dollars in available grants, and that the oversight committees were actively seeking things such as this. He went on to say that arrangements would be made to have Lunderman fly to D.C. and to stay at the Watergate or some similar hotel.

"Naturally," said Mahler, "the government will pick up the tab. All you have to do is keep all of your expense receipts in order to be reimbursed. Will that be satisfactory?"

Lunderman took the bait. "Sure. Okay. I can do that," he said, trying unsuccessfully to conceal his excitement.

Jotting down Lunderman's phone number, Mahler promised to call back as soon as he made arrangements.

A wave of giddiness swept over Lunderman as he hung up the phone. He was energized with the first flush of success. He had visions of all of his dreams and desires falling into place. At last, he would become a respected and integral part of the scientific community. A considered man, an advisor, a consultant to his peers.

*   *   *

Walter Mahler was anxious to get the ball rolling. He left a voice mail message for his supervisor saying that he was not feeling well and that he was going home early. He took the cross-town bus to the northwest section of the city and walked up the three flights to his apartment. Locking the door, Mahler reached for his wallet and took out a worn piece of paper with a phone number written on it. It was a number he called only on special occasions. He sat at his kitchen table and dialed the number.

Someone picked up the line on the other end and said, "T.C.H. International. How may I direct your call?"

"This is Walter Mahler calling. I'd like to talk to Mr. Vincent Parlotti."

CHAPTER TWELVE

L inc parked his Corvette on the driveway where it exited on to the street and walked the lighted sidewalk towards the front door of Preston's mansion. He glanced over his shoulder to take a final look at his automobile. His Corvette was the all new Limited Edition. A fire engine red convertible with the 5.7-liter, small block, V8 engine that had the new high performance modifications and was capable of delivering 405 horsepower. Linc did not have the personality that required him to show off his success, but the purchase of this particular vehicle fulfilled a lifelong dream.

Knowing there was going to be a lot of people at tonight's party, Linc did not want to take a chance of getting blocked in by the other cars in case he chose to leave early. 'Don't allow yourself to get boxed in,' he thought to himself. That had become the motto of his life.

Many other thoughts had passed through Linc's head as he readied himself for the evening. He couldn't stop thinking about yesterday's breakfast meeting. Preston's plea for a relationship between his daughter and Linc seemed quite bizarre. He had always known Preston to be a practical man in most matters. Still, Preston did have a soft underbelly, which tended to manifest itself when he showed his emotions. At those times, the man would allow his feelings to get the better of him. That being said, the dream of Linc fathering Preston's grandchildren had the melodramatic ring of a soap opera.

And what about Emily herself? Over the years, Preston had talked incessantly about his daughter. Linc knew she had been a gifted student and that Preston had sent her to the exclusive Clairmont-Pas School where she had graduated as valedictorian. He remembered Preston saying that she went to Brown University and graduated with a double major in political science and mathematics; an odd combination to be sure. Linc was aware of her affinity for languages and the fact that she was fluent in four or five of them. He wondered whether she was just a geek or, at the very least, a nerdy pseudo-intellectual.

Preston was aware of Linc's position on love, commitment and marriage. After the last of two disastrous and tragic engagements, Linc's attitude toward long-term relationships had become one of extreme caution. He had expressed his doubt as to whether or not he would ever allow himself to fall in love again. Linc figured that, although Preston was only in his mid-fifties, he must have been experiencing a "senior moment" when he thought this one up.

During a more serious time, Preston had confided about the troubling part of Emily's past. He told Linc about the time when she fell in love with an Egyptian tennis pro, Jubal Salaran; how she became pregnant and married him. Preston was extremely unhappy with the match. It was an unsettling time and in talking to Emily, he didn't pull his punches. Preston had been very vocal about his dislike, even hatred, towards "Jube" Salaran which fostered the beginning of the terrible rift between father and daughter. Preston had heard from several reliable sources that Jube was only interested in marrying into money, and Emily was his meal ticket. Expressing his feelings in no uncertain terms, Preston created a constant and furious battle among the three of them. Unfortunately, Emily miscarried and blamed Preston. A few months later, her marriage dissolved and she moved away to Europe.

As far as Linc knew, Jube Salaran still lived in the area. Linc thought he might still be involved in tennis as a teaching pro, giving private lessons to a few Palm Beach residents. Linc recalled that on several occasions, while still with the County Sheriff's Department, Jube had run into trouble with the law. There were a couple of felony charges, having to do with a missing piece of jewelry and a "borrowed" car. It was enough to know that Preston's sources were right about Mr. Salaran. Linc clearly remembered Jube as being a sleaze.

After Emily moved to Europe, a whole year passed before Preston heard from her. Her first few years on the continent produced only sketchy details. It took several years before father and daughter were able to begin to regrow their bond. It was only then that Emily would tell Preston of her life abroad. She had taken a job with NATO, and it was obvious, from what Preston had told Linc, the work involved top-secret intelligence analysis. Because of that, Emily's job was not a topic for discussion. The pair had to find other areas of mutual interest. Linc recalled one of Preston's happiest days, when she asked him to come visit her in Greece. Preston was like a kid getting ready for a birthday party. He bought her so many gifts that the airlines charged him an additional fare for hauling them. Preston visited with Emily often after that. She, on the other hand, never came to the United States. About one year ago, Preston mentioned to Linc that Emily was softening her position and indicated that she might someday return home.

Linc had a strong relationship with Preston, and, at one time or another, had met all of his small family. Linc enjoyed meeting them and felt relaxed in their company. Emily was the only family member he hadn't met and looked forward to the prospect. Of course, now that Preston had expressed his feelings about Emily and Linc having a relationship, he felt uneasy, a little on edge. He did not know whether Preston had said similar things to Emily. He sincerely hoped not.

A couple of years ago, Preston had showed off the old family album. There, Linc had seen childhood photographs of Emily. As a little girl, she had a cute smile, and as a teenager, she had a fresh-faced prettiness. Linc knew that an old photograph was one thing, but felt that time had a way of distorting what once was.

Linc was always interested in having a fling with a good-looking woman, as long as the relationship didn't get too serious. Ever since his broken engagement to Lisa Decker, and the tragic loss of Samantha Broadhurst, commitment was not part of his vocabulary.

Linc walked the path through the front gardens of Preston's home and thought about how the meeting with Emily would go. After all, what do you say to a geek? It shouldn't be hard to figure something out. After all, working for NATO had to have its own fascination. He felt fairly certain they would find a few interesting things to talk about.

Besides, he thought, they had a lot in common. Linc was also a political science buff. Additionally, there was Preston of course and, oh yes, despite Linc being two years older than Emily, they shared the same birthday: August 28th. As far as any likely conversation, he supposed there was nothing to worry about.

One of the tall entrance doors opened as Linc approached, and he was greeted by Louise, "Good evening, Mr. Bradshaw. How nice you look."

Linc was wearing a single-breasted, navy blazer with four silver buttons at the end of each sleeve. Gray slacks and a pair of matching Bali tasseled loafers adorned the lower half. A touch of color was in his shirt. He had found it at a specialty shop on Worth Avenue. It was a combination of the exact gray and navy as his jacket and slacks, but included splashes of white and yellow in the pattern. He hated to pay that much money for a shirt, but it blended perfectly.

"Thank you, Louise. I hope I'm not too early."

"Not at all. Mr. Collingsworth is waiting for you in the Oak Room."

The Oak Room was located on the north side of the house and was Preston's favorite room. A series of very tall, narrow windows overlooked a garden of lush, tropical foliage. Each window had wide slatted Bahama shutters in solid oak. The two walls adjacent to the windows were covered in satin finished oak panels, broken by a thin brass wainscot which ran horizontally near the top and middle of both walls. Opposite the windows was a wall dominated by bookshelves trimmed in brass. A parquet wood floor enriched the room and boasted a central area rug patterned in hunter green and burgundy. The room was appointed with some fine artwork that included an original Rembrandt. Guests could relax in their choice of a sofa, loveseat or four chairs, all in various hues of hunter and pine green, with accents of plum and claret. Recessed lighting, that ran the length of three walls, cast a soft comfortable glow.

Linc walked in and greeted Preston, who was sitting behind a big oak desk trimmed in polished brass. Preston looked dapper with his dark hair, which was graying at the temples and had a narrow silver streak through the middle. He kept it longish and combed straight back. When Preston smiled, he showed very white teeth, which dramatically enhanced his square face and swarthy complexion.

Preston said, "Ah, Linc. I'm so glad you were able to get here early. Emily said that she'll join us shortly. Sit down. Sit down. Let me just finish signing this check."

Preston was very excited. He was generally an enthusiastic person but became more so on the nights he hosted these gatherings. Tonight however, was something special, and Linc picked up on it right away. Before Linc could sit down, Manfred appeared with a rolling bar whose bottles of liquor clinked together as he wheeled it over the threshold. The top tray held an iced pitcher of Tanqueray martinis and a selection of plump green olives, thinly sliced limes and small pearl onions. "Goot evening, Mr. Bradshaw," Manfred intoned in a somewhat more formal air. "Vould you like me to pour you a martini, or vould you prefer zometing else?"

Before Linc could answer, Preston said, "That's okay, Manfred. You can just leave it. We'll help ourselves."

Manfred nodded and left. As he disappeared through the doorway, he could be heard saying, "Oh, Miss Emily. It is really you!"

Linc and Preston could hear Emily's voice as she replied, "Yes, Manfred. It is really me. And look at you. You look wonderful! You haven't changed a bit."

"Zank you," said Manfred, "but you haff changed. You're all grown up. You're so beautiful, if I may say so. It's nice to haff you home."

"Thank you Manfred. It's nice to be home. Is Daddy in the Oak Room?"

"Yes, Miss Emily. He and Mr. Bradshaw, boht."

Linc was fascinated by her voice. It had somewhat of a husky quality to it and she formed her words round and clear. As she came into the room, Linc caught his breath. She was beautiful. His recollection of her old photographs vanished. They seemed to have little resemblance to who was standing in front of him.

Emily was wearing a form fitting sheath dress in a rich jade green, its length falling to mid calf. It was sleeveless and had a high mandarin collar. The dress had a long slit up the left side exposing several inches of her thigh as she walked. Her heels were a matching *peau de soie*. A brunette, she had her hair pulled into an upsweep and held in place with a simple gold clasp. A wide inviting mouth and bow-strung lips were framed by gold button earrings. Her high cheekbones presented a classic look that was further enhanced by her long neck and slender body.

"Hi, Daddy," she said as she went over and put her cheek next to Preston's. "Sorry I took so long."

"Not at all," said Preston. He beamed as he gently kissed her cheek.

Linc moved a step closer and said, "I finally get to meet Emily."

"Yes, yes," said Preston as he steered Emily around. "Lincoln, my boy, this is my Emily. Emily, sweetheart, say hello to Lincoln Donald Bradshaw."

Emily held out her hand. "Hello, Lincoln Donald Bradshaw."

Linc took her hand for a moment, and Emily liked the way it felt. It was warm and comforting and had just the right firmness for a handshake.

Preston spread his arms out and said, "Sit down you two. Sit down. I'm so happy that you two are finally meeting. I feel my family is together at last." Walking to the rolling bar, Preston continued, "I'll pour. I know you'll join me in the martini, Linc, but how about you Emily? Would you like one as well?"

"Just some white wine," she answered. "That Zinfandel would be fine."

Emily sat down on the love seat, and Linc took the chair to her left. He said, "Do you have any idea how happy you've made your father?"

"He has expressed it to me," she said coyly. Then, with a big smile, "Sometimes, he expresses things with more gusto than he should."

Linc recognized the comment as a good-natured gibe and said, "He's been waltzing around here like a schoolboy. Your homecoming has made him very happy. And it does my heart good to see him happy."

Emily looked directly at Linc for a moment and was taken by the sincerity of his sentiment. With a small laugh, she said, "Now, I suppose, we'll have to get together and monitor his liquor intake."

Still pouring the drinks, Preston retorted, "I'm perfectly capable of monitoring my own indulgence, thank you,"

"How long have you known my father?" asked Emily.

Linc started to answer, but was cut off by Preston. "I met Lincoln right after you left for Europe," he said as he handed the white wine and martini to each of them. "For these past seven years, I've been telling him all about you. I'm afraid he knows everything there is to know, Emily darling."

"Well, I hope I've been able to preserve a few secrets," she said pleasantly. "Daddy's told me quite a bit about you as well, but he didn't tell me the origin of your first name. 'Lincoln.' It's so unusual."

Linc hesitated a moment, deciding which of his clever responses he would give, when Preston interjected. "His mother's maiden name was Lincoln. Linc is actually a distant relative of President Abraham Lincoln, but everybody calls him Linc."

Emily turned to look at Linc. "Interesting lineage," she said.

Preston continued, "They used to call him 'Chain-Link.'"

"Chain-Link?" she asked, looking directly at Linc. "Why Chain-Link?"

Preston was so enthused that he wasn't giving Linc an opportunity to respond. With a look of exasperation, Linc sat back in his chair as Preston gave the history. "He played professional football," explained Preston. "American football. He was All-American at Memphis State, and then played professionally for the Miami Dolphins. Just one season, but he could stop anybody from coming through the line. Just like a chain-link fence!"

"Ohh," said Emily as her smile faded, "this is the football player."

Linc saw the change in her eyes even before he heard the change in her tone. Her demeanor switched from curious and friendly to cool and aloof. This was not the way he expected things to go. A little miffed, Linc said, "Stop being so helpful, Preston, and let me speak for myself, if you don't mind."

"Yes, yes, of course," said Preston. "I'm just delighted over this whole thing. I'll try to keep my mouth shut."

"Tell me about yourself," said Linc trying to steer the conversation back on track. "Preston said you've been working for NATO. What was it you did for them?"

Emily was perturbed. Choosing her words carefully, she spoke briefly about her job. She had looked forward to meeting Linc. Preston had told her quite a bit about him, but she did not connect the fact that it was Linc who was the football player. She was disappointed. Another jock. After her experience with Jube Salaran and his buddies, she was convinced that all professional athletes tended to be smug and full of themselves. Even though Linc seemed so pleasant and nice, she remembered having been burned in the past by a different "Prince Charming." Shortly, Louise popped her head in to tell Preston that guests were arriving. Leaving the couple in the Oak Room, Preston went to greet the arrivals.

During their ensuing conversation, Emily shifted in her seat and crossed her legs. The action caused the slit in her dress to fall open, exposing the whiteness of her skin. An air of elegance surrounded her, and Linc hoped to recapture that little bit of playfulness that existed when the conversation first began.

Emily remained cordial but distant. Soon, they could hear the murmuring and laughter of the other guests. Emily said with a sigh, "The inevitable is about to begin. Daddy wants to re-introduce me to half of Palm Beach this evening."

At that moment, Preston came into the room and said, "Come, come, you two. There are people I want you to meet and people who want to meet you!" He took them by their arms and steered them through the living room and into the ballroom, which already had an assemblage of about forty guests. The ballroom was very large and tiled in big squares of high gloss, champagne colored marble. A magnificent crystal chandelier dominated the high ceiling, while the walls featured a plethora of ornate wall sconces. Each window was draped in festoons of peach antique satin with jabots that cascaded down past the sills. A long bar had been set up on one side of the room, and guests were gathered in front of it. Manfred was directing a staff of uniformed caterers as to exactly how he wanted the array of hors d'oeuvres to be presented. A dozen tables were set up around the room, each capable of seating six people quite comfortably. A trio of musicians was setting up their violin, viola and cello. It promised to be a grand evening.

Linc eyed the musicians and felt momentarily disappointed. He was secretly hoping the musical entertainment might have been B.B. King, or at least some other Delta Blues artists. He would just have to live with the string trio.

Preston launched himself into the middle of the mingling crowd and began making hurried introductions. Having attended Preston's parties in the past, Linc knew most of the people. For Emily, it was a very different experience. She did not know or did not remember many of the people who were present. A number of the guests started their conversations with, "Emily, surely you remember the time when . . . ," and they went on to tell a story that happened when Emily was three or four years old. Maintaining her poise and good sense of humor, she became the delight of the ball.

At one point, Preston introduced Emily and Linc to Sidney Aarons and his wife, Lenore. Sidney and Linc shook hands, acknowledging having met previously. Emily remembered Lenore Aarons as a gushy woman, dripping in diamonds and given to spasms of exaggerated personality. She was a "touchy-feely" sort who went on and on about how gorgeous Emily was. Emily smiled graciously and asked Lenore about her son, Scott. Sidney chimed in, "You know Scott? How do you know Scott?"

"We both went to Clairmont-Pas," Emily replied. "I was there the day Scott threw Dr. Sheely's chair out of the window!" Emily turned slightly towards Linc and added impressively, "We were on the second floor at the time."

"Oh, dear!" said Lenore.

"By God," boomed Sidney with a touch of pride, "she does know Scott!"

As Preston took Emily (with Lenore in tow) to the next introduction, Sidney touched Linc on the arm and asked to have a few words with him, privately.

Linc was prepared for this. Preston had filled Linc in on a recent meeting he had with Sidney. During that meeting, Sidney had spoken of his need for a private investigator. Sidney felt that one of his full time reporters, to whom he paid a hefty salary, was selling stories to a tabloid for extra cash. That definitely was unethical. Preston had told Sidney all about Linc, boasting about the solid results that Linc was capable of achieving. Preston also prepared Sidney by saying, "Linc isn't cheap y'know. Be prepared to spend a few dollars!"

Speaking softly, Sidney told Linc of his need for a discreet investigation. In turn, Linc said he would be glad to discuss the matter and, together, they set up a time to meet. Sidney suggested the meeting be held at his offices at the *Sun Coast Ledger.*

Linc balked at the idea. "Sidney, it's probably not a good idea to meet at your newspaper. There's too great a possibility of the reporter in question getting a look at me, and that might hinder any future investigation. Why don't we meet elsewhere?"

"Good point," said Sidney. "Preston said you think of everything." They arranged to meet at nine o'clock the following morning at Sidney's club.

The party went on while food and spirits continued to be consumed in vast quantities. Linc slowly wandered the perimeter of the ballroom, stopping now and then to join a discussion or to meet someone new. At one point during the evening, Linc was introduced to a couple who were presented as "Alex Morgan and the Countess." Morgan was in his middle forties and the Countess looked to be about ten years younger. At first, Linc assumed they were husband and wife. Immediately after the introductions, they both moved in very close to Linc, and Alex, with a distinct effeminate quality, said, "My, you are a handsome devil!"

Linc recalled an investigation he once conducted that required him to go to a gay bar. He spent a good portion of that evening fending off the advances of a young man who was a caricature of femininity. Alex Morgan's demeanor brought back the memory. With his personal space invaded, Linc felt uncomfortable and took a half step backward, saying, "Um . . . right. Thank you."

The Countess closed the gap by moving a half step closer and said, "And look how big he is."

"Now, now, Countess," said Alex with a Cheshire cat grin, "don't expect to have him all to yourself."

Alex Morgan and the Countess were obviously enjoying themselves, while Linc was feeling ill at ease. Attempting to politely excuse himself, he mumbled something about " . . . making the rounds to visit the other guests."

"Don't wander off too far," said the Countess. She put her hand on Linc's chest and sensually moved it down to his stomach. "Oh my God, Alex! Wait until you feel these muscles."

Linc turned and walked away, raising his eyes heavenward in relief. The remainder of the evening was spent having idle chitchat with various guests and listening to the soft music of the string ensemble. Occasionally looking over his shoulder, Linc tried to see where Emily might be. Twice he caught her eye and, at one point, thought he detected a wink. He was determined to break down the cool façade she had developed.

The evening was wearing on Emily. Sensing the conversations were beginning to plod in circles, Emily was looking forward to the end. The night had started off on the right foot when Preston introduced her to Linc. At least, she thought, he didn't say, "My, how you've grown!" Emily ruminated about talking with Linc again. She looked over her shoulder several times for his whereabouts and twice spotted him looking at her. She definitely detected a smile. Emily thought she might have to work a bit to overcome her paranoia of having anything to do with professional athletes.

As the guests were departing, Alex and the Countess wandered over to say their goodbyes to Linc. By this time, it was obvious the Countess had much too much to drink. In the middle of saying goodnight, she grabbed a sizeable chunk of Linc's rear-end, and did it with enough pressure to make him jump. Linc physically dislodged her hand from his rump. Unsteadily, Alex ferried her out the door. Linc turned to find Preston and Emily had both witnessed the uninvited squeeze. Linc felt his cheeks flush.

"Aha!" said Preston. "I see you are the recipient of the favors of the Countess. Did you find the couple a bit bizarre?"

"Who are those people?" asked Linc. "What's their story?"

"She is the Countess Erika," said Preston, making an elaborate bow. "She is actual lineage to the throne of Denmark. Although she is far enough removed so that Queen Margaret II and the rest of the Danes can feel relatively safe."

"And Alex?" asked Linc.

"Alex Morgan makes his money by digging," said Preston. "He owns several mines that produce precious stones."

"Is he the one they call 'Alexander the Great'?" asked Emily, obviously enjoying the embarrassment Linc was feeling.

"Yes, yes," said Preston, "He's the one. When she was a young girl, he took her under his wing and taught her everything she knows."

"Well, he must have taught her how to dig for gold," exclaimed Linc, "because that's what it felt like she was doing to my rear-end."

Emily laughed out loud at his joke. 'Anybody who blushes like that,' she thought, 'can't be all bad.'

Preparing to leave, Linc said, "Emily, you were quite a hit this evening and I, along with the others, enjoyed meeting you. Perhaps you and I can grab lunch some time this weekend."

Cocking her head, Emily looked at Linc for a long time before answering. She liked his height, his good looks, his manners, and his sense of humor. She had come to trust her father's judgment of character, and he had spoken very highly of Linc. Perhaps, she would give him another chance. Perhaps, she would give herself another chance.

"Perhaps," she said.

CHAPTER THIRTEEN

Claude Mendosa was sipping espresso. With his face tilted upward, Mendosa was enjoying the warmth that came from a winter sun. He was seated in the outdoor section of a small café located in an exclusive shopping area of Alexandria, Virginia. Despite the calendar proclaiming the month of February, the temperature had moved up to a balmy sixty-four degrees. The proprietor decided to open the sidewalk section at the request of several of his regulars. Mendosa was pleased. Waiting for the waiter to bring his order of Swiss cheese on toast with spicy mustard, Mendosa began to read the personal ads in the *Washington Post*. Even on days when ads were numerous, it never took much time to scan them. After years of searching the "Post" and *Le Monde,* his eye was trained to catch a particular phrase.

And there it was. The ad read,

> Time to re-hire,
> The lass of Mount Valier.
> Tiger is in the Tower.
> Call within the Hour.

Containing his coded nickname, "The Lass of Mount Valier," made it clear to Mendosa that the ad was meant for him alone. It also meant that it was time to go to work again. Mendosa was meticulous and organized. He spent an inordinate amount of time planning details that others might consider trivial. Continuing to enjoy the lunchtime repast, he relaxed and gathered his thoughts.

Shortly after lunch, Mendosa returned to his apartment, got his attaché case and drove to the hotel which he always used for these contacts. Once settled in his room, he went through his usual preparations before placing his call to Vincent Parlotti.

A man's voice answered. "T.C.H. International," it greeted. "How may I direct your call?"

"This is The Lass of Mount Valier," Mendosa said in a monotone. "Let me speak with Parlotti."

"Mr. Parlotti is not available at the moment, but he would like you to call again at precisely one-thirty this afternoon, Eastern Standard Time."

Mendosa acknowledged the instructions, hung up the phone and checked his watch. Forty-four minutes until he called again. Parlotti was probably out having lunch.

* * *

Professor George Lunderman was on the plane flying from Palm Beach International to Dulles Airport in D.C. Metro. Sitting in first-class and sipping a Chivas Regal and soda, he rehearsed the presentation he would give to Walter Mahler.

Things had gone smoothly during Mahler's return call, and together they went over details of Lunderman's proposal. The only glitch occurred when Mahler said he was anxious to see a demonstration of the device. Lunderman was forced to dance around that particular request. He had already talked to Pitch about flying to Washington to give the demonstration, but Pitch had said it would not be practical on such short notice. There was just too much equipment that would have to be crated and transported. Lunderman was unhappy, but he understood.

Unbeknownst to Lunderman, Pitch had an ulterior motive. Jennifer and he had planned a trip away, and neither one of them wanted to put it off. Making an alternate suggestion, Pitch proposed that Walter Mahler fly down to Florida instead.

Knowing Pitch was right, Lunderman used all of those arguments to circumvent Mahler's request. Even though Mahler was disappointed, he still insisted that Lunderman come to D.C. as soon as possible. Mahler explained that there were other people to whom the Professor needed to be introduced. Mahler said that the Department of Grants and Allocations had no problem reimbursing a scientist of Lunderman's stature, provided he kept his receipts. Mahler also told him, apologetically, that he was not able to reserve accommodations at the famous Watergate Hotel. However, he did arrange a magnificent room at the Dorchester Hotel, which was only a couple of blocks away. Lunderman's instructions were to call upon arrival at Dulles Airport. Then, he was to take a cab directly to the hotel where Mahler would join him for dinner.

Sitting on the plane, Lunderman thought it would be best if he told Mahler everything. After all, the man was not going to be viewing a live demonstration of the listening device. Therefore, it was vitally important to impress this bureaucrat with a presentation that was coherent and convincing. More importantly, the Professor had to appeal to Mahler's sense of imagination. By doing so, Mahler would be able to understand and appreciate the full extent of what the device could do. Realizing that, eventually, he had to mention the name of Pitch Pechowski and his role in the development of the device, Lunderman nevertheless decided that, for now, it would be wiser to downplay that end of it. At the very least, he would play up his own participation. That should be easy. After all, Pitch had been working on the robotics study for almost two years, and Lunderman supervised everything that Pitch did. As Lunderman rehearsed the things he would say, he became more smug and confident by the mile . . . and by the shots of scotch he was consuming.

Lunderman landed at Dulles and called Mahler.

"With the traffic at this time of day," said Mahler pleasantly, "it should take you about forty minutes to get to the hotel. You'll have plenty of time to freshen up. I'll call you from the lobby at precisely six-thirty."

The Dorchester Hotel was located further away from the Watergate than Lunderman had expected. He had hoped for some free time to visit the famous landmark and to relive some of the historic events of the Nixon debacle and the Clinton-Lewinsky tryst. Lunderman was somewhat disappointed in the quality of the hotel into which he was booked. His room left a lot to be desired as well. He supposed Walter Mahler had tried the best he could, considering the arrangements were made on such short notice.

Not thinking ahead, Lunderman had boarded the airplane in Florida wearing his best suit and tie. He had bent over, sat down, stood up and was jostled. He had spilled some of his drink on his tie, dripped food on his shirt and perspired profusely. On top of all that, the plane was late, it took him longer to get to the hotel than he had anticipated and he had to lug his own suitcase. Lunderman plopped his bag on the bed and studied himself in the mirror. He looked like a sweat-drenched slob who had just spent a windy afternoon on a roller coaster. In addition, he smelled bad. Just then, his phone rang. It was Walter Mahler calling from the lobby.

Mahler was appalled at his first sight of George Lunderman. Shaking his hand, Mahler instinctively thought about washing it. "It's a privilege to meet you, Professor Lunderman," said Mahler, mustering all the courtesy he could find. "I've been looking forward to this meeting. I hope your room is satisfactory?"

"It's fine. Just fine," said Lunderman, trying to mask his disappointment. "It's been many years since I've been to this city, and I'd forgotten just how busy a place it is."

"Are you hungry, Professor?" asked Mahler. "We could get started over dinner."

"Call me George, please," requested Lunderman, "and, yes, I am hungry."

"Okay, George, and you can call me Walter."

Mahler had originally planned to take his guest to *Morton's Steak House* for dinner. It was one of Mahler's favorite places. However, he felt certain the maitre d' would never forgive him for bringing such a disheveled and unkempt person to his restaurant. It certainly would ruin his chances of ever getting a good table there again. Instead, Mahler went to the last outpost of a dying restaurant chain called the *Copper Skillet*. It wouldn't be busy, and Mahler knew they could find a quiet table in the back.

After talking a bit about Washington, D.C. and suggesting a few tourist sites, Mahler jumped into the purpose of their meeting by expressing his disappointment. He said it was a shame that he would not be able to actually experience a demonstration of the "bug," but that he understood Lunderman's reasons.

Prior to this meeting, and during his phone call with Vincent Parlotti, Mahler had been told that some extensive research would be gathered on the background of George Lunderman. Just before the two men met at the Dorchester Hotel, Mahler received a fax containing that information. It was an impressive dossier. Armed with more than a dozen pages of background material, he nonchalantly recited the Professor's academic credentials and his work experiences. Eyes wide, Lunderman was duly impressed with the extent and scope of the government's power. Mahler knew enough to feed into Lunderman's ego and kept complimenting the Professor for his brilliance and inventiveness. Trying to get a feel for the invention, Mahler asked many questions. However, his knowledge of electronics was limited, and his questions were very rudimentary.

Lunderman was pleased with how well the discussion was going. Mahler was easy to talk to, but occasionally came up with a technical question that would stump Lunderman. It made him squirm and forced him to maneuver around it. During such times, Lunderman felt like kicking himself for not learning more from Pitch.

"What happens," asked Mahler, "if you try to access a particular telephone and someone is in the middle of using it?"

Lunderman had no idea and had to fudge his answer. "Those are the kinds of things," he told Mahler, "we need to find out in our research study."

Mahler kept mentioning his willingness to give Lunderman enough money for everything he needed. The Professor thought how nice it was to be able to talk to professionals who had vision, unlike the Dean of the University, Albert Chase, who only wanted to cut Lunderman's legs out from under him.

With it all, Mahler was impressed. Very impressed. This invention could have some very far-reaching effects. He could envision all sorts of covert applications. Mahler came to understand that the unique nature of this invention was definitely worth a lot more money, a larger finder's fee than he had originally figured.

Parlotti's instructions were clear. He said that one of his "associates," a man by the name of Skip Nelson, would be contacting Mahler. Parlotti also informed Mahler that Nelson would be playing the role of Mahler's supervisor and was to be introduced to Lunderman as such. In addition, Parlotti stressed that Skip Nelson would make all decisions. Mahler understood that he would have to negotiate with Nelson for his fee. Mahler was waiting to be contacted.

Halfway through his mashed potatoes, Lunderman began talking about some of his other ideas. They were designs he had previously outlined to the Dean of the University, and which had been rejected out of hand. However, this man sitting across from him was much more responsive. Lunderman stopped talking when he heard Mahler's cell phone ring.

"It's Skip Nelson," said Mahler as he looked at the display. "I'm going to take this call outside where the reception is better. You relax and finish eating. I'll be right back."

Lunderman ate with gusto.

Returning to the table, Mahler smiled confidently and said, "I told Skip all about you and your invention, and he's anxious to meet you. He said he's got to be in the vicinity of your hotel around nine o'clock this evening. He said we can wait for him in your room and he'll meet us there. You'll have to give him some idea about how much money you think you'll need."

A worried look crossed Lunderman's face.

"Just a rough estimate," added Mahler, trying to put Lunderman back at ease. "We'll need a written proposal somewhere down the line, but I don't see that as a problem. We'll even help you draft one."

Like a chameleon, Mendosa blended in to his surroundings. He wore a plain charcoal gray suit, white shirt and unobtrusive tie. He walked steadily and calmly and carried nothing in his hands. There wasn't anything to attract attention. If the police were to question witnesses about who was in the lobby of the Dorchester Hotel at nine p.m., Mendosa would not even have been part of their memory. Waiting until some people moved away from the elevator, Mendosa timed his entrance into the lift, allowing him to ride up alone. Checking both ways in the hallway and making sure no one was there, he knocked lightly on the door.

Lunderman opened the door. "Mr. Nelson?" he asked.

"Yes. I'm Skip Nelson," said Mendosa with a big smile as he stepped into the room and pumped Lunderman's hand. "And you must be Professor George Lunderman." Mendosa was taken aback at Lunderman's appearance, but was able to hide his repulsion.

Mahler said, "Hi, Mr. Nelson. Glad you were able to make it on such short notice."

Mendosa replied, "Well, Walter. After what you told me, I just had to meet this gentleman."

Mendosa and Mahler had never met. This little bit of play-acting had been staged through Mendosa's instructions. Mendosa trusted no one and, having never met Walter Mahler, he had even less reason to trust him. The fact that Mahler set up this meeting and agreed to the role-playing was appreciated for the moment, but Mahler's future was written in stone. To that end, Mendosa had to totally control the situation. In a gracious but firm manner, he arranged the seating with Lunderman and Mahler sharing the narrow sofa that sat under a cheap painting of the Washington Monument. Mendosa sat in a straight-backed chair facing them.

"I've had very little chance to familiarize myself with your work," Mendosa began, "other than what Walter, here, has told me. So, before we get into how much grant money I can give you, I'd like to ask you some questions."

Thinking this was a great start, Lunderman gleefully rubbed his hands together and said, "Shoot!"

Mendosa smiled. "I'll probably be asking a lot of the same questions that Walter did," he explained, "so, bear with me."

"No problem," said Lunderman. "Ask away."

Mendosa did indeed ask many of the same questions, but when he got to the technical details, Mendosa's questions took a different track.

"I understand you were not able to bring along your equipment to show me how this thing works," said Mendosa, choosing his words carefully. "But didn't you say you actually do have a working prototype?"

"Yes, I do," said Lunderman confidently.

"And you're able to activate it by using standard telephone equipment?"

"Um . . . yes," said Lunderman.

"Is the microphone in the telephone receiver activated by tone or vibration?"

Lunderman's eyes shifted nervously. "Um . . . a little of both actually. It's the um . . . the software program that controls it."

Mendosa took his time and asked question after question. His knowledge of electronics was much more extensive than Mahler's, and Mendosa was able to delve into areas of theory that were beyond Mahler's capacity. As the minutes ticked by, Lunderman was becoming uneasy.

"How do you prevent the contact phone from ringing?" asked Mendosa.

Lunderman wasn't sure. Instead, he felt as though the questioning process was turning into an inquisition. "We . . . um . . . we use that special computer program I mentioned," he answered shakily.

At that, Mendosa sat back in his chair and just stared at Lunderman for a number of seconds.

Mahler was feeling uncomfortable in the silence.

Lunderman felt his palms getting sweaty.

"I see," said Mendosa after what seemed like an interminable pause. Then, he hesitated again before saying, "I noticed, Professor, that you used the word, 'we,' in your last answer." Another pause. "Who else is involved in the development of this . . . bug?"

"A young man who works for me," answered Lunderman. "His name is Pitch."

"Pitch?" asked Mendosa curiously.

"Pitch, is his nickname," said Lunderman speaking too quickly. "His real name is Peter. Peter Pechowski."

Mahler interrupted the two-way dialogue, "You didn't mention anyone named Peter." Then, looking at Mendosa, he repeated, "He didn't say anything about . . ."

Mendosa's ice cold stare cut Mahler's words off in mid sentence. Realizing that he had overstepped his bounds, Mahler thought he best keep his mouth shut.

"And what role does Peter play in the scheme of things?" asked Mendosa.

"Like I said," answered Lunderman, "he just works for me. He's my computer tech."

When Mendosa did not respond, Lunderman continued, "But he's an exceptionally bright young man."

It had become obvious to Mendosa that Lunderman was not the key. If he had, in fact, invented the device, the man would have been able to answer the majority of the questions. "Peter . . . uh, Pitch helped you invent this," stated Mendosa as a matter of fact.

"Why, yes . . . he did . . . um . . . he did help me," stammered Lunderman nervously.

Mendosa sensed anxiety building in Lunderman. There was no need to let that happen. Lunderman was willing to tell all he knew, but Mendosa would first have to put him at ease.

"Well, this certainly is very exciting," Mendosa said expansively. "With your intellect and your leadership skills, you've accomplished quite an outstanding feat. I don't foresee any problem in arranging grant money for you."

Lunderman breathed a heavy sigh of relief. "All right! That's good to hear," he said wiping a line of perspiration from his upper lip. "You're going to be even more impressed once you actually see it work. How about I call for some room service? Get us all a couple of drinks?"

"Why don't you wait to do that," suggested Mendosa calmly. "I'm only going to be a few more minutes and then I must leave for another engagement."

For the next ten minutes, Lunderman was very cooperative indeed. Feeling certain that he would get the grant, he gladly answered all of Mendosa's questions without any qualms or fear of repercussions. Lunderman felt strongly that Skip Nelson was the kind of man who understood what it meant to be the man in charge. After all, when things go right, it should be the man at the top to receive the bulk of the credit.

Walter Mahler was getting annoyed. Stewing, he thought, 'That fat, sloppy bastard, is telling everything to Nelson. Lunderman didn't tell me jack-shit. Now, Nelson's got the scoop and I look like an incompetent idiot.' Not only did Mahler's dreams of a big payoff vanish, he now hoped that Parlotti did not find it necessary to cut into his finder's fee.

Mendosa was becoming intrigued by the possibilities. A listening device that could remotely activate the microphone in any telephone and enhance it to the point of hearing everything within forty feet, was priceless. Mendosa continued. He wanted to know things like, could the equipment be transported easily? And could the user be traced over standard telephone lines? And what about using the microphones on cell phones?

Lunderman tried his best to be honest and open. He told Mendosa that the entire unit only consisted of a sound mixer, a personal computer and a software program small enough to fit onto a single floppy disc. All of it could easily be transported in the trunk of a car. When it came to talking about issues such as, could the user be traced or did it work on cell phones, Lunderman hesitated. He hadn't spent enough time talking to Pitch about those things and did not know the answers. He got around those questions by saying that part of the research study would look to answer those questions.

Mendosa wanted to know more, but tried to keep the stress level to a minimum by asking some casual questions about the university where Lunderman taught. A few of his questions were ones about Pitch Pechowski, including his personal and private life, but Mendosa was careful not to raise any suspicions. Finally he asked, "Tell me Professor, how much money do you think you'll need to fund this project over the next year?"

With that last question, Lunderman felt as though he was sailing on a cloud. He had done some research on the amounts of money offered by federal grants and knew that some of the figures were astronomical. As he read about the multi-million dollar grants that were passed around, he chuckled at his own naiveté at accepting a mere sixty-two thousand dollar grant from his own university. He felt reasonably certain that he could get ten times that amount from Skip Nelson. He took a quick glance at Mahler, before turning back to Mendosa and said questioningly, "Six hundred thousand dollars?"

Mendosa played his role perfectly when he said, "You obviously haven't taken into account your own salary or the salaries of your staff."

"Um . . . no," said Lunderman as he felt his heart beating with wonderful anticipation.

"Well, I am going to put this request through at an even two million dollars for the first year," said Mendosa convincingly. "You do understand, of course, that it takes a little time to process all the paperwork and such, but do you feel the amount will be satisfactory?"

"Yes! Of course!" Lunderman gushed, clapping his hands and stamping both feet.

Mendosa smiled at the reaction of the academician. "Now, Professor," he said trying to calm Lunderman's enthusiasm, "please remember that we have to deal with the bureaucracy. I'll have to see a demonstration, and then make a presentation to the committee. You know, that sort of thing. So, be prepared to be a little patient."

Mendosa turned to Mahler and said, "Walter, please make arrangements for me to fly down to Florida and view a demonstration of the prototype. For now, write down all the pertinent information so we can get through the red tape quickly."

"Sure, Mr. Nelson," said Mahler, as he took out his pad and pen.

Mendosa said, "All we need from you, Professor, is your name, address, phone number, social security number, that sort of thing. As for me, I'll make preliminary arrangements to meet with the committee. I'm sure they'll be as impressed as I am."

Lunderman turned to Mahler and began dictating the information. Halfway through, Mendosa added, "And Walter, don't forget to jot down similar information on Peter . . . or Pitch."

"I don't know his social security number off hand," said Lunderman.

That's all right," said Mendosa. "Just his address and phone number will be fine. Oh, yes, and the correct spelling of his last name." Then, he added, "Are there any other people who are involved? Anyone else know about this project? Other faculty members, people like that?"

Lunderman thought a moment. There was no sense in mentioning Scott Aarons. He didn't know how the device worked. And Jennifer

Morano and Crystal Richards had nothing to do with it. "No," said Lunderman. "No one on the faculty knows anything about this. We've kept it very quiet. Pitch and I are the only ones who know about it."

Lunderman turned back to Mahler and continued dictating the rest of his personal data. As Mahler wrote the information onto his pad, Mendosa stood up and moved to where he was standing behind Mahler and looking over his shoulder. He bent slightly at the waist, pretending to look at what Mahler was writing. Mahler's body was now blocking Lunderman's view, and neither he nor Mahler could see Mendosa remove the nine-millimeter pistol, with the long silencer, from his shoulder holster.

Mendosa only waited until Mahler had finished writing Peter Pechowski's name and address.

CHAPTER
FOURTEEN

The headline in the *Sun Coast Ledger* read, "D.A. GIVES SWEET DEAL TO RAPIST." Directly underneath the headline was the name of Scott Aarons, informing the reading public that he was the author of this blockbuster. Pitch and Jennifer were reading the article for the second time, scrutinizing it for any clue as to the source of the information. The lead paragraph only said, "*. . . that a source close to the investigation has confirmed that District Attorney, Warren Brock, made a deal with Michael Sharpton, the attorney for accused rapist, John Krum. Krum has been under arrest for allegedly victimizing the little girl who was found raped and beaten while walking home from St. Augustus Parochial School last month.*"

Pitch got through reading the article a little faster than Jennifer. Staring at her profile and waiting for her to finish, he thought about the previous night and the time they spent onboard Scott's yacht. Pitch played it over and over in his mind. Thoughts of Jennifer crept into everything he did. The night had been very special.

The couple had made plans to drive down to the Keys that afternoon to meet Jennifer's grandparents. She had told her grandmother all about Pitch and vice versa. Now, everybody was looking forward to meeting. Jennifer's grandfather had always been an avid fisherman. After twenty-five years as a welder, Grandpa Morano and his wife retired to Key West where he now ran a small fishing charter.

The original plan called for Jennifer and Pitch to meet around two in the afternoon before starting their drive to Key West. She and Pitch had already made hotel reservations on Islamorada, one of the many keys leading to Key West. They would be staying overnight and both were very excited at the prospect.

Plans changed slightly when Pitch called her the previous night. The couple had talked about what had transpired between Pitch and Professor Lunderman after Jennifer and Crystal had left the cafeteria. Jennifer had a barrage of questions, but Pitch had refused to go into any details over the telephone. Instead, he invited her over to his apartment for breakfast. She was very glad he did that. Jennifer could not imagine herself having to wait until two p.m. to find out what happened between Pitch and the Professor. Despite her academic prowess, she was an incurable gossip.

When she arrived at Pitch's apartment, he was already reading Scott's article in the morning paper. Waving the newspaper, he told her there was an article that they were going to discuss. But first, he wanted her to know the events that led up to the writing of the article.

Pitch filled her in on what had happened, how the Professor jumped all over Crystal's comment about his Ultimate Bug. Pitch tried to steer him away from the subject, but Lunderman would not let go. He was like a shark, coming closer, moving in for the kill. Then, the Professor told Pitch about his Washington contacts. Pitch went into great detail, telling Jennifer about how well connected George Lunderman was. Pitch mentioned how the Professor said he knew some high-ranking people at the State Department, not to mention the prestigious National Science Foundation.

When Pitch felt that Jennifer was duly impressed, he continued. Pitch talked about Lunderman's inside track to getting huge amounts of grant money for research; how he was buddy-buddy with the right people, the people who controlled the purse strings. All they wanted in return was for Professor George Lunderman to come up with the right vehicle, a substantive idea that would warrant their investment.

Pridefully, Pitch added, "It turns out that the key to all of this is my invention."

Jennifer was mesmerized. She took a deep breath before remembering to pour the coffee as Pitch explained the Professor's offer. Listening to Pitch detail the proposal, Jennifer ran through a gamut of emotions ranging from curiosity to fascination to shock. The fact that Professor Lunderman offered a complete partnership to Pitch was curious. Jennifer did not trust Lunderman and knew his motives needed to be questioned. Then, there was the idea that the Professor would personally arrange to have this research study become Pitch's doctoral thesis. That part was fascinating. She was proud of Peter's genius and played with the sound of "Doctor Peter Pechowski." Lastly, the concept that Pitch might actually consider partnering up with that hunk of lard was shocking. Jennifer felt that Pitch could accomplish all of his goals on his own, without the aid of "The Lecher."

Pitch continued to bring Jennifer up to date. He told her about demonstrating the bug for Lunderman, and how Scott had come up with this great idea for zeroing in on the meeting between John Krum the rapist, and Warren Brock, the District Attorney. Pitch told her how the Ultimate Bug worked perfectly, and they were all able to eavesdrop on the secret meeting as though they were actually there in the same room. Finally, he told Jennifer of Scott's request to write the article that appeared as today's headline.

When Pitch finished, Jennifer suddenly realized that she had been holding her breath. It made both of them laugh.

Pitch studied Jennifer's face as she continued to read the article. He thought about their night on the yacht. He was wrapped in the memory of moonlight coming through the porthole and illuminating her tanned body, when she interrupted his daydream and said, "I guess your invention is safe. So far."

"Oh. Yes. I suppose so," said Pitch, coming back to the present. "No mention at all about the bug."

Jennifer said, "Scott was being real cute when he wrote, 'A source close to the investigation . . . ' I hope he gets away with that."

Pitch said, "The telephone I activated must have been sitting in the middle of the conference table in Sharpton's office. So, Scott's choice of words was indeed accurate."

"Peter," asked Jennifer, "do you remember what I was saying the other night on the yacht?"

"Every word," said Pitch with a leering smile.

"I'm not talking about that part," said Jennifer with mock exasperation. "I'm talking about your Ultimate Bug and it's ultimate ramifications."

"I know," said Pitch. "I've been thinking about it."

Jennifer ignored his comment and continued, "It's a marvelous little gizmo, Peter, and you're amazing for having invented it. You realize, of course, that all the beer-guzzling bozos on our campus, and campuses everywhere else, would love to have one of these things in order to listen in on the girl's dorm. Get their jollies and whatever else. But after they try it a couple of times, those same bozos will begin experimenting." Jennifer paused for just a moment before continuing. "And where will that lead? Whose private conversation will they want to tap into next?"

"Like Scott," suggested Pitch staring directly into her eyes.

"Yes," she said. "Exactly like Scott."

"It certainly didn't take Scott eons of time to figure out a practical use for it," said Pitch with a touch of pride for his friend.

"Well . . . that's kind of . . . what I'm talking about, Peter," said Jennifer hesitantly.

"What do you mean?" he asked.

"What Scott did, wasn't so much practical as it was selfish. What did he hope to accomplish? Inform the public or aggrandize himself?"

"Scott? Aggrandize?" Pitch questioned, perturbed. "Certainly not! He's just a cub reporter having grown up in a world of reporters. He just did what comes naturally. Scott witnessed an inequity in our justice system and wanted to write about it."

"Think about it, Peter. Think about all the pitfalls that could result from his action. This article might cause such a furor that District Attorney Brock could lose his job or more likely, it could create a prejudiced jury that could, in turn, convict an innocent man. Or how about that murder in Palm Beach a year ago of that widow and her two daughters? Now, that might never get solved. I mean, the writing of this story could be like the beginning of the Domino Theory; all kinds of things could result from this article. Things that I've probably not even thought about. My point is, Scott didn't think about them either. It was just a cheap way to rise to the top."

Pitch was not happy with Jennifer's train of thought. She was being accusatory, and Scott did not deserve it. Pitch straightened up a little and spoke sternly. "Scott's been my friend since childhood. I know him. He is not that kind of person. He wouldn't put his self interest in front of a just cause. He wouldn't do that."

Jennifer sensed immediately that she had crossed the line. She knew that Pitch and Scott had been friends forever and that a strong bond existed between them. Her words had caused Pitch to come to the defense of his friend, and she realized that what she said had put him in an awkward position. She was in love with Pitch and did not want to hurt him. She said, "I'm sorry, Peter. It's just that . . . well, you're probably right about Scott."

"And consider the article he just wrote," said Pitch, still miffed at jennifer's comment and ignoring her apology. "He protected me, Jennifer. He protected me and the bug."

"You're right, Peter. He did. But you know what? I'm scared. I'm scared of what might happen if the wrong people get hold of something like this."

"Now, let's not create Armageddon just yet," said Pitch. "I've already given that some thought. This thing I've invented is not something new. It's just a new version of something old. There are all kinds of listening devices out on the market and what you're worried about could be said about all of them." Pitch paused a moment before adding conspiratorially, "But y'know what? We have a hidden trump card on our side."

"What's that?" she asked curiously.

"The law!" Pitch said exuberantly. "The law is the protection. There are all kinds of laws out there preventing most people from using all those listening devices. If a person isn't authorized to use such a device, it becomes illegal for them to do so. Even the FBI has to get special authorization from a federal judge in order to set up a wire-tap. My invention will fall under those same guidelines. So, believe me, Jennifer, there isn't anything to worry about."

"Mmm," said Jennifer.

"Besides," said Pitch, tapping the breast pocket of his shirt, "I always keep the 'master disc' with me." He smiled brightly as he said, "My little bug just won't fly without it."

Jennifer thought about what Pitch said and realized that he was probably right. She sometimes tended toward being an alarmist and knew she had to work on that particular shortcoming.

The telephone on Pitch's desk began ringing. Jennifer turned the page in the newspaper and stopped at a full page ad depicting ladies undergarments on sale at *Bloomingdale's*. Pitch picked up the phone and said hello.

It was Scott Aarons. He said excitedly, "Did you buy today's newspaper?"

"Yes, actually," said Pitch dryly, but with a smile that Scott was unaware of. "Scoured it front to back. Didn't see a thing. So now, Jennifer and I are using it to start a fire in the fireplace."

"You don't have a fireplace, you asshole!" said Scott, recognizing Pitch's dry sense of humor. "So, what did you think of the article?"

Pitch chuckled at Scott's reply before answering. "Jennifer is here and we both read it. A couple of times. It was brilliant, Scott."

"Thanks, but you have no idea of the flack I'm getting. My story has stirred up a hornet's nest!"

"I can imagine," said Pitch.

"No, you can't." said Scott. "The switchboard here at the paper has recorded more incoming calls than they did during the O.J. Simpson trial."

Pitch was a little apprehensive about his next question. "What did your father say when you told him you wanted to write the story?"

"Naturally, he wanted to know my sources." Scott paused a long time before saying, "But I wouldn't tell him, Pitch. That part of the story is going to come from you."

"So, that was it? You didn't mention anything about my invention being the source for your story, and he still said go ahead and write it?"

"It wasn't quite that easy," said Scott. "First, he had to lecture me on procedure and getting at least two confirmed sources before printing something like this. Then, he read me the riot act about whether I understood the significance of what I was asking him permission for. He really went on and on."

"You must have been relieved when he gave his blessing," said Pitch.

"I sure was." Changing tempo, Scott said, "Guess what?"

"What?"

"This afternoon," said Scott, still flushed with excitement, "I have an interview with Channel Eight. You know, the news show 'Live on the Coast,' with Amanda Dale. She said they'd air the tape at six and eleven. Let's get together for that. I'm picking Crystal up at eight o'clock tonight. Where are you going to be?"

"Jennifer and I are heading down to Key West to spend the evening with her grandparents. I think they're looking forward to meeting a superstar," said Pitch smugly, winking at Jennifer.

"Well, how late will it be when you get back?" asked Scott.

"We're going to be sleeping over. How about we get together for breakfast tomorrow morning? We can go to *Benny's on the Beach,*" suggested Pitch, nodding his head at Jennifer, hoping for her approval.

"Benny's sounds great," said Scott, "but not too early. Let's make it around eleven."

"Okay, sure," said Pitch.

Scott hesitated a moment before saying, "Sooo, your place is going to be empty tonight."

Pitch thought he knew where this was leading and glanced over at Jennifer. She was engrossed in the newspaper and didn't seem to be paying any attention to his conversation when he answered, "Yes, that's right."

"Well, old buddy," said Scott in a lecherous tone. "Crystal and I may just pop in there while your gone."

"Oh, Okay," Pitch said, trying not to reveal Scott's side of the conversation. "*Benny's on the Beach* it is."

"Is Jennifer on your extension?" asked Scott in a whisper.

"Not at all," said Pitch a little too loudly, which caused Jennifer to glance over at him.

"Yes-siree-bob!" said Scott, enjoying Pitch's obvious discomfort. "A little horizontal mambo for this old boy."

"Whatever you say, Scott," said Pitch, nervously.

Scott chuckled as he said, "Just make sure Jennifer doesn't go peeking in the windows."

"Okay. Fine," said Pitch with finality. "We'll go directly to Benny's and meet you there at precisely eleven a.m."

Pitch could hear Scott snorting with laughter as he hung up.

CHAPTER FIFTEEN

Lincoln Bradshaw had been running on an elevated treadmill for the better part of an hour. Arriving at the gym at six in the morning, he spent the first hour working a specific program with weights. He chose lighter weights, which he used with a greater number of repetitions. One of the programs was especially useful for building up the muscles around his bad knee. His daily run on the treadmill gave him an opportunity for an hour of uninterrupted thought. Linc used this time to go over the details of the previous day as well as plan the day ahead.

Linc thought about Preston's party and his meeting Emily for the first time. She was a fascinating woman. There was a quality that made her stand out from the crowd. Having noticed that she sometimes looked at him with a sideways glance and a slightly raised eyebrow, Linc decided that it was very seductive.

Linc wondered about what might have switched Emily off. When they were first introduced, she seemed genuinely pleased to meet him, pert and conversational. Then, something happened. What was it? Linc played the meeting over in his head. Each time Emily asked Linc a question, Preston would supply the answer. Was she upset at the way her father acted? Jealous perhaps at the attention Preston lauded on him? No, he didn't think so. It was something else. If he recalled correctly, Preston was talking about Linc's football days. Going on and on about his old nickname "Chain-link Bradshaw." Maybe that was it. Linc knew from experience that being a professional football player had a very different effect on different women. Some women absolutely swooned as soon as they found out. Others were turned off entirely. Perhaps, Emily was one of the latter.

On the other hand, she had been married to Jube Salaran. He was a professional athlete and yet she married him, for god's sake. She even kept her married name, which was interesting. Maybe, in her head, there was a difference between tennis players as opposed to football players. After all, many of the mansions on Palm Beach had tennis courts as part of the estates. He could not think of a single one that had a gridiron! It just didn't fit the mold.

That was probably it. Linc would have to figure a way to overcome her aversion. At the very least, talk about something other than football. He recalled suggesting they get together for lunch, but he was not specific and she was very non-committal. Maybe, he should call her tomorrow and ask her out. Something casual, such as a cup of coffee. Maybe calling her tomorrow would be too soon. Rushing this woman was probably not a good idea. Someone like Emily needed time. Consequently, he would take his time.

Linc had a very busy schedule, which included juggling several active cases. Besides wrapping up the case for Senator Boyd Williamson against a very perverted Congressman, he had an early morning appointment with Sidney Aarons. The meeting was scheduled for nine a.m. at Sidney's private club, which Sidney and the other members referred to as The Pro Club. It was located on Royal Poinciana Way, and would be less than a ten-minute drive from the gym. Afterwards, he would high-tail it back to his own office on North County Road. Carmen, his secretary, would be there to fill him in on any earthshaking news.

In the middle of his thoughts, Linc's cell phone began vibrating against his waistband. Without breaking stride, Linc unhooked it and checked the incoming number. It was Preston. The man always had a lot to say. Linc would hear from Preston, one way or another, almost every day. In addition to taking on the role of a solicitor for Linc's investigative agency, Preston also had Linc do some personal work. That case involving Senator Williamson, for instance, had Preston's personal signature all over it. Although Linc's fee and expenses were actually paid for by Boyd Williamson, it was Preston and his enormous influence that created the job in the first place. Preston had been hoping to get a certain piece of legislation passed that would be very beneficial to one of his real estate holdings that bordered a section of Yosemite National Park. For a while, it looked as though the committee, headed by Senator Williamson, would pass the needed legislation. However, problems arose when Congressman Jack Higgins, a member of one of the related sub-committees, announced his opposition. From that point forward, it was only a matter of finding a way to get Congressman Jack disavowed. His penchant for luring young girls and boys into hotel rooms made it easy.

Checking the timer on the treadmill, Linc saw he only had a couple of minutes to go. He decided to wait and return Preston's call before jumping in the shower.

Ron Scofield was the owner of Scofield's Olympic Gym, a small chain consisting of eight locations, all in South Florida. Ron and Linc had known each other since their days on the athletic fields of high school. During that time, they were fairly good friends, but lost contact when they went off to separate colleges. While Linc was selected to the ranks of All-American, Ron's prowess was in track and field. He excelled in the 800 and 1500-meter races as well as the high hurdles, and still held Oklahoma's school record in the javelin throw. His real fame, however, came when he made the U.S. Olympic team on two separate occasions and medaled in the Decathlon. They renewed their friendship one evening, quite a few years ago, when they found themselves sitting on the same dais during a gala evening honoring some outstanding local athletes. All the honorees were African Americans except for Linc. Ron kept kidding him about it, saying things like, "What happened Linc? Did they bus you over here?" Shortly after that night, Linc put Ron in touch with Preston Collingsworth, who arranged financing for Scofield's Olympic Gymnasiums. A copy of Ron's Bronze Medal hung in each of his gym locations, and all the walls surrounding it were covered with autographed photos of past Olympians.

Linc poked his head into Ron's office. "Hey," he began. "Okay if I use the office to make a phone call?"

Ron Scofield put his pen down and sat up straight. "Man," he said shaking his head, "look at you, Lincoln! You're sweatin' like a pig, and all you done is that pussy treadmill. You're getting' old, man."

"Good morning to you, too," said Linc.

"Old and fat." said Ron with a serious look on his face.

"Fat? Me?" asked Linc incredulously. "Have you noticed how broad your black ass has become? Sitting all day behind your desk has made it spread like a blanket."

"Are you kiddin' me?" said Ron, standing. "Those pretty young 'boo-jum' out there love my black ass!" He continued as he strutted past Linc and out of his office, "They say, my ass got dimples."

Linc was still smiling as he sat down at Ron's desk and dialed Preston's number. Louise answered.

"Good morning, Louise," said Linc. "May I please speak with Mr. Collingsworth?"

"Certainly, Mr. Bradshaw," she replied. "One moment, please."

Mopping the sweat from his brow, Linc waited for Preston to pick up the phone.

"Linc! Good to hear from you," said Preston in a voice that was more enthusiastic than usual. "What's up?"

"Good morning, Preston," said Linc. "Just returning your call."

"My call?" questioned Preston. "I didn't call you."

"Well, my cell phone has your num . . ."

"Emily!" interrupted Preston gleefully. "I'll bet it was Emily."

Linc was silent. For the moment, he couldn't think of anything to say.

"Hello? Linc? Hello, are you there?" Preston asked in a staccato.

"Oh . . . yes, Preston," said Linc. "I'm still here."

"Hold on. I'll get her. Now hold on, y'hear?"

"All right, Preston," said Linc gathering his senses. "I'll hold."

Seemingly waiting a long time, he finally heard the click of the receiver followed by Emily's, voice. "Lincoln Donald Bradshaw. Whatever did you say to my father to make him so giddy?"

Linc was not prepared for that question and stammered, "Nothing, Emily. I didn't say anything. Really."

"Oh, come now, Linc," Emily said smoothly. "You must have said something. He's rubbing his hands together and . . . prancing!"

By this time, Linc had gathered himself and said, "He's just happy that we're talking. In Preston's eyes, we're both family."

"Well, in that case," said Emily, "how about we two family members meet for lunch?"

"Family members?" Linc asked hesitantly.

"Yes. You and I," said Emily.

"Having lunch?"

"Mr. Bradshaw," Emily said emphatically. "Do you want to take me out to lunch, or what?"

"Yes, of course," said Linc quickly. "When?"

"Noon at *Charlie's Crab* on South Ocean Boulevard."

"Okay. Sure. That'll be great," said Linc still unsure of just what happened. "I have a morning meeting at the Pro Club, but I'll be free for lunch."

"See you there. Bye for now," said Emily, hanging up before Linc could respond.

Linc sat there staring at the dead telephone. "How do you like that," he said out loud to the empty office. He had been so sure it was going to take time and a great deal of effort to get back into Emily's good graces. This was certainly easier than he thought it would be.

Ron Scofield walked back into his office and said, "Man you look like you just bet more money than you should have on the Knicks. Either that or you just been talkin' to a woman."

Linc looked up, amazed that Ron could read his face that well and said, "Yup. A woman."

"Man, what would a woman see in you?" said Ron lowering his head and shaking it back and forth.

"It's my butt," said Linc as he stood up, grabbed his towel and headed for the shower. "It's got dimples."

CHAPTER
SIXTEEN

After showering, Linc dressed in a pair of pleated, tan slacks, a taupe shirt, open at the collar and a cocoa colored sport coat with a very fine herringbone pattern and drove straight to his meeting with Sidney Aarons. Although Linc had never been to the Pro Club, he nevertheless was certainly aware of its reputation. It was located near the magnificent and opulent mansion of Henry Flagler, who some say was responsible for creating Palm Beach and its singular attitude. The Pro Club was instituted, just after World War II, as a wry, dry literary club with an odd twist of irony. The real name was The Protagaras Club and was named for the Greek philosopher who espoused literature and who charged great sums of money to those who would hire him as a guest speaker. The wealthy charter members of this very exclusive club found that fact, somehow, very satisfying. Over the years, the club had seen the likes of Ernest Hemingway, Dashiell Hammett, John Steinbeck, Isaac Asimov, Kurt Vonnegut and James Michner pass through its doors. These days, it was a haven for wealthy people who enjoyed the proximity to literary genius. The membership boasted a few mildly successful authors, as well as journalists like Sidney Aarons.

Linc arrived about five minutes before the appointed time, and Sidney was already waiting. Linc did not know the man very well, but sensed that he was a bit nervous. Certainly more on edge than the previous night at Preston's party. After greeting each other, Sidney led Linc to one of the "chat rooms" that the members used for private conversations. The room was small and cozy but very well appointed with a lot of fine leather and a Chippendale settee upholstered in a cut velvet. Sidney closed the big double doors before sitting in the chair next to Linc. It was a plush Queen-Anne style that looked quite comfortable, but Linc noted that Sidney was sitting on its very edge.

Sidney began by saying, "Linc, I don't want you to think I brought you out here under false pretenses." Then, he paused a long time gathering his next thoughts.

Linc did not think that false pretenses were unusual at all. As a matter of fact, it was the basis of his work. If everybody was open and above board, there would be no need for undercover investigations. He chose to sit quietly and listen.

Sidney continued. "I told you about this reporter fellow who works for me, and whom I feel is stealing stories from me. Well, that part is true. His name is Henry Drummond and I hate the son-of-a-bitch, even though he's a damn good reporter."

Linc remembered having seen Drummond's name listed as the author of several lead articles in Sidney's newspaper.

Sidney went on. "You and I are going to have to talk about Drummond . . . someday, but not today."

It all sounded a little cryptic, but still Linc thought it best to keep quiet. His experience taught him that there were certain people who needed some mental ranging room and Sidney seemed to be one of those folks.

Sidney lowered his voice and said, "I've been doing a lot of soul-searching this past week, and now I've decided that I need help. Your help."

The two men just looked at each other. It was obvious to Linc that Sidney was fighting with himself about divulging the details of the story. Linc was already ahead of him. Perhaps it was his years with the Palm Beach County Sheriff's Department that gave him a healthy dose of cynicism, but to Linc, it looked like Sidney was embarrassed. That led Linc to think that it probably had to do with some kind of involvement in drugs, a woman or perhaps extortion. Finally, Linc spread his hands questioningly and asked, "With . . . what?"

Sidney spoke slowly, "About six months ago, I met this young woman named Elana. Elana Velez." Sidney paused. Swallowing a couple of times, he continued, barely audibly, "She was beautiful, and . . . and I got all turned around."

'So, there it was,' thought Linc. 'A woman.' Linc was sure he was going to hear a story he had heard many times before, but he focused intently on what Sidney had to say and tried his best to be objective and compassionate.

Once Sidney warmed to the task, he went on to tell his account in great detail. Elana Velez was voluptuous and sophisticated. A cosmopolitan model who had eyes that bore right through you. She was easy to talk to and laughed at Sidney's jokes and made him feel good about himself.

Occasionally interrupting with a question or two, Linc nevertheless allowed Sidney to tell the story in his own time.

Sidney continued. Within a matter of weeks the relationship grew, and Sidney would arrange modeling jobs for her that would appear as specialty ads in his newspaper. This setup gave Sidney access to her whenever he wanted, and they arranged to be together often.

Linc asked about any background checks that might have been done. Sidney sheepishly admitted that his own human resource department came to him with questions about her past, but he ignored them. She was gorgeous, passionate and seemed to know his every desire. Whatever her past, it seemed unimportant.

As Sidney talked, Linc became aware that time was slipping by. He did not want to jeopardize his lunch date with Emily, but this was taking more time than he had expected.

Sidney went on. Being editor and publisher of a large newspaper, he traveled quite extensively. "It was a simple matter," explained Sidney, "to fly Elana to any of the locations I planned on visiting." In the past six months, Sidney had been to a dozen of the finest hotels around the world, and he had arranged to have Elana Velez waiting for him in each one.

Linc asked about any records that Sidney might have kept, receipts for meals or gifts, vouchers, tickets, that sort of thing. He also asked

Sidney if it was all right to take notes, although, Linc put it more in the form of a statement.

Sidney asked, "Does this mean you'll become my private investigator? Help me work out of this jam?"

"Sidney," said Linc, "at this point, I still don't know what kind of jam you're in. The story you're telling me is very interesting, but you haven't yet told me what it is that I can do for you."

"You're right," concurred Sidney. "I didn't mean to take up this much time, but I wanted to set the stage, so to speak. Y'know, help you to understand my state of mind." Sidney was preparing to come to the crux of his tale and agitation was beginning to show. "We had become more that just lovers, you see. She was my confidante, my soul-mate, my trusted partner, my intimate . . ."

Linc interrupted, "I'm getting the idea, Sidney. Go on with the story. Then, what happened?"

Sidney now stood up and began pacing as he said, "It started out so innocently. The first time it happened was in London. We were at a little street bazaar. I was kissing her, playfully, and this vendor took our picture. It was just a Polaroid snapshot, and it was so meaningless. I gave the man some money and we kept the picture. Elana and I laughed about it. It was wonderful . . . at the time."

Linc watched Sidney's countenance change as he paced the floor in silence. Sidney suddenly thumped his fist on the back of the chair and said angrily, "We looked so goddamned cute in that picture! Who could have known?"

"Take it easy, Sidney," Linc said. "Was the guy who took the snapshot part of a setup? Is that what happened?"

Before answering the question, there was a knock at the double doors. Sidney was so startled by the sound, Linc thought the man would have a heart attack. A member of the staff poked his head in and asked if they would like some refreshments.

"No!" Sidney shouted. "Not now, goddamnit! And close the door!"

"Easy, Sidney!" Linc said with a marked firmness that caused Sidney to back off.

"I'm sorry," said Sidney. "I'm sorry. It's just that . . ."

"Sit down, Sidney, and finish telling me what happened."

Sidney took a ragged breath and said, "To answer your question, the guy who took that snapshot was a nobody, but we got such a kick out of it, I went out and bought our own camera. A digital. We went back to our hotel room and . . ."

"And you took pictures of each other," Linc said in conclusion.

"Yes," said Sidney despondently.

"And now, she has the pictures, and you want them back."

Sidney looked dolefully at Linc and said, "It's worse than that."

Linc thought to himself, 'Well, now . . . there's more to this Sidney Aarons fellow than meets the eye.' Linc sat forward and said, "Go on, Sidney. Let's hear the rest of it."

"After a couple of weeks, we got bored with the snapshots, and I bought a video camera." Sidney's voice trailed off during the last part of the sentence.

Linc waited.

"I had rented a large yacht, crew and all, and we were moored off the island of Capri. It was beautiful that night, and Elana was so sultry. One young man who was catering to us, kept commenting on how in love we were. He was telling us stories and making us laugh. I asked him if he would be kind enough to videotape us."

Looking sadly at the publisher, Linc rubbed his forehead and sighed.

Sidney went on. "Elana even said to me, 'Can we trust the crewman to keep it secret?' and I was the one to say 'What's the difference? We'll never see him again, and we'll have the videotape, not him.' Can you imagine that?"

Sidney was starting to choke up, and Linc had a passing thought about calling for one of the club's staff to bring Sidney a brandy. Instead, Linc asked some questions about the yacht leasing agency and the name of the crewman who did the videotaping. He jotted a few things down and waited.

Sidney said, "That videotape is devastating. I was doing some really stupid stuff with one of my socks and some cherry cordial chocolates . . ."

Linc quickly interrupted, "Have you actually seen the tape?"

"Yes," said Sidney. "She mailed it to my office about a week ago with this letter attached." Taking the letter out of the inside breast pocket of his sport-coat, Sidney handed it to Linc.

Unfolding the letter, Linc asked, "How about the quality of the tape? Are you recognizable on it?"

"Oh hell, yes!" replied Sidney. "Everything. Clear as a bell. It looks like it was produced in a goddammed Hollywood studio."

Linc read the letter. Elana Velez made it very simple. She wanted ten million dollars and the original tape would be turned over to Sidney. She promised never to ask for anything more, and she swore that there were only two copies. She had one. Now, he had the other. She would contact him again in one week to arrange the payoff. She signed it, "Love forever, Elana."

Linc rubbed his face and smoothed down a cowlick in the back of his head. He felt as though he could have used at least a cup of coffee, but it was too late to ask for that now. It was almost time for him to leave, but first he asked, "Have you told your wife about this?"

Sidney's eyes went wide and two veins began to protrude on his neck. "Good God, no!" he gasped.

"Okay," said Linc. "Then, let's get down to business." Linc went over the details of Sidney's story. First making sure he had all the facts, Linc next laid out what his services would cost. He also went over his expense account, which he explained might become considerable, depending on where he had to travel and whom he had to interview. Sidney agreed to all of it.

Next, Linc spelled out the possible consequences of this extortion demand. Not wanting to candy-coat it, Linc spoke frankly of the devastation this kind of thing could cause; the failure of a marriage, the loss of a business, not to mention the complete collapse of one's lifestyle. Linc added a small ray of hope by saying that there were ways to solve these kinds of problems. However, it was important that Sidney remain realistic.

Linc looked at his watch and saw that it was already noon. Even if he left right now, he would still be ten to fifteen minutes late. He had to cut this short.

He stood up and his action caused Sidney to do the same. Linc said, "It is very important that you keep two things in the forefront of your mind."

"What's that?" asked Sidney, hopefully.

"Be tough and be silent."

"Tough? What do you mean, tough?"

"You're under a lot of stress, Sidney. This whole affair has obviously brought you some sleepless nights. But as bad as it's been, it's going to get worse. Now, comes the waiting. While I'm doing my thing, all you can do is sit on your hands and wait. It's a tall order for a man like you. That's what I meant when I say, be tough."

Sidney nodded his head.

Linc said, "Here are the rules, Sidney. Do not speak to anyone else about this. We must contain the damage. Next, call the phone company and have them install 'Caller I.D.' on the phone you suspect that the Velez woman will use to call you. We need to trace where she's calling from. If she does call, do not agree to anything. Understand? Give her some excuse. Any excuse. Try to get her to meet with you in person, so you can work this thing out. If she won't, try telling her to call back the next day at a specific time and then, hang up. After that, call me immediately. I want to be at your side when she calls back."

Sidney was a dynamic and decisive man and, most of the time, a man of action. This disastrous debacle had wilted his resolve, but Linc's firm voice and positive instructions were making him feel better. Sidney felt that there might actually be a light at the end of this dark, dark tunnel.

"Where is the videotape?" asked Linc.

"It's locked up in my desk at the office,"

"Get it delivered to my office this afternoon," ordered Linc. "It's not a good idea for it to be in your possession."

Sidney nodded his agreement. "Yes. All right."

"In the meantime," said Linc, "if you can think of anything else, call me. If I don't hear from you, I'll get back to you in two days with a plan of action."

CHAPTER SEVENTEEN

After the two men shook hands, Linc took off for his lunch date with Emily. He was going to be at least fifteen minutes late, regardless of how fast he drove and he hoped that she would understand. Pulling up in front of *Charlie's Crab,* he let the parking attendant take the Corvette. While waiting for the ticket stub, Linc glanced over the sea wall at the waves cresting on an incoming tide. Four to six foot breakers were crashing over the pale yellow sand, leaving a blanket of white foam that retreated and disappeared into the surf like a movie reel running backwards. The lonely sound of the gulls, swooping low and searching for morsels, rose above the roar of the waves. True, he was late, but he paused a moment to take in the scene. Perhaps, he thought, there would be time to get Emily reacquainted with the beauty of Palm Beach.

Emily was sitting at a table by the window and staring out at the turbulent ocean. The tablecloth obscured most of her outfit, but she was wearing a blouse that befit the Florida tropics. It was a shimmery material of muted pastels, dominated by the colors of teal and shrimp. A wide open collar showed off her long neck and soft, white skin.

"I'm sorry I'm late," said Linc standing at Emily's table. "I just came from a business meeting that took much longer than I intended. I hope you haven't been waiting long."

Emily broke away from her view out the window. Slowly lifting her chin to look up at Linc's face, she said, "I hope this is not your usual habit."

Linc replied quickly. "No, not at all. It's just that when you called this morning . . ."

Emily interrupted, "Do sit down, Mr. Bradshaw. You can't expect me to continue to crane my neck like this."

"No. Of course not," said Linc, feeling like a school boy as he sat down opposite her. "And please, call me Linc."

"Chain-link?" asked Emily with her lips pursed tightly to prevent a smile.

Linc studied her face and saw the twinkle. It was at that moment, he recognized her charade. She was just twisting his tail. He relaxed and broke into a broad boyish grin. Feeling a slight flush in his cheeks, he said, "No. Just plain Linc. My old nickname, 'Chain-link', is long gone."

The waiter came over and took Linc's beverage order. Since Emily already had a diet cola, the server took a moment to acquaint them with the lunch specials. Emily waited for the man to depart before asking, "Do you realize that's the second time I've seen you blush?"

Emily's comment reminded him of the incident at last night's party when the Countess Erika grabbed a sizeable chunk of his buttocks. With an uneasy chuckle, Linc said, "Y'know, I don't usually blush. I am in the wrong business to be a blusher."

"Yes. Daddy told me you're a private investigator. Anything like 'Magnum, P.I.?'"

The absurdity of the comparison made Linc smile. "Magnum, P.I. is more like Hollywood than real life. My cases are much more boring than that." Linc had a sudden memory flash of the meeting he had with Sidney Aarons and realized that Sidney's story sounded pretty much like a Hollywood script.

"Give me an idea of what a typical case is like," requested Emily. "I'd be interested. The meeting you had with Sidney Aarons this morning, for instance. What was that about?"

Astonished, Linc raised his eyebrows and stared at Emily. "What makes you think I had a meeting with Sidney Aarons?"

"Oh, come now, Linc. Give me some credit. I'm a pretty good detective, too."

"Really? Go on," prodded Linc, with a half-smile on his lips. He was extremely interested in what she had to say.

"Well, first," said Emily, "at last night's party, Daddy was talking to Sidney and made some oblique references to your ability as a detective. I overheard parts of the conversation, but I'm afraid I didn't pay much attention. However, after you and I had that little chat with Sidney and Lenore, I saw you hang back and caught a glimpse of him bending your ear. And lastly, during our phone call this morning, you mentioned a meeting at the Pro Club. I happen to know that Sidney has been a member there for years. So, I just put two and two together."

"Very good," said Linc. Impressed with her powers of reason and deduction. "Now, you know what my typical workday is like."

"What do you mean?" asked Emily.

"I put two and two together. Just like you did."

Emily liked his mannerisms. She was aware that she flustered him somewhat, but she liked the way he was regaining his composure. "So, tell me about this meeting," prompted Emily.

Linc smiled at the brashness of the question and said, "You realize, of course, that there is such a thing as confidentiality."

"Of course there is," said Emily, "and believe me, I wouldn't expect you to break that rule willy-nilly. But there are times, I'm sure, when you could use good help. Help from someone who knows things. Someone who would have access to information that, otherwise, would not be available to you."

It was quite obvious that Emily was baiting him. She had something up her sleeve, something else she was trying to get across. Linc gave her a slight sideways glance and said, "What are you talking about?"

"How much has Daddy told you about me?"

"Well, frankly, quite a bit. You've been a part of our conversation for the past six or seven years." Linc paused to study her face. Although Emily had a classic beauty, serene and angelic, there were many more complex layers beneath that surface. He continued, "He's told me all about your personal life, your marriage to Jube Salaran, your divorce and the reason you left home. But somehow, I don't think any of that is what you're referring to."

When Emily had asked the question, she was referring to her Top Secret security clearance at NATO. Linc's answer, referencing her personal life, took her by surprise. "Daddy has told you all that?" Emily asked incredulously.

"Yes."

"Huh! The two of you are even closer than I thought," said Emily. "I've never known Daddy to talk about . . ." Her voice trailed off followed by several seconds of silence. Suddenly, she said with renewed vigor, "Well, I'm glad you know all that. It means you and I have a special bond."

Linc thought of her comment about getting along like members of the same family and asked, "Really? What kind of bond?"

Before Emily could answer, the waiter came back with Linc's ice tea and asked to take their order.

Linc said pleasantly, "We haven't had a chance to look at the menu yet. If you could give us several more minutes, we would appreciate it."

The waiter left and Emily asked, "What were we talking about?"

Linc was sure Emily remembered his question, but she obviously wanted to play coy. He said, "You were remarking about a special bond between us. What kind of bond?"

Emily tilted her head just slightly and said with a soft smile, "A close one."

Linc felt fairly certain that Emily's comment was not the kind that a sister would make to a brother. He returned her smile and said, "Oh. I see."

Emily spoke briefly about the nature of being a private investigator and how she viewed the future of that business. She had obviously done her homework. Emily spoke of the correlation between the growth of the economy and the growth of people's discretionary income. As personal wealth increased, so did the demand for services like private investigations. People preferred not to go to the police if they didn't have to. Ending her dissertation, Emily sat back and said,

"Daddy told me that you've been thinking about hiring someone to help you. Have you found anyone yet?"

"No," said Linc. "I haven't even interviewed anybody yet. I'm still thinking about it."

Emily decided to be more specific when she asked, "Did Daddy tell you about what I did for NATO during my years in Europe?"

"Actually, he was kind of vague about that part of your life. Almost as though he didn't know exactly what you did for them. But if you recall, you were kind of filling me in last night, just before the party started."

"Did you come away with a clear understanding of the work I did?" asked Emily.

Linc studied her face again, this time concentrating on her eyes. "No. I did not. Interestingly enough, I didn't realize just how vague you were until after I went home and played our conversation back again in my head. That's when I figured you must have been doing something that was highly classified." Linc paused and smiled. "Or, you just didn't feel like talking to me."

"You do put two and two together," she said admiringly.

"Elementary, my dear Emily,"

"So? Could you?" Emily asked.

"Linc had a blank look on his face. "Could I . . . what?" he asked.

"Could you use someone who knows how to access vital information that would aid your various investigations?" she queried patiently.

"What are you telling me? Are you saying that you are that someone?"

"I most certainly am," said Emily with an air of confidence. "I could give your profession a new dimension."

Linc was dumfounded. He said, "Emily, I just thought we would have a pleasant lunch together. Get to know each other, that sort of thing. I didn't know this was going to turn out to be a job interview."

As Emily was getting ready to reply, the waiter was approaching the table and, at the same time, a female voice called out from the direction of the entrance, "Emily?"

Emily looked up.

"Emily Collingsworth?"

Recognizing her old friend, Laura Parsons, Emily sprang to her feet and rushed to embrace her. They had their elbows linked as they walked back to where Linc was sitting. The waiter continued to wait patiently.

Linc stood as the two women approached the table. He had a sinking feeling about how things would progress from this point forward. Emily was about to make the introductions when Linc said, "Hello, Laura. How are you?"

"Linc!" Laura screeched. "Fancy meeting you here." She quickly turned towards Emily and said, "Fancy meeting the both of you here . . . together."

Emily had a look of curiosity on her face as she turned to face one, then the other and said, "How do you like that. You two know each other."

"Are you kidding?" Laura said. "Linc and I go way back. Not as far back as you and I," she amended as she wrapped her arm around Emily's shoulder, "but pretty far back."

Linc looked at Emily and explained, "We've shared information on a couple of jobs."

"And we've shared other things," Laura said cryptically, reminding Linc of matters of which he did not wish to be reminded.

Emily caught Laura's comment and filed it under, 'things to be discussed later.'

The waiter interrupted and asked Laura, "Will you be joining them for lunch?"

Emily turned to Laura and asked, "Are you here with someone? If not, you'll definitely join us for lunch."

Linc was hoping she had come with someone, but Laura gave her beverage order to the waiter and sat down.

"Emily Collingsworth," Laura said excitedly, "the last thing I heard was that you were sunning topless somewhere in the Greek Isles. What's been happening?"

"Well, first of all, my name isn't Collingsworth anymore. It's Salaran. And I was not sunning myself topless. I was working."

"Oh, yeah. I remember," said Laura. "You married that old snake-in-the-grass, Jubal. Did you ever legally split from that slime-ball?"

Emily smiled at the memory of Laura's salty vocabulary and realized the woman had not changed a bit. "Yes," she confirmed. "We actually filed for divorce before I left for Europe."

"Why did you keep the name 'Salaran'?" Laura asked. "I mean, Collingsworth is such a hoity-toity name here on the island."

Emily answered, "I was upset and angry with my father at the time and . . . well, by then, too many years had passed by and it would have been such a god-awful hassle to change it back."

"Well, I'm glad you're not with that piece of crap anymore." As Laura said this, she stuck out her tongue as though she had just eaten something rotten. She continued, "Jube Salaran is one of the cases Linc and I both worked on."

"This is so strange," said Emily, again turning to look at each of them as she spoke. "I mean, last week the three of us were all so far removed. I haven't seen you," she said to Laura, "in almost seven years." Turning to Linc, she said, "And we didn't even know each other." Emily shook her head at the coincidence. "And now, I don't know . . . it's just that having the both of you here and finding our lives so intertwined, seems phenomenal."

Laura's eyebrows went up in surprise. "You mean, you two just met last week?" she asked with the evilness of a gossip columnist.

The phrasing of Laura's question made Linc begin to squirm.

"No," said Emily. "We just met last night."

"Well, ain't this something!" said Laura glancing between the two of them. The hint of wickedness in her voice became more pronounced. "Emily, honey, you just better hold on to your panty-hose and watch out."

Linc folded his arms across his chest and glared at Laura.

Emily sat back in her chair. "You don't say? Tell me, Laura," Emily said while staring directly at Linc, "what is it about this man that should worry me the most?"

Knowing that Laura had an unstoppable mouth, Linc was beginning to dread this lunch. He unfolded his arms and put his elbows on the table.

Laura leaned forward and said in a conspiratorial stage whisper, "Well, he has this well-founded reputation among all the horny ladies in the area for having . . . a really big . . ." Laura mimed looking both ways as if to ensure privacy, "I mean, a huge . . ." Laura paused for maximum effect.

Linc glanced at Emily and saw her leaning forward in her seat.

" . . . Ego!" Laura blurted and began to laugh. "He has a huge ego!"

Emily began to laugh with Laura.

Linc just smiled weakly, slowly shaking his head and hoping this particular vein of conversation would soon come to an end.

The waiter brought Laura's drink, a basket of warm rolls and an extra menu.

Then, Emily asked, "What was it about Jube that brought the two of you together?"

"Linc had the weasel arrested," Laura replied, "for having possession of stolen property. I was the prosecutor on the case."

"My goodness!" exclaimed Emily. "You actually arrested my ex-husband? Did he go to jail?"

"Nah," said Laura. "He's as slippery as an oil slick."

Linc added, "He managed to get a key witness to change his testimony."

"Yeah. The pawn shop guy or something," said Laura, squinting and trying to remember the details. "He's had some other brushes with my office."

"Someday," said Linc, "he'll make a mistake."

The waiter came by again and the three of them finally gave their orders. He wrote them all down and hustled off toward the kitchen.

Emily turned to Laura and asked, "Tell me what you've been up to? What's going on in your life?"

Emily and Laura had known each other since seventh grade. Having both attended Clairmont-Pas, they had been fairly close in their youth. After going off to college, they lost contact with one other. Laura went to FSU in Tallahassee to study pre-law before continuing on to Georgetown to complete law school. There, she had a torrid love affair with a fellow law student who went on to become an FBI agent. Wanting to be close to him, Laura joined the Bureau herself and was doing quite well until their relationship broke apart.

Heartbroken, she left the FBI and moved back home where she found employment as an assistant district attorney for the county.

She and Emily were able to renew their friendship until Emily married Jubal Salaran. Once again, contact was lost and Laura was only able to get smatterings of information about her friend.

"You mean, other than losing my job," Laura stated sarcastically.

Linc looked at Laura. He always felt that her sharp tongue would get her into trouble.

Emily said, "What are you talking about?"

"Have you been following the John Krum rape case?" asked Laura, angrily.

Linc knitted his eyebrows and said, "There was that big headline in the paper about the D.A. giving some kind of deal to the rapist. Did you have something to do with that?"

"Jesus Christ, Linc! You know me better than that. I wouldn't give any kind of deal to a shit bag like him! Cut his pecker off and feed him to the alligators . . . that's the kind of deal I'd give him."

Laura's voice had risen dramatically. Some patrons at one of the nearby tables grew uncomfortable at the outburst.

"Cool it, Laura," said Linc in a hushed tone. "I don't want to get thrown out of this restaurant because of your mouth."

"I'm just so pissed," Laura whispered.

"So, how did you lose your job?" Linc asked.

"Well, I didn't actually lose my job," said Laura. "But Brock threatened to fire me for leaking the story to the press."

"What did you hope to gain by leaking the story?" asked Linc.

"I didn't leak the story!" Laura said exasperated. "That's what this whole thing is about. For some reason, he thinks I did. But I didn't leak it."

Linc said, "Then, why . . ."

Laura continued, "I kept saying, 'Why would I leak it? For what purpose?' But he wasn't listening. Brock is such an asshole."

Emily smacked the table with the flat of her hand. Both Laura and Linc looked at her. "Will one of you kindly tell me what is going on? I was in Europe up until two nights ago."

Linc and Laura each took turns telling the story to Emily. They filled her in on the rape of the little eleven-year old girl and the events that led up to John Krum, the accused, trying to finagle a deal.

"What kind of deal?" asked Emily.

Laura explained the part about the unsolved homicide.

When Emily asked for details, she was informed that the victims were the widow Jeanne Blakely and her two teenage daughters. Emily was aghast. She said that she knew Jeanne Blakely. Not well, but well enough to say hello by name. "My father knew her quite well. I understand she was a very generous woman." After a pause, Emily added, "I only vaguely remembered the Blakely girls. They were very young when I left for Europe."

Linc said, "Since the Blakely murders have never been solved, there's been a lot of pressure on the police."

Laura picked up the story. "So, when Krum said he had information that could break the case wide open, my boss grabbed at the bait."

"My goodness," said Emily.

Laura turned the conversation back to her own dilemma. "So, like I was saying, there were only two of us in that room who were not in favor of a deal. Me and Gary Gifford."

"Who's Gary Gifford?" asked Emily.

"Gifford is the attorney for the little girl who got raped."

"Okay. And . . . ?" coaxed Emily.

Laura took a roll from the breadbasket, broke off a small piece and popped it into her mouth. "So," she continued, "Gifford must have been the one to leak the story. By leaking the story, he gets public sympathy on his side. That's what he's going to need when he goes to trial."

Linc sat back in his chair and sipped his iced tea. He had to think about that explanation. He thought about everyone who was in the room with Laura while the deal was being hatched. The leak certainly would not have come from John Krum, nor his attorney. It definitely would be in their best interest to make the deal along with as few waves as possible. As for D.A. Brock, he was going to be under a lot of scrutiny no matter what he did. But the public would be clamoring for his head if they thought he were giving away the farm. It was a good bet that it wasn't Brock who leaked the story. Besides, Laura said that it was Brock who threatened reprisal if anyone leaked the story.

Linc also felt that Laura was telling the truth when she said she didn't do it. Consequently, that left Gary Gifford as the possible source of the leak. Or did it?

Linc knew through his contacts with the police force that the chief of police was under a tremendous amount of pressure to solve the Blakely murders. Linc also knew where that pressure was coming from. Preston had told him. Being a friend and neighbor of the murder victims, Preston had spoken about Jeanne Blakely and all the money she had spread around. Not only was she philanthropic towards the community, she was also a most generous contributor to the governor of the state of Florida, the democratic senator for the State of Florida, and the mayor of Palm Beach.

These high-ranking politicians knew all there was to know about putting pressure on people. Linc had no doubt that the chief of police and the District Attorney had very little room to maneuver. Eventually, they were going to have to make some kind of deal with the devil. The devil, in this case, was John Krum. And in order to accomplish that feat, it meant getting Gary Gifford on their side. He was representing a little girl who had been bludgeoned and raped and whose parents were certainly not wealthy. That meant that this case wasn't going to generate a lot of money for Gifford. It was possible, Linc thought, that a sizeable cash payment was one way to get Gifford to switch sides. Of course, if six months from now, Gifford should suddenly get an appointment to a judgeship or some similar nugget, that would be another way to move him onto their side of the street.

Linc could not be sure how the mayor and the D.A. were going to swing Gifford into the deal-making lane. However, Linc felt certain that with the help of the governor's office, plus the influence of a senator, Gifford would probably get some kind of sweet offer.

Linc waited for a pause in the conversation between the two women. "I don't believe Gifford leaked the story," he stated.

Laura spun her head to glare at Linc. "Goddamnit, Linc!" she burst out. "What the hell are you saying? That I leaked it?"

Linc turned to Emily and said with a look of exaggerated surprise, "Boy, oh boy! Your friend is ve-ery touchy today,"

The waiter approached and served lunch. A little calmer, Laura said, "Nah, not touchy. Just hungry."

Emily took a forkful of her broiled snapper and chimed in, "Linc, who do you think gave the story to the newspaper?"

Linc directed his question towards Laura. "Was there anybody else in the room besides Krum, Sharpton, Gifford and Brock?"

"Just me," said Laura. "And that was only until Brock threw me out for getting pissed."

"No secretary or stenographer?"

"No," said Laura. "Sharpton has this 'little-miss-wide-eyed-and-blonde' sitting in the outer office, but that's all."

"Could she have had an intercom turned on or something?" Linc asked.

"Nah." said Laura. "Even if she was listening, she definitely doesn't have enough brain power to pass on the story to the paper. Did you read the article? I mean, there were a lot of details in the article. Those details came from somebody who was inside that room."

"Well, it wasn't Gary Gifford," said Linc. "But you're right about one thing, Laura. It would have been to his advantage to leak the story in order to get public sympathy, *if* he were going to trial. However, he is not going to trial. Instead, Brock will offer some kind of deal to Gifford. He'll agree to a plea bargain in return for a plum. For that reason, he's going to keep his mouth shut and not talk to the press, no matter who the reporter is."

"And that's another thing," said Laura, reminding herself that there was more with which to be upset. "Can you believe the reporter on this story was Scott Aarons, that little twerp?"

"Our Scott Aarons?" asked Emily, skeptical.

Linc asked, "Is this the same Scott Aarons you were talking about at the party last night?"

"Y'know," said Laura, still disgusted, "he's just some goddamn little rich kid with an attitude who now thinks he's a reporter. All he really is, is some silver-spooned bull-shitter whose daddy happens to own the freakin' newspaper."

Emily answered Linc's question, "Yes. Scott went to school with Laura and me."

Linc tilted his head slightly and, with a puzzled look on his face, tried to recall the conversation of the night before. "He's the son of Sidney Aarons, and you said something about an incident where he threw a chair out of a second story window."

Emily was becoming more and more impressed with Linc. He had shown his ability to exercise logic and reason when he spoke about the people who were present at Laura's meeting. Now, he demonstrated his powers of recollection by reciting the conversation she had with Sidney and Lenore Aarons. "You don't miss a thing, do you, Linc?"

Linc smiled at Emily's comment. Turning to Laura, he said, "It sounds to me as though you don't think too highly of this Scott Aarons."

Laura started to open her mouth to let out some sort of tirade, when Emily interrupted with a stage whisper of her own. "Laura actually dated 'the little twerp!'" she enunciated.

"First of all, it was only one date, and besides, I felt like I was robbing the cradle. He's such a baby. And thanks a lot for reminding me, Emily."

"Well, there it is!" said Linc expansively. "You hate Scott. Scott hates you. He just wrote this story to get you into trouble."

Emily laughed at the simplistic fantasy, and soon, Laura was chuckling along with them.

"Seriously," said Linc, "It's possible that Scott or his father had some sort of bug planted there in order to get a jump on the story. It's been done before, y'know."

"A bug?" asked Laura.

"Yes," said Emily. "A listening device."

"I know what a 'bug' is," said Laura, annoyed.

Emily was fascinated by the idea. "How do you manage to get a bug into a lawyer's office?" she asked.

"Yeah," added Laura, "and without a court order at that. Wouldn't that be highly illegal, Mr. Detective, Sir?" said Laura, sarcastically.

"Hell. I wasn't the one who did it," Linc said defensively. "All I'm saying is that these kinds of things are used all the time." Then to Emily, he said, "It's a fairly easy matter to plant the simple ones. Glue it to the bottom of a coffee table, drop it into a waste basket or put it in a flower vase and leave it on the table. There are more sophisticated devices that can get a little tricky. Some of them get hooked up to cameras, while other models are designed to be placed inside a telephone receiver. They even have special directional antennas that you can aim and tune into conversations that are taking place a hundred feet away. All kinds of sophisticated equipment."

"When I was working for NATO," said Emily, "there was a whole section that monitored all sorts of military transmissions. Even some covert stuff. And just like you say, Linc, very complex. Very sophisticated. It takes real genius to invent things like that."

Laura brightened, "Yeah," she said, snapping her fingers in recollection. "Remember that Pechowski kid? The one who used to invent all kinds of things?"

Emily nodded at the memory of Pitch and said, "You're right. He could have grown up and gone on to do something like that. What ever became of him?"

"He still lives local," replied Laura. "Last I heard, he had a job working for the university. Some kind of research or something."

"Who is Pitch Pechowski?" asked Linc.

"A local boy," said Laura, "and a certifiable genius."

"He went to our school," added Emily, "although he was a couple of years behind us."

"Clairmont-Pas," commented Linc, "Home of the really smart people."

"Clairmont-Pas touted itself as an elite school for gifted children," explained Emily, "It certainly had its share of talented students, but Pitch Pechowski stood out head and shoulders, above everyone else."

Laura chimed in. "When he was just a kid, he invented this amazing burglar alarm. He was actually able to capture a couple of scumbags. Made the newspapers and everything."

"And when he was still a teenager," Emily said, continuing the tale, "he invented some sort of electronic device that gave everyone in his neighborhood free cable."

"I think he got his ass whipped for that one," said Laura.

Leaning forward, Linc said, "So, if your school was for gifted people, then I'm sitting in the presence of greatness."

Emily put a smirk on her face. "You most certainly are," she said emphatically.

"Did you know," asked Laura, "that Emily was valedictorian?"

"Really?" said Linc, trying to sound genuinely impressed even though he had learned that fact from Preston.

"Oh, come on now," said Emily, slightly embarrassed. "I only made it by a tenth of a point. Anyone of my classmates could have been valedictorian."

"Yeah, right!" said Laura sarcastically. "Like Homer-what's-his-face. You know, that asshole who used to drool all the time."

"Oh, my gosh," said Emily smiling at the memory of someone she had almost forgotten.

"And Elaine Velachuk, that dumb bitch who couldn't tie her own shoes."

"Boy, she was a piece of work," recalled Emily.

"And how about Geoffrey-the-fish?" asked Laura. "Like, he could have been valedictorian, right?"

Emily and Laura were laughing and enjoying the memories that were now flooding their minds. Linc sat back and enjoyed the moment of a friendship being renewed.

After taking another bite of her Caesar salad, Laura asked, "So, what do you think I ought to do?"

"You're probably best off doing nothing," advised Linc. "If Brock was going to fire you, he would have done it already. This thing will probably blow over."

Emily turned to Laura. "Or . . ." she said thoughtfully, "you could get hold of Scott Aarons and use your charm and your sex appeal. See what he has to say. See if he'll give you any sort of hint as to the sources of his story."

"I like that idea," said Laura. "Want to come with me? I could use your moral support."

Linc looked at his watch and realized, alarmingly, that he had spent too much time over lunch. He would not have had much of a problem with that, if the lunch had only included himself and Emily. However, Laura's sudden appearance, and the fact that so much of the conversation swirled around her dilemma, annoyed him. He had been hoping for a more private and intimate get together with Emily. He said, "I'm going to have to get going. I have a ton of things waiting for me back at my office."

There was a moment of silence as Linc stood. Emily held eye contact while she said, "Call me later, Lincoln."

Linc smiled at Emily and said, "I will." Then, looking at Laura, he squinted and said, "Kinda nice to see you again, Laura. You take care."

Linc turned to walk away and heard Laura say loudly, "Don't fall down the stairs, you big blockhead!"

CHAPTER EIGHTEEN

Standing behind his desk, Vincent Parlotti gazed out at the Washington, D.C. skyline. He was upset. Very upset. Although his face showed no emotion, his eyes seemed to change color. Parlotti looked like a fireplug. Broad shouldered, barrel-chested and no waist. Balding in the pattern of a monk and having absolutely no neck, he gave the illusion of being shorter than his five-foot eleven-inches.

John Anderson sat in a chair facing Parlotti's desk. Anderson watched Parlotti's back as he continued to stare out the window. Parlotti was wearing a white shirt and tie under his suit jacket, but the fact that his gene-pool didn't allow for a neck made the shirt collar invisible.

Anderson absent-mindedly mulled over this mundane fact while noticing that the bald spot on the back of Parlotti's head was redder than usual. Parlotti often took his time pondering the variables in difficult situations, and Anderson was used to waiting.

Still looking out the window at some rain clouds gathering to the south, Parlotti finally spoke. "I wonder what it would be like to have a job that didn't spring so many goddamned surprises on me." He started the sentence in a quiet manner, but by the time he got to 'goddamned surprises," he had raised his voice to an alarming level.

Anderson, who was relaxing in his chair, sat up straight at the unexpected outburst. Choosing not to respond. Anderson sat motionless.

Parlotti turned and said, "I'm getting too old for this horse shit."

"What are you talking about, Boss?" asked Anderson, still confused by Parlotti's flare-up.

"I'm talking about 'Harpoon,'" said Parlotti, "and why the hell he decided to take out 'The Weasel.' His instructions were to remove only Lunderman."

Parlotti lived in a world of passwords and codenames. "Harpoon" was the agency's codename for Claude Mendosa. "The Weasel" belonged to Walter Mahler. Even though Mendosa had worked for Parlotti for several years as a contract assassin, Parlotti still had not learned Mendosa's real name. Over the past couple of years, Parlotti had used Harpoon for several highly sensitive projects. Ones that involved the assassination of some very public and influential people. Harpoon had proved himself to be very capable and efficient. Still, he had an advantage over Parlotti, and that was something Parlotti could not and would not tolerate. Not knowing Mendosa's true identity had become a thorn in Parlotti's side. Parlotti was a man who had to have power and control over others in his realm. Parlotti had always known the assassin by one of his aliases, Skip Nelson, and by the nickname that Mendosa requested, "The Lass of Mont Valier." However, he did not relish allowing an operative with the lethal capabilities of Harpoon to keep any secrets.

As for Walter Mahler, Parlotti was not concerned about the loss of The Weasel's life. He was gravely concerned about two other things. Number one, Harpoon acted contrary to orders and, on his own volition, killed Walter Mahler. Secondly, every time there was an unauthorized assassination, the local police came prancing through the homicide scene, always asking too many questions. Sometimes, that led to reporters and that, in turn, led to trouble.

Walter Mahler was a low-level informant and rarely came up with anything of value. In the past four years, he had produced exactly two decent leads. One of those was taken over by the CIA in a midnight exchange of an Israeli scientist for a former KGB agent. The other lead spawned by Mahler, turned out to be a windfall. Not only was it profitable for Mahler, but it led to a planned assassination that was extraordinarily timely for the then Attorney General of the United States. Parlotti was able to bask in some short-lived glory over that one.

This time, Mahler had uncovered a tantalizing piece of information. In the last conversation with Parlotti, Mahler had talked about Lunderman and Pechowski's little invention. It was a gem. An unrivaled little device that had possibilities and implications that were very far reaching. Parlotti had been hopeful that Mahler had finally turned the corner and was actually becoming a useful informant. Now, it was too late. Harpoon had taken him out.

Parlotti's face turned crimson as he growled, "He better give me a goddamned good reason for doing what he did!"

Anderson remained calm. "Y'know, Boss, thinking about it now that it's over, it almost hadda happen that way."

"You're referring to Harpoon's demand for anonymity." Parlotti said it more as a statement than a question.

Mendosa had always made it clear that he would do the work cleanly and efficiently, but he always insisted on working alone. He did not want any witnesses to his deeds or identity.

"You know how he's dead-set against anybody being able to finger him," said Anderson.

"He'll be calling in," said Parlotti. "Tell the desk to have him call me back precisely at four p.m."

Anderson stood up and started to leave. Parlotti halted his exit when he said, "And have the boys set up the trace again."

"Another trace?" asked Anderson, his eyebrows raised. "Y'know it's a waste of time."

Parlotti shrugged, "We have to keep trying. Maybe he'll make a mistake."

CHAPTER NINETEEN

L inc was surprised to hear himself humming, as he drove to his office. His feelings of annoyance about Laura Parsons showing up at lunch were dissipating. Until last night, the sum total of his knowledge about Emily came from Preston. As much as he respected Preston's ability to read into a person's character, the man was still her father. Fathers tended to have a very different perspective when it came to their daughters. Preston had raised Emily in a puritanical fashion, trying to impart traditional, even old-fashioned values. Linc, on the other hand, was interested in a different side of Emily. He wanted to get to know her sense of humor, her sense of style, her likes and dislikes, her "hot-buttons" . . . so to speak.

While rehashing parts of the lunchtime conversation, Linc was bewildered by Emily's notion of wanting to become part of his investigative agency. At first, that seemed like such an odd thing. Then, he recalled a fact that he had originally learned from Preston, that Emily had worked several years for NATO, ostensibly in communications. Preston thought she had a top rated security clearance, and Emily herself, made it clear over lunch that she had access to "covert" information. Linc wondered if following up on that issue was something he should consider. Deciding to take a wait-and-see attitude. Linc nevertheless was curious to know if Emily would bring the subject up again.

Emily had asked Linc to call later, and he intended to do just that.

Perhaps, he would suggest they take a drive. That would certainly prevent any interruptions from flakes like Laura Parsons. If Emily was willing to join him for dinner, Linc would make sure to go somewhere off the island. Palm Beach was too confining, and he knew too many people who lived and worked in the community.

Then a thought came into Linc's head that jolted him. He suddenly realized that when he left the restaurant, he left Emily alone with Laura. What would be the ramifications of that? Laura had a wicked mouth and loved to gossip. Worse than that, she had a tendency to exaggerate. Linc shook his head. Being the first to leave the restaurant meant that he would certainly be the topic of conversation.

As Linc drove to his office, a look of dismay crossed his face. He began to chew his lip in anticipation of the awful things Laura might be telling Emily right about now. After all, he and Laura did have a short-lived affair and, ever since then, there had been an edge to their relationship. There was a distinct possibility that Emily might not ever speak to him again.

*   *   *

"Oh, my god!" exclaimed Emily, wide-eyed. "Are you serious?" Laura just nodded.

"So . . . who did he end up with?" asked Emily, her face all scrunched up into a question mark. "The mother or the daughter?"

"Both," replied Laura emphatically. "Old 'Blinkin'-Lincoln' continued to squire the both of them until one night, mother and daughter were working a skin club out at the airport. That's the night Linc happened to be part of a police raiding party that came in and arrested all the strippers. That's what ended the three-way relationship."

Emily had been listening with rapt attention. "Whatever became of them?"

"Lilly Saint-Kitts moved up north, somewhere," Laura answered. "Jacksonville, I think. I understand she's still doing the lap dance circuit, although that news is about two years old. I later heard that her daughter, Tiger, got involved with a 'speed' crowd and died of a drug overdose, although I don't know how true that is."

"Well," said Emily taking a deep breath, "Lincoln Donald Bradshaw certainly has had a diverse love life."

"Ahhh," growled Laura, "don't take it to heart, Emily. All those things I just told you happened a while back, when he was still sowing his wild oats."

"Sowing his wild oats?" remarked Emily. "It sounds more like he was planting his wild seeds!"

Laura giggled.

"Does he have any redeeming features?" asked Emily.

"Yeah, actually. He's become really good at police work, now that he doesn't let his hot head get the better of him."

"Hot head?" asked Emily, picking up on the phrase.

"Yeah, well, Linc's a big guy, y'know. Strong and quick and definitely not afraid of anybody. He used to be a real hard-ass, y'know what I mean? Very aggressive. He used to get disciplined a lot, when it came to how he handled the bad guys. If they were stupid enough to give him a hard time, he would think nothing of kicking the crap out of the dumb shits."

Emily was fast getting reacquainted with Laura's colorful metaphors.

Laura continued. "After he left the Sheriff's office, he became a U.S, Marshall. I had heard he was doing pretty good until the incident."

"What incident?"

"Hey, Emily." exclaimed Laura, her hands spread questioningly. "I thought you said your father told you all about Linc?"

"Well," replied Emily, "he obviously seemed to have left out some pertinent details. Now, what incident are you referring to?"

"Did you ever hear of Henri Petite?" Laura asked, pronouncing it 'On-ree Pah-tee."

"No," said Emily.

"Well, he was a big time Haitian drug dealer. A real scum-bag, but very well connected. In fact, he was so well connected that he had some kind of around-the-corner connection with that Aristide guy.

Do you remember him? He was the guy our State Department gave asylum to and eventually got him reinstated as President of Haiti."

"Yes, of course," said Emily. "Jean-Bertrand Aristide. Salesian Priest. He had about one year in office and was overthrown by General Raoul Cedras in a military coup. After the U.S. helped to get Aristide back in office, he caused some sticky diplomatic problems by joining an alliance with Cuba, and we ended up with egg on our face. He finally gave up the Presidency to his hand picked Prime Minister, Rene Preval."

Laura just stared at Emily for a moment before saying sarcastically, "Right . . . Miss Valedictorian high-brow smarty-pants. I just forgot for a minute who I was talking to."

Emily smiled at her snide sense of humor and said, "So, tell me about the incident."

"Anyways, Petite had been in a Miami jail on drug related charges, but was released because of some heavy string-pulling. Right after that, it was discovered that Petite had pulled some really nasty shit involving a couple of kids and some crack cocaine. So, another arrest warrant was issued. Linc was part of the team that went down to Miami to find Petite and to haul him back to the slammer. When they finally found him, he was in the company of some Haitian Ambassador, or something. Petite began resisting arrest and claiming diplomatic immunity. Now, this Haitian drug lord, Petite, was a big dude and began causing a lot of commotion and confusion between the agents. No one was sure how to handle him, and he was being a terrific asshole. Y'know pushing our guys, cursing, even spitting on them."

"Oh," whispered Emily.

"Well, you know Linc. He ain't afraid of anything or anybody. So he grabs this guy, Petite, and body slams him into the pavement. But in doing so, he cracks the guy's head open. They haul the slime bucket off to the hospital and then off to jail. But the next day, the lawyers and the suits from our nation's capitol get involved. Next thing you know, the phrase 'police brutality' hits the newspapers and our poor Lincoln is right in the middle of it. Everyone on the Marshall's team comes to Linc's defense, but the incident takes on a life of its own and just grows out of proportion. Suddenly, the whole thing is front-page photo-ops swirling around a couple of congressmen, some State Department lawyers, official Haitian diplomats, and . . ." Laura paused and sighed before concluding, "Well, Linc didn't stand a chance."

Laura took a sip of her drink while Emily asked, "So, what was the outcome?"

"He got canned. When they found out that he'd been in trouble before for mistreating prisoners, the newspaper reporters beat him up real bad, and, as you would say, he was summarily discharged."

"And that was the end of it?" asked Emily. "He couldn't get his job back?"

"Nope," said Laura with finality. "That part of his life was over. He came back to this area, got his P.I. license and opened his own business."

Emily made a mental note to have a long talk with her father regarding all the details he had so conveniently left out when talking about Lincoln Donald Bradshaw.

"Fascinating," said Emily. "What else can you tell me about Linc?"

Laura just stared at Emily. As Laura did so, her eyes narrowed and a wry smile formed on her lips. "Oh my God! You're getting the hots for the guy. Aren't you?"

"Don't be silly," said Emily.

"Don't be silly, my ass," said Laura. "You should see your face. You're practically drooling!"

Emily felt a sudden flush come to her cheeks.

Laura continued, "Look, Emily. If you want to be smart, you'll take my advice. Forget it. Forget him. Sure, he's good looking and all that, but you're not going to be able to break through his wall."

"I'm not so sure about that," replied Emily. "He was trying desperately to be charming, and I actually made him blush."

"Yeah?" Laura said smugly. "Well, it wouldn't make a difference if you were Julia Roberts and Katherine Zeta-Jones all rolled into one. You're still going to get hurt."

"Why are you saying that?" asked Emily.

"Two reasons," replied Laura, cryptically. "Samantha Broadhurst and Lisa Decker."

There was a moment of silence as Emily waited for more information, and Laura let the suspense deepen.

"I give up," said Emily. "Who are Samantha Broadhurst and Lisa Decker?"

"Samantha Broadhurst is the woman he lost and Lisa Decker is the bitch who ruined him for every woman who followed. Between the two of them, they broke his heart and caused him to build that freakin' wall of his."

"What happened?" asked Emily.

"About twelve years ago, Linc was engaged to the Broadhurst woman. They were in college. She was homecoming queen, perfect couple, love of his life . . . y'know, the whole nine yards. Anyways, it was a Sunday afternoon. Linc was watching a football game and Samantha was out at the supermarket buying groceries. She never returned. Linc got frantic, took off looking for her, but no luck. No sign of her. He called everybody. Police didn't know, hospitals didn't know and her friends didn't know either. Finally, around midnight, Samantha's father called Linc to tell him that she'd been killed by a drunk driver."

Emily was speechless. She never expected such a tragic story. A chill ran through her.

Laura saw the anguish on Emily's face. "Wait," said Laura. "There's more."

Laura went on. "About seven, eight years ago, while he was still bleeding, he's now engaged to Lisa Decker. She was one of the try-outs for the Dolphin's Cheerleaders. Beautiful girl, very athletic and they shared an apartment down in Miami so that they could be together for the home games. One day, he comes home early and hears some sounds of passion coming from their bedroom."

"I don't think I'm going to like this story either," interjected Emily.

"Well, to make a long story short," concluded Laura, "she was doing the dirty deed with, not one, but two of Linc's so-called buddies."

Emily was not prepared for the ending of either tale. She held her hand to her mouth and softly whispered, "Oh, no."

"He's never been the same since," added Laura. "He can still walk and talk okay, probably even charm you out of your bra and panties, but the word 'commitment' ain't in his vocabulary anymore."

When Emily didn't reply, Laura said, "My advice to you is, if you want to have a fling, go ahead, but keep it light. Otherwise, he'll just break your heart. After losing Samantha, I think his ability to love or trust another woman, completely disappeared in the bedroom with Lisa Decker."

It was getting late and the waiter was sending out vibes by hovering around their table. Emily asked for the check, only to be informed that it had already been paid for, " . . . by the gentleman who was sitting with you." After that, the two women began their good-byes. The conversation turned lighthearted as they reiterated how wonderful it was to run into each other and renew their friendship. They both agreed to pick up where they left off. Emily renewed her suggestion that they seek out Scott Aarons and see if they could convince him to divulge the source of his story.

"What time do you want to get together?" asked Laura.

Before Emily had a chance to answer, Laura interrupted with another thought. "And remember," said Laura wagging her finger, "tomorrow is Sunday. I don't do 'early' on Sundays."

"Come over about lunch time," suggested Emily. "I'll make some sandwiches and we'll go from there."

Laura's mouth dropped open. "You? In the kitchen?" uttered Laura in disbelief. "This, I've got to see."

CHAPTER TWENTY

M endosa put two ball-point pens, along with a note pad, into his breast pocket. Grabbing the attaché case with the equipment inside, he headed out the door. Driving by the entrance to the Amity Hotel, he slowed to check for anything that looked out of the ordinary. After two more left turns, Mendosa pulled his car into the rear parking lot of the hotel. He slipped unnoticed into the back entrance and let himself into room 114. Mendosa had this room rented on a long-term basis under another of his aliases, specifically, one James Milligan.

The room was sparsely furnished. One double bed, a closet without a door that held several wire hangers, an old television set, and a painted dresser with three drawers. A pair of rubberized blackout drapes covered the single window. The only things in the room that looked new were the telephone and the metal bridge table upon which it sat.

More than a year before, Mendosa had made arrangements with the management of the Amity Hotel to have this telephone installed. Rather than it being a phone that had to be routed through the switchboard, it was a second and separate line for the hotel. Any calls that Mendosa made on that particular phone were billed directly to the hotel. Originally, the manager was very reluctant to allow such an arrangement, but Mendosa gave the manager five hundred dollars in escrow plus a hundred dollars for his own pocket. He also assured the manager that the telephone bill would never exceed the amount in escrow. The hotel merely billed Mendosa for the occasional phone calls he made, along with his regular hotel bill. Mendosa always paid his bill in advance and in cash. The arrangement kept Mendosa one step ahead of anyone who might be looking for him.

Mendosa plopped his briefcase on the bed, opened it and took out the Multi-Cordex Line Reverter. Bending to reach the phone box on the wall, Mendosa skinned back the plastic sheath on the protruding wires, exposing two little yellow splicing caps. Unscrewing both caps, he quickly spliced in the line reverter.

Mendosa had a list of more than six thousand telephone numbers from all around the world. It was a wide variety of numbers, including government agencies and Fortune 500 companies, as well as private residences. Some numbers were unpublished and others were of famous people. More than forty of the numbers on his list were from telephones that existed inside the Pentagon. His list also included actual phone numbers inside the offices of the KGB, MI-6 and the Mossad organizations.

Mendosa started with a pre-programmed list of fifteen random numbers and input them into the line reverter. He was now ready to call Parlotti at the appointed time.

Parlotti had tried many times in the past, to trace Mendosa's calls. He could not blame Parlotti for trying, since he still did not know Mendosa's true identity. Even though the two men had a fairly compatible relationship up to this point, this was the type of business where the boss needed to maintain control. For Parlotti, that meant knowing as much about his operatives as possible. For Mendosa, that meant that Parlotti would try again to trace his call.

There had been a time in the past when tracing a call was a matter for the FBI or CIA. It was a complicated procedure, requiring the services of highly skilled technicians. At that time in history, if a trace were initiated, it could take several long minutes to discover the number and several more to route it to its location. Then, along came the modern era of telephone technology, and the telephone company itself, offered instant tracing though "Caller ID." Read a number on your display window, punch that number into a special www-dot-com address and "zap," instantly, there is a name and address to go along with the telephone number.

The Multi-Cordex Line Reverter was a slippery chunk of communication technology. Besides making the tracing of a call very difficult, the unit allowed the user to program in one or more false numbers. When someone activated a trace, it would "revert" the tracer to the stored false number. Mendosa started with fifteen false numbers as he dialed Parlotti.

It was almost four p.m. Vincent Parlotti sat at a desk in the "phone-room," waiting for the call from Harpoon. He knew what he wanted to say, and he knew what he had to say. Parlotti would be crystal clear in his instructions for the next phase of this operation. In addition, Parlotti needed to get the point across of how pissed he was at Harpoon, for taking out one of Parlotti's own people.

The two technicians, along with John Anderson, were ready.

The phone rang. Parlotti picked it up and an operator said, "He's on line one, Mr. Parlotti."

Parlotti nodded to the three men to get ready before he hit the number "one" button.

"Parlotti," he barked.

"The Lass of Mont Valier," said Mendosa identifying himself. He knew that Parlotti wanted everyone to use their code name, but he always chose to ignore the instructions. "What have you got for me?" he asked.

"Never mind what the fuck I have for you," growled Parlotti. "First, tell me what went wrong in D.C. You were only supposed to take out Lunderman. Why the hell did you kill Mahler?"

There was a long pause before Mendosa said, "Is this what we're going to be talking about?"

"I want to know why you took out one of my own people," boomed Parlotti.

Mendosa paused again. Longer this time. Then, he hung up, and the phone in Parlotti's hand went dead.

Parlotti slowly put the phone back into its cradle. He looked over at John Anderson and asked in a tightly controlled tone, "Anything?"

Anderson shook his head and said, "He's hooked up to a line reverter again. The first trace showed him calling from inside the Museum of Natural History in New York. After working through that one, it showed he was calling from some pub in Dublin, Ireland. I didn't have time for anything else."

Parlotti rubbed his face and chin. He sighed, before saying, "He'll be calling right back. Have the operator put him through."

Mendosa sat at his little bridge table looking at the phone and thought about the nature of the call. The fact that Parlotti was upset didn't bother Mendosa. The fact that he had killed Parlotti's agent, Walter Mahler, bothered him even less. However, it seemed that Parlotti was losing sight of their "arrangement" and that fact was bothersome. Mendosa was a contract killer, an independent agent, not one of Parlotti's employees. Parlotti had to follow Mendosa's rules, not the other way around.

Mendosa had made it clear on many occasions that he would keep his identity a secret at all costs. If Parlotti chose to test Mendosa's resolve by putting someone like Mahler in harm's way, that was too bad for the one who had to die. Obviously, it was time to reinforce that particular criteria.

Mendosa reconfigured the Multi Cordex line reverter and entered a pre-programmed list of two hundred random phone numbers. It would now take a major effort from Parlotti's team to trace his call. After all, this next call might take a while to complete.

Just as Parlotti expected, Harpoon did call back in short order. The first minutes of their conversation were dedicated to Mendosa telling Parlotti what the ground rules were for any future assignments. Parlotti managed to get his point across that he could not afford to have Mendosa remove anymore of his agents. Parlotti stopped short of using the words, "or else."

The talk continued with Parlotti spelling out the details of the follow-up job that had to be done. "Now listen," explained Parlotti. "This kid, Pitch Pechowski, has all we need on one disc. One single disc. Professor Lunderman made it clear that whoever holds the disc, holds the key to making his listening device work."

Mendosa interrupted, "You seem to forget that I'm very familiar with the details. After all, I was the one who got you all this information."

"Yes, I know," snapped Parlotti. "At the price of one of my best agents."

"First of all," said Mendosa, "we have already covered this ground. Second, if you had relied on Agent Mahler's information, you would have been following Lunderman, not Pitch Pechowski. And third, if you don't get to the point quickly, I'm going to hang up again." Parlotti breathed deeply through flared nostrils. He was furious and frustrated at being boxed into a corner with no room to maneuver. He said, "Harpoon . . . get me that disc. Quickly. And I don't care how you do it. Just make sure there are no loose ends."

"Payment?" Mendosa asked simply.

"The usual," replied Parlotti. "The money will be wired tonight at nine p.m. eastern standard time."

"Anything else?" asked Mendosa.

Parlotti hesitated a moment, as he unconsciously squeezed the phone until his knuckles turned white. Then, he simply said, "No."

Mendosa hung up.

Parlotti looked over at Anderson who had been diligently working on trying to trace the call. Anderson just shook his head.

Parlotti inhaled a ragged breath. Slowly enunciating each word, he said, "One day, we're going to have to set him up and take him out."

Anderson busied himself logging off the computer and motioned for the other technicians to break down the tracing equipment. Parlotti barely heard Anderson as he said, "I'm surprised it's taken this long, Boss."

CHAPTER
TWENTY ONE

Carmen Delgado had worked for the Bradshaw Agency for the past four years. Several times during every workday, Lincoln Bradshaw found himself blessing the woman, her family and, most of all, her efficiency. She was great. Before Carmen started working for him, his office always looked like the aftermath of a ticker-tape parade. Important papers and documents, the lifeline of his business, were always misplaced. Carmen turned his life around from her first day on the job. On day one, she straightened up the files. After that, she remained diligent and kept them that way. Within six months, Carmen, attempting to save herself aggravation, instituted the 'read and initial' policy. Linc had a habit of reading something in a case file and, several weeks later, complaining, "Carmen, you never showed this to me before." Now, every time Linc read something, Carmen would insist that he initial it. After it was initialed, she would date-stamp it and file it away. Carmen's memory for detail was superb. There were many instances when Linc would ask her for a shard of seemingly insignificant information relating to a case. On each of those occasions, Carmen would manage to produce the appropriate answer. Linc learned to trust her judgment, her memory and her expertise.

Carmen was a round woman, in her late forties and of Cuban heritage. Speaking English with a rich Spanish accent, she nevertheless was completely fluent and eloquent in both languages. She owned a wicked sense of humor and wielded it like a rapier.

Occasionally breaking into song, her musical selection could always be relied upon to be endemic to the situation at hand. Her taste in clothing leaned to bright, gaudy, island colors. Linc often commented that she looked like she was on her way to some Cuban version of Mardi Gras. Carmen thought nothing of launching into a tirade about what a mess Fidel Castro had made of her beloved Cuba.

Her husband had died a dozen years before. As a single mom, she raised two daughters who were now both nurses in a local hospital. Her eldest daughter had married about a year ago and was soon to give birth to Carmen's first grandchild.

Linc was listening while Carmen went over all the important messages that had come through that morning. As was her habit, she created elaborate memos about the telephone conversations she had with clients. Still in all, she liked to go over them with Linc in more detail, so she could explain what she meant in her memos. Sometimes, she would even describe the inflections in the caller's voices.

Linc initialed the last of the papers and said, "Carmen, put in a call to Eddie Strickland and then run a Comprehensive report on someone named, Elana Velez."

"Ooo," exclaimed Carmen. "Elana Velez, huh? That's an exotic sounding name. Who is she?"

Linc went on to explain, in considerable detail, the events leading to the extortion demand on Sidney Aarons. Linc also told her about the videotape. "Sidney's arranging to have the smoking videotape delivered this afternoon."

Carmen said with a straight face, "You know, when you're not here, I usually get to watch *General Hospital* and *As the World Turns*, but this videotape sounds like it will be much more interesting."

Ignoring her put-on, Linc finished by asking her to start a confidential case file on Sidney Aarons.

"Excuse me, Mr. Simon Legree," said Carmen, referring to Linc as the notorious slave driver. "It is Saturday, you know. I was supposed to be home an hour ago."

"Oh, yeah. Right," said Linc upon her reminder. "Okay. Just put a call in to Eddie. The rest can wait."

"So . . . Sidney Aarons," Carmen said dreamily. "The big-shot newspaper man."

"Yep, that's him," agreed Linc.

"Oooo, *caramba*, Mr. Linc," cooed Carmen. "That is a good account to bring in. It sure will help to pay the rent."

Linc rolled his eyes. He knew she would never talk like that if clients were present. "Okay, Carmen. Back to your cage. Don't forget to dig me up something on that Velez girl on Monday."

As Carmen walked back to her desk in the reception area, Linc heard her say, in a stage whisper, "Maybe even a bigger Christmas bonus. Sure was a little meager this year."

Linc listened a moment to her singing, "We're in the money . . ."

She would soon be aware of all the remaining dirty details in this new case. Trustworthy, loyal, and smart, Carmen had earned the responsibility to be privy of all the cases the office handled.

Linc picked up the phone and called Preston. Louise answered, and said that she would give the message to Mr. Collingsworth. Next, he left a voice mail for Sidney Aarons. No sooner had he hung up, Carmen informed him that Mr. Collingsworth was on the line.

"Preston," began Linc. "I just wanted to keep you informed that Sidney Aarons and I were able to strike a deal. I'll have him sign the client contracts on Monday. Thanks for the lead."

"Good for you, Linc," blared Preston. "It's a grand start with the Aarons' account. Are you familiar with the expression 'Still waters run deep?'"

"Sure."

"Well," said Preston, "that expression seems to best describe Sidney. In private conversations, he regularly intimates what an exciting lifestyle he leads. He hints at illicit affairs in exotic places. Or perhaps exotic affairs in illicit places. I can't remember." Preston chuckled at his own humor before continuing. "Especially, when he goes abroad. I know this first job is a rather cut and dry one dealing with that droll reporter fellow who works for him, but if you do a good job, this could lead to a major account."

"Having to do with his exotic and illicit lifestyle?" Linc queried.

"Oh, yes. Absolutely," said Preston. "You could be busy for a lifetime keeping Sidney's fishing pole out of the well, if you know what I mean."

Linc found it annoying that Sidney had even hinted about his affair. It also made Linc wonder about whom else the newspaper mogul might have told and how much sordid detail he might have divulged.

"Yeah, right," said Linc. "Someday it will make a great chapter in my book."

Preston paused just a moment before asking, "Uh . . . so tell me, Linc. How was lunch with my dear Emily?"

"Is she home already?" Linc asked in return.

"No, no. It was just that one of my contacts told me you two had lunch at *Charlie's Crab.*"

"Preston, is there anything in this world you don't know?" Linc said with mock exasperation.

"Hah! Try to be serious, Linc. We're living on the island of Palm Beach. It's just a tiny little town in the middle of a bunch of gossips. You can't keep secrets in a place such as this."

"Yes, Preston," said Linc. "We had a very nice lunch."

"Well, I was told that it sounded like there was some kind of argument going on at your table."

"Damn!" said Linc, smiling to himself. "Since you found out, I might as well come clean."

"What was it, Linc?" Preston asked with concern. "What happened?"

"Emily really went off on you, Preston," Linc said, making it up as he went along. "She was complaining bitterly about what a busybody you are, and how you can't keep your nose out of her love life. As for me, I spent the entire lunch hour vigorously trying to defend you."

There were two full seconds of silence on the other end of the phone before Preston said in a grave, fatherly tone, "Lincoln . . . ?"

At that moment, Carmen gave Linc a signal that one of his pages was being returned. Laughing to himself and knowing that his friend, Emily's father, must be feeling midway between baffled and frustrated, Linc said a quick goodbye and hung up.

Before picking up the next call, Carmen said, "I called Eddie Strickland. The desk sergeant said he'd be back in about twenty minutes. Between you and me, he'll probably come back with powdered sugar on his mustache. I left a message for him to call you. I am outta here. *Hasta luego, Señor* Linc."

"Enjoy your street festival," Linc called after her as he picked up line two. It was Sidney Aarons returning the call.

Linc explained that he had had a chance to go over his notes from the morning's meeting and had some additional questions regarding the time line of the events. More importantly, he recalled that Sidney talked about the newspaper's human resource department questioning the veracity of Elana Velez's application. Linc asked that they fax over Elana's paperwork. He planned going over it with a fine tooth comb, hoping to turn up a location for this female extortionist. Next, Linc asked for a couple of still-photos of the model. Sidney confirmed that he had already dispatched a courier with the videotape and Linc should have it within the hour. He agreed to do the same with the requested pictures on Monday.

It wasn't much, but for Sidney, this phone call gave him a feeling of gratification. Hearing from Linc so soon after their meeting was unexpected and appreciated. Although Linc kept cautioning the publisher, Sidney could not contain a growing feeling of hope.

As the man talked, Linc wondered about Sidney having bragged to Preston about the affair. Linc decided not to reveal any of what Preston had told him. Linc simply reiterated the importance of not talking to anyone. Even though Sidney promised again and again that he would comply, Linc was glad to get off the phone.

Linc was thinking about the newspaper magnate when his phone rang again. He answered, "Lincoln Bradshaw."

"Why do you keep pestering me?" said a gruff voice on the other end of the line.

"Hey, Eddie," said Linc in a matter of fact tone. "Is it true you have powdered sugar on your mustache right now?"

The running joke about cops and donuts was getting old. "Up yours," said Eddie emphatically. "What's going on?"

A friend of long standing, Eddie Strickland was another one of Linc's high school jock-mates. The two of them were "three-letter men" having been teammates on the football, basketball and baseball teams. After high school, Eddie went to the University of Miami on a baseball scholarship where, for his four years, he put together some good statistics. Eventually, he was drafted by the Dodgers and given a ninety-thousand dollar signing bonus.

Eddie played Triple-A ball for three years before meeting a girl who changed his life. He loved her and she loved him. Despite being an exceptional young woman, she did not understand that thing called baseball. To her, it was just something you played as a kid. Hopscotch, hide-and-seek, and baseball. They were just games, not something for a grown up, responsible person to do for a living.

Try as he might, Eddie could not convince her otherwise. Not wanting to lose her, he had no choice but to give up the game and marry her.

Although he never said it, Linc was convinced that Eddie did the right thing. The love the bride and groom had for each other was good. However, Linc knew the decision was best because Eddie was missing that extra spoonful of talent it takes to make it to the big leagues.

Eddie went on to become a cop and was instrumental in getting Linc a position on the force.

Ten years and two kids later, Eddie got divorced. The wounds of the split were still fresh and painful. His wife took the kids and moved back to Boston, leaving Eddie very bitter. He ranted and raved about having been forced to give up the life of baseball for no reason. After all, he was now in his early thirties, much too old to get back into the competitiveness of that sport.

The separation from his family was still a fairly fresh wound. Eddie had just recently crawled out from under his rock and was beginning to live life again.

Not long ago, Eddie had been promoted to detective and was now privy to all the dirt that passed through police headquarters. Eddie was not the smartest of the detectives on the force, but he was a good guy and tried hard. Now that he was getting his head back on straight, Linc was, once again, enjoying his friend's company.

"I'm looking for someone named Elana Velez," said Linc. "Ever hear the name?"

"Spell it," said Eddie.

Linc spelled out her name and added, "Late twenties, maybe thirty, professional model and maybe a background in blackmail, extortion or larceny."

"I keep telling you Linc," chided Eddie. "If you're looking for a long term relationship, you gotta stay away from this kind of woman."

"I assume that's a 'no,'" said Linc.

"Well, it ain't ringing no bells, or nothin'. Did you already run a 'comp' on her?"

A 'comp' or Comprehensive Report was the first step for an organization like the Bradshaw Agency. The report was used to get the background and history of a person and could be done on a state or national level. Besides containing standard data such as social security and driver license numbers, the comp also listed assets like real estate, cars and boats. The body of the report went into great detail regarding any arrests, indictments, and convictions. A completed comp went a step further and included information on ex-spouses, relatives, and even roommates. It was a very special tool.

"Carmen is going to run the comprehensive on Monday," said Linc.

"So, who is this woman?" asked Eddie. "What's the deal?"

"I can't really talk about it Eddie," said Linc. "Suffice it to say, she's attempting to extort money from a prominent Palm Beacher."

"Got any X-rated photos?" asked Eddie lasciviously.

"I'm actually getting a videotape, but I can't show it to you," said Linc. "But, I'll show you some photos of the girl."

"Y'know, you're a real prick," said Eddie. "Keeping all the good stuff for yourself."

"What's going on in your world?" asked Linc. "Anything earthshaking?"

"I suppose you know there's a whole task force working on the John Krum rape case," said Eddie. "The newspaper had that article about the D.A. making a so-called deal, and now the heat is really on."

"Yeah," said Linc. "I just met Laura Parsons and she's on the verge of losing her job over that article."

"The Chief is really pissed," said Eddie. "He's demanding that the task force find out who murdered the Blakely family, or heads will roll."

"So, the squeeze is on."

"Well, not on me personally," said Eddie, "As a matter of fact, the Captain just asked me to fly up to Washington, D.C. to investigate a murder."

"D.C.?" asked Linc. "Isn't that a little out of your jurisdiction?"

"Yeah, well it seems like a local college professor got himself all shot up in a sleazy hotel room in that town."

"No kidding?" said Linc. "Anybody we know?"

"I don't think so. Supposedly, it was a professional hit. I don't have to really do anything with it. The Captain is just throwing me a bone for being such a good boy. The primaries on the case are still the D.C. cops. Me? I'm just the guy who gets wined and dined."

"Sweet deal," said Linc. "When are you leaving?"

"Monday morning, first thing. In and out. I should be home sometime Monday night."

"Give me a holler when you get back," said Linc. "We'll go grab a beer or something."

"Yeah, right," said Eddie sarcastically. "If I deem you worthy of my time."

Then Eddie hung up.

CHAPTER TWENTY TWO

Crystal looked hot! Scott could barely keep his eyes off of her. She was wearing a black and white patterned, cocktail length dress with just two thin spaghetti straps holding it in place. Cut low, it dramatized the line of her cleavage. Her shoes were black satin with a three-inch heel. Even though Crystal had a magnificent figure and very shapely legs, the heels somehow managed to accentuate her lines even more. The little gold cross that nestled at her throat was like a period at the end of a poem.

Scott had taken her to dinner at *Chuck and Harold's*, a well-known landmark restaurant in Palm Beach and had chosen to sit at one of the outdoor tables. Although Scott found the food and service excellent, the stares from the wait staff, as well as passersby, were distracting. Crystal didn't seem to mind. She only had eyes for Scott.

After dinner, Scott took her to *Ta-boo's*, a local restaurant and nightclub, for some drinks and dancing. His original plan was to take his date to his parent's yacht for the night, but it was Saturday evening and Scott's mother had informed him that plans had been made for a dinner party onboard. Instead, he told Crystal about Pitch and Jennifer going away to visit her grandparents in the Keys. When Crystal understood that she and Scott could spend the night in Pitch's apartment, she was thrilled. She giggled and murmured and held tightly to Scott's arm. She longed for any chance to be alone with him.

Scott had told Crystal all about his interview with the anchorwoman,

Amanda Dale, and that it would be aired during tonight's eleven o'clock news. "When we get back to Pitch's apartment," Scott said, "I just want to take some time to watch that segment on TV."

Crystal nodded. She was happy doing whatever Scott wanted.

They finished their first dance and were heading back to their table when a man called out, "Hey Scott! Scott Aarons!"

Scott turned to see Henry Drummond, one of the reporters who worked for his father. Looking somewhat disheveled, Henry had removed his suit jacket, and his tie was loosened at the collar. One side of his shirt had become untucked, and he reeked of alcohol.

"Hello, Henry," offered Scott. "How you doing tonight?"

Slurring his words slightly, Henry said, "You've been having yourself quite a day, young man."

Scott didn't like Henry Drummond on several levels. The man was always too patronizing and Scott had heard his father speak negatively about the reporter's bad attitude and lack of loyalty on more than one occasion. "Yes, Henry. It's been very exciting," said Scott as he turned away to guide Crystal back to their table.

"I saw your interview with that Amanda chick," Henry said trying to squelch a belch. Then, he continued with a sharp edge to his voice. "That was quite a story. Who do you got on the inside, Scottie?"

Turning back towards Henry, Scott held up his hand and said, "Now, now, Henry. You know I have to protect my sources."

"Well, if your sources are legitimate, that's one thing," said Henry, "but if you just had Daddy lay out a bushel of cash for your story . . . hey, what the hell."

Scott felt a flash of anger and his temples began to throb. He stared at Drummond. A moment passed. Then, he said as politely as he could, "Take care, Henry. Have somebody drive you home."

Scott turned and, once again, he and Crystal tried to head back to their table, but Henry began following. "Aren't you gonna introduce me to your beautiful blonde, model friend?" Henry slurred, as he stumbled over another customer's foot.

Before Crystal could sit down, Scott had an immediate change of plans. "Henry," he said, as he reached into his pocket for his billfold, "you've had much too much to drink, and you're becoming obnoxious."

"How'd you get that story, huh?" asked Henry. "Daddy get one of his judge pals to do a wire-tap?"

Scott did not reply. He took out a twenty-dollar bill and laid it on the table. It would be more than enough to pay the tab and a very generous tip.

Henry continued his badgering. "You don't know the meaning of the word 'sources,'" he said raising his voice.

Scott still chose to ignore him.

Henry went on, his voice becoming shriller. "You don't know shit about the newspaper business."

Scott took Crystal's arm and, without saying a word, he forcefully directed her toward the exit.

Henry was still following them as he shouted, "I've been a reporter for twenty goddamned years. You couldn't even shine my shoes!"

Scott spotted his open topped convertible and told the valet he would get it himself. He had preplanned the evening and had taken the Chrysler Sebring. He did not want to leave his Rolls Royce parked outside of Pitch's apartment all night long. He told Crystal to get into the car. As he started the engine, he could hear Henry yelling, "Big man! Where's your fuckin' Rolls?"

They drove away hearing Henry's fading shouts, "Goddamn little rich kid! You don't know jack-shit!"

Scott and Crystal drove in silence. He tried to calm himself, and get his mind back to where it was before Henry Drummond's drunkenness almost ruined his date. Henry's words kept bouncing off the inside of his head.

Crystal was the first to speak. "He actually thought I was a model."

Scott turned fully to look at Crystal, "What?"

"He thought I was a model," repeated Crystal, pleased with the thought. "'A beautiful model,' he said."

"Crystal," Scott said exasperated, "the man was drunk, for Christ's sake."

A hurt look appeared on Crystal's face, as she crossed her arms and said, "I know that. What do you think, I'm stupid?"

Scott knew instantly that he said the wrong thing. He gripped the steering wheel tighter as he drove towards Pitch's apartment. He did not want this night to turn sour.

Scott glanced at Crystal. She had her head turned away from him and was looking out the passenger side window. He was taken by her beauty. The fine lines of her face could be on the cover of any magazine. The shapeliness of her body could adorn any centerfold. And all of that magnificence without even a whisper of lipstick.

Crystal was gorgeous, but there was more. Besides all that loveliness, Mother Nature had also given her passion. Scott and Crystal had been together a few times and had toyed with each other during the inevitable petting sessions. Her movements and actions hinted at much more to come. When the four of them spent the night on the Aarons' yacht, Scott's anticipation was answered. Crystal was extraordinarily passionate. When the two of them made love, she threw away all inhibitions and gave of herself completely. She was a consummate lover, enjoying the pleasures she got from him and giving pleasures from the depths of her soul. Scott had been lusting for her ever since that night on the yacht.

"You know what, Crystal?" said Scott softly. "You do look like a model."

Crystal turned to look at him, but still had her arms crossed under her breasts.

Scott continued. "With your face and your body, you could be on the cover of Cosmopolitan."

"Are you just saying that?" asked Crystal trying to break the dark spell that hung in the car.

"No, no. I'm serious," said Scott. "You are one of the most beautiful women I have ever known."

"Really?" said Crystal smiling and uncrossing her arms. "You mean that?"

"I most certainly do," Scott said as convincingly as he could.

Crystal had fallen in love. She knew now that she would work to make Scott happy. He made her feel wonderful and gave her butterflies whenever he complimented her. She also felt very secure and protected when he stood close, especially when he put his arm around her. Unabashed desires were flip-flopping through her; mothering him at one moment and making wild passionate love the next. Crystal would willingly spend the rest of her life with this man if only he would ask.

"There's something I need to tell you, Scott."

"Yes?" said Scott as he looked away from the road and glanced into her eyes.

"I love you."

Scott knew the words were coming. He just didn't know when. It was okay, he thought. Timing is everything. He was on his way to the apartment, and he was going to make sure the rest of the night went as smoothly as a sailboat on a sea of glass.

So, he said the words that would ensure a perfect night, "I love you too, Crystal."

*　　*　　*

Mendosa had driven to Pitch's apartment complex earlier in the day. First driving around the building, Mendosa next went around the development, before exploring the rest of the neighborhood. Studying the flow of traffic on the side streets and how it allowed for access onto the highway, Mendosa timed the traffic lights and memorized the best route for escape. Mendosa watched the apartment from every possible angle trying to determine the best spot from which to observe the subject. He went up onto the roof of several adjoining buildings to see if there was a vantage point from which to spy into the apartment. On the roof of a building across the parking lot, Mendosa found excellent concealment. It was behind an air conditioning vent on the near side of the roof.

He had walked past the front door several times and saw that the lock would not be a problem. Double checking the contents of his black satchel, he assured himself that he had all the tools he would need.

Mendosa thought about his orders from Parlotti, including the instructions to get the disc at all costs. This was obviously a very valuable disc. As he thought about the information he had extracted from Professor George Lunderman, Mendosa began to realize the full implications of this device. Wire-taps were used to listen in on telephone conversations, but this thing was designed to listen in on any conversation being conducted in any room. Whoever controlled this device, this very special bug, had the ability to listen in on every private conversation in every home in the world. It would allow anyone to listen in on any conversation in any boardroom in the corporate world. It would even allow anyone to listen to secrets as they were discussed in every political leader's private office. Whoever controlled the disc could do all that, just sitting at a desk and simply punching in some numbers on a keypad.

What was the value of such a device? Certainly more than Mendosa was getting paid for this job. The more he thought about the device, the more he realized that it was priceless. If he went to sell it, he could not think of a price that would be commensurate with its value.

The true worth of this device was in its ability to gather information. One man alone could use it judiciously to find out what the KGB was planning to do to the Chechen rebels, or to uncover the names of the Mossad agents working as undercover Palestinians, or the CIA plans for the assassination of Colonel Muammar al-Qaddafi. How much was that information worth? Certainly, a lot more than just selling the device outright. Information such as that would give the provider a continuous cash flow. Various groups of militants and terrorists around the world, and there were hundreds of them, would stand in line with money in their hands waiting to have their questions answered.

Mendosa began to think of a different tack. Insider trading. This device would allow anyone to know when a company was planning a spin-off or an IPO, an Initial Public Offering, before it became general knowledge. The owner of this device would be able to find out if one company was going to acquire another, or if a corporation was about to be the recipient of a big government contract. Garnering that sort of information could earn untold millions . . . even billions of dollars.

Parlotti was right. Get the disc at all costs. All costs, indeed. Since Parlotti understood the value of such a device, it seemed strange that he would send only Mendosa, a single agent, on such an important mission. Perhaps, this was just a wild goose chase and the listening device was bogus. Or, more likely, Parlotti had dispatched another team somewhere. Maybe, even to this very location. With that thought, Mendosa grabbed his infrared night vision binoculars and scoured all the parked cars and windows within his line of sight. It seemed to be all clear. If there were another team, they weren't at this location.

Thinking about the kind of adversary he would encounter in Pitch Pechowski, Mendosa suddenly realized that he had neglected to get a physical description. It was a minor mistake, but still Mendosa silently berated himself for it. He would have to concentrate on remaining focused for the duration of this job, if he were to continue to be successful.

His mind went to other things. Mendosa recalled that Professor Lunderman had said, " . . . Pitch always keeps the disc on him." Mendosa wondered if young Mr. Pechowski had the foresight to encrypt the disc, thereby preventing anyone from copying it. Mendosa's mind was roaming around the various possibilities, as he waited for Pitch Pechowski to come home.

CHAPTER TWENTY THREE

I t was ten-thirty p.m. when Linc finally got around to calling Emily. He hoped it wasn't too late to call, although he could not fathom that she would be sleeping at this hour on a Saturday night. As Linc dialed her number, a thought crossed his mind. There was a better than even chance that she would give him a hard time for not having called earlier. Knowing that she really wouldn't object to the time, it still seemed that the woman enjoyed making him feel uncomfortable. So far, she had managed to do just that on each of the occasions they had met.

"Hello?" Preston mumbled, gruffly.

Preston's voice sounded different and for a moment Linc did not recognize it. Linc asked haltingly, "Preston? Is that you?"

Preston said, "Yes, Linc. It's me. I must have dozed off." Then, realizing the hour, he asked, "Is everything all right?"

"Oh, yeah. Sure," Linc said quickly to alleviate any fears. "It's just that Emily had wanted me to give her a call this evening. I hope I'm not calling too late."

"No, not at all," said Preston. "As a matter of fact, she isn't even home yet."

Linc had a momentary flash of Emily out on a date somewhere and found the thought somehow disturbing.

Before that supposition could develop further, Preston continued, "She went next door to the Campbell's. They were upset that they didn't get to spend enough time with her at the party. They practically helped raise her, you know."

"Well, when she comes in," said Linc, "just tell her I called."

"Where are you now?" asked Preston. "Do you want her to call you back?"

"Believe it or not," said Linc, "I'm calling you from my cell phone, and I'm just leaving the office as we speak. I'm on my way home and dragging my butt. So, if she wants, she can reach me on this cell phone in the next fifteen minutes. When I get home, I'm going to bed after the eleven o'clock news."

"Before you hang up," said Preston, "I just want to fill you in on the call I received from Boyd Williamson."

Preston spent the next five minutes telling Linc about the Senator's call and the outcome of Linc's investigations into Congressman Jack Higgins' philandering. "Boyd told me to pass on regards to you," said Preston. "He thinks you're an extraordinarily capable young man and told me he offered you a job."

"He did," confirmed Linc. "When I told him I was happy doing what I was doing, he said he would pass my business card on to some of his cronies, and I should expect a flurry of phone calls."

"He's a good man to have in your corner," remarked Preston.

Linc recited a philosophy he had formulated several years earlier. "To wield influence is to wield a broadsword. To offer influence is to offer a dagger. To refuse influence is to cut your own throat."

"That's pretty good," said Preston. "Who said that?"

"I did," said Linc, emphatically. "It's a truth I've become very aware of over the past decade. But the opportunity to recite it just doesn't come up very often. Anyway, I'm really pleased that things are turning out well for you, Preston."

It was getting late, but Preston was on a roll. It was obvious that he was now fully awake and wanted to talk about how the Jack Higgins investigation would be beneficial to Preston's real estate holdings. Linc was ready to cut him off when Preston stopped in mid sentence and said, "It's Emily. Emily is home. Hold on, Linc."

Linc could hear Preston telling Emily who was on the phone, but her reply was muffled. Linc held the phone tightly to his ear, in hopes of hearing what was being said, when Emily suddenly said, "Good evening, Lincoln."

"So, you finally come waltzing in," said Linc in a scolding tone. "Do you have any idea what time it is, young lady?"

"One father is quite enough, thank you," said Emily. "Daddy just told me you're still at the office."

"Actually, I'm on my way home even as we speak," said Linc.

"Don't you know that all work and no play makes Jack . . . etcetera, etcetera?" quipped Emily.

"That's the price I have to pay for having long lunches when I should be working," said Linc.

"Speaking of lunch," said Emily, "Laura Parsons had some interesting stories to tell me after you left. I'm quite anxious to hear a confirmation or denial on your part."

Linc had realized that this particular subject matter was inevitable. "Since it was Laura who told you," said Linc, a little miffed despite the realization, "I can probably deny most of it."

"I don't know, Linc," said Emily with a tone of exaggerated doubt. "She said some pretty sweet things about you as well."

"Sweet things?" asked Linc. "About me? Are we talking about the same Laura Parsons?"

"The Laura Parsons I'm talking about," said Emily, "seems to know the details of a few of your . . . escapades, shall we say?"

Linc was looking forward to seeing Emily once again but had the feeling that he would be walking into a bear trap. He took a deep breath and said, "Okay. Tell you what. You tell me the yarns and I'll confirm or deny. How about we do that tomorrow? It's Sunday. What are your plans?"

"I'm meeting up with Laura in the late morning," said Emily.

Linc scrunched his face, mortified at the thought.

Emily continued, "Then, we're off to find Scott Aarons so that she can ask him about his sources for his newspaper story. But I'm free for dinner."

"Dinner it is," said Linc a little too enthusiastically. "Do you like really great cheesecake?"

"Oh God, yes," said Emily.

CHAPTER TWENTY FOUR

Mendosa glanced at his watch. He was sitting in his car at the far end of the parking lot from where he had an unobstructed view of the front of Pitch's apartment. It was exactly ten-thirty p.m. As he watched, the Chrysler Sebring convertible made a wide turn and pulled into the parking spot. He studied the young couple while they exited the car and went inside the apartment. Although focusing his attention on the young man, Mendosa took a moment to admire the blonde in high heels. During the couple's short walk to the apartment, Mendosa's practiced eye scrutinized their physiques and closely watched their movements. He was calculating the strengths of his adversaries, determining their athleticism and deciding how tough they might be. The assassin did not like surprises.

Mendosa saw the lights go on in the living room first, followed by those in the bedroom. Despite not being able to see details, he could make out their movements quite clearly through the blinds covering the windows. Between the wide-angle of his binoculars and the illumination in the apartment, he was satisfied with his view.

It looked to Mendosa as if they were settling into the sofa in the living room. Perhaps, they planned to watch television. He waited.

Not more than ten minutes had elapsed, when the blonde girl began to crawl all over the young man. They stood up and, with their faces seemingly locked together, began to discard their clothes as they shuffled to the bedroom. The lights in the living room went out. Mendosa hoped they would leave the light on in the bedroom.

They did.

When the couple lay down on the bed, they disappeared from Mendosa's view. He left his car and stealthily made his way to the roof of the adjoining building. Sitting down behind the vent stack, Mendosa once again removed his binoculars from his satchel. Because of the angle of the slats on the mini blinds covering the bedroom window, Mendosa had an almost unobstructed view of Scott and Crystal as they made love on the bed. To a man with a normal libido, this act of voyeurism could have been an erotic fantasy. Not so for Claude Mendosa. He watched as this young couple began their amorous foreplay and sensuously moved into the throes of passion. Mendosa observed them closely, but with an other purpose in mind. He was waiting for the moment of attack. Acutely aware of all that could go wrong, Mendosa was waiting for the ideal point in time to sneak into the apartment and subdue these two unsuspecting lovers. He was dispassionate. He focused on getting the disc, and only the disc, at all costs.

Time was passing, and Mendosa was hoping the couple would eventually fall asleep sometime before daybreak. But these two lovers had stamina. Scott and Crystal brought each other to a passionate crescendo and fell, seemingly exhausted, into the pile of rumpled sheets and pillows. Yet, after a short respite, the fondling and kissing resumed, and they began to arouse each other again, and once more dove into their private sea of ecstasy. This pattern of love-making continued until just before three a.m. when Crystal rolled out of bed, got a drink of water and shut off the bedroom light.

Mendosa hurriedly switched to his night vision binoculars and saw that they truly were going to sleep. He decided to give them one hour, time enough for deep sleep, before he would enter the apartment. It was the advantage for which he was waiting.

At four a.m. Mendosa tore off eight pieces of duct tape, each about two feet long. He carefully stuck them to his clothing so that they did not overlap, but could be quickly and easily removed. He made his way to the front door, skillfully picked the lock and let himself in. Hesitating a moment, he listened to the sounds of regular, deep breathing coming from the bedroom. Satisfied that the young couple were both asleep, he searched through the piles of clothing that were strewn across the floor in the living room. Remembering the words of Professor Lunderman, that Pitch always kept the disc on him, Mendosa hoped to make this easy by finding it somewhere between the various pockets of the discarded clothing. A quick search revealed that the disc was neither in the pile of garments nor in the woman's pocketbook. Cautiously crossing the floor to where the computer terminal sat, Mendosa saw dozens of discs, some labeled and others not. There wasn't anything written on any of them that identified it as the one he wanted.

Preparing his nine-millimeter pistol with its long silencer, Mendosa moved forward. Like a leopard on the prowl, he slowly moved into the bedroom. Crouching over his black satchel, he removed a full roll of duct tape and a roll of high tensile strength fishing line.

He fashioned a loop out of the non-twist, monofilament line and tied the other end to the slats on the headboard just behind Crystal's head. Next, Mendosa took another length of fishing line and again made a loop. With this one, he tied the loose end onto the bed frame just below Scott's feet. Moving back to Crystal, who was sleeping on her side, Mendosa slipped the big loop around her face and the top of her head, carefully avoiding touching her cheeks. The rhythm of her breathing was barely broken when the bottom of the looped line touched her neck and came to rest on her little gold cross. Mendosa knew she would soon awaken with a start and instinctively sit up in the bed. The loop would tighten and, hopefully, she would not decapitate herself. He intended to use her, if necessary, to get the information from the young man sleeping next to her.

Moving back to the foot of the bed, Mendosa looped the secured line over Scott's feet. Now, the assassin was ready.

Immobilizing two people without killing them or leaving yourself in jeopardy was quite a trick. Mendosa needed to prevent either of them from attacking. It was also necessary to keep them from shouting out too loudly and disturbing the neighbors. Most importantly, the victims needed to be reasonably conscious, allowing them to give up what he was looking for.

Mendosa removed one of the pre-cut lengths of duct tape from his pant leg. With one fluid motion, he flipped off the sheet covering Crystal's naked body and bound her ankles with the tape. The action, as predicted, made her sit bolt upright in the bed. Mendosa was already waiting with a second piece of tape for her mouth and another for her wrists. Crystal sat up with such force that the fishing line created a garrote-like action around her neck, cutting her skin very deeply. Unpredictably, the line also became entangled with her necklace and the sharp edge of the gold cross pierced through her cricoid cartilage and punched a hole in her trachea. The shock and sudden pain of the tourniquet around her neck caused her to snap back onto the bed, her partially bound fingers flailing at the constriction. A pool of blood formed quickly and began dripping through the laceration in her neck and into the hole in her windpipe. It created a gurgling, interrupted by an occasional whistling sound.

Scott was slow to react. He was obviously in a deep sleep and, despite the commotion, was having trouble waking. He tried to roll towards Crystal, but the loop tightened around his ankles. That obstacle made him grunt and roll back over as he tried to get out of bed. Still groggy and moving spastically, he only succeeded in having his head and shoulders slip off the bed and onto the floor leaving his feet seemingly roped to the mattress.

The assassin moved with the quickness of a striking cobra. Jamming his left foot into Scott's throat, Mendosa wrapped duct tape around the young man's ankles.

Scott was confused and incoherent as another constriction was applied to his wrists. He began calling out in panic, "Ahhh! What's happening? What's going on?" But before Scott could say another word, he felt a piece of tape violently pressed across his mouth, making further speech impossible.

Mendosa wound a second piece around his victim's wrists, immobilizing his hands. Mendosa darted back to Crystal. She was gasping for air and writhing on the bed. This time, he was more methodical. Ignoring the spray of blood that came with each exhale from the hole in her neck, Mendosa bound her wrists with a piece of the tape he had pre-stuck to his pant leg. Next, he used the roll of tape from his satchel to further bind her just above her knees and to reinforce the places he had taped previously. Her face was turning bright red from the fishing line choking off the blood supply to her brain, and her eyes were beginning to roll back in her head. Taking out his stiletto knife, Mendosa cut the line around her throat allowing the passage of blood to begin again. Mendosa's actions barely eased her discomfort, but in a moment he felt fairly certain that she would not die prematurely.

Bound as she was, Mendosa pulled her off the bed and dragged her body around to where it was in Scott's full view. Mendosa then reinforced all of Scott's bindings before finally removing the piece of tape from his captive's mouth.

Immediately, Scott hollered, "What the fuck do you think you're doing? Who the hell are you?"

Mendosa moved in close and Scott fell silent as he momentarily stared into the man's eyes. It was like looking into the eyes of a snake. Without a hint of emotion, the cold-blooded intruder smacked Scott across the mouth with the butt of his pistol. The sudden strike broke two of Scott's teeth and caused a gush of blood to spurt from his bottom lip.

Scott was shocked by the ruthlessness of the action. Eyes brimming with tears and wide with fear, he chanted, "Oh shit. Oh no. Oh shit." His eyes met Mendosa's once again. "What . . . what do you want?" Scott trembled.

Mendosa spoke softly, "Where is the disc?"

Scott did not understand the question and said nothing.

Mendosa asked again, this time more emphatically, "Where . . . is the disc?"

Scott was lying partially on his back and the blood from the gash on his lip was running into his mouth. He sputtered the blood and was flitting his tongue at the gaping hole left by the broken teeth as he asked tenuously, "What disc?"

Mendosa leaned forward and menacingly raised the butt of his pistol as he said, "Do not be glib with me. Where is the disc that controls the telephone listening device?"

Scott became bewildered. His fear was causing him to panic, and he could not think clearly. He kept glancing between Crystal and this stranger who was about to hurt him again. All he could manage to mumble was, "Telephone . . . telephone, disc . . ."

Mendosa moved closer to Crystal who was bound and helpless on the floor. She seemed semi-conscious. He laid a hand on her naked stomach and said, "You wouldn't want to see her die, would you?"

Scott shook his head violently as he stammered, "No. Please . . . no!"

"Then, I will ask you for the last time," said Mendosa, making it clear that his patience was limited. "Where is the disc that controls the listening device?"

Scott's head was beginning to clear. He was starting to fully realize the danger of this situation. Dozens of thoughts were sparking in his head, and he was trying desperately to sort them out, to make sense of what was happening. His whole day had been spent with people who were trying to get him to divulge the source for his story. Then, there was Henry Drummond. Had Henry followed him here? Did he hire this hit man to do this? Did Henry find out about the listening device? Scott was experiencing a little more clarity as he silently mouthed the words, 'telephone listening device'.

Looking into Mendosa's eyes, Scott mumbled through his heavily swollen lip, "You're looking for the bug! "Are you looking for the Ultimate Bug?"

Mendosa had not heard it referred to as such, but was pleased that this inquisition was finally going in the right direction. "Yes," he said. "Where is the disc that controls it?"

Scott felt a tinge of relief as he realized what was happening. He relaxed the tightened muscles in his neck and let his head slump to the floor as he said, "Pitch. You want Pitch. You're looking for Pitch."

There was a moment of absolute stillness, broken only by the irregular gasps for air coming from Crystal. Mendosa just stared at Scott. Cynical thoughts flashed through Mendosa's mind. Could this boy be lying? Is it possible he's just trying to throw me off track? Then, just as quickly, Mendosa realized that this person was not Peter "Pitch" Pechowski. This young man, who was bound and beaten and whose countenance and demeanor were just moments ago filled with fear, could not possibly be lying. Mendosa knew that, at this moment in time, this victim lying naked on the floor did not have the capacity to lie. He was not Pechowski.

Berating himself for not doing a better job of pre-planning, Mendosa cursed the fact that he hadn't bothered to get a photo of his prey. Thoughts of Parlotti jumped into his head, and Mendosa questioned if he were being set up. He had been harboring a growing suspicion that one day Parlotti would turn on him. Perhaps that time was now. If so, then Mendosa's salvation was the disc. Parlotti was right. Claude Mendosa needed to get the disc at all costs.

He turned his attention back to the victims, lying naked and trussed before him. He needed to find out who they were and what they were doing here. Most important of all, where was Peter Pechowski and where was the disc?

"Who are you?" asked Mendosa.

"Scott," said Scott with his eyes half closed, nursing the pain in his mouth, "Scott Aarons."

"And her?" asked Mendosa with a nod of his head in Crystal's direction.

"Her name is Crystal," replied Scott. "She's my girl . . ." His voice trailed off.

Mendosa nudged him, using the muzzle of the silencer on his pistol to jab into Scott's ribs. "Pay attention," he said menacingly, "What are you doing here in Pechowski's apartment?"

Scott opened his eyes wide and craned his neck upward. The reality of the situation came rushing back to him, and he understood that it wasn't over yet. "Pitch went away," he whined. "He just let me use the place."

"When will he be back?"

"In the morning," volunteered Scott. "We're meeting in the morning."

It was approximately four thirty in the morning. There were only about two more hours before daybreak. There was not a lot of time to question the victims, but Mendosa needed to find out a few more things. Asking several questions, Mendosa was pleased to hear that Scott was somewhat familiar with the apparatus and the disc, although he did not seem to know the details of how it worked.

Finally, Mendosa asked, "Where does Pitch keep the disc?"

Scott was feeling better. He had not been beaten or smacked around for a while and was regaining his courage. He said, "He keeps the disc on him. He always carries it with him." Scott looked over at Crystal and saw that she was doing very poorly. "Listen," he said pleadingly, "I've got to get her to a hospital. I can't help you any more. Let me get her to a doctor, please."

Mendosa, who was sitting on the corner of the bed, stood up. That simple action somehow gave Scott a feeling of instant relief. He knew now, that everything was going to be all right. Briefly playing with the idea of asking this stranger to untie them, Scott quickly dismissed the notion, realizing there was no possible way that this man was going to aid in their release. Scott would just have to wait for the intruder to leave before figuring a way to untie himself and getting help for Crystal.

Turning his head toward her, a genuine longing came over Scott. She looked so pitiful lying there suffering and helpless. He had to do something to help her. He desperately needed to save her life. At that moment, Scott realized he never wanted to lose her. Like an epiphany, Scott suddenly knew that Crystal was the one woman with whom he wanted to spend the rest of his life.

Those were the very last thoughts that floated through his mind.

CHAPTER TWENTY FIVE

There always seemed to be a long line of people waiting to get into *Benny's on the Beach*. However, once your name was on the list, the staff of this unique restaurant made certain that your complimentary cup of coffee was always filled. The eatery was an immensely popular establishment that overlooked the Lake Worth Beach and pier. John Tsakon and Peter Thano, the two round and personable owners, had long ago mastered the secrets of a great restaurant. Two dining areas, each with a casual Florida ambiance, featured ocean breezes and picture postcard views of the beach, the pelicans and the waves. The surroundings couldn't help but stimulate your appetite, and the food was colorfully presented and always twice as much as you expected to eat. The variety of breakfast fares included an outstanding rendition of french toast made with combinations of crushed almonds and a host of secret ingredients that would make Colonel Sanders jealous. Jennifer had full intentions of ordering the delicately battered bread.

Pitch and Jennifer had arrived there just before eleven in the morning and knew that they would not be seated for at least a half-hour. Pitch felt pleased with his timing. He had arranged to meet with Scott and Crystal at precisely eleven a.m. Consequently, he felt confident that, by the time he and Jennifer were seated, their friends would be showing up.

Pitch and Jennifer were having a grand time. Conversation flowed easily without ever suffering through that halting awkwardness that so often marks the patterns of a newly dating couple. Being considerate of each other, they constantly found themselves asking what one could do for the other.

Pitch was experiencing an odd emotion. It was the realization of being mature and responsible. He liked the feeling of being responsible for another person, specifically Jennifer, her safety, her well being, and even her happiness. It had the added benefit of giving him a purpose.

Waiting for their name to be called, Jennifer stood by his side and held tightly to his arm. Occasionally, she turned to look at his profile, and felt a comforting warmth sweep over her. These last twenty-four hours were like a honeymoon. From the romantic ride to Key West to the introduction of Pitch to her grandparents, it was all part of an idyllic fantasy that made her feel like her childhood dreams were coming true. Looking at Pitch, she smiled. Jennifer's mind flooded with the memories of the previous night when their feelings had exploded into passion. Pitch was a considerate lover and she would do her best not to disappoint him. With her hands wrapped around his arm, she knew she was very much in love.

The time slipped by quickly and soon they heard their names being called. "Pechowski? Party of four?"

They approached the maitre d' and waited to be seated. When Pitch saw the man grab only two menus, he said, "There'll be four of us."

Grabbing two additional menus, the host asked pleasantly, "Is everybody in your party here?"

Pitch glanced at Jennifer, then back to the man with the menus. "They're just parking the car," he lied.

Without any further conversation, the maitre d' walked the couple to their table and left four menus. The waitress came by with four glasses of water and took their drink orders.

Jennifer absentmindedly opened the menu and asked, "Peter, what time did you say they would meet us?"

Pitch looked at his watch and said, "We agreed on eleven o'clock. Scott was precise. He did say eleven."

"They're about a half hour late," Jennifer noted. "I hope everything is all right."

Pitch wasn't too worried about Scott and Crystal. He was more concerned about telling the host that they were a party of four and now there were just two of them. He didn't want to cause any trouble. Pitch was also beginning to feel a little guilty about not telling Jennifer everything that was happening between Scott and Crystal. He began, "Listen, Jennifer. I think I know why they might be running a little late."

Jennifer looked up and seemed mildly surprised, "Really? Why is that?"

"Yesterday, when Scott called," Pitch said tentatively, "he asked if he and Crystal could spend the night in my apartment."

Jennifer waited to see if Pitch was finished or if there was more to this story. Then, she said, "Is that it?"

"Um, yes." said Pitch squirming a bit in his seat. "They were, uh . . . you know."

"Peter," said Jennifer, her brow beginning to knit, "How come you didn't tell me this before?"

Pitch suddenly felt like a Cub Scout who was keeping the wrong secret. He had no idea why he hadn't told her before. There certainly was no need for secrecy, not after the four of them had spent the night on the Aarons' yacht.

"I don't know," Pitch blurted out defensively. "It was just the way Scott asked me . . . like it was a fraternity prank or something. Just a stupid . . . guy-thing."

"Peter," Jennifer said somberly, "I hope this won't develop into a pattern."

Pitch swallowed and hurriedly said, "I apologize, Jennifer, for not telling you. That won't happen again."

Jennifer did not want this to turn into a grovel-fest and said brightly, "Tell you what. I'll order for both of us and you go give them a call. Shake their asses out of bed."

Pitch smiled a toothy grin as he stood and said, "Order me the 'Sunrise Special' with a side of corn beef hash, well done."

Striding off to the public phone, he heard Jennifer call after him, "Tell them I was hungry and couldn't wait."

Pitch dialed the phone to his apartment and let it ring four times until the answering machine picked up. After listening to his own voice announce that no one was home, Pitch waited for the beep and said, "Scott? Scott, this is Pitch. Pick up the phone. Wake up and pick up the phone." Pitch waited several moments before saying, "You'd better be on your way down here to *Benny's on the Beach*, you incorrigible asshole, or I'm going to kill you!"

Pitch came back to the table and told Jennifer that there was no answer. They surmised that their two friends were probably on their way. Pitch and Jennifer went ahead with enjoying their brunch and dawdled over coffee until the waitress asked for the second time, "Will there be anything else?" The time was nearing twelve thirty and both Jennifer and Pitch were becoming concerned. After paying the bill, they drove back to Pitch's apartment. In route, they each took turns coming up with different scenarios as to what caused Scott and Crystal to miss their appointment.

Pitch rounded the corner and spotted Scott's Chrysler Sebring. "That's Scott's convertible," he said. "He uses it sometimes when his Rolls is in the shop."

Jennifer's only reply was a barely audible, "Oh." She reached over and touched Pitch lightly on the arm. Pitch parked the car and got out. Jennifer came around and caught up to him as he walked to the entrance. Approaching the front door, an uneasiness came over Jennifer and she tightened her grip on Pitch's arm. The door was slightly ajar. Pitch stood flat-footed on the step and pushed the door open. With Jennifer at his heels, he tentatively stepped inside. An unexplained feeling of dread washed over them as they stared at the clothes strewn on the living room floor. The door to the bedroom was open, but nothing was visible from where they stood. A shiver run through Jennifer and she took a step closer to Pitch.

Without moving from their spot just inside the entry, Pitch called into the bedroom, "Scott?"

After a moment of silence, Jennifer reached out to touch Pitch. Her grip tightened involuntarily as she called softly, "Crystal?"

CHAPTER
TWENTY SIX

L aura Parsons had called and said she was on her way. Emily was keeping a watchful eye on the driveway. Seeing the car pull up, Emily threw open the front door and embraced her old friend. "Come in, come in," said Emily enthusiastically. "Welcome to my quaint little Quonset hut."

Walking into the huge house, Laura looked up and around at the opulence that surrounded her. The last time she was in this majestic home, both girls were still in high school and Emily had invited her to a party of some sort. It seemed like a long time ago and Laura had forgotten just how impressive the home was. Whistling through her teeth, Laura said, "So, you still living in this same dump? When are you going to split this rat trap and get your own place?"

Emily ignored her quip and said, "Are you hungry? It's Manfred's day off, but I can fix us some lunch."

Emily led the way to the kitchen and rummaged through the refrigerator looking for Manfred's corned beef. "Yesterday afternoon," explained Emily, "when I told Manfred that I was having a friend over for lunch, he suggested the corned beef he had just finished making. The kitchen smelled *so* good."

Manfred's recipe was the best Emily ever had. It could have been world famous had he owned a delicatessen. As it were, only the Collingsworths and their guests were privileged to sample the fine delicacies resulting from Manfred's culinary talents.

Trying to keep the slices as thin as possible, Emily used one of the big kitchen knives to carefully shave off about half a pound. She only succeeded in making a mess.

Laura, who was picking and nibbling occasional scraps of the tender meat, watched her friend hopelessly hack at the corned beef. She shook her head in mock sorrow as she said, "Hey, Emily. You're making a bigger mess than the *Exxon Valdez.*"

"What's the difference how it looks," said Emily, as she laid out some pickles, olives, mustard, Russian dressing and several slices of fresh Jewish rye bread. "It'll still be delicious." The two of them ate their lunch and sipped their iced tea, while they began making plans for tracking down Scott Aarons.

"Why are we making this such a big deal?" asked Laura. "All we have to do is call him and ask him."

"Definitely not," said Emily through a mouthful of sandwich. "It's much too easy to deny things over the telephone."

"You think he'll just blow us off, eh?" asked Laura slicing off a piece of pickle.

"From everything you've told me, this is Scott's first big story. And I must say, it sounds like a doozy. I've known other reporters and they're instinctively protective of their sources. We're going to have to be face to face with him in order to have any chance of breaking him down."

"Eyeball to eyeball," said Laura biting into a big Spanish olive.

"I kind of envisioned that we would sit him down, get him to relax, talk about old times . . . you know, that sort of thing."

Laura's eyes went wide as she said, "Then, we could sit on his chest and beat the crap out of him till he tells us the source for his story!"

Emily laughed picturing the scene.

Laura continued, "I'm pretty sure he's still living home with Mommy and Daddy. Let's give a call and see if he's there."

"I think we'll be better off if we just drive over there," said Emily. "After all, isn't surprise our best ally?"

"What if the slug ain't home?" asked Laura. "Then, it's just a wasted trip."

"Not really," said Emily. "We'll probably be able to find out where he is, or at least what time he'll be back."

"Okay, let's do it," said Laura. "I'm pumped!"

Taking practically no time to clean up, they next made the decision to use Laura's car.

The big iron gate blocked their entrance to the driveway. Laura pushed the button on the intercom.

It crackled open and a man's voice said, "May I help you?"

Emily leaned across from her passenger seat and spoke loudly into the speaker, "Hello. This is Emily . . . Collingsworth," she said, deciding to use her maiden name. "We're here to see Scott."

"One moment, please," said the voice.

Less than a minute passed before a woman's voice sounded clearly through the speaker, "Emily, dear. Is that you?"

"Yes, Mrs. Aarons. I'm here with a friend to see Scott."

"Do come in," said Lenore.

The wrought iron gate slid open automatically, allowing Emily and Laura access to the long driveway that led to the house. Approaching the front entryway, they were greeted by one of the staff who asked the young ladies to follow him to the sitting room.

Lenore Aarons sat in a comfortable loveseat, a beautiful Angora cat in her lap and a stack of crossword puzzles at her side. The fluffy feline barely complained as Lenore stood and placed it on the floor. "Oh, Emily," gushed Lenore as the girls approached. "How nice to see you again."

"Thank you, Mrs. Aarons," said Emily. "Nice to see you as well."

"Please, dear, call me Lenore."

"Lenore," said Emily, "I would like you to meet a friend of mine, Laura Parsons. She also went to Clairmont-Pas with Scott and me."

"How nice to meet you, my dear," said Lenore extending her hand. "What a pretty thing you are."

The three of them sat down and the cat began walking around Lenore's feet. Meowing softly, it rubbed its long fur against her legs.

"I haven't seen Scott in years," said Emily. "Laura and I were just reminiscing about old times and wanted to visit with Scott in order to catch up. Is he home?"

"No, I'm afraid not," replied Lenore. "He left last night and hasn't been home since."

Laura and Emily glanced at one another and Laura said, "I hope everything's all right."

"Oh, goodness, yes," said Lenore with a wave of her hand. "He does this sort of thing on a regular basis."

Laura nodded her understanding.

"He had plans," Lenore continued, "to get together with his friend, Pitch. Do you girls remember him? He also went to school with you."

"Sure," said Laura. "Pitch Pechowski."

Emily added, "I didn't realize they still maintained a friendship."

"Oh, yes," stated Lenore. "The two of them have been friends forever. Pitch is such a fine young man, very clever and all. And he seems to have both feet on the ground. I do believe he's a good influence on my son. Scott tends to be a little head-strong and . . . well, you know . . ."

"Isn't that funny," said Emily. "We were just talking about Pitch over lunch yesterday."

"Well, the two of them were running off somewhere with a couple of young chippies from the college," said Lenore. "It's a very different world, you know."

"Gee," said Laura. "I hope he has enough sense to protect himself."

Emily's mouth fell open at the rudeness of Laura's remark. She could not believe that Laura would actually say such a thing to Scott's mother.

Lenore, on the other hand, never batted an eye. She seemed to take Laura's comment in perfect stride, as she smiled at the comment and said, "Oh, not to worry. My Scott may be head-strong, but he's not stupid. Besides, every time he gets into trouble, he somehow manages to extricate himself." Lenore bent over and lifted the cat back onto her lap. "That boy," said Lenore, stroking the cat, "has nine lives, just like 'Bagels,' here."

The cat began to purr and Emily was astonished at how loud the sound was.

CHAPTER TWENTY SEVEN

After dialing 911, Pitch and Jennifer were waiting in his car as the police and ambulance arrived. Finding it impossible to stay in the apartment, they chose to wait outside. The wait had seemed interminable when in actuality the first patrol car arrived in less than ten minutes. They said little to each other during the interim, choosing instead to comfort each other by hugging and holding hands. Pitch was devastated and Jennifer inconsolable as she sobbed intermittently. They were both confused and in shock.

When Pitch had called in and notified the authorities, he used the phrase, 'they were murdered.' As a result, three police cars showed up with a total of five uniformed patrolmen who began the initial tasks dictated by such a call.

Pitch came out of the car to meet them. One of the policemen walked around the building, while two others went inside the apartment. A fourth cordoned off the crime scene with yellow police tape while the last one, a sergeant, began questioning Pitch and Jennifer after having taken a quick look at the murder scene.

After explaining who he and Jennifer were, Pitch added that the apartment was in his name. He gave the sergeant the names of the victims and mentioned that Scott worked as a reporter for the *Sun Coast Ledger,* while Crystal had been a student at the local university. Describing the relationships among the four of them, Pitch choked up. He had to stop several times to compose himself before going on.

After countless questions, the cop lowered his pen and pad and asked, "Do either of you have any idea who might have done this thing?"

In unison, Pitch and Jennifer looked at the questioner and slowly shook their heads. Jennifer added through her tears, "I was about to ask you that question."

A van had arrived with the words "Crime Scene" written on the side. The sergeant told Pitch and Jennifer to relax while he went to speak to the forensic specialist and the photographer. The three of them disappeared into the apartment. A small crowd of on-lookers gathered as two of the policemen opened their trunks and took out barricades to help control the growing contingent. Some people in the crowd were asking questions, but the vagueness of the answers just titillated them into postulating their own theories.

Pitch glanced at Jennifer who was sitting in the front passenger seat of his car with the door wide open. Her left foot was resting on the seat and she had her arms wrapped around her bent knee. Her other foot was out the door and resting on the pavement. Pitch walked over to her, knelt down in front of her and lightly touched her thigh. Once again, she began crying softly and reached to put her arms around him. Hugging awkwardly, they were only vaguely aware of two more cars arriving.

Jimmy Dalton, a portly man in his early forties, was the first detective to arrive on the scene. His partner, Eddie Strickland, was on his way. Speaking to the sergeant in hushed whispers, Detective Dalton kept looking in the direction of Pitch and Jennifer. Finally, the two officers turned and walked into the apartment. Neither Pitch nor Jennifer was able to hear any part of their conversation.

An older, gray haired man in a dark suit occupied the second car, which had arrived at the same time as Detective Dalton. Getting out of his car, the old gentleman walked around, opened his trunk and took out what appeared to be a rather large, black medical bag. A couple of the patrolmen nodded to him as he stepped into the apartment and seemingly vanished into the darkened doorway.

Pitch and Jennifer were left outside to worry and wonder. Jennifer, who had been immersed in her grief, looked up at Pitch and plaintively asked, "Why, Peter? This just doesn't make any sense. Just a stupid killing . . . and for what? To rob a couple of bucks?"

Pitch had not taken the time to think about what might have been stolen from Scott or Crystal or his apartment. In his mind, he began to inventory all the valuables that he owned. Suddenly, Pitch was overcome with guilt for having such materialistic and selfish thoughts at a time such as this. He said, "I don't know why, Jennifer. Maybe an addict just trying to get enough money for another round of crack cocaine. I just don't know."

As they talked through their confusion and sorrow, another car pulled up and Detective Eddie Strickland emerged. Eddie was tall and lanky with long arms. He had an angular face, aquiline nose and a bushy mustache that covered a good portion of his upper lip. His hair was light brown, which he referred to as sandy, and combed straight back. He had a habit of constantly running his fingers through it in a vain attempt to nullify its unruliness and to keep it out of his eyes.

Pitch watched this newcomer stand by his open car door and take in the scene. One of the uniforms called, "Hey, Eddie."

Eddie answered in a gravelly voice, "Hey, Bronco. You taking care of things?"

"You bet, Eddie," answered Bronco.

Eddie closed the door to his car and slowly walked toward the entrance to Pitch's apartment. Hesitating in the doorway, he glanced from side to side absorbing the scene before moving inside.

The masses of neighbors and curiosity seekers were growing at the barricades. Quiet whispers were turning into bold statements, as the murmurs grew in intensity. It was difficult to make out exactly what was being said but occasional words like "murder" and "dead bodies" kept floating up through the susurration.

Another five or six minutes passed before Eddie and his partner, Dalton, emerged from the murder scene and approached Pitch and Jennifer.

Eddie spoke first, "Hi. I'm Detective Eddie Strickland and this is my partner, Detective Jimmy Dalton. Are you guys all right?"

Jennifer looked as though she had just been trampled. Her eyes were puffy and her cheeks were streaked. Pitch appeared to be holding up a little better, but he was obviously tormented by what had transpired. He said, "Not really. Those are our . . ." He paused at his use of the word "are" and thought he should probably re-phrase it to the past tense "were", but continued, " . . . our two best friends in there."

"We're sorry about what happened," said Eddie as he ran his fingers through his hair, "but I have to ask you some questions. Probably going to be a lot of the same questions the other cop asked you."

Jennifer spoke to Eddie for the first time, "We understand."

Eddie asked the majority of the questions, with Dalton interjecting a few of his own. As promised, many of them were the same as had been asked by the sergeant. Then, Eddie asked a new one. "You know anybody might have wanted either of them dead?"

Jennifer said, "Maybe a drug dealer or something."

"Why?" asked Eddie. "Were either of them into drugs?"

Pitch and Jennifer both began saying "no" simultaneously. Pitch tried to clarify her statement by saying, "We just thought they might have been killed by someone who was robbing them for drug money. You know, to buy drugs." Pitch thought that might have sounded confusing and added weakly, "The killer, I mean."

Eddie paused a moment before saying, "This wasn't a robbery. Nothing was taken. They each had money and credit cards in their wallet and purse."

Pitch and Jennifer looked at each other. Jennifer asked, "Then, why were they murdered?"

Dalton spoke up. "We were hoping you could tell us."

One of the basic tenets of police work is that everybody connected to a murder is a suspect. Even though this was obviously the work of a professional, Eddie was not about to dismiss anyone, especially Pitch and Jennifer. While Eddie and his partner were inside the apartment, they discovered a message on the answering machine. When they played it, they heard Pitch's voice saying, " . . . I'm going to kill you." It was a fact that stayed in the forefront of Eddie's mind. He had a few more questions.

Eddie began asking Pitch and Jennifer about their personal lives; where they worked, where they lived and when was the last time they saw Scott and Crystal alive. Jennifer told Eddie about school and how she and Crystal had been friends and roommates for a couple of years. As Jennifer spoke, she cried often at the onrush of so many memories.

When Pitch talked about Scott, who he was and where he lived and worked, Dalton interjected a question, "What are you telling me? He was the reporter responsible for yesterday's blockbuster headline about the Krum case?"

"Yes," said Pitch. "He told me he'd been under a tremendous amount of pressure because of it."

"Pressure?" asked Eddie. "From where? From who?"

"He wasn't real specific," replied Pitch. "He only said a lot of people wanted to know his source for the story."

"And who was the source for his story?" asked Eddie.

There was a long moment during which Jennifer stared at Pitch. Finally, he said, "I don't know. He didn't say."

Detectives were tuned in to recognizing lies and Pitch's words did not pass unnoticed. Both Detectives waited as they stared at Pitch and Jennifer, hoping that the uncomfortable silence would make them add something to clarify or rectify Pitch's last comment.

At last, Eddie continued, "Where do you work, Peter?"

Pitch was beginning to feel uncomfortable and deliberately decided to keep his answers short. "I work at the college," he said.

"What do you do there?" asked Eddie.

"I work on a research project for Dr. Lunderman."

Eddie's eyebrows went up. "Lunderman? Professor George Lunderman?"

"You know him?" asked Pitch with mild curiosity.

"Only by reputation," said Eddie, concealing an excitement that arose whenever he was able to uncover a vital clue in an investigation. It was only the day before that Eddie's Captain had received a call from a police officer in Washington, D.C. who was investigating the murder of George Lunderman. Eddie was scheduled to fly there tomorrow to gather information on the case.

Now, he was being hit with this coincidence. In police work, a coincidence is an open invitation to probe. Eddie felt this new revelation would definitely be something to dig into.

He was finished with his questions here in the parking lot. The time had come to take these two witnesses back to the station house for further interrogation. There, in a controlled environment, they would be separated and made to sweat. Eddie would ask each of them for their alibis and the meaning of Pitch's words on the answering machine. He needed to get their individual statements, but hoped for a confession that would lead to arresting one or both of them.

Eddie said, "We're going to need the both of you to come down to the station house to make statements. Why don't you hop into the back of this patrol car and we'll drive you downtown."

Pitch asked, "Would it be all right if we just followed you in my car?"

"Nah," said Eddie in a fatherly way. "You guys are too shook up to do something like that. When we're all done, I'll have somebody drive you back here. Besides, it's procedure."

Dalton had already opened the rear door to one of the cruisers, allowing Pitch and Jennifer to get in. Jennifer suddenly became nervous and hesitated getting in. She did not like the idea of having to ride in the back of a police car with its cage-like appearance. Eddie spotted the trepidation and said, "You two guys are going to help us crack this case."

It was the right thing to say, for it had a calming effect. With their trust level bolstered, Pitch and Jennifer both slid into the back of the patrol car, while Eddie gave instructions to the driver.

Eddie watched as the car pulled away. Then, he walked toward a couple of uniformed cops who were standing together. He ran the fingers of both hands through his hair as he called out, "Hey Bronco."

"Yo, Eddie," said Bronco. "What's up?"

"I want you to notify the parents of the deceased," said Eddie, handing him a piece of paper with the pertinent information.

"Oh, man," whined Bronco reluctantly.

Eddie ignored Bronco's aversion to the task and said, "The girl's parents live in Wellington. Give them a call. Have them meet us at the station. As for the parents of the dead guy . . ." Eddie paused and pursed his lips, "they are the rich and powerful Aarons' family of Palm Beach. Here's their address. Don't, I repeat, don't call them. Drive directly to their home and tell them personally."

CHAPTER TWENTY EIGHT

There was pandemonium inside the Aarons' estate. After the uniformed patrolman, known as Bronco, proffered the bad news to Lenore, she began wailing. The cries of grief were high-pitched and long and they caused Laura Parsons to panic. Emily and Bronco moved quickly to help Lenore.

Bronco was prepared. He reached into his pocket and took out an ammonia packet of smelling salts. Deftly snapping it open, he passed it in front of Lenore's nose. Although she responded to the pungent salts, Lenore was still in no condition to speak. She continued to cry out and sob.

The few staff who were working that Sunday came running at the eerie sound and were thrown into a state of shock upon hearing what had happened to young Scott Aarons. Lenore's inability to function catapulted Emily to take over and ask each of the staff if they knew the whereabouts of Mr. Aarons. Although there were some guesses, none knew for sure. She directed one to get some brandy, ice and a washcloth while the others were asked to make phone calls and try to locate Sidney Aarons as quickly as possible.

As Emily and Bronco worked side by side to calm Lenore, Emily quietly asked him some questions about what had happened. Refusing to go into detail, Bronco kept his answers simple and straightforward. To several of Emily's queries, he answered, "I'm not sure," or "I don't know," but followed up by saying, "You'll have to ask Detective

Strickland about that." Emily did learn that Scott's girlfriend, Crystal Richards was also found murdered and that it all happened at Pitch's apartment. Bronco also said that Pitch and his girlfriend, Jennifer, had been taken to police headquarters for further questioning.

After feeling reasonably certain that he would not have to call an ambulance for Mrs. Aarons, Bronco asked Emily if she had everything under control.

Emily replied, "I suppose so. Mrs. Aarons will be better off once we locate Mr. Aarons."

"If you don't think you'll be needing me," said Bronco, "I've got to get back to the station."

"Sure," said Emily. "I understand. Thank you for your help."

Emily walked with Bronco to the front door where he gave her a card with the address and phone number of police headquarters. He took a moment to write Eddie Strickland's name and direct telephone number on it before handing it over.

Emily looked at the card. "Could you write your name on it as well?" she said, handing it back.

"Everyone knows me as 'Bronco,'" he said as he wrote out the additional information. "But my real name is Robert. Robert Clydesdale." Handing the card back, he instructed Emily to remind the Aarons' that Detective Strickland would need to talk with them and they would probably have to identify the body. Emily shuddered at the thought.

Bronco exited as Laura, who was standing nearby, shivered against a non-existent chill. Face pale and eyes filling with tears, she said, "Emily . . . listen. I'm no good here. I don't think I can handle this."

"Are you all right?" asked Emily, taking Laura's hand into hers. It felt cold and clammy.

"I gotta get out of here," Laura said, jamming her words together. "You'll be able to find Mr. Aarons, right? I mean, Mr. Aarons will be home soon, don't you think?"

Emily saw the near panic. Some people just cannot handle certain situations such as the death of someone they know. Laura was one of those people. As an assistant D.A., she dealt with situations that were far more devastating. However, in her work, she was personally removed from those tragedies. The rapes and murders that came across her desk were just names on a blotter. But here in this room, it was all too real.

Emily understood. Before leading Laura to the front door, Emily half turned and slipped an arm around Laura's waist. "It's all right Laura. You go ahead. Take a deep breath as soon as you get outside in the fresh air."

Laura was immediately grateful for Emily's understanding. "Okay," she said. "I'll do that. Thank you, Emily. Are you going to be able to get home all right?"

The comment reminded Emily that they had both arrived in Laura's car. "Yes, of course," said Emily assuredly. "No Problem. No problem at all."

Laura drove off while Emily went back inside to check on Lenore's condition and to see if anybody had made any progress in locating Sidney. The staff wasn't having any luck so far. Lenore asked Emily to please help her to the bathroom.

While Lenore was washing her face and trying to compose herself, Emily felt a need to call Linc and tell him what had happened. She dialed his number.

Linc picked up after the second ring.

Emily began a rapid-fire dissertation of everything that had just occurred. She was speaking quickly, wanting to get the worst of the situation explained before Lenore came out of the bathroom.

Linc listened intently as the tale unfolded. At Emily's first pause, he asked, "Emily? Are *you* all right?"

She found the sound of his voice reassuring and was able to take a ragged breath and say, "Yes, Lincoln. I'll be fine. Thank you."

Heinous crimes such as murder had been a part of Linc's life a number of times in the past. He wasn't easily shocked or dismayed. Nonetheless, he found this situation to be disturbing. He had just been to a party with the parents of one of the victims and, as of this morning, Scott's father was now a client. But what bothered him most of all, was that Emily was in the middle of it. Linc had formed an early impression of Emily as someone who had a delicate nature. He felt that she had a vulnerability that needed to be protected and shielded from the offenders, malefactors and scoundrels of this world. He was experiencing a feeling of helplessness, knowing that she had just been tossed into the role of comforter and consoler. The gruesome circumstances of a murder now surrounded her and he wasn't there to protect her from that. Linc was suddenly aware of this feeling and was surprised that it had surfaced. A memory of the death of his first fiancée, Samantha Broadhurst, crept into his mind. That was followed by the recollection of being engaged to Lisa Decker and the wrenching memory of her infidelity. He worked to clear his head.

Linc had a lot more questions about the crime, but thought it would be best if he asked Emily in person. "Give me twenty minutes," he said. "I'll throw something on and be right there."

Emily sighed. "I was hoping you were going to say that," she said.

"Have you called your father?" Linc asked.

"Not yet," she replied. "That was going to be my next call."

They said goodbye and Emily dialed her father's cell phone. When there was no answer, she left an awkward message saying only that there was an emergency and for him to call back as soon as possible.

Linc was rummaging through possibilities and probabilities, as he quickly prepared to head over to the Aarons' home. He was recalling parts of yesterday's lunchtime conversation with Laura Parsons, Emily and himself. Laura had talked about the terrible trouble Scott had caused her by writing his blockbuster headline story. Realizing that Laura was wrapped up in her own troubles, Linc shook his head knowing that those problems were insignificant compared to what happened to Scott. However, Laura had insisted that Scott Aarons was at the root of her almost getting fired. Sometimes, thought Linc, the writing of a story can lead to unpredictable results, and he wondered if there was any connection between Scott's article and his murder.

Another thought came creeping into Linc's consciousness. Sidney Aarons was in trouble. He was a target. A target of blackmail. Linc knew that blackmailers would go to great lengths to ensure they got their money. There was a distinct possibility that the murder of Scott Aarons was really a message to Sidney.

*   *   *

After listening to the emergency message on his cell phone, Preston immediately returned Emily's call. Hurriedly, he asked if she were all right.

First assuring Preston that she was fine, Emily told him of the circumstances leading to this point in time including the murder of Scott Aarons.

Preston was stunned.

After telling Preston that Lenore was near collapse, she said, "We're trying desperately to locate Sidney. I have everybody in the house working on it. Do you have any idea where he might be?"

"Yes, Emily," said Preston haltingly, his voice still shaking with the shock of her news. "He's here. With me."

CHAPTER TWENTY NINE

It looked exactly like an interrogation room one would see on any cop show on TV. *Law and Order, N.Y.P.D Blue* or *The District* all could have been filmed in this very room. It was stark, bare and cold with only a steel table and a couple of steel chairs as furniture. There was a small window in the entrance door and a mirror on one wall. Pitch guessed correctly that the mirror was actually made of one-way glass.

The police had spirited Jennifer away to another room, which bothered Pitch greatly. He did not yet understand the significance of what was going on, but he knew there was more to this situation than just giving "statements." A long time had passed and Pitch was experiencing a growing anxiety at not knowing what lie ahead and would have preferred that Jennifer be at his side.

The upside of this delay was that it gave Pitch time to think. Taking a deep breath, he attempted to get his thought processes moving in the right direction. He would feel better if he could work out the variables to this strange and shocking day. Pitch knew the job of the police was to solve the crime and that meant looking for suspects. Eddie Strickland had said this was not a robbery since nothing of value had been taken. Those words hung in the air like a bad smell. So, who would have killed Scott and Crystal? It was hard to think straight. The enormity of the tragedy kept looming up in front of his eyes. Pitch had just lost his best friend. Violently murdered. It was a difficult time to exercise logic and reason. He had no idea who might have killed them. Pitch struggled to regroup his thoughts.

Perhaps a better question to ask himself would be, who do the police think did the killing? Thinking about it that way, caused a sensation of coldness in the pit of Pitch's stomach. He suddenly realized that he was the suspect. Could it be that the police even suspected both himself and Jennifer?

Of course, thought Pitch. It made sense. That was why they brought them here. That was the reason they had separated them. That was why they were making him sit all alone, trying to unnerve him. Detective Eddie Strickland would have been pleased to know the strategy was working.

Eddie Strickland was just on the other side of the one-way mirror, peering in on Pitch. He and his partner, Dalton, had been discussing the case with their lieutenant, as they waited for the initial forensics report.

Nodding in Pitch's direction, the lieutenant, said, "So, you actually got that kid on tape saying that he was going to kill Aarons?"

"Yeah," said Eddie reluctantly, "but we won't be allowed to take it out of context. If you listen to the whole message on the answering machine, it loses some of its impact."

"So, what else have you got?" asked the lieutenant hurriedly, anxious to get back to other things.

"Well," said Eddie turning to look directly at the officer. "You know how the Captain asked me to fly up to D.C. tomorrow and check on that Professor Lunderman murder?"

"Yeah. So?"

"Get this," said Eddie, pointing by jabbing his thumb toward Pitch, "This Pechowski kid worked for Lunderman!"

"Well, don't that sorta stink," said the lieutenant. "Stay on that track, Strickland. See what it gets you."

Before Eddie could say something else, another cop approached the trio and handed Eddie the early forensics report. Among other things, it stated that both murder victims died between three and six a.m. Armed with copies of the report, Jimmy Dalton went to question

Jennifer while Eddie Strickland entered the room to continue Pitch's interrogation.

Eddie settled himself into a chair adjacent to Pitch and asked, "How ya' doing, Pitch? Okay if I call you Pitch?"

"Certainly," said Pitch, a little off guard by the friendliness of Eddie's tone.

"Great," said Eddie enthusiastically. "Let me ask you about the message on the answering machine. The one we found in your apartment."

Pitch furrowed his brow for just a moment. Then, he immediately recalled the message he had left. In a flash, he understood why he was a suspect. Now, he knew the direction of Eddie's upcoming inquisition. Pitch put both hands flat on the metal table and threw his head back with a moan.

"What's the matter, Pitch?" asked Eddie innocently. "Something bothering you?"

Pitch gathered his courage, straightened up and said, "Yes, something is bothering me. You have me labeled as a suspect based on that message. Isn't that correct?"

"Tell me about it, Pitch," said Eddie softly. "Tell me about the message and what you meant when you said, 'I'll kill you.'"

Pitch tried to compose himself by taking a deep breath. He knew he was entering some dangerous ground and had a fleeting thought about asking for a lawyer. However, he felt that by doing so, it would send the wrong message to Eddie. It would sound as though Pitch was someone who had something to hide. He did not want to give that impression to this policeman.

Pitch told his story to Eddie, starting at the point where Scott had called and asked to use the apartment while Pitch and Jennifer were visiting her grandparents. He filled Eddie in on the details of the plan to meet Scott and Crystal at *Benny's on the Beach* at eleven a.m. Pitch related how he became upset when his friends missed their appointment and didn't show up on time. Pitch finished by saying, "That's what prompted me to call and leave that message."

Eddie chose not to respond right away. There was a long silence while the Detective just stared at Pitch. Even though he had a growing feeling that he should add something, Pitch could not think of what it should be. If this Detective was going to pressure him any further, Pitch would definitely ask for a lawyer.

Eddie finally broke the stillness. "What time did you and Jennifer leave to go see her grandparents?"

"Around ten thirty or eleven, Saturday morning," said Pitch with a slight break in his voice.

"Where do they live?"

"Key West," answered Pitch.

"Key West?" asked Eddie. "What did you do? Stay over-night?"

The importance of an alibi was coming at Pitch like a head-on freight train. "Yes!" he said excitedly. "Yes, we did!"

Eddie started to say, "I'm going to need the details of . . ."

Pitch was already three steps ahead as he interrupted the Detective. "The Morano's!" Pitch shouted. "Her grandparent's names are Angelo and Theresa Morano!" Trying to get all the information out as fast as possible, Pitch spoke quickly as he told Eddie about Jennifer's grandparents, including their address and directions to their home. He could not remember their phone number but assured Eddie that he could get it from Jennifer. Emphasizing the late hour that they left Key West, Pitch related how he and Jennifer stayed over Saturday. They spent the night at a motel on Islamorada Key, one of the many islands in the chain between Key Largo and Key West. Pitch told Eddie the approximate time they arrived at the motel as well as the time they left in the morning.

Eddie asked, "Did anybody see you leave the place?"

Pitch was still excited and began a frantic search of his pockets for his receipt. "Yes, of course," he exuded. "When we checked out, she signed my . . ." Pitch was unfolding the receipt he had been given by the front desk clerk. "Here it is! Darlene! That's the woman who checked us out and signed my receipt. You can verify it with her." Pitch handed the receipt to Eddie.

Eddie stood up and started to walk to the door. "Relax. I'll be right back."

"I want the original of that receipt," said Pitch confidently. "You can make yourself a copy."

Eddie was only gone for a short time. When he returned, he handed the original receipt back to Pitch and sat down. "Okay," said Eddie. "Let's talk about something else. When was the last time you saw George Lunderman?"

Pitch was somewhat confused by this sudden change in direction. "Last Wednesday," he said.

Eddie continued. "Did he say anything to you about going to Washington, D.C.?"

Pitch was troubled. He wanted to cooperate with the police, but he was not sure that he wanted to divulge any information regarding his listening device. He had been having some second thoughts on the long-range implications of his invention and doubt was creeping into his mind. Jennifer had said some things that gave him an uneasy feeling. Pitch was unsure how to answer that question without giving this Detective a new line of interrogation.

"Yes," said Pitch. "He did."

"Sightseeing or something else?" asked Eddie.

It was the opening Pitch was looking for. "Sightseeing, I suppose," he said calmly. "I don't know for certain."

Eddie continued to ask several additional questions, but he felt somewhat deflated. He had anticipated somehow implicating Pitch in the murder of Scott Aarons and Crystal Richards. Now, it looked as though the alibi was going to prove iron clad and, in addition, he hit his first stone wall with the Lunderman investigation.

Eddie's mind began to churn. He needed another scenario to explain the murders of Scott and Crystal. Moreover, the killings certainly looked like a professional hit. Jimmy Dalton had mentioned that Scott was one of the reporters on the John Krum rape case, and Pitch had said that Scott was under a lot of pressure to reveal his sources. The Aarons kid might have been killed for those reasons. It was quite common for people to get themselves killed for sticking their noses where they didn't belong. Maybe, there was a connection between Scott Aarons and John Krum. Maybe, the hit-man was one of Krum's cronies. Or better yet, Krum's lawyer, Michael Sharpton, might have arranged this whole thing in order to make sure that his client got his deal. After all, the attorney had a bad reputation for always doing things on the edge of the law.

Eddie sighed and wondered if he might be getting too carried away with his theories. Then again, the Aarons kid was dead and it sure wasn't Pitch or his girlfriend who did it. Eddie's thoughts wandered back to the idea of Scott being killed through a John Krum connection. That had possibilities. Krum was bad through and through with a rap-sheet that extended to hell. He was the kind of person who would know, and could hire, a professional hit-man. Yes. John Krum was probably the man behind the murder. Besides, the storyline would make more sense and also explain the death of Crystal Richards as just an unlucky bystander.

Eddie felt good about his line of reasoning. There was a kind of order to it, like the pieces of a puzzle falling into place. As a result, Eddie began asking Pitch a lot of questions hoping to get a handle on this new direction. It sounded very plausible. After Krum arranges the murder of the Aarons kid, the hit-man kills the Richards girl in the scuffle. It became the new focus of Eddie's investigation.

CHAPTER THIRTY

Mentally checking off a myriad of details and making certain not to forget anything, Linc rushed to get ready. He had planned on showering before his date with Emily, but now there would not be enough time. He put on a pair of slacks and managed to get a pull-over sport shirt halfway on before remembering his deodorant. Linc tucked in his shirt before running one brush through his hair and another through his teeth.

Stepping into his loafers, Linc thought about the directions to the Aarons estate. He had never been there, but knew where it was. One of the sprawling, tourist-gawking, stone monstrosities, the home was located right on the Atlantic Ocean.

Linc hopped into his Corvette and turned onto South Ocean Boulevard. His mind was racing over the events that Emily had just related to him. Feeling badly for Lenore and Sidney, he thought about what he might possibly say, how best to console them. Were there any words to alleviate the utter grief they must be experiencing? Saying "I'm sorry" could not possibly do anything to make them feel better, but speaking some kind words was far better than expressing nothing at all. He would offer whatever help he could.

Linc's thoughts turned to Emily. She was stuck there, trying to take charge and directing the staff to locate Sidney. Linc could still hear her voice, lonely and vulnerable, calling out for help. Realizing she was under a lot of pressure, he somehow felt a need to be there with her, to put his arms around her and to let her know everything was going to be all right.

Linc tried to snap back to reality. After all, he had just met her three days ago, and he wasn't sure if things were going all that well. Between the party at Preston's and their lunch with Laura Parsons, he seemed to be having a problem connecting with her. He had been hoping that their upcoming dinner date would give them a fresh start.

Linc was, once again, surprised at the depth of his feelings towards Emily. It had been a long time since experiencing similar emotions and Linc was not sure he liked it. Since losing one fiancée to a drunk driver and another to the girl's inability to control her adulterous behavior, Linc felt that relationships were akin to walking a tight-rope without a safety net. A person might find that exhilarating, but nobody liked the prospect of falling and getting hurt. His mind told him that there was no sense in letting his heart run away with his head. He would just make sure to keep his emotions in check and to keep things under control.

Sidney had a personality as volatile as a roller-coaster, and it was going to be a question as to the man's reaction when he found out that his only child was dead. Linc was hoping that the importance of Sidney sharing grief with his wife would take priority over emotions such as anger or revenge. Linc did not envy the unfortunate detective who happened to draw this case. The cop would undoubtedly be under a lot of pressure from his superiors as well as the Aarons' family to solve the case straight away. Linc also hoped that, before he arrived, Emily had been able to reach Sidney.

Pulling his Corvette into the long circular driveway of the Aarons' estate, Linc saw more cars than he had anticipated. Perhaps they belonged to neighbors or relatives. That would be good. The consolation of friends and neighbors can be a welcome comfort. Looking about, he noticed Preston's royal blue Bentley parked near the entrance and was glad that he had arrived. The Collingsworth and the Aarons' families had been friends for years. Sidney and Lenore were going to need that bond.

Seeing that the front door was open, Linc let himself in. He could see a small crowd of people milling about in a room off to his right. As he walked toward them, he could hear voices and an occasional cry of anguish coming from within the room. Standing at the arched entry, Linc saw about a dozen people surrounding Sidney and Lenore who were sitting together on a sofa.

Emily moved out from behind two people and spotted Linc. She came rushing towards him and, without saying a word, threw her arms around him.

Putting his arms around her, Linc could feel her shaking. He tenderly pulled her closer. For the first time since Patrolman Bronco had arrived with the devastating news, Emily let herself go. Linc could feel her start to cry even before he could hear it. Crying softly and gripping him more tightly, the crescendo of Emily's tears increased. They stayed in each others' arms until Linc felt her sobs subsiding. Then, he gently led her to an adjoining room and they sat together on one corner of a large overstuffed piece of furniture.

Linc held both her hands and asked, "Are you all right, Emily?"

She nodded without speaking, as the tears continued. Linc did not have a handkerchief to offer and felt awkward.

Just then, one of the staff poked his head into the room and asked if he could get anything for Emily. She said, "Thank you, Barkley, but I'll be all right."

Linc turned toward him and said, "Barkley, would you please bring us some tissues?"

The tissues arrived in short order and Emily was able to compose herself. Linc asked first about Sidney and Lenore. "I'm glad you were able to locate Sidney," he said. "How are they holding up?"

"Barely," Emily replied. "He just broke down completely. They've been holding each other and sobbing since I told him."

"You mean, you told him in person?" asked Linc. "Rather than on the phone?"

"Yes," said Emily, shuddering from the memory. "Right after I spoke to you, I left a message for Daddy. When he called me back, it turned out that he and Sidney were together. I never said a word until they were both here."

Linc gently touched her arm. "I know this is hard for you, Emily, but tell me again what happened. What did the detective say?"

"It wasn't a detective who came by," explained Emily. "It was a patrolman by the name of . . . Clydesdale. Robert Clydesdale. He basically told me what I told you on the phone."

Linc was hoping for more information. "Did he say anything about how Scott was murdered, or where? Anything about any suspects or leads?"

Emily related the whole story, beginning when Patrolman Bronco had arrived. She told Linc about the murder being committed at Pitch's apartment and that Scott's girlfriend had also been murdered. Emily finished by saying that Bronco seemed evasive when it came to answering some of her questions.

Linc asked one last question, "Did he happen to mention the name of the detective who was in charge of this case?"

"Yes," said Emily, brightening at being able to offer something concrete. "Someone named Strickland. I have his direct phone number written on a card. I just gave the card to Daddy. We can . . ."

"Eddie Strickland," Linc said with obvious recognition.

"You know him," said Emily.

"Yeah, sure do," said Linc. "I'm kind of glad he's got the case. He's pretty good at his job, and . . ." Linc paused while he put his thoughts in order. "Well, more importantly, Eddie will let me know exactly what's going on each step of the way."

"Well, I'd sure like to know what's going on," said Emily. "That policeman told me that Pitch and his girlfriend were brought down to the station for questioning. Does that mean they're suspects?"

"Probably," answered Linc as a new thought came to him. "This fellow, Pitch . . . same guy you and Laura were talking about over lunch? The boy-wonder?"

"He couldn't possibly be the murderer!" said Emily, agitated at the thought. "Not Pitch."

"Emily," said Linc, "You've been gone for quite a few years. People change."

Emily looked at Linc and with barely a smile said, "Wait until you meet him, Linc. In less than one second, you'll realize he's not a murderer. It'll be very obvious."

Emily excused herself and went into the bathroom to freshen up.

Linc went into the sitting room to offer a word of sympathy to Sidney and Lenore. Preston spotted Linc and stood to solemnly shake his hand and to thank him for coming. Pulling over a straight-backed chair, Linc sat close to Sidney and Lenore and quietly offered his deepest condolences. Sidney was regaining his composure and thanked Linc for coming. Lenore barely had the strength to nod her head in gratitude.

Linc told Sidney that he had contacts at the Police Department and that he would keep them updated on the events of the investigation. Sidney thanked him again.

Linc stood and pulled Preston aside. "Preston, I happen to know the detective who's in charge of this case. I'm going to head over to the police station to talk with him, see how he's doing on the investigation."

Preston thanked Linc for whatever help he could offer before saying, "I'm going to take over here. Sidney is in no shape to do anything. I intend to make all the funeral arrangements."

Preston continued to talk as Emily came back into the room and stood close to Linc. Preston was asking to be kept informed about the disposition of the body and reminded Linc that the family was Jewish. That meant that they had to have a quick burial. He also told Linc that the Jewish faith frowned on autopsies.

Linc said, "I doubt if I'll have any influence on whether or not the body is autopsied, but I may be able to do something about the timetable. I'll see what I can do."

Preston turned his attention to his daughter. "Emily, sweetheart, Linc is on his way downtown to Police Headquarters. If you would be so kind . . ."

Emily interjected, "Daddy, I'm going with Linc. You'll need to take over here."

Knowing there would be a laundry list of things to do, Preston felt slightly overwhelmed. He had hoped that his daughter would be lending her support and organizational skills to the situation. A fleeting thought about making a last ditch appeal, disappeared when Preston took one look at her face and realized that she had been through enough.

Emily's decision to accompany Linc to the police station would be all right with Preston. In a sense, he was pleased that she felt close enough to want to be by his side at a time like this.

For his part, Linc was surprised that Emily had chosen to stay with him rather than Preston and the Aarons' family.

On the other hand, thought Linc, perhaps Emily was warming up to him. Maybe she had an opportunity to re-think her loathing of athletes and was now giving herself another chance. Waiting for Emily to pay her respects to Lenore and Sidney, Linc realized there were more pressing matters to think about.

Emily was holding the hands of Lenore and Sidney and whispering her heart-felt feelings of sympathy. The scene made Linc focus on the upcoming trip to the police station. Emily had seemed so certain that Pitch was not someone capable of murder. Having never met him, Linc could not share that view. However, Emily had proven herself to be bright and intuitive, and Linc thought there was a better than even chance that she was right about Pitch.

Linc knew that he was not going to have any problem being kept up to speed on the findings of the investigation. Rather, he perceived the problem being with Eddie, himself, and his investigative skills. Eddie had only recently been promoted to detective grade and had not yet mastered all the techniques for success. Plus, he had not quite healed from the emotional wounds of having his wife and children move away. He was a good cop, to be sure, with good gut-instincts, but he also had some glaring deficiencies. One of them, was his ineffectiveness as an interviewer. Some cops excelled as interviewers. Not Eddie. Linc had seen some detectives question witnesses and demonstrate the ability to squeeze their memories beyond what the witnesses would have thought possible. A few of those same detectives had the ability to question suspects in such a way as to render their lies into fairy tales. With a few expertly phrased questions, they could poke holes in a story that seemed to be wrapped in piousness, sitting on an altar in the middle of the Vatican.

That was not the case with Eddie Strickland.

CHAPTER THIRTY ONE

A smooth-faced, rookie cop, fresh out of the academy, was nervously waiting for Eddie Strickland to stop yelling at the coffee vending machine. Eddie was screaming profanities and physically manhandling the dispenser. Aside from not being able to defend itself, the machine had taken, without permission, another pair of Eddie's hard-earned quarters. When Eddie's tirade finally subsided, the young cop ventured, "Eddie?"

Eddie spun around and glared down at the rookie.

Realizing his error, the rookie tensed up and started again. "Detective Strickland?"

"What?" growled Eddie.

"There's someone here to see you," he said timidly, pointing in the direction of the glass partition that separated the desk area from the visitor's anteroom.

Linc and Emily had come in to see Eddie and were stopped by the fresh faced, young cop who insisted they remain in the waiting area until he had informed Detective Strickland of their presence. Linc and Emily had both watched the unmerciful scene of intimidation as it unfolded.

Eddie looked up and spotted Linc. Without missing a beat, Eddie leaned in close to the young man's face and said conspiratorially, "Do you mean that big guy standing in the doorway?"

"Yeah," said the rookie, looking over in that direction just to make sure. "Him and the girl. They're here to see you."

Eddie suddenly hollered at the plebe, startling him into a spastic jump, "Well, just don't stand there, you idiot!" he shouted as he pointed at Linc. "Arrest that man!"

Emily was also alarmed by Eddie's outburst and became confused as to the meaning of his orders.

Jabbing his index finger in Linc's direction, Eddie continued to yell at the rookie, "Goddamn-it, boy, move it! Put the cuffs on him! Throw his ass in jail!"

The rookie began fumbling with his handcuffs and, in his nervousness, was not able to unfasten them from his utility belt.

Taking Emily's hand, Linc stepped through the doorway towards Eddie's desk. Linc noticed Emily's reluctance and pulled her along with a firm grip. "Man, you are some piece of work," said Linc shaking his head in disbelief. "Scaring the crap out of this poor kid just to get a rise."

There was scattered laughter coming from a few of the other cops in the squad room.

"When this is all over," Linc continued, "you are absolutely going straight to hell."

"How ya doin', Linc?" asked Eddie, as he casually plopped one corner of his rump on an available desk and ran a hand through his unruly hair. Eddie looked at Emily for a moment then, back to Linc and asked, "What are you doing with such a pretty girl?"

"You remember the name Preston Collingsworth?" asked Linc. "Palm Beach?"

"Sure," said Eddie. "I know the name."

Linc said, "This is his daughter, Emily." Turning to face her, Linc said, "Emily, this is my buddy, Eddie Strickland."

Emily cautiously extended her hand and said, "How do you do?" She was breathing easier now that she realized that the previous scene was just a charade. Still, she felt an odd mixture of relief and excitement. It was as though she were waiting for the next round of action and finding a thrill in the anticipation.

Linc jumped into the purpose of the visit. "I hear you've been given the Aarons' murder case," he said.

"Sure have," replied Eddie. "You know anything important about it?"

"I'm not sure," said Linc cryptically. "Tell me about what you found out there."

Eddie folded his arms across his chest and looked at Emily for a full beat before turning back to Linc. The signal was unmistakable, but before Linc could say anything, Emily said, "Eddie, am I to understand that you're holding Pitch Pechowski and his girlfriend?"

"Well, they're here, if that's what you mean," said Eddie. "Right now, I've got one of my boys verifying their alibis. I've got a feeling I'll be letting them go."

"Would it be all right if I go see him?" asked Emily politely.

Eddie glanced up at Linc, who nodded almost imperceptibly. Emily caught Linc's subtle nod in her peripheral vision.

"Sure, why not," said Eddie. He turned back to the rookie cop, who had recovered from being humiliated, and directed him to escort Emily to Interrogation Room Two.

As the rookie led Emily away, Eddie called after them, "Tell him I'll be there in about twenty minutes."

Sitting at his own desk, Eddie proceeded to talk about what he knew from investigating the murder scene as well as what he learned from interviewing Pitch and Jennifer. There were no eye witnesses and none of the neighbors had heard or seen anything. No sounds of a scuffle or a gunshot. Nothing.

When Eddie began to tell about the killer's "modus operandi," his M.O., Linc listened with rapt attention. Eddie talked for quite a while with Linc asking an occasional question.

Eddie wrapped up by saying, "It was a very professional hit. Good quality duct tape applied perfectly, fishing line around the neck, very few signs of a struggle and one bullet in the brain for each of them."

"The place wasn't ransacked?" asked Linc. "Nothing stolen?"

"Nope. Nothing," said Eddie emphatically. "Looks like he was there just for the killing."

"So, what's your take in all this?" asked Linc.

"Right now," said Eddie, "it's too early to tell. The crime scene boys are out there as we speak, doing their dusting, but I don't think they'll come up with any prints."

"Do you think the Aarons boy was the target?" asked Linc. "Or the girl?"

"The girl?" Eddie said, surprised at Linc's suggestion. "Nah. I'm betting they were after him, and she was just the innocent."

"Who's 'they', Eddie?" Linc asked, emphasizing each word.

Eddie was quiet for a moment after which he said, "Well, that's the real fly in the ointment, isn't it?"

They were quiet for a moment longer and Eddie added, "Pechowski told me that Aarons had written the headline article about John Krum maybe getting off. He also told me that his dead buddy was under a lot of pressure to divulge his source for the story. So, maybe that's the angle. Maybe, he got himself killed because the 'source' didn't want to be identified." Eddie stroked his mustache as he said, "So, who stands to benefit from not being tapped as the source? Someone in the D.A.'s office? Someone in the Mayor's office?"

Linc smiled and said, "Boy, oh boy, Eddie. You are really reaching on this one."

"Okay, so talk to me," said Eddie. "You obviously have something to say. Spit it out."

Linc suddenly felt like he was between a rock and a hard place. He suspected that the murder had something to do with Elana Velez. Linc figured that it made sense for Velez, along with any partners she had, to put the squeeze on Sidney. That way, she could make sure that Sidney didn't balk at paying the ten million dollar blackmail demand. It probably meant that Sidney would be receiving a note of some sort letting him know that if he wasn't quick about paying the money, someone else close to him would die.

The problem that faced Linc was divulging any part of this theory to Eddie and having Elana Velez become a full fledged murder suspect. If that became the case, there was no way he could protect Sidney. The information would become public knowledge, and Sidney's picture would be wallpapered on the front page of the tabloids along with a half-naked photo of Elana Velez. That was not a pretty prospect.

Linc chose his words carefully, "I'm working on a couple of things that might, I say *might* shed some light on this thing. Don't get your hopes up. It's probably nothing."

An older cop, with gray hair and a paunch, approached Eddie's desk. "Here's the information you asked for on Pechowski's alibi," he said as he handed some papers to Eddie. Turning to Linc, the older cop said, "Hey Linc, what you been up to?"

"Just managing to keep my head above water, Roscoe," said Linc. It had been several years since Linc had worked there, but the old-timers still remembered him.

"Yeah, right," Roscoe laughed sarcastically. "Now that you're hob-nobbin' in Palm Beach, you ain't got time for us peons."

"Well," said Linc with a straight face, "if you showered more regularly, I might show up more often."

Roscoe slapped Linc on the back. "Good to see you again, Linc. Next time, let's go grab a beer."

After reading over the information sheets, Eddie looked at Linc and said dejectedly, "Just like I figured. Their alibis check out. I'm gonna have to let them go."

"Why do you sound unhappy about that?" asked Linc.

"Because there's something bothering me," replied Eddie. "Remember we were talking yesterday and I told you I have to fly up to Washington, D.C. to investigate a murder of a local man?"

"Yes, I remember," said Linc. "You said it was some professor at a local college."

"Right," said Eddie. "Well, that Pechowski kid, I have in Interrogation Room Two, not only was best friends with the two kids found murdered in his apartment, but it turns out he works for, or I should say worked for, the dead Professor."

A long time passed in silence. "Eddie," said Linc slowly, "maybe the Aarons boy wasn't the target after all. Think about it. They were found dead in Pitch's apartment. Maybe Pitch was the target. Maybe Pitch and the Professor were working on something worth killing over."

Cognizance seemed to rise up in Eddie. "You know something, Linc?" he said without smiling, "Behind that ugly face of yours, you still have an active brain cell or two. I'm going to go ask him before I let him go."

The two men headed down to the interrogation rooms where Emily had been visiting with Pitch. He had been very glad to see a friendly face. Emily was not only a friend out of his past, she was someone he could trust; someone who was not there just to gouge him or to squeeze out information. Her presence gave him a sense of calm and he cherished it. Things would have been somewhat better if he and Jennifer had been allowed to remain together. As it were, Pitch didn't know how she was doing and was deeply concerned over her well being. Emily's presence was softening his worry. Her compassion and tenderness were like a godsend.

It didn't take long before Pitch was pouring his heart out to Emily about the double murder and how terrible he felt. Pitch went on about his friend's hopes and dreams for the future, lamenting that it was a future that poor Scott would never know.

When Emily asked about Crystal, Pitch spoke only briefly. His main thoughts about Crystal Richards were as Jennifer's best friend and, as a result, he launched into a discourse about Jennifer. Pitch talked about his girlfriend in such detail that Emily quickly recognized how much in love he was. Frustrated, Pitch complained about being held at the police station for more than five hours and all during that time he and Jennifer had been separated.

Emily was in the middle of asking a question when Eddie, suddenly appearing in the doorway said, "Emily, if you'll excuse us . . . I need to ask Pitch a couple of more questions."

"I am not answering any more questions without a lawyer," Pitch said, defiantly. "Where is Jennifer? What have you done with her? Aren't I entitled to a phone call or something?"

"You won't need a lawyer," Eddie said. "I'm going to be letting you go. But I need to ask you just a few more questions."

Eddie turned to face Emily and pointed to the exit. "Go out the door and turn left, then left again at the second door. Linc is waiting for you in the lounge."

Emily reached over and touched Pitch gently on his hand and said, "I'll see you in just a bit."

When the door closed, Pitch became defiant again. "What do you mean, 'a few more questions'? Is this going to mean another five hours? Do you plan on charging me with this crime?"

Eddie spoke softly, trying to disguise the natural gruffness in his voice. "Relax, Pitch. You're no longer a suspect."

"Does that mean I can get Jennifer and leave?" Pitch asked, still upset.

"Yes, it does," said Eddie. "But first, I need your help."

"What is it?" said Pitch grudgingly.

"Was there anything that Professor Lunderman might have been working on in his lab that would have put him in danger?"

This was the second time that Eddie Strickland skirted the edges of this particular topic. Pitch felt uneasy, as he thought about Professor Lunderman being in some sort of trouble. He answered, "No, I don't think so."

"What kind of things are you working on in his lab?" asked Eddie.

"It was a simple robotics study," said Pitch. "Nothing special, that's for sure. As a matter of fact, Professor Lunderman had just lost his funding and had informed me that I was out of a job."

Eddie asked Pitch several more questions about the robotics study and why Lunderman had lost funding for his work. Pitch talked freely about the robotics study and how it failed to meet its original expectations. He told Eddie that Professor Lunderman was not getting the kind of results that had been anticipated by the school. Pitch went on to say that Dr. Albert Chase, the Dean of the University, had similar thoughts and did not feel that the school was getting its bang for the buck.

Pitch decided not to divulge any of George Lunderman's shortcomings. Since Pitch was contemplating a partnership with the Professor, there wasn't any reason to deride the man any more than he had to.

Finally, Pitch asked, "What's going on with Professor Lunderman that's making you ask these questions?"

"He's dead," said Eddie, stone-faced.

Pitch's eyes went wide and he exclaimed, "What? What do you mean 'dead'? What happened?"

"Frankly," said Eddie, "I have no idea. All I can tell you is I'll be flying up to D.C. tomorrow to investigate."

Pitch was very concerned and felt a deep seated fear building in his gut. He looked directly at Eddie, "Is there anything that Jennifer or I can do to . . . um, help?"

"After I find out exactly what happened to Lunderman," said Eddie, "I may have some more questions for you guys."

Linc and Emily had been sitting in the lounge area. She filled Linc in on Pitch's state of mind. Linc could see the toll that stress had taken on Emily and he had her sit back and relax. The bristling atmosphere inside a police precinct added to the stress of her day. Policemen with weapons on their belts, interrogation rooms, one-way mirrors, the undercurrent of criminals and their heinous crimes all added to her anxiety and now, exhaustion. This was old hat for Linc, but the events of the day were beginning to tell on Emily.

With the questioning of Pitch complete, Eddie led the young man down the hall to a private room. "Hang here for just a minute," said Eddie. "I'll get Jennifer and be right back." True to his word, Eddie brought the two of them together.

Eddie poked his head into the lounge and said, "I'm all set for now, Linc. You guys can go get them. They're both in the little room across from the copier."

As Linc led Emily to where Pitch and Jennifer were waiting, he said, "Well, Emily, a penny for your thoughts."

Emily let out a heavy sigh. "Those poor kids," she said sorrowfully. "Pitch and Jennifer have been through hell today. Their best friends have been murdered, and they've been mentally tortured for the past five hours. Let's go see what we can do to help."

Linc was learning more and more about this woman. So far, he liked what he saw. Emily had proven to be clever, inquisitive and witty. He had no trouble talking with her at all. He was also impressed with her compassion, for true compassion was a rare attribute.

Jennifer had arrived in the room just before Linc and Emily. Sobbing, Jennifer was locked in an embrace with Pitch. Linc and

Emily waited. A short interval later, Jennifer tried to compose herself and managed to regain some of her dignity, as she wiped her tears. Emily and Pitch lightened the moment by introducing Linc and Jennifer. Sitting down to chat, Linc and Emily asked the young couple about any immediate plans they might have made.

Pitch said he had not thought about it. Jennifer answered that she did not want to go back to her dorm room on campus, and neither of them wanted to go back to Pitch's apartment.

"Here's what I suggest," said Emily. "The four of us will go out for dinner and then back to my house." Emily reached out and put her hand on Jennifer's shoulder as she said, "I want the both of you to stay with me until you can get a semblance of order back into your lives."

Jennifer objected weakly, but Pitch knew it would be best. Emily tried to allay Jennifer's concern about all of them living under one roof, by briefly explaining the size of her home and the fact that there was a staff of people working there. She assured Jennifer that having both of them as houseguests would not be any inconvenience.

"You don't quite realize the expansiveness of my home," said Emily. "Truth is, we probably won't even bump into each other."

Linc was impressed by how Emily was handling the situation. She was calm and reassuring. Linc noticed how Emily was able to garner trust from the distraught couple and how quickly they became dependent on her strength. With Emily having made that decision, Linc was pleased that she was going to be able to nurture them and to provide a safe haven.

Linc was grateful with the decision for another reason. He had been thinking about what Eddie had said, the business about Pitch's boss being found dead in Washington, D.C. Linc had a gnawing feeling that without the aid of Emily's home substituting as a safe-house, Pitch and Jennifer's lives might be in danger.

CHAPTER THIRTY TWO

Eddie Strickland could see the lights of Palm Beach, as the plane he was on loomed out of the darkness that was the ocean. Commercial airliners that approached Palm Beach International Airport from the east, crossed a hefty chunk of the Atlantic Ocean before skimming the pale yellow sands of the beaches that were the playgrounds of the jetsetters.

Nighttime arrivals took on a different beauty. At night, the ocean was always black. Colorless and non-reflective, the ocean seemed like a void, a vast emptiness that lacked even a twinkling of light. A passenger staring out the window would soon lose any perspective of where he was or even if he were moving. Sometimes, it was disorienting and often created an eerie feeling of loneliness. Then, as though suddenly a curtain were being lifted in some darkened cosmic theatre, a fine string of lights would appear. Looking at first like reflecting dew drops on a gossamer thread, the approaching pin-points would grow larger. Soon, their appearance would help to dispel the feeling that one had been alone in the vacuum of space.

It was Monday night, eleven p.m. and Eddie was hoping that his partner, Jimmy Dalton, would not forget to pick him up at the airport. Eddie had just flown in from his day trip to Washington, D.C. where he had met and spent the day with two detectives from homicide division. One of those detectives, a young man by the name of Chris

Belcher was exceptionally welcoming, and Eddie felt as though he might have made a new friend.

Eddie's mind had been churning over the facts of the case. A West Palm Beach professor of science, along with a government employee, found murdered in a seedy hotel room. Both of the victims were fully clothed, nothing was disturbed, no sign of robbery and both had been executed professionally.

Chris Belcher had been very cooperative and forthcoming, offering whatever help he could, but it was precious little. It turned out that his hands were tied. The investigation had been taken over by some sort of division of the Secret Service who had roped off the hotel room, refusing access to all outsiders. Even though Detective Belcher and his partner had been the original investigating officers, they were no longer allowed to participate. Pleading that Detective Eddie Strickland had just traveled all the way from Florida, made no difference. To Eddie's surprise, Chris and his partner seemed very nonchalant about the whole thing. Eddie caught the impression that this sort of thing happened quite often and it was viewed by the local constabulary as a windfall for reducing their caseloads.

Eddie was troubled. There seemed to be a question about Pitch Pechowski being tied into this by virtue of him knowing Scott Aarons, Crystal Richards, and now, Professor George Lunderman. Eddie was confronted with another parallel. The Washington, D.C. murders were also committed by a professional assassin, and the victims, just like Scott and Crystal, each died from a single bullet to the head.

The D. C. cops had taken Eddie to lunch, after which they showed him what little information they had. After looking over the crime scene photos, Eddie was given a copy of the meager background check the detectives had compiled on the second victim, a man named Walter Mahler. It was an unproductive afternoon. The only bright spot happened when Detective Chris Belcher took Eddie out for dinner to a nice steak restaurant in Georgetown. Then, he was driven to Ronald Reagan Airport in time to catch his 8:20 p.m. flight back home.

Even before coming to the escalator that led to ground transportation, Eddie heard Jimmy Dalton's voice.

"Eddie! Hey Eddie!" shouted Dalton as he waved his arm trying to get Eddie's attention. "Over here!"

It was late and Eddie was tired. Noticing that Dalton seemed wide awake for this time of night, Eddie approached his partner and said, "Jimmy, you look like you've been taking caffeine injections. You gotta start laying off that shit."

Dalton ignored the comment, "How was your flight, big shot?" Ever since the Captain had tossed Eddie this plum of an assignment, Dalton had taken to referring to his partner as "big s hot." It was not very often that a detective got to fly around the country, be wined and dined and not have to show any real productivity for his time. Dalton had been on the force longer than Eddie, but realized that Eddie was the poster-boy in the eyes of the brass. Dalton would be retiring in a couple of years and only wished well for his partner.

"No turbulence," said Eddie, "and that suits me just fine."

"So, what did you see in the big D.C.?" asked Dalton, sounding as though he was performing a rap song.

The two men were walking towards the exit, and Eddie looked directly at Dalton, "What's with you?" he asked. "You sound like you been taking drugs or something."

Dalton made a face of disgust at the ridiculousness of Eddie's comment and said impatiently "Come on. Tell me about what you found up there."

Relating the events of his day, Eddie spoke about the mystery that was surrounding the deaths of Professor Lunderman and the other victim, Walter Mahler. Eddie told Dalton about how the Secret Service took over the investigation, closing the door so that the regular cops were stymied. After going over the details, Eddie finally said, "There might be one small break."

"Yeah? What's that?" asked Dalton.

"Before the Feds took over," said Eddie with cautious optimism, "the cops had forensics do some tests on one of the bullets from the murder weapon."

"And . . . ?" asked Dalton.

"It's too soon to tell," replied Eddie, "because they didn't get the report back yet.

"What are you talking about?" asked Dalton.

"The detective up in D. C., a kid named Belcher, said if the Feds don't confiscate that report, he'll fax me a copy."

"Then what?" asked Dalton.

"Then, we'll be able to compare the bullets from the D. C. killings to our own little murder," said Eddie expansively. "We'll be able to see if the killer was the same person."

"Well," said Dalton excitedly, "I've got a news flash for you."

"Yeah? What is it?"

Dalton and Eddie were in the covered, short-term parking lot and just a few steps away from Dalton's car. Preparing to unlock the passenger side door, he said, "I solved the Aarons murder case."

Eddie replied in sarcastic disbelief, "What the hell are you talking about?"

"While you were ballet dancing up in the nation's capitol, big shot," said Dalton, "I solved the goddammed murder of those two kids. I even made the arrest."

"You made the arrest?" shouted Eddie. "Who the hell did you arrest?"

Dalton had a big smile on his face. He was obviously proud of what he had accomplished and was getting a kick out of Eddie's astonishment. "His name is Henry Drummond," said Dalton. "Ever hear of him?"

Eddie and Dalton had been partners for almost a year and Eddie knew Dalton's limitations. He was a good detective when it came to research and interviewing, but he was not a "closer." If you wanted to get information from the street, Dalton was your man. He had the reputation for having a vast army of snitches that could dig up vital information on everything from drug deals to art theft. But he had trouble when it came to putting two and two together. Although he had broken a couple of cases in the past, it just didn't happen very often.

"Henry Drummond," repeated Eddie. "Nope. I never heard of him. Who is he?"

Dalton unlocked the door to the car, allowing Eddie to toss his small duffle bag into the back and climb in. Starting the engine,

Dalton said, "Drummond is also a reporter for the *Sun Coast Ledger,* the same paper that the Aarons kid worked for."

"Okay, okay," said Eddie. "Enough with the suspense already. Tell me what happened. How did you accomplish this stunning breakthrough?"

Dalton's face was beaming as he drove. "When I got to work this morning, there were two messages on my desk from people who said they had a lead in the Aarons' murder. When I called them, they both told me the same story."

"Go on," said Eddie.

"It turns out, there ain't no love loss between Drummond and the Aarons kid. Drummond hated Scott Aarons with a vengeance. I was told he said things like 'Aarons was no good' and 'the world would be better off if he were dead.'"

"You got statements from witnesses?" asked Eddie.

"Yup. Sure did," said Dalton smugly. "Quite a few of them. I spoke to four witnesses that heard Drummond threaten Aarons on Saturday night in *Taboos.* Two of them also told me that Drummond made a play for Scott's girlfriend, y'know, the Richards girl. I also interviewed people at the *Sun Coast Ledger* where Drummond worked."

"And . . . ?" coaxed Eddie.

"They confirmed that Drummond had a hard-on for the Aarons kid. And get this; when I told Sidney Aarons about the Drummond connection, he went ballistic. He was carrying on and yelling that he should have known it was Drummond all along. Seems that Drummond was no good from the get-go. Listen to this; he was stealing stories from the 'Ledger' and selling them to the tabloids. When old man Aarons got wind of it, he started an official investigation. He also told me that Drummond drank too much, and that when he drank, he got mean and vicious. Aarons told me he was certain that Drummond was the kind of man that could easily have committed the murders."

"So, then you went to talk to Drummond?" asked Eddie.

"You bet," confirmed Dalton. "And guess what?"

"I give up," said Eddie patiently. "What?"

As Dalton drove, he held up his index finger and said, "First, he was trying to cover up illegal trafficking in stolen stories." Dalton held up two fingers and said, "Second, he hated Scott Aarons, so there's no question about motive." Dalton put both hands back on the wheel. "Third, he has no alibi for where he was at the time of the murders, and get this . . ."

Eddie waited.

Dalton turned to face Eddie as he said, "After searching his house, we found a .32 caliber pistol that had recently been fired."

"Watch the road!" said Eddie pointing forward.

Dalton swerved slightly to get back into his own lane and added, "And . . . some fishing line and a started roll of duct tape!"

They drove in silence for a while. Dalton was waiting for some kind of reaction from Eddie.

Eddie finally said, ".32 caliber, huh?"

"Right," said Dalton speaking quickly. "Remember when we first got to the crime scene how we both said it looked like a nine-millimeter bullet hole?"

"Yeah, I remember," said Eddie knowing what was coming next.

"Well, .32 caliber . . . nine-millimeter . . . they both make the same size entry wound," said Dalton emphatically. "Right?"

"Did you call the D.A.?" asked Eddie.

"They're sending someone over first thing in the morning," said Dalton with finality.

Jimmy Dalton drove in silence, as he waited for what he hoped would be Eddie's approval.

Finally, Eddie spoke, "Well, I'll be goddammed!"

Dalton looked at Eddie and smiled.

"Jimmy Dalton, you are one lucky son of a bitch."

Dalton's smile became a toothy grin. Turning fully to face Eddie, he said "Yeah? Y'think?"

Eddie nodded enthusiastically. "Way to go," he stated.

Dalton was energized. He continued to talk about all the minute details of his triumph while Eddie just listened.

Soon, Eddie slumped down in the passenger seat and closed his eyes. He was pleased that his partner had been so successful. The drone of Jimmy's patter faded and Eddie began thinking about how the pieces of the puzzle were struggling to fit together. There definitely seemed to be some unanswered questions. Eddie worked on the problem a little longer, but it was late and he was tired. Thoughts of rationalization bounced around in his head. So what if there are some loose ends? There are always some loose ends.

CHAPTER
THIRTY THREE

T he breeze off the ocean was gentler than usual. The tempera
ture was an eye-opening sixty-two degrees, but the bright
morning, Florida sun was working hard at correcting that. The humidity
had risen several points but had not reached the discomfort level that
would be prevalent during the summer months. Instead, it only served
to augment the aroma of salty ocean air to a level that was most pleasing.

It promised to be the kind of day that drew all the wintertime
visitors, the "snowbirds," as they were referred to by the natives, to this
weather perfect paradise. Linc marveled at how easy it was to spot the
tourists from the year round residents. When the temperature hovered
in the low sixties or less, all the true Floridians wore long sleeved
shirts and jackets, while their northern brethren pranced around in
tank tops and shorts.

Linc was one of the few exceptions. He was dressed in a muted
teal, short sleeved pullover. It was solid, broken only by a coral colored
band of fabric on the inside of his collar and a nondescript emblem of
the same color over the left breast pocket. His slacks were of a light
coral tone and perfectly creased. Tan leather moccasins finished off
the outfit. Preferring casual clothes, Linc rarely wore a blazer or a suit,
and it was rarer still to see him sporting a tie.

Carrying a hot cup of coffee, Preston came out to the pool deck.
He was wearing a long sleeved shirt and a wind breaker. He hesitated

before sitting down next to Linc and said, "Aren't you cold dressed like that?"

"Oh, just sit down, Preston," said Linc. "You've known me too many years to ask a question like that."

Careful not to spill his coffee, Preston sat down and said, "Emily will be joining us directly. She was just putting the finishing touches on her face. I told Manfred to hold off serving breakfast until she gets here."

"Did you have any luck arranging Scott's funeral?" Linc asked.

"Yes," said Preston. "I think I've finally been able to make some headway."

As promised, Preston had taken charge of making the funeral arrangements. It allowed his friends, Sidney and Lenore, to grieve over the loss of their son without having to wade through that particular quagmire. However, Preston had run into a conflict. The Aarons' family, being Jewish, required the funeral to take place within twenty-four hours. The police had a different timetable. Because this was a murder investigation, an autopsy had to be performed. Preston had been fighting with the police and the bureaucrats at the medical examiner's office to speed up the process of the autopsy.

"I had to pull some strings," said Preston, "but I got them to promise that they would release Scott's body to the funeral home this afternoon."

"When is the funeral?" Linc asked looking at the deepening lines in Preston's face.

"Tomorrow afternoon. Three o'clock."

Linc changed the subject. "How have your guests been holding up?"

Preston brightened. "Pitch and Jennifer? They are a delightful young couple. They're going through some trying times right now, but they have an awful lot going for them. Very engaging. Very engaging, indeed."

Explaining that he and Pitch were both about the same size, Preston had been able to loan the lad some clothes just to tide him over. Preston mentioned that Emily had been able to do likewise with Jennifer but, late last night, had taken both of them shopping for some personal items.

Preston paused a moment before continuing. "That Pitch is an exceedingly bright young man. Very clever . . . no, strike that. Brilliant! That's what he is. Brilliant. Did you know he has this theory . . ."

Preston's sentence was interrupted by Emily's entrance onto the pool deck. "Good morning, gentlemen," she announced.

She was followed closely by Manfred who was wheeling a small cart containing orange and tomato juice, a pot of hot coffee and a small stack of cups and saucers. Both men stood while Linc pulled over another deck chair forming a small circle for the three of them.

While Manfred took everybody's breakfast order, Linc admired Emily's outfit. She wore a white, long sleeved sweater with a scoop neck. The sweater was partially covered by a black and white plaid jumper that came just below her knees. Emily wore thick white socks and a pair of bright white, delicate looking sneakers. Her only other accessory was a short, black pearl necklace and a pair of matching earrings.

After the morning pleasantries were completed, Emily looked at Linc and asked, "Did Daddy tell you about the funeral arrangements?"

"Yes," answered Linc. "He filled me in on all the details. We were just discussing Pitch and Jennifer. Are they still sleeping?"

Emily took a sip of her tomato juice. "They most certainly are *not* sleeping!" she said emphatically.

Linc crossed his legs and said, "Um . . . should I take a chance and ask what they are doing?"

Emily lowered her voice an octave and said, "They're in the middle of a raging argument. I couldn't hear what it was about, but as I passed in front of their bedroom door, they were going at it."

Preston interjected, "Couldn't you have stopped and listened for a moment, Emily?"

"Daddy!" Emily exclaimed, exasperated at the audacity of his suggestion. "Their lover's spat, or whatever it is, is no business of ours."

"I'm not so sure about that, Emily," said Linc, carefully choosing his words. "You invited them here because they didn't have another acceptable place to go. Even though you did that out of the goodness of your heart, you're now kind of responsible for their well being."

"What are you saying?" asked Emily. "That I should have done what Daddy asked and listened at their door?"

"No," said Linc. "Not exactly. But I do believe there's a danger here, and we've now become responsible to see that Pitch and Jennifer remain safe."

"A danger?" asked Preston slightly alarmed at Linc's choice of phrasing. "What kind of danger?"

Linc saw that the two of them were both paying close attention to what he was about to say. He mulled over his thoughts before speaking. "There are too many things about this murder that just don't fit. The fact that it was a professional hit, coupled with the motive that the police have put forward, don't mesh. Think about it. If someone were really upset with Scott Aarons for not divulging the source of his story, would they go through the trouble of hiring a professional hit-man to do the job?"

Linc paused to let that question sink in before continuing, "And another thing; Scott's story hit the papers on Saturday morning. He was found dead less than twenty-four hours later. That just doesn't wash. It takes more time than that to set up a kill with a pro."

Preston was astounded. Emily was shocked. Neither had thought much about the "how" and "why" of the murder. Their thoughts had focused on the aftermath, all the things that needed to be done to help the living.

Emily sat forward in her chair. She was fascinated by Linc's ability to break down a problem into minute segments and put it back together in a different configuration. Having witnessed this process during lunch with Linc and Laura, she once again studied his eyes as his mind churned.

"There's more, isn't there?" asked Emily pointedly.

"Yes," said Linc solemnly. "I don't think Scott and Crystal were meant to be the victims."

Emily was startled by this revelation and put a hand over her mouth, trying to prevent any sound of surprise.

Preston found his voice, "Linc, what are you suggesting?"

Before Linc could answer, Emily softly declared, "He's saying that the targets were supposed to be Pitch and Jennifer. Isn't that right, Linc?"

"Let me tell you something that neither of you know about this case," said Linc. "It seems Pitch has been working in a laboratory for a Professor George Lunderman. Some kind of robotics study or something. I'm not familiar with the details. Anyway, late last week Professor Lunderman goes up to Washington, D.C. He checks into a hotel and the next morning, he's found . . . murdered. Eddie Strickland flew up there yesterday to get the facts in the case, but I suspect . . ."

At that moment, Manfred appeared through the sliding glass doors, pushing a huge rolling cart. Clattering across the patio stones, the wheeled table held a sumptuous breakfast. As they moved their chairs to the table that Manfred was setting, Preston and Emily were eager to return to the conversation. They wanted to hear what else Linc had to say. Manfred put out five place settings. Before he had finished, Pitch and Jennifer walked out to the pool deck to join the group.

"Good morning," greeted Jennifer. This was immediately followed by a combination of hugging, hand shaking, additional "good mornings" and inquiries into how everyone slept. Prior to departing back into the kitchen, Manfred scurried around making sure that everything was laid out just right. A short awkward silence was broken by Preston. He filled Pitch and Jennifer in by somberly announcing the latest news about the funeral arrangements.

Linc was studying the faces of Pitch and Jennifer while Preston talked. Pitch looked a little uncomfortable and somewhat distracted, but was nodding his head approvingly at the things Preston was saying. Jennifer was literally sitting on the edge of her seat, seemingly waiting for her turn to speak.

When Preston finished reciting the planned sequence of events, Jennifer cleared her throat. "Emily has probably filled you all in," she began, "on the conversations the two of us had yesterday . . ."

Emily interrupted, "Jennifer, I'm sorry. I haven't had the chance to tell them anything yet."

Gathering her thoughts, Jennifer bowed her head for a moment before looking up and proceeding. "Yesterday, Emily and I spent a number of hours discussing trust and friendship and things of that nature."

Jennifer reached over to take Pitch's hand as she continued, "Peter and I are feeling a little alone right now and have come to realize just how much we appreciate all that you're doing for us. We also realize that we need your help in another matter." She looked first at Preston, then at Linc and added, "Help from all of you."

Preston was very curious, but eager to help in any way he could. Emily was absorbed by Jennifer's sincerity and was feeling "sisterly" towards the pair. Linc was experiencing a slight case of cynicism and had a fleeting thought that Jennifer sounded as though she were about to confess to the murders. Linc wondered just how open and honest Jennifer was about to be. He waited.

Jennifer went on. "Peter and I have been . . ." Jennifer pursed her lips and hesitated, thinking about her choice of words. She and Pitch looked at each other for a moment before continuing. "We've been discussing what we're about to tell you. It's very important and . . . and confidential. Even though I've only known each of you for just a short time, I feel a need . . . we feel a need to trust you. Thanks to Emily's insights and sincerity, we feel that we *can* trust you."

Preston could not contain himself any longer, "This all sounds very cryptic, Jennifer. What are you trying to say?"

All during Jennifer's halting preamble, Linc had been staring at Pitch. Linc suspected that this entire discussion could be cleared up as soon as Pitch decided to talk. Meeting Linc's eyes, Pitch realized that it was his turn. He sat up straight in his chair and spoke for the first time.

"I have invented something," said Pitch with clarity in his voice that surprised Linc. "A device. A device that we feel is responsible for all the killings."

Preston leaned forward and asked, "How can that be? What is it?"

Jennifer picked up the explanation. "It's this . . . thing," she said haltingly, "that intrudes into your privacy. It's a . . ."

Pitch interrupted, "Jennifer, please," he said softly. "Let me tell it."

Jennifer nodded her head.

"Jennifer is right," said Pitch, squeezing her hand. "It does have to do with intruding into one's privacy, but it's much more than that. Much more. I just didn't realize . . ." Pitch hesitated, gathering his thoughts before continuing.

For the next hour and a half, Pitch told them everything. How he invented the bug and his motivation for doing so. He went into great detail explaining why his listening device was so far superior to anything else that might be available.

"If you want to listen in on any conversation," explained Pitch, "I mean, any conversation, in any home or any office anywhere throughout the world, now it's just a simple matter of clicking into my program and dialing the number of the telephone in that room. It automatically activates the microphone that's in the handset."

Jennifer added, "And Peter has figured out a way to prevent the target phone from ringing once it's activated. So this way, a person would never know when they're being listened to."

Pitch rubbed the back of her hand and went on with his story. He told the group about the device's first test. "It was Scott who had the idea for the first real live test of my prototype. He suggested that we try it on the telephone in Jennifer and Crystal's dorm room. It worked perfectly. I could even hear Jennifer speaking when she was in the closet choosing an outfit for that night."

Next, Pitch spoke about Professor George Lunderman's connection, and Jennifer added a comment regarding his slovenly appearance. Relating the incident when Scott, Lunderman and he were in his apartment, Pitch told how he tapped into the office of John Krum's attorney. "There was no problem whatsoever," explained Pitch. "Once the connection was made, Scott, Professor Lunderman and I were able to eavesdrop on every word of the District Attorney's secret meeting."

Emily looked over at Linc, but he was listening intently to everything Pitch was saying. She was amazed by the fact that Linc had been able to figure out that there must have been a listening device in the lawyer's office during that meeting. She was further astonished that Linc had it figured out by the time they met for lunch last Saturday. Emily wanted to ask Pitch if he remembered Laura Parsons, but decided not to break the continuity of his story.

However, Pitch's tale was briefly put on hold when Manfred came out to refresh the hot and cold beverages and to clear away some of the dishes. As Manfred departed, Pitch went on to tell how Lunderman was planning to go to Washington D.C. to get funding for their joint research project. Pitch also related how Scott had used the information gathered through the device to author his big headline story.

Pitch's voice dropped half an octave. "Just before Jennifer and I left for the Keys, I gave permission for Scott and Crystal to use my apartment."

Pitch took a moment to sip his coffee. "I have this dreadful feeling," he said, "that whoever killed Scott and Crystal was actually looking for me."

"That is precisely what Lincoln said," exclaimed Preston, "just moments before you got here."

Both Pitch and Jennifer looked at Linc with surprise. "You were able to deduce that?" asked Pitch.

"There were just too many parts of the puzzle that didn't fit," said Linc. "After the police told me about Lunderman's death, it had to be something like that."

Pitch turned to Jennifer and declared, "See, the police have figured this out as well. That's another reason why we're no longer suspects."

Jennifer asked Linc, "Who do the police suspect? Are they about to make an arrest?"

"The police aren't looking at this the same way you are," said Linc. "They're working under the premise that Scott was the intended victim."

"Shouldn't we go tell them?" asked Jennifer.

Everybody was looking at Linc, awaiting his reply. A few seconds ticked by and Pitch put both hands around Jennifer's, as he asked, "Why don't you think we should tell them, Linc?"

Linc was troubled. "It's that device of yours," he said. "You've invented something that is potentially so dangerous, I'm having trouble imagining all the problems that will arise. You've invented something that, in effect, creates the total absence of privacy. There can't be any more secrets."

Linc paused to think how best to finish answering Pitch's question. "The more people who know about this," said Linc, "the more dangerous things become for you. Think about the kind of people who might want a device like that. The answer is, everybody you don't want to know. Drug dealers, terrorists, blackmailers, bank robbers; the list is endless."

"Don't forget crooked politicians," added Emily.

"Right," said Linc. "Any one of these people would torture you for the information you have in your head."

Pitch reached into the breast pocket of his shirt and pulled out a three and a half inch floppy disc. "Or the information that's contained in here," he said.

There was a dumfounded silence, broken by Linc as he asked, "Are you telling me, that floppy contains everything you want to know about your invention?"

The continued absence of conversation caused Pitch to look from one to the other. It slowly dawned on him that they were thinking that this invention was something very complicated. "You people must recognize that this thing I've invented is really rather simple."

"Rather simple?" queried Preston.

"Absolutely," said Pitch. "It was just a simple matter of calculating the proper harmonic frequency and converting that to an electronic signal that I could tie into my computer."

"Unbelievable," said Preston, shaking his head. He turned towards the others and said, "He actually thinks of it as 'simple.'"

Pitch spoke defensively. "It was simple," he said, trying to make it sound like anybody could have accomplished the feat. "It's not like calculating the trajectory and gravitational vectors of a space probe, you know. I actually obtained all my formulas right off the Internet."

Emily commented with a smile, "Pitch Pechowski . . . you are something else. Ever since high school, you've been in a class by yourself. And part of your charm is that you don't even realize it."

Jennifer nodded her head in agreement.

Emily continued. "But charming or not, Linc is right. This little invention of yours sounds dangerous. It's just that it's so easy for people to be corrupted these days. Everywhere you look, you see evidence of looser morals, a willingness to stretch the law, people who are quick to rationalize their lies. It would be a very short step for those kinds of people to want to take advantage of your invention. A device like yours can be so . . . I don't know . . ."

"Tempting?" offered Preston.

"Are you kidding?" asked Linc rhetorically. "This thing could tempt the Pope."

Jennifer had been vigorously nodding her head during the discussion. She had tried to convey some of those very same thoughts to Pitch, but felt that she had been unsuccessful because of how defensive he became. Now, as the discussion broadened and encompassed other people's values and ideals, she was feeling vindicated. Jennifer eagerly added, "And not only that, think about what it means if these corrupt people have such easy access into your daily life. No one could ever be sure they were having a private conversation. No one could ever feel safe. It's a way of invading your soul. You might as well take the Fourth Amendment and set fire to it. It would just be a useless piece of paper. It wouldn't make any difference at all."

"George Orwell's, *1984*," said Emily.

"Exactly," said Jennifer. "It's a matter of privacy. Big Brother might not be watching, but he certainly would be listening."

Preston, who had been quiet for a while, said, "There's another aspect here. Money. Whoever controls a device such as yours can easily tap into any boardroom in the country. I know a group of investors who are, right now, clamoring to find out about a particular licensing agreement. It would be child's play to gather advance knowledge about proposed mergers, acquisitions or patent rights. A few judicious investments and one would seemingly have the Midas Touch. It could guarantee wealth."

"That is precisely the kind of corruption I'm talking about," said Emily emphatically.

"I suggest," said Linc, "that the first order of business is to find a safe place for that disc. Any suggestions, Preston?"

"How about a safe deposit box?" asked Preston. "Do you have one, Pitch?"

Before Pitch could answer, Linc said, "Even if you have one, you can't use it. It would be a simple matter of tracing which bank you use, and there are ways to gain access into the box."

The five of them sat in silence for a moment. Linc was trying to think of a solution that would be acceptable to Pitch. Understanding that Pitch had been reluctant to divulge any of this to begin with, Linc felt that trust was a defining issue.

Emily offered, "Why don't we have Jennifer open a safe deposit box and Pitch can store his disc in there?"

It was a smart idea. The disc could be stored under Jennifer's name and reduce any possibility of Pitch being tied to it. Everyone agreed to the plan. Preston said he would take the couple to his bank where he was sure they would get speedy cooperation.

Linc took a moment to talk about security measures. He told Pitch and Jennifer that they should confine themselves to the house and grounds. It wouldn't be safe to go wandering off. He requested that either Preston or Emily be in close proximity to the young couple and that Preston talk to his staff regarding taking extra precaution. Jotting his private cell phone number onto his business cards, Linc gave one to each of them. In case of any sign of trouble, Linc made it clear that he was only a phone call away.

Jennifer said, "Since we're staying here, we'll need to go to the store and buy a few additional personal items."

"All right," said Linc. "Preston will take you when you all come back from the bank. I just don't want you lolly-gagging around the mall."

Pitch and Jennifer thanked everyone for their kindness and their help. Standing, they excused themselves and went off to get ready.

A half hour later, Linc and Emily were alone on the large patio overlooking the pool. "Linc," asked Emily as she came out of a thought, "how are you going to reconcile not telling the police about Pitch and his invention?"

Linc took a deep breath. "I've been thinking about that very problem," he said. "By not coming forward with this information, I'm coming very close to the definition of 'obstruction of justice.'"

Emily waited silently. She did not know what kind of solution Linc would come up with, but she now felt confident in his ability to think of something resourceful.

"Unfortunately," said Linc, "we're going to need the resources of the police department to help us track and find the killer. For that reason alone, I really should let them know. But, here's how I think this thing should play out. I'm only going to tell Eddie Strickland. No one else. I'm sure Eddie will keep it between us for as long as he can. That way, Eddie, acting like a one man investigating machine will be able to help solve this."

"Linc," said Emily, "I have an alternate suggestion."

"Let's hear it."

Emily stared intently into his eyes and said, "I'll help you find the killer."

Linc had a recollection of Emily saying that she wanted to be part of his detective agency. "Emily," denounced Linc, "we're not playing games here. This is the kind of thing for professionals. We're playing for keeps."

Emily never wavered. She continued to stare at Linc and said, "Mr. Bradshaw, I am a professional."

"What are you talking about Emily?"

"For the past seven years, I've been working for our government in various capacities. The one thing that all of my positions had in common was that I specialized in criminal research."

Linc had been well aware of Emily's connection with NATO, but did not know the specifics of her job. "What do you mean when you say, 'criminal research?'" he asked.

"During my tenure, I've been on loan to the CIA, the FBI and a couple of other organizations that I'm not permitted to divulge. NATO Intelligence and I have been wrapped in the same cocoon for the past three years. Not only was I a division head, but I was the one who developed and taught a course in advanced search techniques."

"So, you're familiar with looking under rocks for the scum of the earth," said Linc still trying to absorb all the new information about this woman.

"Yes," said Emily, confidently. "And I have a lot of experience dealing with assassins, bombers, terrorists and run of the mill murderers. I'm very good at what I do."

Linc was impressed. "That's quite a résumé," he stated.

"Y'know," said Emily with a big smile and her arms spread wide, "this ain't just fluff you're looking at! Now, are we going to get started, or what?"

Linc could not keep from grinning. As each day passed, he found more and more to appreciate in this woman. Obviously, there were many layers to peel back. One part of him wanted to explore, to find out all he could about her. He had a yearning to embrace her and try to recapture feelings he had not thought about for a long time. Another part of his psyche put on the brakes. Knowing that he needed to be cautious, he couldn't take the chance of allowing himself to replay a disaster. He wanted no more of the pain that came from exposing his raw emotions.

Linc just looked at Emily for several moments and slowly began nodding his head. "Okay," he said. "Now I get it. This is what you were referring to last Saturday when we had lunch, isn't it?"

Emily sat silently.

"You want to be a detective, like Magnum, P.I., don't you?"

Emily just stared into Linc's eyes.

Linc continued to dissect her motivation. "Preston told you all about what I did for a living, and you figured that once you got back to the good old U. S. of A., you would just turn on your charm and become a part of it."

A slight smile came to the corners of Emily's lips.

"All this time," Linc said raising one eyebrow, "you've known the ins and outs of police work and procedure, and you were just looking to become a part of something. Am I right?"

"Daddy told me more than just what you do for a living," said Emily. "He told me about the kind of man you are, the pride you take in your work and the confidence he has in your ability. He has total trust in you. If you decided to work closely with someone, wouldn't you want that someone to have those same attributes?"

Although Linc felt a flush of pride, he decided to tweak her sensibilities. "Well, that certainly explains why you want to work with me. I appreciate that vote of confidence, but what makes you think I'm going to want to work with you?"

Emily never missed a beat. "First of all, I'm the best there is at what I do. Your agency will definitely benefit from my talents." She leaned over close to Linc and said in a sultry voice, "And besides, I'm an international spy. Doesn't that make me alluring and hard to resist?"

They stared into one another's eyes, each hoping for the momentum of this conversation to lead to a touch or a kiss. "Okay," said Linc, breaking the spell, "let's give it a try. We'll go over to my office and I'll introduce you to Carmen. There's an empty office. You can have that one. You'll have your own computer and Internet access."

Emily stood up, slightly disappointed in Linc's lack of an emotional response, but still excited at the prospect of working with him. She saw a slight frown appear on his face. "What's the matter Linc? What is it?"

"I'm still going to have to bring Eddie into this," he sighed. "After all, he has access to some things that are going to be vital."

"Such as?" asked Emily

"Such as forensics, finger prints, eyewitness reports and the crime lab technicians."

"I understand," said Emily. "I think it's a good plan of attack."

Emily then decided to wait in silence. She had spoken her mind and made her statements. Now, it was up to Linc to actually make a final decision.

There was a long moment of silence as Linc just stared at Emily. He was mulling over the ramifications of what he was about to say. "Come on," he blurted while standing up. "Let's go catch us a bad guy!"

CHAPTER THIRTY FOUR

There was no question that Emily had a complete understanding of computers as well as a unique ability to wander around the Internet. Linc watched over her shoulder as she accessed files into the FBI and Interpol. Without any hesitation or reference to any written notes, she delved into sub-routines that required additional passwords.

Linc was astonished at some of the proprietary items that appeared on her screen. "How did you get into that file?" Linc asked.

"You mean, this little old Top Secret thing?" replied Emily, coyly.

"Yeah," said Linc still fascinated and leaning in for a closer look.

"You have to remember, Linc, I've only been in the States for less than a week. My head is jammed full of all kinds of secret passwords, access codes and account numbers." Glancing over her shoulder and smiling, Emily added, "You ain't seen nothin' yet!"

Watching her work, Linc had a growing suspicion that she might be worth her weight in gold.

Linc and Emily had arrived at the office less than an hour before. The introduction of Emily to Carmen went exceedingly well, and the two women seemed to develop an immediate rapport. Knowing that Linc contemplated the hiring of another operative, Carmen had been worried that it would end up being some frumpy, old, demanding ex-cop. She was concerned about whether she would be able to get along with someone like that and, if not, how it was going to affect her job. Carmen loved her job and thought the world of Linc.

After learning that Emily would be working at the agency, Carmen was delighted. Emily appeared to be the exact opposite of Carmen's worst fears. She jumped up from her desk, hugged Emily and said excitedly, *"Con mucho gusto!"*

To Carmen's surprise, Emily replied in Spanish, and the two of them chattered for several minutes in Carmen's native tongue. Carmen was ecstatic.

Linc had given Emily a heads-up on what to expect upon meeting Carmen. Having been filled in on Carmen's work ethic and personality, Emily had been anxious to meet her. What Emily found was a warm hearted woman who was refreshingly sincere. During their little chat in Spanish, Carmen had said that she would do whatever she could to make Emily's job easier. The comment made Emily think about all the dreadful office politics that can be so distracting, even in small offices. However, on the contrary, Emily felt that this work environment would be perfect.

After the introductions, Linc had shown Emily the office that she would be using. It was fairly large and had a big window that faced north. If a person stood at the right side of the window and pressed their forehead against the glass, they could get a glimpse of the intercoastal waterway. Emily was pleased with the physical layout. She watched as Carmen ran around made certain there was enough paper in the copier and in the bubble jet printer. Emptying out a few drawers, Carmen prepared a file cabinet. She set out a stapler, paper clips, desk calendar and a dozen other things before Linc finally told her to stop and go back to work. Linc and Emily laughed as Carmen went back to her desk singing, "Happy days are here again . . ."

Linc continued to watch as Emily did her thing on the computer. She was setting up the system to allow her easier access in the future. Occasionally, Linc interrupted with a question. Emily answered most of them directly, but declined to answer others stating, "Sorry, Linc. That would be a breach of my security clearance."

Linc understood. He would have enjoyed spending the afternoon watching her, but he needed to get his own work done. After about a half-hour, he excused himself and went into his own office to tackle the growing pile of paperwork. Sitting at his desk, Linc realized that he was very pleased with the way Emily and Carmen got along. After thinking about the possibility of having Emily become a permanent fixture in his agency, Linc decided to take a wait-and-see attitude. He wanted to see some actual results and thought that waiting an extra week would be prudent.

Carmen put in a call to Eddie Strickland at Linc's request. He planned on filling Eddie in on this new information regarding Pitch and his invention. Linc had some serious misgivings about doing so, but he felt that Eddie's investigation was not going to produce any concrete results without it.

It was late morning when Eddie returned Linc's call. "What's up, jocko?" inquired Eddie.

Linc said, "We need to talk, Eddie. Got any time today?"

"Sure. Meet me here at the station house after lunch."

"How about we grab a cup of coffee somewhere . . . private?" Linc countered.

"Okay," said Eddie, picking up on the urgency. "The coffee shop in the lobby of the Hilton. Two o'clock."

"See you there at two," said Linc.

Emily, Carmen and Linc remained busy for the next hour at their individual desks. Carmen had presented Linc with a stack of letters and papers that he needed to read, initial or sign. Although incoming phone calls were considerable, Carmen was able to handle the majority of them. Linc only needed to speak twice with clients.

The approaching noon hour spurred Carmen to holler out, "Hello, you two! *Que pasa?* It's almost lunchtime. Are we going out to celebrate?"

Emily came out of her office and walked into the reception area. Standing at a spot near Carmen's desk that offered a view into Linc's office, she said, "I'm in the middle of downloading some files, and I need to be here when they're completed. Why don't you folks go to lunch, and I'll join the two of you some other time?"

Before Linc could respond, Carmen said pleadingly, "Please, Miss Emily. Don't force me to go to lunch with Mr. Linc alone. He always makes me eat asparagus and rutabagas and then makes me pay the check."

Emily giggled.

Linc tried to ignore Carmen's humor. "I've got a two o'clock over at the Hilton with Eddie Strickland," he said. "I plan to just have a sandwich or something here in the office."

"Sounds good to me," said Emily.

Carmen offered a suggestion. "How about I run across the bridge to 'George Carballo's restaurant for some Cuban sandwiches? He makes the best."

Linc and Emily agreed. Carmen took their orders and called them in to the sandwich shop. She left moments later to pick them up.

Linc and Emily worked independently for the next quarter hour. While Emily waited for more of her files to download, she wandered into Linc's office. Linc began filling her in on his upcoming meeting with Eddie. He told Emily about some of his private thoughts, specifically his uncertainty in telling Eddie about Pitch's invention.

"Are you having second thoughts about trusting him?" asked Emily.

"No," said Linc. "It's not a matter of trust. I trust him completely. Eddie's proven himself to be a good friend."

"Then, what is it?" asked Emily, taking a seat in a comfortable chair facing the desk.

"Two things," said Linc. "First of all, it's that damn bug. I don't think Pitch has fully realized it yet, but he's opened up Pandora's Box with that gizmo. Jennifer has a better understanding of the seriousness of the situation than he does. The more I think about it, the more I realize just how insidious a device it is."

"Wasn't it you who told me that listening devices are commonplace?" queried Emily.

"Yeah," said Linc nodding his head. "They are commonplace. Did you know that 'John Q. Consumer' can actually get a catalog of these devices, place an order through the mail, and get any number of them without restrictions?"

"No," said Emily, slowly becoming aware of the public danger. "I didn't know that."

Linc continued. "Thanks to the Internet, it's a piece of cake. But there's a major difference. When you go out and buy one of those mail order bugs, you still need to place it somewhere. Y'know, actually install it or hide it. It takes a certain amount of guts or moxie to sneak into someone's house or office and hide one of those things. The bug-man always runs the risk of getting caught, and that in itself is a major deterrent."

"But with Pitch's invention . . ." Emily started to say.

"But with his invention," said Linc nodding his head as he picked up her words, "the risk is gone. Whoever holds that damn disc is home free. No sneaking around, no midnight break-ins, no disguises, nothing. No risk. Anyone can do it. And you know what the biggest problem is?"

"Tell me," said Emily.

"This particular device just doesn't bug telephone conversations. Remember, this thing is activating a microphone inside a room. And there are telephones everywhere. Hundreds of millions of telephones. That means hundreds of millions of microphones! How many people do you know who have a telephone in every room of their house?"

"Oh," exclaimed Emily wide-eyed. "Oh, my. I'm beginning to understand, Linc," she said with a worried look. "It's almost like having someone hiding inside your house. Or should I say, inside your head."

"Exactly," said Linc.

"Privacy vanishes," mused Emily.

"Well, the point I'm making is that the fewer people who know about this thing, the better off we're all going to be. That's one reason I'm not so anxious to tell Eddie."

"And the second?" asked Emily raising her eyebrows.

"Damage control," stated Linc emphatically.

"What do you mean?"

"Once I've told Eddie," said Linc, making a helpless gesture with his hands, "there's no way for me to control what he says. I'm sure he won't volunteer that information to anybody, but what if he loses control of the situation? What if the investigation demands that he divulge the existence of the bug? Or the existence of the floppy disc that contains its secrets? Or how about when the time comes that he has to re-question Pitch, and the session becomes open to the other cops?"

"Does that have to happen?" asked Emily. "Won't Eddie have a way around it? You know, a way of protecting you and Pitch?"

"Not if the bug or the disc becomes the motive," said Linc. "Here's how it works. The police have a murder on their hands. Their priority is solving it. One of the main things they look for is motive. That's one of the keys that very often lead to the identification of the killer. Once Eddie knows that the disc, for instance, might be the motive, he'll have no choice but to divulge it in order to catch the killer. And for sure, Laura Parsons, or someone else in the D.A.'s office will have to present that information as evidence in order to prosecute the murderer."

Suddenly remembering that her computer was downloading classified material, Emily jumped off her chair and rushed into her office. Linc followed. Satisfied that she wasn't logged off, Emily asked, "So, what do you intend to do? I mean, about Eddie?"

Linc was standing next to her swivel chair as he said, "I'm just going to play it by ear. I need to see where Eddie is in the investigation, how far along he's come and what direction he plans to take." Linc turned his attention to something out her window. "Whether I tell him or not is just going to depend on a gut feeling."

Emily finished and spun her chair to face Linc. As she stood up, Linc, still staring out her window, neither stepped back nor gave her space. As a result, they were now standing near one another. Because they were in such close proximity, Emily had to tilt her neck to look into Linc's eyes. "I'm sure you'll do the right thing," she said softly.

Linc felt her hand slip into his, and he took a half step closer. It was at that moment they both heard Carmen approaching the outer door to the office and singing a line from the song 'Cabaret', " . . . Come pour the wine . . ."

Lunch included some good-natured, three-way banter. Emily enjoyed Carmen's sharp sense of humor, as she talked about her daughters and the upcoming birth of her first grandchild. When Emily asked if Carmen was planning on having any of her relatives from Cuba come to the festivities, she launched into a diatribe on Fidel Castro and the mess he had made of her homeland.

"Emily," Linc said with a mouthful of sandwich, "you just tapped into one of Carmen's hot buttons. Shell go on and on for hours."

"It's just that Castro, that pompous ass," ranted Carmen, "has made it almost impossible for me to see my family. Cuba is so close to Florida, but yet it might as well be on the other side of the world. Our government needs to send a castration-squad on a midnight run to Castro's villa . . ."

Linc and Emily's laughter drowned out the rest of Carmen's suggestion.

At one forty-five, Linc got ready to leave for his appointment with Eddie. "Emily," he said as he stood up and brushed some of the lunchtime crumbs from his slacks, "this shouldn't take too long. I'll see you in a little while."

"Now, don't you forget about me," said Emily with a smile. "Remember, it was you who drove me here, and I'm relying on you to take me home."

Linc opened the door to exit the office and hesitated. He turned to Emily and said, "I couldn't possibly forget about you." Then, he left.

Linc walked into the coffee shop and spotted Eddie sitting at a table by the window. Eddie looked up as Linc approached and said, "Well, Bradshaw, I got good news and bad news. Which do you want first?"

"Okay," said Linc, easing himself into one of the cushioned rattan chairs surrounding the table. "I'll play your silly game. Give me the bad news first. Let's get that out of the way."

"The bad news is . . ." said Eddie, pausing for effect, "you're ugly and no amount of surgery will ever make it right."

Linc smiled. "And the good news?"

"Jimmy and I solved the Aarons' case. We have the killer in custody."

Linc gawked at Eddie in disbelief. With his mind racing, Linc asked for details. Eddie told him the whole story, admitting to the fact that it was his partner, Jimmy Dalton, who actually made the bust. Eddie told Linc about the various leads that came in attesting to the threats that Henry Drummond had made on Scott Aarons' life. Eddie spoke about the argument that took place at *Taboos* nightclub the night of the murder and that there were several witnesses to the fact.

Eddie also mentioned finding the duct tape and the fishing line in Drummond's house. Finally, Eddie talked about the arrest and how Dalton was able to uncover and confiscate the murder weapon.

Linc had been listening intently, waiting for Eddie to finish. "Henry Drummond, huh?" asked Linc. He remembered the man's name from a couple of snippets of the conversation with Sidney Aarons. Sidney had said that he hated Drummond even though he was a good reporter. Linc shared a gossip line. "Y'know," he said, "there was no love loss between Drummond and Sidney Aarons to begin with."

"That's what Jimmy told me," said Eddie. "But, what do you know about it?"

Careful not to divulge too much, Linc explained. "Sidney hired me to do some investigative work. He told me that he suspected Drummond of doing some very underhanded things. Really unethical. Sidney wouldn't have put anything past him."

"Yeah, I know," said Eddie. "Getting a salary from the 'Ledger' and selling your stories to the tabloids. Jimmy questioned old man Aarons and found out all about that." Eddie leaned back in his chair, draping his arm over the chair next to him. "Is that what you wanted to talk to me about?" he asked.

"Kinda," Linc lied.

"Linc," said Eddie with a brotherly tone. "I've known you too long. You've got something else on your mind. What's up?"

Linc had met Eddie with the possible intention of telling him about Pitch's listening device. Now that Eddie thought he had the killer behind bars, Linc no longer felt a need to tell Eddie about the bug. On the other hand, Linc had a gut feeling that Drummond was not the murderer. After listening to a description of the murder scene, Linc surmised that it had to have been committed by someone who did that sort of thing on a full time basis. This was not "Amateur Night in Homicide Heaven.

Linc said, "Well, now you know I'm working for the Aarons' family. I told Sidney I would keep him posted on the progress of your investigation. After all, Scott was his only child. I want you to keep feeding me anything new regarding this case. Anything that comes up."

Eddie narrowed his eyes. "Sure, Linc. No problem. There's nothing special about this case that I can't let you in on. But, remember this works both ways, right? If you had pertinent information, you'd tell me. Right?"

"You'd almost be the first to know," said Linc.

"So, talk to me," said Eddie. "There's something else bothering you. What is it?"

Linc just stared blankly. He had to give Eddie something to satisfy his curiosity. After all, it was Linc, implying a sense of urgency, who called for this meeting. Eddie would have been expecting something important.

"Well, frankly," said Linc with his head down, "it has to do with Emily."

Eddie leaned forward, putting both elbows on the table and said, "Yeah, go on."

"Remember," said Linc, "you told me about the time you were 'doing' your sister-in-law, your wife's sister?"

"Yeah," said Eddie stretching out the word.

Linc cleared this throat. "Well, y'know the kind of relationship I have with Preston. He's kind of like my father."

Linc paused.

As Eddie sat staring, his eyes became squinty and his eyebrows knitted into a single line of thatch. He finally spoke. "And that would make Emily . . . what? Kinda like your sister? Is that what your saying?"

"Right," said Linc straight faced. "I need your advice."

Eddie gave his advice. He started off by calling Linc " . . . the stupidest son of a bitch I ever met," and then lambasted him further " . . . for even making such an idiotic comparison." He called Linc " . . . a dumb-ass fool for thinking of Emily as a sister," and, finally, after a thorough tongue lashing, began giving Linc some serious advice.

Linc sat quietly and listened with half an ear. He had succeeded in diverting Eddie's attention from the original agenda and allowed him to go on and on. And on and on he went. Eddie had a load of advice to offer, and all of it with good intentions.

Linc looked at his watch and remembered that Carmen had to

leave early that day. He did not want to leave Emily alone in the office. Thanking Eddie for his good counsel, Linc reminded him to forward any new information regarding the Aarons murder case. They shook hands and parted.

Pulling into his parking garage, Linc glanced at his watch. Thinking that he probably arrived just as Carmen would be leaving, Linc planned on wrapping things up and taking Emily home. He remembered the fleeting moment of intimacy that had passed between them earlier that afternoon and was planning to ask her out for dinner that evening.

Linc came through the entrance door to find Emily sitting in Carmen's swivel chair behind the reception desk. "Hi, Emily. Where's Carmen?"

"She had to leave," said Emily. "I would have thought you passed her in the hall or something. She just left, not more than a couple of minutes ago."

"Sorry I'm so late," said Linc. "Eddie was in one of his rambling moods. Are you ready to get out of here?"

As Emily pushed herself away from the desk, the swivel post under her seat tilted precariously. She uttered a little gasp, as Linc moved toward her swiftly. Making sure that she would not tilt any further, he grabbed her upper arm and pulled her out of the chair. His motion was smooth and strong, and his action, coupled with her momentum, propelled her into him. They stood like that, face to face, almost touching for a moment, and he felt her eyes boring into his. He was conscious of her hands touching his arms and moving up toward his neck. He released the grip on her arm and moved his hands to her waist.

Emily was captured by this moment. She was feeling her heart race and pound in her chest. Her temples were throbbing as she put both hands around his neck and pulled herself closer. Emily felt him responding. She sighed at the feel of his hand going to the small of her back and pulling her toward him. Their lips met in a gentle kiss, parted and met again, this time for a moment longer. When they kissed for the third time, a deep passion engulfed them. Their eyes were closed, and they were lost in time and space until the office door burst open, and Carmen stopped in her tracks and uttered an embarrassed cry.

Linc and Emily were speechless.

Carmen spoke haltingly. "I suppose it would be politically incorrect for me to sing a song right about now . . ."

Linc smiled wanly and Emily brushed absently at her black and white jumper.

Carmen moved towards her desk. "I forgot to bring the rest of my sandwich home," she said apologetically. "If I'd left it in my desk, the place would stink to high heaven by the morning."

"It's all right, Carmen," said Linc, all the while looking directly at Emily. "Go ahead and get your sandwich."

Carmen opened the drawer and removed the half sandwich.

Linc started, "Emily . . . I . . ."

Emily averted her eyes. She was clearly embarrassed. "Linc," she said turning towards Carmen's desk to retrieve her purse, "if you would be so kind as to drive me home now, I would greatly appreciate it."

CHAPTER
THIRTY FIVE

I t was seven a.m. on the morning of the day of Scott's funeral. Linc was in the process of perspiring profusely, while running on an inclined treadmill. Nearing the fifty-five minute mark of his one-hour goal, his thought pattern was disrupted when his cell phone vibrated against his waistband. He checked it without breaking stride. Preston's telephone number appeared on the little display window. Even though Linc wished it was Emily calling, he knew, after yesterday's embarrassing episode, that there was a possibility that she would never talk to him again.

Chauffeuring Emily back home yesterday afternoon was an uncomfortable situation marked by very few words. Long intervals of silence dominated the trip. Carmen's sudden appearance during the kiss was an obvious embarrassment to Emily. Linc was at a loss as to how best to break through her humiliation. He decided it would be best not to ask her out for dinner. Instead, he chose to drop her off, drive home and take a cool shower.

Linc was finishing his run when Ron Scofield, the proprietor of the establishment, came into the gym. He stopped by the treadmill, and the two men gabbed briefly.

"Okay if I use your office to make a call?" asked Linc.

Ron seemingly changed the subject. "I'm going to be increasing your annual dues, Lincoln," he said.

"Really? Why's that?"

"I've got to start charging you for the use of my office and for the sweat you're dripping on my floor in here."

Smiling at the droll humor, Linc shut down the treadmill and followed Ron into his office. Unhooking his cell phone, Linc asked, "Ron, have you ever been caught in an awkward situation? I mean, with a woman?"

Ron put down the piece of paper he was holding, as a look of surprise came over his face. He had never heard this type of question from his friend. "Lincoln," said Ron leaning back in his chair and interlacing his fingers behind his head, "each of us has been caught with our hand in the cookie jar at one time or another. You get bummed by a bad scene?"

"Yeah," lamented Linc. "Yesterday afternoon. It was pretty embarrassing, but it really upset my . . . girlfriend. Ever have something like that happen to you?"

"Well, I don't usually talk about this sort of thing," said Ron, trying to sound a little put off by Linc's intrusive question, "but seeing as we been friends for so long, let me tell you what happened about three weeks ago."

Linc nodded and put his elbow on the desk.

"You remember my woman, Leticia?" asked Ron.

"Sure," said Linc. "Pretty face. Long fingernails. I've met her."

"Well, I was closing the place up that night and Leticia, she come bargin' in to this very office and ended up catching Wanda cleanin' my pipes. You know what I mean?"

"Wanda?" asked Linc, a smile beginning to form on his lips. "Who's Wanda?"

"She's one of the pretty little 'boo-jum' that come in here to work up a sweat," explained Ron. "All gussied and tight and always wearing one of them thongs and shit."

"So what happened with you and Wanda?" asked Linc. "I mean, how did she react the next day? Did she stop coming here, or what?"

"What you talking about, 'stop comin' here?'" exclaimed Ron, puzzled by Linc's question. "There wasn't no problem with me and Wanda."

"No problem?" asked Linc.

Ron grunted a sound of exasperation. "You ain't getting' this Bradshaw," he answered. "Of course there wasn't no problem with Wanda. Think about it Lincoln. Wanda was the 'catchee.'"

Linc had a puzzled frown on his face.

Ron continued. "There ain't never a problem with the 'catchee.' Now, Leticia . . . she was the 'catch-er.' There's always a problem with the 'catch-er.' Leticia got so pissed at catching Wanda on her knees and under my desk, and me with a big-assed smile on my face . . . , hell, she just split."

"And that was it," stated Linc, awed at the simplicity of Ron's philosophy. "She just split?"

"Well," added Ron with a dour look, "I mean, she said a few choice words and threw some shit, and then she split. But the bottom line is, Leticia is outta my life."

Linc just shook his head in disbelief.

"Now," Ron continued, "what you got to ask yourself is . . . who do you want to be with: the catchee or the catch-er?"

"Definitely, the catchee," said Linc as he picked up the cell phone and dialed Preston's number.

Louise answered. "Collingsworth residence."

"Good morning, Louise," said Linc.

"Good morning, Mr. Bradshaw," offered Louise, recognizing Linc's voice. "If you will just hold on a moment, I'll tell Emily you've returned her phone call."

Linc held the receiver to his ear, waiting for Emily to come to the phone. He looked at Ron and smiled a toothy grin. Vigorously nodding his head, Linc gave Ron a thumbs-up letting him know that his "catchee/catch-er" philosophy was right on the money.

"Good morning, Lincoln," said Emily, brightly. "I'm glad you got an early start and returned my call so promptly. How are you?"

"I'm fine, Emily," said Linc, pleased to hear a lilt in her voice. "I'm happy to hear from you."

"Daddy needs your help with some things this morning," said Emily, "and when he told me he was going to call you, I asked to place the call instead."

"I'm glad," said Linc trying to suppress a grin.

Emily never mentioned the incident in the office. Instead, she went on to tell Linc about Preston's favor. It dealt with the last minute funeral arrangements for Scott. Emily said she intended to go back to the office for a couple of hours this morning and get some "real work" done. Now that she had certain prerequisite files downloaded, she felt she could start making headway with her search. "Would you please do me a favor and call Eddie Strickland," she asked. "Could you have him fax me a copy of his report on the murder? Oh, and make sure he includes any fingerprint and DNA analysis."

"I didn't have a chance to tell you this," said Linc, "but, Eddie told me yesterday that they caught the killer."

"Really?" asked Emily incredulously. "That was fast."

Linc went on and explained the details of the arrest.

After learning that the suspect was Henry Drummond, a reporter for Sidney Aarons' newspaper, Emily said, "That'll never hold up, Linc. Within the week, Eddie will be back on the street looking for the real killer. So in the meantime, would you have Eddie get me the information?"

Linc agreed with Emily's assessment and said he would arrange it. Then added, "When do I get to see you?"

"I'm only going to be at the office until around eleven," said Emily. "Then, I must get back here to the house. I promised Daddy I would help him with some of the last minute details. And of course, I have to change into something more appropriate."

"All right," said Linc. "I'm looking forward to seeing you."

"Linc," asked Emily after a momentary pause, "would you do me a special favor, and ride with Daddy and me to the funeral? I would like it if you were near me."

The way Emily phrased the question put a surprised look on Linc's face as he mouthed a silent "wow." "Of course," he said.

Chatting a while longer, Emily spoke proudly of how the entire staff at the Collingsworth household was being so cooperative and sympathetic with the advent of the funeral. Speaking of Pitch and Jennifer, Emily mentioned how their emotions were keeping them on a roller coaster. She filled Lincoln in on everyone's plan to attend Crystal's funeral on Friday.

After telling Linc about the successful procurement of a safe deposit box for Pitch's disc, she added, "One thing that's helping to keep Pitch on an even keel is that Daddy has taken an acute interest in everything Pitch has to say. They stay huddled for hours and Daddy seems to start every conversation with, 'You know what Pitch told me . . . ' I'm glad they're keeping each other occupied."

"One thing I've always appreciated about Preston," said Linc, "is his amazing appetite for learning anything new."

"I know," said Emily. "Have you ever been with him when he stops complete strangers and begins picking their brains?"

"Are you kidding?" said Linc, eager to tell his tale. "One time, there was this hooker in Miami, and your Dad . . ."

"What!" exclaimed Emily.

"Well," said Linc with a chuckle, "he just wanted to learn about everything she did. How much she charged, what she did for the money, y'know, how she ran her business. I never saw a hooker try to get away from a man before. It was really rather comical."

Emily paused before saying, "I'm looking forward to seeing you later, Linc. I miss you."

*　　*　　*

Carmen was very happy to see Emily arrive at the office. After offering some exuberant good morning wishes, Carmen said, "I am so sorry, Miss Emily, for bursting into the office last night. When I came through the door, I was about to say, 'I hope I am not interrupting anything,' but it was quite obvious that I certainly was interrupting something."

Emily replied with a sincere smile, "Carmen, you don't have to apologize."

"If someone were kissing me like that," said Carmen dreamily, "I would be thinking of giving him the key to my heart."

Emily nodded at the thought and appreciated Carmen's depth of understanding.

Carmen continued, " . . . and the key to my chastity belt!"

Emily burst into laughter and Carmen joined in, happy that there was someone who appreciated her sense of humor.

Shortly after the two women started working, Carmen received Eddie Strickland's fax detailing the investigation into the Aarons murder. Carmen brought the documents into Emily's office. Carmen loved the idea of having someone else in the office with her. Linc spent so much of his time out of the office doing fieldwork that sometimes it got a little lonely. With Emily now being a part of the team, Carmen would have someone with whom to gab. She was happy that the decision was made to bring Emily on board.

However, there was one small detail that was bothering Carmen. Linc had not yet asked her to fill out all the necessary paperwork to get Emily's actual employment started. There was a load of forms that needed to be processed: name, address telephone and social security numbers, withholding information, health insurance forms, just to name a few. The next time she saw Linc, Carmen decided to remind him that all that needed to get done to facilitate Emily's employment.

Emily took the report from Carmen and began to look it over. She spotted the two areas on the report that were labeled "Fingerprints" and "DNA." The fingerprint section contained results showing the prints of Pitch, Jennifer, Scott and Crystal, but no information about a possible suspect. The section labeled DNA was blank. Emily assumed that the laboratory technicians had not yet had time to compile those results. The report did contain the initial ballistics study, and it identified the murder weapon as a nine-millimeter pistol that was fired through a silencer. The other part that she found interesting was that Crystal had been choked with fishing line to the point of piercing her windpipe.

Armed with that information, Emily logged into Interpol's files and requested a list of known assassins who used a nine-millimeter and had an M.O. that included a garrote.

Waiting for some response to her search request, Emily glanced around her new office. Her eyes came to rest on the printer that sat next to the computer. It was an ink-jet type that gave an excellent copy, but was far too slow for the kind of file she hoped to build.

She walked out to where Carmen was sitting. "Carmen, I'm going to need a laser printer like yours. Do you have an extra one?"

"No, Miss Emily," said Carmen with a wry expression on her face. "Mr. Lincoln was too cheap to get one when he bought the computer in your office. I told him, but, nooo. He said, 'Why should we spend the money for a second laser printer?' And here you are, asking for exactly that."

"Well," stated Emily, "if you speak to him before I do, tell him I'm going out to buy one, and I expect to be reimbursed."

Carmen pumped her fist and said defiantly, "You go, *muchacha*!"

Emily got ready to go to *Office Depot* for her printer purchase. Carmen asked if Emily would please pick up a short list of office supplies while she was there. Shortly after Emily left, Carmen prepared to attack the files that had piled up over the last three days. Just as she pulled her chair over to the filing cabinet, the phone rang. It was Linc. They exchanged the usual pleasantries after which Linc said that he was going to be tied up all morning helping Preston with a few pre-funeral details. Linc added that he would not be coming into the office. He asked her to do a couple of things that he had intended to do himself.

After making sure she understood what had to be done, Linc said, "Carmen, I'm awfully sorry about yesterday. I didn't mean to embarrass you like that."

"You didn't embarrass me, Mr. Linc," said Carmen with a touch of mischief in her voice. "It wasn't me who was about to indulge in the vertical mambo!"

"Cute, Carmen," said Linc. "How's Emily doing this morning?"

"She is singing like a yellow bird," said Carmen. "Oh, by the way, Mr. Linc, Emily has gone out to buy another laser printer. Her printer is too slow for what she has to do. It's going to cost about six hundred dollars. Are you prepared for that?"

Linc did not relish the thought of spending that kind of money on another laser printer. He knew there was a way to get each of the computer terminals in the office tied into the one laser printer that sat near Carmen's desk. "Carmen, why can't we all just use your laser printer?" he asked.

"Because I'm always using mine," said Carmen with a hint of exasperation. "And besides, Emily has much to print. That poor girl will definitely be needing her own."

Carmen listened while Linc took a deep breath and said, "Okay, Carmen. See to it that she has anything she wants."

Those were the words Carmen was waiting for. It meant that Emily was officially a part of the Bradshaw Agency. Carmen knew that having "anything she wants," meant no more secrets. Now, their conversations could include work as well as personal topics. Carmen would be able to share with Emily the details of all the cases the agency investigated. Even thought she was an incurable gossip, Carmen's loyalty to Linc, along with her unwavering work ethic, prevented her from talking about the intimate nature of the business. This long-suffering silence had been extremely frustrating, but now it was over. She would be able to talk freely with Emily about some amazingly titillating things to which she was privy. Carmen assumed that Emily, like most women, would be excited and intrigued by scandalous news and looked forward to the chance of bringing it up.

Emily returned within the hour, holding a small bag filled with the office supplies that Carmen had requested. "Okay," said Emily rubbing her hands together, "The printer will be delivered tomorrow. Now, all I have to worry about is getting paid back."

"Don't you worry, Miss Emily," said Carmen knowingly. "I spoke to Mr. Linc and he said, not only can you have the printer, but that you can also have access to anything you want."

"Really?" asked Emily, pleased to know that there would not be a conflict.

"His exact words," said Carmen, "were, 'anything she wants.'"

Emily went into her office to see if any results had been forwarded to her from Interpol. She checked her coded e-mail to find a response from Gunnar Hansen, a Colonel who headed a division in one of NATO's Intelligence units.

Emily had spent three years stationed in Germany. It was a NATO base located on the western border in a small town called Geilenkirchen. Emily and Colonel Hansen had worked closely for the past several years and had come to respect and admire one another.

Gunnar Hansen was a Swedish national who had been with NATO his entire career. Colonel Hansen had an assistant, a young woman by the name of Ilisa Kleiner. Holding the rank of Major in the NATO military, Ilisa hailed from Belgium, which was less than fifteen kilometers away. She was blessed with an unbelievable capacity for remembering facts. Remarkably detail oriented, Ilisa could rattle off names, dates and tens of thousands of unrelated bits of data at the drop of a hat.

As Emily checked her computer screen, she saw an additional e-mail from Major Kleiner that read, "Hello. Wish I was there. IK."

Emily smiled at the fond memories of Ilisa Kleiner and began to read the response from Colonel Hansen. He wrote that he had received Emily's request and would do his best to accommodate it, although the process would take a little extra time due to some back ups on the server.

Returning to the reception area, Emily said, "Well, I'm on hold for right now. Anything I can do to help you?"

"I'm just getting rid of this little bit of filing," said Carmen. "I was going to set fire to it, but Mr. Linc prefers that I put it in the file cabinet."

"Here, let me help you," offered Emily.

Carmen took a step backward to allow Emily room to get to the pile. Reaching for the top group of papers, Emily saw the name "Sidney Aarons" typed boldly across the heading.

"Sidney Aarons," said Emily with a hint of curiosity. "I was just talking with Linc last Saturday about Sidney being an active account here at the agency."

"Oh, yes," said Carmen. "An ongoing investigation. Did Mr. Linc tell you about his girlfriend?"

Emily became momentarily confused. "Linc has a girlfriend?"

"No, silly," said Carmen as she shuffled down into the stack of papers and pulled out a big glossy of Elana Velez. "Sidney Aarons' girlfriend," she said, as she handed the photograph to Emily.

Emily was stunned. She stared at the picture of Elana Velez. The woman was modeling seductive lingerie that looked like something out of "Fredericks of Hollywood."

Emily waved the photo in the air. "This is Sidney Aarons' girlfriend?" she asked skeptically.

"Yes. Can you believe it?" said Carmen excitedly, as she opened the file drawer and took out a fat manila envelope. "Wait. Take a look at this video. You won't believe your eyes!"

Carmen led Emily into Linc's office and slipped the video into the VCR. Without any fanfare or prelude, the video began immediately with a scene showing Sidney and Elana in a partial state of undress, uncorking a bottle of champagne. Obviously playing to the camera, the two of them were laughing and fondling each other. The cameraman followed them to a bedroom where the couple collapsed onto an unmade bed and the erotic lovemaking began in earnest.

Emily was glued to the TV monitor. The sex scene unfolding in front of her was mesmerizing. She was having trouble digesting the fact that it was Sidney Aarons who was starring in this production. After all, this was a man she had known all her life, or at least thought she knew. This man was one of her father's best friends.

"Stop the video!" blurted Emily. "Carmen, stop the video!"

Carmen had the remote in her hand. She clicked the stop button and said, "What is it? What's wrong?"

Emily's mind was racing. She could not quite fathom what was going on. What else was going to shock her? She had a terrible premonition of her father suddenly appearing on screen. Was it possible that her father was a part of this debauchery? Emily could not stand the thought of seeing her own father in a production of this sort. Trying to catch her breath and regain her emotional balance, Emily realized she had been watching an incredibly disgraceful X-rated movie starring someone she knew. And what about Lenore, thought Emily? Where was Lenore during this libidinous fiasco?

Emily turned her back to the TV and asked Carmen, "Does anybody else show up in this movie? Or is it just the two of them doing . . . this thing?"

"It's just the two of them, Miss Emily," said Carmen, concerned and noticing that Emily was visibly shaken. "The girl is blackmailing Sidney Aarons for some pretty big bucks, and it's our job to put a stop to it."

Emily tried to gather her wits about her. In just a few hours, she would be attending the funeral of Scott Aarons, the son of the man in the video. Emily wondered how she was going to find the wherewithal to handle the situation. How could she approach Sidney, hug him and offer her sympathies? Slowly shaking her head, Emily realized she would never again look at Sidney in quite the same way.

Taking a ragged breath, Emily calmed her frazzled nerves. She straightened up and said, "What did you say her name was?"

"She uses the name, Elana Velez," replied Carmen, "but we haven't been able to come up with any information about her. She's obviously using an alias. Of course, with a body like that, who could possibly forget her?"

Still holding the eight-and-a-half by eleven glossy, Emily sat down to rest her trembling knees. She studied the photograph.

Carmen started to rewind the video, disappointed that Emily was not more intrigued by the erotic scandal that had been presented.

Looking at the photo, Emily experienced a vague feeling and suddenly said, "Carmen, could you run that video again, please?"

Carmen smiled broadly and re-inserted the tape. She hit the play button, all the while singing a verse from the tune, "Hernando's Hideaway".

Emily watched intently as the opening scene again showed Sidney and Elana drinking the champagne. At one point, Elana dipped her middle finger into the glass of champagne and sensuously sucked it. As soon as she completed the erotic gesture, Emily said, "Carmen, rewind that. Let me see that again."

The two women watched as Elana repeated the gesture.

"Carmen," asked Emily, with curiosity and concern, "what do you and Linc actually know about this woman?"

"Only what Mr. Sidney Aarons has told us," replied Carmen. "And I'm afraid it's not too much." At that moment, the video monitor was showing a visibly excited Sidney Aarons exploring Elana's belly button with his tongue. "As you can see, he showed much more interest in her front-ground, than he did in her background."

Carmen's comment caused Emily a sudden rash of nervous giggling that she had trouble controlling. It took a full minute before Emily was able to ask her next question. "Well, where did he meet her? How long has he known her? What *do* we know?"

Carmen answered as many of Emily's questions as she could. They shut off the video and went back into the reception area where Carmen pointed out the stack of papers that had already accumulated on the Aarons case. Filling Emily in on Elana's employment at the newspaper, Carmen spoke about how that was the start of the affair. Emily learned that Elana was a model specializing in lingerie, and that Sidney conveniently took her with him when he traveled on business. Carmen produced a couple of "tear sheets" that Sidney had sent over. They were entire pages torn from the *Sun Coast Ledger* and each of them contained an advertisement that included a full-length picture of Elana Velez modeling some kind of undergarment.

Carmen watched Emily's face as she studied the newspaper clippings. Then, Carmen said, "You're onto something, aren't you, Miss Emily?"

"It's just a hunch," said Emily. "Too soon to tell."

Emily thanked Carmen for the tear sheets and went into her own office. She listened as Carmen began singing, "This could be the start of something big . . ."

Sitting at her desk, Emily called the D.A.'s office and asked for Laura Parsons. After connecting, the two women chatted about the upcoming funeral. Laura admitted that she was finding the whole thing very upsetting and that she had decided not to attend. She told Emily that she had already made arrangements to send flowers and a personal card. "That's going to have to do," said Laura. "I just can't deal with it any other way."

Emily expressed her understanding, and Laura somehow felt better.

Changing the subject, Emily invited Laura to come over to the Collingsworth estate later that evening. Laura said she was not sure she could make it, but that she would call first to let Emily know.

"Since you're not going to the funeral," said Emily, "I need you to do me a favor."

"Sure," said Laura. "What is it?"

"Go to the offices of the *Sun Coast Ledger* and look up two old newspapers. Got a pencil?"

"Yeah," said Laura. "Fire away."

"One is from last October second, page eight-D," said Emily. "That's the fashion section. The other is from October twenty-first, page five-D, also the fashion section. On each of those pages you will see a photo of a young woman, a model."

"Yeah . . . so?" asked Laura.

"Study the woman closely," said Emily emphasizing each word, "and let me know if she looks familiar."

CHAPTER THIRTY SIX

B lack was the dress code for the afternoon. Black dresses, black suits, black scarves and hats, all arriving in black cars. The mood was lugubrious and somber. Mendosa stood on a small knoll, where he was partially obscured by some low branches of a ficus tree. Even though the foliage protected him from being seen by others, he held an unobstructed view of the funeral procession as it gathered at the graveside of Scott Aarons.

Mendosa was becoming frustrated by the growing size of the gathering. Already, there were hundreds of people who had surrounded the Aarons' family, and more were arriving every minute. Mendosa thought the burgeoning crowd resulted from either the deceased being a very popular individual, or his parents being extremely influential. Regardless of the explanation, the sheer number of people was making his task more difficult. He was intent on spotting the face of Pitch Pechowski somewhere in that multitude of mourners.

After realizing he had murdered the wrong person, Mendosa had gone to the public library and used its computer to contact Parlotti. He had persuaded one of Parlotti's tech-boys to over-night a photo of Pitch Pechowski. Armed with that picture, Mendosa was scanning the faces of every male at the graveside. There would be no mistaken identity this time. He had staked out Pitch's apartment, but doubted that he would return there anytime soon. Reasoning that Pitch would be present at this funeral, Mendosa would be given the perfect opportunity to track Pitch back to wherever he was staying. Mendosa had locked onto the idea that getting the disc was his once-in-a-lifetime opportunity to grab the brass ring and create an incredible cornucopia of cash. He would get the disc that contained the secret to the listening device. Nothing was going to stop him.

*   *   *

Preston had hired a stretch limousine and driver to ferry his daughter and her guests to and from the funeral. The services at the funeral parlor were over, and the massive procession was now heading toward the cemetery. Emily sat in the middle of the rear seat, with Preston on one side and Linc on the other. She had looped her arm through Linc's and was holding on firmly. Facing the three of them, were Pitch and Jennifer who sat in the pullout jump seats. A small refrigerated bar that separated Pitch and Jennifer. Nevertheless, they held hands across its top.

Looking at both Pitch and Jennifer, Linc said, "Listen you two. I want you both to kind of stay in the middle of the crowd. Try and keep close to Preston or myself. Whatever you do, don't go wandering off."

Jennifer had been dabbing a tissue at her tears and asked, "Do you know something you're not telling us?"

"No," said Linc shaking his head. "It's just that things have been unusually quiet for the past couple of days, and that's been making me a little uneasy."

"What have you been expecting?" asked Pitch.

"Nothing specific," said Linc, suddenly aware that Emily had tightened her grip on his arm. "But we have to remember that a couple of your friends have been murdered and probably over that disc of yours. If I'm right, then I can assure you it's not over yet."

Pitch moved the position of his hand allowing him to interlace his fingers with Jennifer's. "Do you think it's dangerous for us to be here?" he asked.

"Probably not," replied Linc. "Preston tells me there's going to be a lot of people here . . ."

"Hundreds," interjected Preston. "Hundreds of people."

"It'll be too busy and too public for anyone to try anything," Linc continued. "But like the old saying goes, don't talk to strangers."

The burial service was a doleful event. There was a dark green canopy, as prescribed by Jewish law, that had been erected over the grave. The covering had the added benefit of shielding the immediate family from the elements. Of course, it was nowhere near large enough to accommodate the masses who had gathered. One of the poles that held a corner of the canopy had started to weaken from age and was being held in place by an orthodox Jew in full regalia of long black coat, beaver hat, sideburns and beard. Everything was dull, pasty and dark, except for the coffin. The gleaming reflection from the high polished wood and brass seemed wrongfully out of place at this dark gathering. The rabbi chanted in ancient Hebrew and the cantor sang the mournful dirges to the dead. Weeping, sobbing and an occasional wail of anguish emanated from the crowd. Lenore Aarons was near collapse during the entire proceeding. Sitting in a metal chair next to Sidney, she kept throwing herself from side to side in a pitiful expression of abject grief.

Turning to Linc, Emily whispered, "I'm going to make my way over to where the Aarons are sitting and try to think of something consoling to say."

After wending her way, Emily bent to whisper something to the grieving parents. Whatever words Emily chose to say were not as comforting as she had hoped. Lenore cried out and partially fell over into Sidney's arms. Visibly shaken, Emily quickly moved back to where Linc was standing and pressed herself very close to him. Linc put his arm around her shoulder and felt a shiver run through her. He scanned the crowd looking for anything unusual or suspicious. His gaze fell upon Pitch and Jennifer who were sitting in chairs on the opposite side of the gaping hole into which Scott's body was about to be lowered. Pitch was sitting hunched forward, white knuckled and ashen faced. Jennifer had her arm draped over his back and her head was resting on his shoulder. The ceremony seemed to last forever.

*   *   *

Dark clouds were starting to roll in. A particularly ominous looking one was rapidly approaching from the west, casting a shadow over a major portion of the Beltway. Washington D.C. was in for some rain this evening.

Vincent Parlotti swiveled his chair around and away from the window. Speaking in a low, portentous voice, he said, "That's it. I've lost my goddamned patience. Get a team ready."

Looking up at Parlotti, John Anderson felt a twinge of excitement course through his fingertips. He said, "No problem, Boss, but let's make sure we're clear on this. Do you want my team to go after the disc or do you want them to go after Harpoon?"

"Fuck the disc!" barked Parlotti, his nostrils flaring. "I'll get the goddamned disc myself! You go get Harpoon."

"You want me to send anyone in particular?" inquired Anderson, trying to suppress an eagerness about the upcoming manhunt.

"How about Prince and Dutch?" suggested Parlotti.

"I just sent Prince to Baton Rouge this morning," said Anderson. "How about I send Gator with the Dutchman instead?"

Parlotti nodded his head in agreement.

"Okay," said Anderson. "One more time. Let's be clear. Do you want us to bring Harpoon in? Or do you want us to take him out?"

Parlotti was quiet for a while. The light from the window was coming in over his shoulder and casting his face in shadow. Anderson was not able to see any expression in the man's eyes.

In an attempt to contact Harpoon, Parlotti had instructed Anderson to place the usual ads in the usual newspapers and run them for several days. Harpoon/Mendosa had chosen not to respond. That created an untenable situation for Parlotti. He now had a "rogue" on his hands. One of the most dangerous rogues on Earth. It was time to slam the door shut.

Parlotti stood up and started putting some papers in his briefcase. He hesitated long enough to say, "Harpoon is no longer salvageable. Take him out."

CHAPTER
THIRTY SEVEN

P reston's enthusiasm was near its peak as he expounded on the many talents of Pitch Pechowski. Referring to some glitches that had plagued Preston's personal computer from day one, he lauded Pitch's ability to solve them. Linc was sitting with Pitch and Preston in the Oak Room of Preston's Palm Beach mansion, waiting for Emily and Jennifer to return from freshening up their faces.

"Do you realize," said Preston, "that I must have called tech-support two dozen times and each time a different technician told me a different story? It's been unbelievably frustrating."

Self-conscious about the praise that was about to be heaped upon him, Pitch put both hands over his face.

"Then," continues Preston, "Pitch here, walks in, as smug as can be, turns on my computer, hits a few buttons and . . . Eureka! Problem solved. Just like that," said Preston, snapping his fingers in exclamation.

Linc said to Pitch, "All right, Houdini, what's your secret?"

Pitch leaned back into the comfortable love seat and slumped down until his head rested against the upholstery. "It's just Microsoft's version of Windows. If the technicians had stopped a moment and thought logically about the problem, there wouldn't have been a problem."

Preston jumped up out of his chair. "Okay, okay" he said gathering his thoughts. "God looks down on Earth and realizes He doesn't like what He sees. Too much poverty, too much war and too much famine. He decides to create a conflagration and destroy all human life. But before He does, He chooses three men to summon to heaven so that He can tell them personally, and they, in turn, can go back to Earth and prepare their people. God summons George W. Bush, Vladimir Putin and Bill Gates."

Linc already had a big smile on his face. He knew Preston's jokes were not the absolute funniest, but they were always apropos for the moment.

Preston went on. "God says to these three guys, 'In one week I am going to destroy the Earth and there's nothing you can do to stop it. I'm only telling you three so you can go back and give your people some advance warning'. Then, with a puff of smoke, the three men are back on Earth."

Preston was very animated as he continued. "George W. gathers his Cabinet," said Preston making an appropriate gesture with his arms, "and announces, 'I've got some good news and some bad news. First, the good news. Like I've been telling you, there is a God. The bad news is, He has decided to end life as we know it, in one week!'"

Preston stood up and began speaking in his best Russian accent. "Vladimir Putin gathers his inner circle in the Kremlin and says, 'Comrades, I've got some bad news and some very bad news. The bad news for all of us good Communists is, there is a God! The very bad news is, He is going to destroy Mother Russia along with all humankind on Earth in one week!'"

Now Preston actually began to strut during the last portion of his story. "Lastly, Bill Gates gathers his staff at Microsoft Headquarters and tells them, 'I've got some great news and some really great news. The great news is, God thinks I'm one of the three most important people on Earth. But the really great news is, we don't have to bother ourselves about fixing the bugs in our Windows Program!'"

With a wide grin, Linc shook his head at the uniqueness of Preston's style. Pitch was laughing uproariously, and Preston was beaming like a little boy who had just given his first recital.

Laughter subsiding, Pitch said, "That was very good, Preston. I needed that. The timing was right in more ways than one."

"At your service," said Preston bowing to the compliment before re-seating himself.

Linc had watched the growing camaraderie between the two men over the last couple of days and was pleased for the both of them. Preston always had a yen to learn all that he could from as many people as would allow it. The more knowledge they possessed, the more captivated he became. Preston had seemingly found a wellspring of knowledge in Pitch.

As for Pitch, the traumatic events of the past few days had put him on edge. He needed familiar faces around him. Although, initially, Emily provided that, it was the developing rapport between the three men that offered Pitch a bond of trust, something he needed very badly. Pitch and Jennifer had spoken privately about the possibilities of Linc, Emily or Preston having ulterior motives in their decision to take them in. However, the couple agreed that it was not something they had to worry about. Pitch and Jennifer looked to Preston for the safe haven he could provide, while Linc's presence was like a sentinel guarding against any unseen harm that might come to them. On more than one occasion, Jennifer confessed to wishing that Linc lived in the house as well. She expressed her feeling that Linc represented a barrier, even a deterrent, against some unknown evil that lurked outside.

Linc was growing to like Pitch and Jennifer, and wished he could spend more time with them. They were an interesting couple to talk with. Pitch had a black-and-white way of looking at the world, clear cut, concise and not too many shades of gray. Jennifer, on the other hand, was very idealistic and saw all of humanity as a delicate garden in need of nurturing and protection.

Linc was a pragmatist. He saw things for what they were. He also had the ability to see events as they developed and was often able to predict the outcome by playing out those events in his head. People thought it uncanny that Linc had the capacity to be right as often as he was.

Linc knew that the killer was still out there. He also knew that Pitch and Jennifer were not going to be able to stay in Preston's house forever. Sooner or later, they were going to have to leave this nest.

When that happened, they would both become extremely vulnerable. Linc had no idea as to the identity of the killer, but he had no doubt about the assassin's competence. It was obvious from the report and photos of the murder scene that he was a cold blooded and efficient executioner. Linc knew that, alone, Pitch and Jennifer had zero chance of survival against that kind of man. Their survival depended, in part, on being surrounded by others.

Linc was not looking forward to any sort of confrontation with this killer, but he realized that by protecting Pitch and Jennifer and remaining in such close proximity, he was putting himself in harm's way. Subconsciously, he had been preparing himself for awhile. If he ever came face to face with the killer, Linc knew that any decisions would have to be lightening fast and decisive.

Emily and Jennifer returned from their respective powder rooms and joined the three men in the Oak Room. Jennifer sat on the love seat next to Pitch and cuddled up close to him. Linc was sitting in a big upholstered chair, and Emily perched herself on its arm, lightly draping her hand on his shoulder.

It was very early evening and the conversation ebbed and flowed over several subjects. Movies, shopping and the traffic jams caused by the snowbirds, kept the mood light. At one point, the discussion became quite serious while they talked about the John Krum rape case, as it had come to be known. That brought about some bittersweet memories for Pitch and Jennifer. Speaking about Scott and the writing of his first feature article, Pitch was able to convey to the others just how proud and excited Scott was. The recollection of the moment made Pitch smile.

The spell was broken when Manfred popped his head into the room to announce that dinner would be served within the hour. That altered the discussion to include the subjects of food, restaurants, and the proper amount to tip the waiter or waitress for service.

At six forty-five, they all moved into the dining room where Manfred served a wonderful dinner consisting of an appetizer of chilled shrimp with a lemon pepper sauce, a cup of hearty vegetable chowder and a main course of poached salmon sprinkled with ginger and Caribbean seasonings. Jennifer found the salmon a little too spicy for her taste, and that prompted the others into some good natured ribbing. Preston took center stage for a while and told some interesting stories about various foods he had to tolerate during some of his world travels.

They were still sitting at the dining room table when Louise entered and said, "Excuse me, Emily. There's a telephone call for you."

Linc watched as Emily excused herself and left the room. He wondered who might be calling and ran several possibilities through his mind. For some reason, not knowing who the caller might be, bothered him. He remained distracted until Jennifer asked him a direct question. Jennifer wanted to know if Linc had ever tried chocolate covered pretzels or strawberries.

Before he had a chance to answer, Pitch excitedly chimed in, "Forget pretzels and strawberries. Did you ever have chocolate covered roaches or spiders?"

"Or any kind of insect covered in chocolate?" added Preston.

The shock value of the questions immediately brought Linc's focus back to the discussion at the table.

Shortly after Emily returned, the dessert was served. It was an array of delicate, individual pastry shells, filled with vanilla custard and laced with a rich Belgian chocolate. Everyone enjoyed the dessert course and no one made any more mention of creepy crawlies covered in chocolate.

Preston was first to excuse himself. Pitch and Jennifer followed his lead by retiring to the library. Linc partially re-folded his napkin and placed it on the table. "Emily," he said, "why don't you and I take a drive? It's a beautiful evening, and we could both use some fresh air."

"We can't leave yet," answered Emily. "Laura is on her way over."

"Laura Parsons?" asked Linc, not sure of what was going on.

"Yes," said Emily. "That was her who called before. She has some important information to tell us."

Linc was beginning to wonder if he would ever get to spend time alone with Emily. "I don't understand," he said.

"Let's go someplace where we can talk privately," said Emily, as she led him from the dining room and out onto the pool deck.

A crescent moon hung low over the darkened eastern sky. The night air was a little warmer than it had been, and a soft breeze was coming in off the ocean. The reflection of the lights from the house shimmered in the pool and cast a soft glow over the patio stones. Emily arranged two cushioned patio chairs side by side and facing the house so they could see anyone coming out.

When they were seated and Linc had his legs stretched out and crossed over a footstool, Emily took Linc's hand. She then told him about the incident that occurred that morning when Carmen showed her the X-rated video of Sidney Aarons and Elana Velez.

Linc sat bolt upright, pulling his legs back off the footrest. "Carmen showed you that video?" Linc asked with an accusatory tone. He took his hand away from hers and grabbed the arms of his chair. Carmen's actions seemed to be totally out of character, and Linc was having trouble absorbing Emily's statement.

Emily had a lot of ground to cover with Linc, but stopped short at his reaction. "Before I go on with the rest of what I have to tell you," she said, "why are you acting so shocked?"

"Because I wouldn't have expected that from Carmen," said Linc. He was sitting forward in his chair and half turned so he was directly facing Emily. "That was a breach of trust. Why did she do that?"

Linc was quite upset and Emily had not seen this side of him before. She did not understand his agitation and felt it to be unjustified. Furthermore, she was feeling put upon, as though he were expecting her to answer for Carmen's actions. Emily stood up and faced Linc. She raised her voice indignantly as she said, "What do you mean, 'why did she do that?' Do you have various levels of clearance that I have to go through before I can have access to certain things? Is it all right for certain employees to work on some cases but not others? If so, you certainly haven't spelled out any of those parameters to me."

Linc seemed a little dumfounded by her anger, as he sat back in his chair and said "Employee?"

Emily put her hands on her hips and stared at Linc with a quizzical look. "Are you suffering from some kind of dementia? Have you already forgotten that you hired me?"

"I thought that was tentative," said Linc weakly.

"Lincoln Donald Bradshaw," stated Emily in a formal tone, "The first day, you introduced me to Carmen as your prospective new hire. The next day, Carmen told me you spoke to her and made your decision to bring me on permanently. Carmen told me that you said I was to be given access to anything I wanted. Carmen was very explicit. I will add that she was also very excited about the fact that I was coming on board." Emily paused. The decibel level of her next sentences came down a notch or two. "I thought we all were. What's going on in your head, Linc?"

Linc's mouth fell open, as his mind quickly backtracked over several different conversations he had had relating to the subject. Slowly, he began to realize that the misunderstanding stemmed from a gap in communications. "Emily," he said, "sit down . . . please."

As Emily sat down, Linc said, "You and I were on two different planes. In my head, I was going to officially make you a part of the team next week. This coming Monday to be precise. At that time, I was going to officially welcome you and give you an orientation of my agency, including the cases we're working on. I certainly didn't want you to learn about Sidney's escapades from Carmen. That wasn't even close to my intention."

"So," said Emily, "you haven't changed your mind about me working with you?"

"No, of course not," said Linc. "But, do me a favor and put my mind at ease."

"What would you like to know?" she asked.

"Please tell me that Laura Parsons does *not* know about the Sidney Aarons case," pleaded Linc. "She hasn't seen the video, right?"

"Linc," said Emily with a patient smile, "you're just going to have to give me more credit than that."

Linc was able to take a deep breath, while Emily settled back into her chair. She went on to tell Linc about her insights into the Aarons investigation. Emily spoke about the initial shock of seeing the video. After pulling herself together, she had a vague recollection of Elana Velez, but couldn't quite place her. Emily related her feeling that it seemed to be someone whom Laura might be familiar with as well.

Distracting the conversation, the sliding glass doors opened and Laura Parsons walked out onto the pool deck. Emily stood and the two women embraced briefly. Glancing at Linc while he pulled over an additional chair, Laura greeted him with, "Hey, chump."

Linc slid the chair forcibly into the back of Laura's knees, causing her to plop into the seat. "Hello, mouth," he said by way of a return greeting.

Laura began the conversation by asking about the funeral and the general emotional state of Sidney and Lenore. Linc noted from her tone that she knew nothing about the video or any of the details of Sidney's affair.

After chatting for a while, Emily brought the conversation around to Elana Velez. "Laura," said Emily, "earlier, you said that you had some success learning a few things about that lingerie model in the newspaper."

Nodding, Laura took on a Cheshire cat grin.

"Like . . . what?" asked Emily.

"Like who she is," replied Laura, coyly trying to build the anticipation.

"So . . . who is she?" asked Emily.

"She goes by the name of Elana Velez," said Laura, "She's one of those free-lancers who does occasional modeling for the *Sun Coast Ledger*. But her real name is . . . ." Laura paused for effect and to look at both of them in turn. "Elaine Velachuk."

"Of course!" exclaimed Emily, her hands coming together in a single clap. "Elaine Velachuk. I knew she looked familiar."

Linc spoke for the first time, "Why is that name familiar to me?"

"It's someone we both went to Clairmont-Pas with," said Laura.

Emily looked at Linc and added, "We mentioned her name during our lunch last Saturday." Turning back to Laura, Emily said, "Elaine Velachuk. Can you believe it?"

"At least she kept the same initials: E.V." said Laura.

"True," said Emily. "But you've got to admit, Elana Velez is a lot more exotic than Elaine Velachuk."

"Yeah, well, from what I saw," said Laura in classic cat-like fashion, "she's been working real hard to make herself a lot more exotic. She definitely had her boobs pumped up," said Laura with a wave of her hand, "and she might have had one of those injections to puff her lips a bit, but that's her. No doubt about it."

Linc asked, "What else can you tell me about her?"

"Well," said Laura, "I can tell you when she was fifteen years old, she bragged about how she was giving blow jobs to her orthodontist."

"Oh, my God," squealed Emily. "That's right. Dr. Myron Shandelman. I had forgotten."

"He was in his thirties," said Laura. "A real doofus. They had a regular thing going. Humping each other once or twice a week for a couple of years. Then one night, he took her away to Las Vegas or someplace like that."

"She was still in high school," remembered Emily. "No more than seventeen. Shandelman got into all kinds of trouble when her parents found out."

"Oh yeah," recalled Laura. "They cut off the good doctor's balls. He lost everything. His wife left him . . . took the kids. He lost his dental practice and had to move away. And as for Elaine Velachuk, she thought the whole thing was just a hoot."

"Was she ever in trouble with the law?" asked Linc.

"I recollect something about that," replied Laura, "but I don't remember the details. I can look it up tomorrow. What's she done? Why are you two guys interested?"

Emily answered. "We can't say, Laura. At this time it's a private matter."

"Oh, bullshit, guys," said Laura throwing her hands in the air in frustration. "Come on. I'm in law enforcement too, y'know. Remember? Assistant D.A.? Duh? You can tell me."

"Laura," said Emily emphatically, "I cannot tell you. It would be a serious breach of ethics."

Linc was glad that Emily had taken it upon herself to deny Laura any further information. Emily was proving her mettle.

"Goddammit," snapped Laura. "Y'know, I hated that bitch. When we were in the eighth grade, she told Bobby Campitelli that I didn't know how to kiss. Then, she proceeded to kiss him, tongue and all, right in front of the lockers, for me and God and everyone else to see. And that was the last time Bobby paid any attention to me. Today, he's a friggin' doctor and if it wasn't for that slut, Velachuk, I could have had him!"

Linc and Emily both started laughing.

"So now what?" continued Laura. "She's having an affair with one of the hoity-toity citizens of Palm Beach and you guys can't let the cat out of the bag? Is that it?"

Linc and Emily were both smiling and silent.

Laura looked from one to the other waiting for a response. When none came, she folded her arms across her chest and said, sullenly, "Y'know what? Bite me! The both of you!"

CHAPTER THIRTY EIGHT

Arriving early the next day to pick up Emily, Linc chauffeured her to the office. He had decided it would be much more efficient to use one car, since his new plan was to drive around and introduce her to a few of his business contacts and support agencies. Linc had several accounts he worked with on a regular basis, and he hoped to make those introductions as well if time permitted.

Emily was dressed conservatively. A white blouse contrasted with a suit consisting of a taupe colored jacket and skirt, trimmed in a fine hairpin welt of chocolate brown. Her shoes and handbag matched the trim and sported the *Gucci* label. The ensemble was very business-like, but left no doubt as to her femininity.

"I'm glad I won't be driving you to work every day," said Linc, opening the door of the Corvette for her.

"Oh?" said Emily. "Why is that?"

"You look beautiful," he replied. "I'd never be able to concentrate on what I'm supposed to be doing."

"Why, thank you, Lincoln," she said demurely.

Carmen was already in the office preparing a fresh pot of coffee when Linc and Emily strode through the door. Glancing over her shoulder and spotting Emily's outfit, Carmen stopped what she was doing and said, "Oh, wow, Miss Emily! Look at you. I can tell right away you don't shop at K-Mart."

"Thank you, Carmen," said Emily as she turned a pirouette. "Do you like it?"

"Yes, indeed," she said. "You are going to make this place very professional and chic."

Carmen herself was wearing what looked like a party dress with a solid black background and huge colorful chrysanthemums spread evenly throughout. The dress was quite short and sleeveless. A black netted shawl hung over the back of her chair. "Mr. Linc likes me to wear this type of dress," Carmen said, spreading her arms, "so I can show a little skin,"

"All right," said Linc. "Enough with the jokes. Emily has figured out why we haven't been able to track that Elana Velez woman. Seems she's using an alias, and Emily has come up with her real name: Elaine Velachuk. So, let's run another Comp on that name and see what we come up with."

As Emily wrote out the spelling of the name, Carmen joked, "Ooo, an alias. I like it when we find an alias. It makes it seem like we're working in a detective agency."

Linc and Emily busied themselves in their respective offices. Linc had a message that Eddie Strickland had called. Emily logged onto the Internet and left an e-mail for Colonel Gunnar Hansen, asking him for the name of the primary contact person at the FBI Archive Division in Des Moines, Iowa. Next, she filled out the daunting pile of employment forms and paper-clipped them together before handing them back to Carmen.

After Linc had completed a few priority tasks, he was able to get in touch with Eddie Strickland. They had a lengthy conversation during which Eddie expressed frustration over being a cop. Linc listened with a sympathetic ear. He understood that some days were better than others. The end of the conversation included an agreement to meet for coffee later that morning. Hanging up, Linc went into Emily's office to see if she were ready.

Preparing to leave, Linc and Emily first stopped at Carmen's desk. Linc announced, "We're off. I'm going to introduce Emily to Mike Prosco and Demetrius. We also have a tentative appointment with Ferdie Dumay. From there, we're going to meet with Eddie."

Carmen looked at Linc. "I'm glad you're starting her out gently." Then, she looked at Emily and said, "Those are nice people he's introducing you to. But wait 'till you meet 'Pink-eye' and 'Mongo.' Oh, and let's not forget 'Hacker.' He's another good one."

Emily looked at Linc and asked, "Who are Pink-eye, Mongo and Hacker?"

"Informants I occasionally use, but don't worry. You'll never meet them," said Linc. "And as for you," Linc said to Carmen, making an attempt at intimidation, "stop trying to scare her. It's only her first day. We'll be back in time for lunch, and the three of us will go out and celebrate."

They walked out the door and down the corridor leading to the garage. They listened to the fading strains of Carmen singing, "Cel-le-brate good times . . . Come on . . ." Emily smiled upon hearing the familiar *Kool and the Gang* tune.

The morning went smoothly, and Linc was pleased with the way the introductions were going. Mike Prosco was a CPA. He was known as "The Number Cruncher" and had an investigative agency that specialized in accounting fraud. Linc used Mike's services on many occasions, and they had a good working relationship. Linc was somewhat surprised that Mike began acting like a high school kid at meeting Emily. Linc had never recalled Mike being so clumsy, and he seemed to start every sentence with "Oh, boy" or "Jeez." Emily handled herself professionally, but with a hint of coyness. When they left, Linc had no doubt that Mike was anxiously looking forward to working with Emily.

Linc had a long time relationship with Demetrius Kaltarakis. Demetrius had a multi-faceted business that dealt with import-export. His offices were at the ports of Palm Beach, Port Everglades and Miami. He was a walking encyclopedia regarding anything and everything that went out or came in by ship. The introduction of Emily went extremely well. Showcasing his European sophistication, Demetrius was debonair and charming, as he bowed at the waist and lightly kissed her hand. Emily was gracious, but showed her knowledge of international shipping by asking some very pointed questions. When the meeting was over, Demetrius escorted the couple out of his office.

In his rich Greek accent, he whispered to Linc, "She is smart *and* beautiful. Be careful, my friend, that you do not find yourself tied to her bed, or out on the street."

Ferdie Dumay headed up one of the largest agencies in South Florida. Linc did business with the Dumay Agency whenever he required additional manpower. If there were jobs that called for things such as a protective motorcade or a large number of bodyguards, Ferdie was the man to call.

Unfortunately, Ferdie was on his way to the airport to catch a commuter flight, and he only had time for a fast "hello." Nonetheless, Ferdie was never one to forget a face, and Linc was satisfied with the introduction.

The meeting with Eddie Strickland was interesting. Things were not going well for him, and he was in a foul mood. Brightening slightly at the news that Emily was now working for the Bradshaw Agency, Eddie quickly fell back into the doldrums when he announced that a shake-up was going on at police headquarters. The John Krum rape case was creating huge waves and there was a strong probability that Eddie's captain was going to be replaced. Eddie knew the person slated to take over the position. His name was Baumgarten. Eddie was nervous because he did not like Baumgarten, and Baumgarten did not like Eddie.

Furthermore, Eddie said that they had to let Henry Drummond go free.

"Go free?" said Linc, feigning surprise. "How come? I thought he was your prime suspect in the Aarons murder case."

"Ballistics came back with the information on the murder weapon," explained Eddie. "It was definitely a nine-millimeter and the only weapon we could find at Drummond's place was a thirty-two caliber."

"Same size hole," stated Linc.

"Close, but no cigar," said Eddie smoothing his mustache. "So his lawyer was all over us like flies on . . ." he glanced at Emily and checked the rest of his sentence. "Anyways, I also got the report from that murder up in D.C. Y'know, that Lunderman guy? The professor?"

"Right," said Linc.

"Well, he was found murdered in this hotel room along with this other dude named Mahler. Walter Mahler. Turns out, Mahler worked for the government. Some low-level bureaucrat or some shit. Anyways, one of the government agencies is preventing the local cops from doing their job and I can't get any more details about the case."

Emily jumped into the conversation, "What kind of things are you looking for?"

"Well, like I was saying," said Eddie with a dubious look on his face, "one of the things I did get from the D.C. cops was the initial ballistics report. It turns out Lunderman and Mahler were killed with the exact same nine-millimeter that took out Scott Aarons and Crystal Richards."

Linc and Emily flashed a glance at one another.

"So," continued Eddie, "I need to interview some more people regarding these murders, but the Feds are blocking the way up in D.C., and my pal up there can't get to first base."

"Eddie," Emily interjected again, "when you say 'The Feds,' are you referring to the FBI?"

"No," he replied. "The FBI ain't involved. It's that NSA outfit. They do that cloak and dagger shit, right? I have no idea what they're doing in this mess. Maybe that Mahler guy has something to do with it. I don't know. I'm not even sure what NSA stands for."

"National Security Agency," said Linc and Emily in unison.

"Eddie," asked Emily, "can I get a copy of the ballistics report from Washington, D.C.?"

Eddie glanced over at Linc, then back to Emily. "A copy? Why?" he asked, barely concealing his sarcasm. "You writing a book or something?"

"I may be able to get you some additional information," said Emily. "Some good stuff that might help you."

Eddie ran a hand through his hair and said "Yeah?"

"Don't sell her short," said Linc. "She keeps coming up with surprises. She's very good."

Armed with copies of the latest ballistic reports on the murders in D.C. and Palm Beach, Linc and Emily started the drive back to the office.

"Linc," started Emily, a little tentatively, "what do you think of Eddie's expertise as a policeman?"

Looking at Emily, Linc raised his eyebrows, smiled and turned his attention back to the road in front of him.

After a short silence, Emily said, "I doubt if you're ignoring me."

Linc's smile got broader. "No," he said. "It's just that I know where this conversation is headed."

"Really?"

"Emily," said Linc, "one of the things that fascinates me about you is that nothing gets past you. You're very perceptive. You seem to be able to . . . read people, and you think you see something missing in Eddie's ability."

"Linc, please . . . I know he's your friend and I don't want to create . . ."

"No, no," said Linc with a wave of his hand. "You're not creating any rift or anything like that. The simple truth is that Eddie is not one of the golden boys. He ranks at or near the bottom of the detective pool."

"I rather thought so," said Emily.

"What was your first clue, Sherlock?"

"I actually picked it up that first day when he was interrogating Pitch. I thought he failed to ask, what I would have considered, several important questions. He should have been able to come away with much more information than he did."

Linc expelled a nasal huff. "Eddie's a good cop," he said, trying not to sound apologetic. "Time and again he's proven his worth. When we were on the force together, he was physically aggressive and never afraid. And he seemed to have a knack as to where to look for clues. Right after he was promoted to detective, his personal life started to fall apart. It seemed as though his ex-wife messed up his head and he lost something. That 'edge' he used to have was gone."

Linc looked at Emily for her reaction. She just nodded her head.

Linc continued. "If there is some salvation, it's in the fact that he hasn't been an actual detective all that long. I'm hoping that he'll grow into the job. I'm really hoping he'll be able to turn things around."

They arrived back at the office well past the noon hour and Carmen was eager to get out and celebrate Emily's new position. Emily asked if it would be all right if they delayed going for about ten minutes. She just wanted to create a search program based on these latest reports she had received from Eddie. She logged onto the Internet and contacted her mentor at NATO, Gunnar Hansen. She faxed him copies of the ballistics reports and asked him to search the records for any other crimes that were committed using the same weapon. Then, they all went to lunch.

Lunch turned out to be a raucous affair. The three of them went to a local delicatessen called *The Gourmet Deli-House* where a transplanted Bostonian, named Lester, seated them. They ordered smoked meat sandwiches with all the fixings. Carmen was in rare form, and kept Linc and Emily in stitches. Good-natured banter flew around the table like a three-act show at a comedy club. Carmen poked fun at Linc, Linc razzed her back and picked on Emily, and Emily proved to have a sharply honed sense of humor. They laughed until their stomachs hurt. Some of the nearby customers couldn't help but get into the act and that added to the enjoyment of the celebration.

Lunch lasted for over two hours. The cashier was ringing up the lunch check when Carmen said, "Miss Emily, I am so glad you are now part of our staff. This business of having two hour lunches is wonderful."

"Yeah, well enjoy it," said Linc. "It'll be a long time before we do this again."

Carmen twisted her face and said in a stage whisper, "He's right, you know. The last time he allowed me two measly hours for anything was when I had to have a hysterectomy."

They were still chuckling when they went back to work. Linc and Emily disappeared into their respective offices while Carmen checked for messages. There were several, including one from Preston Collingsworth for Emily. Bringing the note into Emily's office, Carmen was about to hand it to her along with a funny remark. She decided against it when she saw how engrossed Emily was in her computer screen. Simply putting the note down, Carmen said, "While we were at lunch, your father called."

"Thank you, Carmen," said Emily without looking up.

Gunnar Hansen had come through again. He had received her e-mail along with the copies of the ballistics reports and had quickly done his homework. His reply was actually written by his assistant, Major Ilisa Kleiner and started with, "I have never seen a real live palm tree. Please invite me to Florida." It was signed, "Ilisa." The heart of the reply told Emily about another killing that had been committed with matching ballistics from the same nine-millimeter. It was also a multiple murder that had taken place in a suburb of Memphis, called Germantown. The family's name was Blanchard. The victims included the head of the house, Roger Blanchard, his wife, Sandi, and Mary Franzheimer, whom the police determined was the babysitter.

Fascinated by the information, Emily read that all the victims were bound with duct tape and that the killing shots were single and directly into the head. The similarities with the Aarons' murder were unmistakable. Anxious to share the news, she jumped up from her desk and went into Linc's office. Even though he was on the phone, Linc held up two fingers signaling that he would be through with his call in two minutes. Emily hesitated a moment before going back into her office and clicking the print icon in order to make a hard copy of this report.

Seeing that Linc was still on the phone, Emily called her father. Preston had called to say that he had a pre-arranged appointment and, not wanting to leave Pitch and Jennifer all alone, needed Emily to come home. Louise had taken off for the day and only Manfred would be there. When Emily balked, Preston reminded that it was entirely Emily's responsibility to baby-sit the couple, and he was only doing it out of the goodness of his heart. Emily knew her father was right. After all, it was her idea to invite the couple to be guests in her home. Preston certainly had done more than his fair share by keeping Pitch and Jennifer company.

"All right, Daddy," she said. "Why don't you go ahead and take off. I'll get there as soon as I can. Linc drove me over here in his car, so I'll have him drive me home as soon as he's free."

"You won't be long, will you?" asked Preston. "I hate the thought of leaving them all alone."

"No, Daddy," she answered. "I won't be long. I'll be home in twenty, twenty-five minutes. Tops."

Emily once again went to check on Linc. He was still on the telephone, but this time he held up only one finger and silently mouthed, "one minute."

Emily ambled back to her office and called the Memphis Police Department. After being connected numerous times to various extensions, she finally got to speak with a Detective Laramie. She introduced herself and began asking about the Blanchard murders. Laramie had a deep southern accent. As her questions continued, Laramie became suspicious, then evasive and finally curt. Emily tried again to explain who she was, hoping for a little professional courtesy. Instead, Laramie became downright rude and hung up.

Emily put in a call to Eddie Strickland. Informed that it was Emily on the line, Eddie answered the phone with, "Hey. What can I do for you, darlin'?"

"Eddie," replied Emily, "we can do something for each other."

"This kind of talk will get you a hot Saturday night," he said.

"Listen," said Emily, ignoring his remark, "I've received some very pertinent information for you regarding the Aarons case."

"Yeah? Shoot."

"I've uncovered another murder," said Emily, "that was committed with the same nine-millimeter."

Eddie was silent as he absorbed this news.

"It was another multiple murder," said Emily, "committed up in Memphis, but with the same M.O. Those victims were also tied up with duct tape."

Eddie finally spoke. "You guys know more about this case than you're letting on. What are you guys doing? Slowly feeding me information?"

"No, Eddie," said Emily indignantly. "I just found this out a few minutes ago."

"Yeah? How?"

"This is what I do, Eddie," she said. "This is why Linc hired me. Now, I need you to do something for me."

"Yeah? Like what?"

Emily spelled out the details of her request. She asked Eddie to contact Detective Laramie in the Memphis P.D., for a copy of his report on the Blanchard murders. Then, she made sure that Eddie, in turn, would forward the reports to her.

Linc came into her office, as she was saying good bye. Emily hurriedly began telling him about the details of her findings, trying to get it all in, before Linc had to answer the next phone call. She told him about her conversation with Detective Laramie in Memphis and how he was so completely uncooperative.

Linc chuckled. "Welcome to the world of private investigators," he said. "You'll find that most cops won't even give us the time of day."

"Well," explained Emily, "I called Eddie and asked him to call Detective Laramie. Hopefully, Laramie will be more forthcoming with a fellow officer of the law."

Linc was quite pleased with all that Emily had accomplished in such a short period of time. He smiled at his good fortune in getting her to work for him. At the same time, he was becoming acutely aware of a growing bond between them and wondered just how far it would go.

Emily told Linc about Preston's phone call and his request for her to come home early.

"No problem," said Linc. "Give me half a minute and we'll be on our way." Stopping at Carmen's desk to say good bye, Linc said, "My cell phone battery is low, so if there's anything earth-shaking, you can reach us at Preston's number. Otherwise, I'll see you in the morning."

"*We* will see you in the morning," corrected Emily.

CHAPTER THIRTY NINE

T he doorbell seemed to be ringing for a long time. At first, Manfred did not pay any attention to the sound, knowing that Louise always answered the door. It was her usual responsibility to greet new arrivals at the Collingsworth residence. However, as the doorbell continued its incessant chiming, Manfred suddenly remembered Preston's instructions that Louise would be off for the day, and that he, Manfred, had the additional duty of receiving any guests.

Making his way to the front door, Manfred passed the bank of sliding glass doors that led out to the pool deck. He spotted Pitch and Jennifer playing Scrabble under an umbrella. Noticing that Jennifer was wearing a rather skimpy bikini, Manfred slowed his pace and became aware of the way her long, auburn hair cascaded over her back and shoulders.

Manfred turned his gaze towards the front door. Through the many small panes of glass that were part of the magnificent entryway, Manfred could see the figure of a lone man. Opening the door, Manfred said, "Goot afternoon, Sir. May I help you?"

Standing before him was a man in a dark gray business suit, a starched white shirt and a conservative, diagonally striped tie.

"I'm Special Agent Brant Sheffield, FBI," he said holding up his identification badge with his photo prominently displayed. "I'm here to talk to Peter Pechowski." Then added, "Pitch Pechowski."

Brant Sheffield's tone was firm, but very business like. Opening the door wide to invite him in, Manfred reckoned the Agent to be about six-foot tall and noted his boyish good looks. As Agent Sheffield came through the entrance, he thanked Manfred and nodded his appreciation. Manfred was impressed with the manners of this FBI policeman. As a youth in his native country, Manfred's experiences with police was not particularly favorable. As a result, he was appreciative of the man's pleasant and non-threatening style.

Manfred led Special Agent Sheffield to the library and instructed him to make himself comfortable. "I vill tell Mr. Pechowski dat you are here und vaiting to see him." Manfred went out to the pool deck to inform the young couple.

Learning that there was an FBI Agent waiting to talk to him, Pitch got a cold feeling in the pit of his stomach. "The FBI?" he asked, somewhat intimidated by the title. "What does the FBI want with me?"

Manfred made a helpless gesture with his hands and said, "He did not say."

Jennifer was standing. "Manfred," she asked in a conspiratorial whisper, "When is Preston coming home? Will he be here soon?"

"Also, he did not say," whispered Manfred in return. "But he told me dat Mr. Bradshaw und Miss Emily vould be coming home early."

Jennifer was distraught. "Peter," she said, "Could you please wait to speak to the man until I've gone upstairs and changed?"

"Oh, Jennifer," said Pitch, putting on his short, white, terrycloth robe, "don't be such a mother hen. I'm sure it'll be all right. You go on upstairs and change, and then meet us in the . . ." He looked at Manfred questioningly.

"In za library," answered Manfred. Then, looking at Jennifer, he repeated, "He's vaiting in za library."

Jennifer grabbed her sunglasses and towel and hurried off to change out of her bathing suit, while Manfred led the way to the library. With his feet slapping along in his sandals, Pitch followed. Agent Sheffield was standing just inside the arched entry to the library, and saw Manfred and Pitch approaching. Pitch noticed that, although

Agent Sheffield was standing casually, he seemed to be intently scrutinizing the approaching pair and never wavered his gaze.

Manfred spoke first; "Mr. Pechowski, zis is Special Agent Sheffield from za FBI."

Pitch put his hand out and said, nervously, "Um, hello. You're from the FBI?"

"Yes," said Sheffield taking Pitch's hand for the obligatory shake. "Special Agent Brant Sheffield."

Pitch was surprised by the firmness of Sheffield's grip, and during the brief handshake, Pitch was momentarily startled when Sheffield pulled him forward, just slightly. The barely discernable action almost drew Pitch off balance before the Agent let go. "Sit down, Pitch," said Sheffield motioning towards a straight-backed wooden chair, one of a pair that sat by a substantial reading table. "Is it all right if I call you Pitch?"

"Sure," Pitch said as they both sat down. "Pitch is fine." Pitch was feeling fractionally more relaxed. Agent Sheffield had smiled slightly and didn't seem particularly menacing. All in all, Pitch felt he could handle the upcoming interrogation.

Conducive to reading and quiet conversations, the library was a large room with a very high ceiling. Two walls were completely covered with bookshelves. The books extended from wall to wall and from floor to ceiling, broken only by two tall, narrow windows that were centered on each wall. There was an angled ladder that had a spindly platform midway up its height, and the whole contraption was attached to a motorized rail at the top and bottom. The ladder and platform assembly was designed to allow easy access to the books on the higher shelves. The third wall had a similar bookshelf running from floor to ceiling but only extended half the width of the room. The remaining half had numerous reference books, but was dominated by a huge globe that sat in a beautifully carved, antique, wooden globe well. The globe itself was colored for geographical use, but was also steeply textured for anyone interested in the Earth's topography. The sounds of spoken words tended to be absorbed by the thousands of books on display.

"Let me get right to the point," said Agent Sheffield, crossing his legs. "You're the subject of a very intensive investigation."

"I know," interrupted Pitch. "The police have already questioned me about Scott and Crystal and . . ."

Sheffield held up his hand causing Pitch to stop mid-sentence. "I'm not just talking about the recent murder of your friends," said Sheffield, uncrossing his legs, "I'm talking about . . . everything, Pitch."

Pitch just looked at this FBI Agent and knew what was coming next.

Sheffield leaned forward and rested both elbows on his knees. He put his fingertips together and said, "I'm talking about the death of Professor George Lunderman and . . . your disc."

"My disc?" asked Pitch, surprised. Pitch had anticipated being asked about the details of his listening device, his Ultimate Bug. However, he was astonished that the FBI was referring specifically to the disc. "What do you mean?" asked Pitch.

Sheffield sat up straight and became very serious. Sternly, he said, "Don't try to be evasive, Pitch. The Bureau already has a couple thousand hours in this investigation, and we know what's going on. We know everything, Pitch. You following me?"

Pitch nodded his head.

Sheffield continued. "Your device has caused the death of four people already. You understand?"

Pitch bowed his head and nodded affirmatively. As Special Agent Sheffield uttered his words, Pitch was reminded that he and his disc had caused the death of his best friend.

"Now, I can't tell you the details of what we've uncovered," said Sheffield, "but there are some very sinister forces at work here and more people are going to die unless you cooperate."

"I understand," said Pitch almost inaudibly.

"Good. Now, let's start by giving me the disc," said Sheffield, holding out his hand.

"I . . . I don't have it here," said Pitch.

"Where is it?" asked Sheffield, drawing back his extended hand.

"It's in a safe deposit box . . . at the bank," replied Pitch, thinking he was in real trouble now.

Agent Sheffield leaned back in his chair and re-crossed his leg. He stared at Pitch trying to determine the validity of his statement.

The moment of silence was broken by the sound of footsteps and

Emily calling out, "Pitch? Jennifer?"

"In here, Emily," called Pitch in return. "I'm in the library."

Linc and Emily appeared in the doorway. As they entered the room, Agent Sheffield stood up and unbuttoned his jacket.

"This is Special Agent Grant Sheffield," said Pitch visibly unnerved.

"Brant Sheffield," corrected the Agent.

"Sorry," said Pitch. "Brant Sheffield. He's from the FBI."

"The FBI?" said Emily. "What's the FBI's interest in Mr. Pechowski, here?"

"I'm afraid it's a personal matter," said Sheffield. "Official business. I'm not at liberty to discuss the details."

"They're asking for the disc," volunteered Pitch.

Linc spoke for the first time, "Could I see your ID, Agent Sheffield?"

Sheffield eyed Linc's size and asked, "And who might you be?"

Before Linc could answer, Jennifer strode into the room, looked from face to face and sensed the tension. "What's up?" she asked.

Pitch started explaining to Jennifer about the FBI wanting the disc, but was interrupted when Emily took a half step towards Agent Sheffield and said sternly, "We are the people who live in this house. This is Mr. Bradshaw and I am Miss Collingsworth." Emily felt it would be prudent, for the moment, to use her maiden, rather than her legal married name. "So," she went on, "may we please see your identification?"

Agent Sheffield held out his ID. Emily took it and was perusing it, while Linc looked over her shoulder. Handing it back, Emily said, "With which office are you connected?"

"Washington, D.C.," he answered.

"No," said Emily, "I mean, to which office, here in Florida, are you reporting?"

"Oh," said Sheffield, his eyes darting during a fractional hesitation. "When I got here to Florida, I reported to the Miami office."

Manfred had been working in the kitchen. It was an area of the house with which he was very familiar. He liked creative cooking and was uncomfortable with other chores. With Louise having taken off for the day, Manfred worried about what other duties he had to be responsible for. He suddenly remembered that there was a guest in the house, and it would be proper to offer everyone some refreshments. He began making his way towards the library.

Hearing Sheffield mention the FBI office in Miami, Linc put a big smile on his face and said expansively, "The Miami office, eh? Well, you obviously got to meet the man in charge. How is old Morty Markham? I haven't seen him in about a year."

It was a trap and Claude Mendosa knew it instantly. There was no use continuing this charade, pretending to be FBI Agent Brant Sheffield. If he only had more time with Pechowski, Mendosa could have brought this matter to a conclusion. But Bradshaw and this Collingsworth woman knew too much about the FBI for Mendosa to try to carry his act any further. He wasn't going to take any more chances either. Mendosa thought it was very possible that Pitch was telling the truth, and realized that the disc probably was in a bank vault. That meant he was not going to get it today. Mendosa's priority changed in a flash. His immediate concern was getting out of there, but not empty-handed if he could help it.

Taking a hostage would be the answer. If he grabbed Pitch's girlfriend, Mendosa could eventually demand the disc. Better yet, he could take Pitch himself. Then, Mendosa wouldn't need the disc. He knew he wouldn't have any trouble torturing the information out of the young man. Mendosa had already tested Pechowski during their initial handshake and was certain the lad would be no match.

Mendosa moved quickly. Very quickly. In a motion almost too fast to follow, he slipped his right hand under his jacket and whipped out his nine-millimeter with its long silencer. He started to level out the pistol just as Manfred appeared at the doorway to the library. Seeing the gun as it swung around, Manfred shouted, *"Goht in Himmel!"*

Manfred's loud cry caused Mendosa to re-direct his first shot. The bullet caught Manfred in the neck, spinning him around as a blood trail burst from his jugular vein.

Emily, Pitch and Jennifer were frozen in their tracks. The only movement was the blur of Linc's motion as he bolted like a sprinter out of the starting blocks. Covering the five-foot distance in a microsecond, he charged into Mendosa full bore. Linc never took his eyes off the weapon and grabbed it with both hands, as his right shoulder smashed into the imposter.

Mendosa was agile and quick. Cushioning the blow by stepping backward at precisely the moment of impact, enabled Mendosa to maintain his balance.

While Linc was amazed that the assailant never went down, Mendosa was shocked at the speed at which the big man moved.

Linc had a death grip on the pistol, and Mendosa was desperately trying to free it. They began spinning across the room like two dervishes dancing around a central point, a loaded gun in this case. They crashed into furniture, destroying it in their wake. First, a bookstand holding some large reference books and then, an elaborate glass floor lamp that splintered into flying shards. Next to topple over was the big reading table, and yet neither man lost enough of his balance to go down. Although each man pulled at the pistol, Linc's greater strength was causing him to move backward. They were heading for the very chair on which Pitch had just been sitting. Pitch suddenly reached out and grabbed the chair, pulling it out of Linc's path, preventing him from toppling over it. The wildly spinning dance drew them to the ladder and platform assembly. Their bodies heaved into the structure causing the platform to break loose and crash to the floor. An ear-splitting sound was followed by a tangled avalanche of pipes and railing pieces.

Unexpectedly, each man altered his strategy, and the change happened simultaneously. They had been trying to pull away from each other, each one attempting to win possession of the pistol. Now they went after each other. Linc was still holding tightly, his big hands wrapped around the hand and fingers of Mendosa. Lurching forward, Linc tried to knock Mendosa down with a mighty shoulder blow. At the same time, Mendosa tried to flip Linc off balance by moving in and sweeping his right foot, hoping to cut Linc's legs out from under him.

It was Mendosa who had the better tactic. Linc felt his feet being swept out, and he went down. But in doing so, he gave a mighty effort and a guttural cry, as he forcefully twisted the pistol.

Linc thought he felt the bone break in Mendosa's hand. At the same time, he heard Mendosa emit a painful grunt. Linc tumbled into what was left of the ladder and platform apparatus and felt a hot, searing pain in his left shoulder. He became all tangled up in the wreckage. He tried to get up, but his feet were snarled between the bent pipes, and his hip was jammed under a metal crossbar. Looking helplessly at Mendosa, Linc wondered why the man just didn't shoot him. Surely a broken bone in his hand wasn't going to stop this killer. Instead, Mendosa turned and started to run toward Emily and the others. It wasn't until that moment that Linc realized that it was he who was holding Mendosa's pistol.

Lying on his back half twisted like a pretzel, Linc tried to free the pistol from the broken obstacles around him. He did so, just as Mendosa was turning the corner out of the room. Linc barely had time for one shot and took it. The bullet missed by some two feet and shattered a chunk of plaster near the door frame.

Emily ran to Linc as Mendosa's fading footsteps disappeared out of the house. "Oh, my God!" she cried, "Are you all right?"

"Manfred," Linc said hoarsely between gulps of air, "He took one in the neck." Linc used the pistol to point at Pitch and Jennifer as he shouted, "One of you put pressure on the wound, and call nine-one-one. Hurry!" Then he let his head fall back, his breath still coming in ragged bursts.

Emily was standing awkwardly in the middle of the twisted wreckage. "Linc," she said with tears in her eyes, "You're hurt."

"Something is sticking me in the back," he said. "Help me out of here, Emily."

A large pool of blood had formed on the tile floor around Manfred's head. He wasn't moving and didn't seem to be breathing. More blood was now pumping out from the bullet wound.

Pitch bent to try to stop the flow and called out, "Jennifer, you call nine-one-one! I'll see what I can do for Manfred!" Pitch stood up and removed his terrycloth robe. He took one sleeve, rolled it into a ball and jammed it into the side of Manfred's neck. The white cloth quickly absorbed the blood, but Pitch ignored the staining and continued to apply pressure to the wound.

Jennifer was in a tizzy. She grabbed the phone to make the call and was dialing over and over, not understanding why the call was not going through. After the fourth or fifth attempt, she yelled, "Shit!" and bolted from the library. During the struggle, the phone wire had been yanked out of the wall, and it no longer had a dial tone. Jennifer made the call from the telephone in the Oak Room.

Linc seemed to be jammed in pretty tightly, and Emily did not have the strength to pull him out. Each time they combined their efforts to sit Linc upright, the pain in his left shoulder became very severe causing Emily to release her grip.

Jennifer came back into the room, as Emily looked up forlornly and said, "I need help. I can't do this by myself."

Pitch called out, "Jennifer! Come here and hold this tight to Manfred's neck so I can give Emily a hand. I think the bleeding has finally slowed down."

"Are you sure he's not dead?" asked Jennifer as she tentatively knelt alongside Pitch.

"Not yet," he said. "He's still breathing. A little shallow, but still viable. Medics on their way?"

Jennifer confirmed that the Emergency Medical Services had been dispatched immediately. She told Pitch how she had emphasized the dire importance of the emergency. "When I told them that Manfred had been shot, they said they were going to dispatch the police as well."

Jennifer put her hands around the makeshift terrycloth roll, while Pitch guided them into applying the correct amount of pressure. "Hold it there," he said. "Just like that. Let me just go help Linc."

Pitch started by removing some of the debris from around Linc. It made it easier for both Pitch and Emily to get a good grip. As Pitch worked, he said to Linc, "That was a good shot, Linc. You got him as he was running away."

"No such luck," said Linc. "I missed him and hit the door frame."

"Well, something hit him," replied Pitch. "He left a trail of blood right out the door. Should make it easy for the bloodhounds to follow."

Pitch and Emily each put a hand under Linc's upper arms.

"Wait, wait," said Linc, as they began their extrication. "There's something pinching me hard in the back. See if you can tell what it is."

Pitch maneuvered himself to where he could look underneath Linc. "Uh-oh," he said.

"What," said Emily anxiously. "What is it?"

Pitch straightened up into a kneeling position and said, "Lincoln, it looks like you have a lance sticking out of your back! Not too much bleeding, but it looks like it might be in there pretty deep."

"Is it a long piece of metal?" asked Linc.

"About like this," said Pitch holding his hands about eight inches apart.

Holding out the nine millimeter, Linc said, "Take the gun, Emily, but don't get any more fingerprints on it. Mine are mostly on the handle but his are probably on the silencer." Then, he turned to Pitch. "Okay Pitch, old buddy. Get yourself a good stance and grab my right hand. You're going to pull me out of here."

Pitch readied himself, as each man took a firm grip on the other. There was a moment of hesitation, as they all became aware of the sound of approaching sirens. Then, grimacing in pain, Linc pulled hard with his right hand, while Pitch gave a mighty heave and a loud grunt. Linc came to his feet, but was slightly off balance and leaning far to his left. Emily started to move forward to steady him, only to stop short and gasp when she spotted the metal bar sticking out of his back. Linc regained his balance and smiled at Emily. "Whew," he exhaled. "That's much better. It doesn't hurt anywhere near as much now that I'm not lying on it."

They helped Linc step away from the tangled metal platform, just as the first ambulance pulled into the driveway. The sound of the siren ground to a stop.

Three paramedics came in and did a quick triage. Although they were fascinated at the sight of Linc casually standing around with what looked like a short javelin protruding from his back, they immediately tended to Manfred.

Manfred was bleeding profusely and his breathing had become labored. Quickly giving up on the idea of applying direct pressure, the ambulance attendants, instead, decided to attempt the placement of a couple of hemostats. The tallest of the two men, along with the one woman paramedic, were kneeling side by side near Manfred's head.

The tall man said, "Michelle, you need to blot this area a little faster. I can't find the upper bleeder."

The Paramedic, Michelle, reached into her kit and took out a handful of gauze pads. Her hands darted in and out of the injured area, trying to clear the view. "There," she said softly. "There it is, Mark."

Mark said, "Okay . . . just a little faster . . . I'll try to place this hemostat on the jugular."

Michelle was working quickly, but still tried to do more. "Go ahead, Mark," she said in a hushed tone. "Just be careful of the carotid. It's just behind the jugular and slightly to the middle."

Bending his head in very close, Mark struggled to line up the hemostat, trying to get the advantage of a clear shot, "Well, this guy's got . . . another carotid . . . just in case I accidentally . . ." There was a tense moment of silence. "Got it!" said Mark triumphantly. "I think I got it."

Michelle continued to use gauze pads to blot the area. "Good," she remarked. "The bleeding has slowed. I can see it clearly now. Go ahead and place the lower one."

While Mark and Michelle struggled to prevent death, the third paramedic had intubated Manfred in order to keep his airway open. As soon as that task was complete, Mark applied electrodes to the patient's chest and began monitoring his cardiac function.

Michelle continued to blot the injured neck wound, even after the second of the hemostats was in place. Mark looked up from his patient and surveyed the room. He said, "Our initial dispatch report said that this man was shot. Is that right?"

"Yes," answered Linc.

"By one of you?" he asked, looking from one to the other.

"No," said Linc. "The shooter's long gone. Took off for parts unknown."

"The cops will be here pretty soon," said Michelle, as she prepared an IV solution of normal saline. "We heard on the radio that they were running about five, ten minutes behind us."

Mark stood up and approached Linc. "How you doing?" he said with a smile.

"Actually," said Linc, "pretty good. Right now, it's more annoying than painful."

The Para medic looked at the wounded area. Careful not to touch the short piece of metal, Mark gently felt the area around the shoulder to determine the extent of the damage and to see how deeply the shaft might be lodged. "It doesn't look too bad," he said. "But you can bet we ain't going to lay you down on a stretcher when we ride you to the hospital."

Linc smiled. "I was thinking you guys might just be able to yank it out."

"Nope," said Mark emphatically. "We're going to transport you just like you are and let the doctors do the yanking. But I'll tell you what I will do. I'll cut away your shirt so the movement of the fabric doesn't aggravate it."

"I'll help," said Emily, as she moved around in front of Linc to assist the medic with the removal of Linc's shirt. Linc did the unbuttoning while Mark took a pair of scissors and began cutting a big hole in the back of the shirt. Next, the Paramedic carefully cut away the small threads that were hooked on the jagged piece of metal. That done, Emily gingerly helped Linc remove what remained of his shirt. Biting her bottom lip, Emily sucked in an audible breath each time Linc winced. It seemed to be as painful for Emily as it was for Linc.

"So far so good," said Mark. "I'm going to put some tape around it to kind of hold it in place. Y'know, so it won't get jostled."

Emily could not help notice Linc's physique. His chest was well defined with wide lats and cut pectorals. His stomach was flat and slightly ridged into a washboard effect. Looking up into his face, Emily was immediately aware that his eyes were locked on hers. She became self-conscious and her cheeks flushed when she realized that she had been caught staring. She took a ragged breath and tried to smile.

"Are you all right?" Linc asked.

"I'm still very unnerved by what just happened," she said. "I thought you were going to get killed. And I don't know what's to become of Manfred. I'm still shaking inside."

Linc reached out with his good hand and gently placed it against the side of her face. Emily closed her eyes and covered his hand with her own.

Mark, the Paramedic, said, "I think the old guy's going to make it." Then, to his two partners, "Are you people almost ready to go?"

"In just about one minute," answered Michelle.

Double-checking Linc's injury, Mark wrinkled his nose. Even with all the careful handling of the shrapnel, the wound began bleeding in earnest. He worked quickly to clean and bandage the injury, trying to get it to hold together long enough to transport Linc to the emergency room. The other two Paramedics had placed Manfred on a stretcher and were ready to wheel him out to the waiting ambulance.

Mark tapped Linc gently on his right shoulder and said, "Come on, big guy. Let's go. We're off to the hospital."

Linc took the first two steps and stopped. "Wait," he said. "Emily, you can't stay here alone with Pitch and Jennifer."

Emily looked at Pitch and Jennifer. They had the look of willing participants just waiting for a decision to be made. "Of course not," said Emily. "We're all going with you to the emergency room. Right?"

The decision was made without further discussion. Heading out the door, Linc said to Mark, "Radio ahead and have the cops meet us at the E.R. at Good Sam Hospital." Then, to Emily he said, "While you're following us, put in a call to Eddie. This needs to be his case."

Emily started to walk out with Linc and the rest of the crew when another thought came to her. "I guess I'd better call Daddy," she said, turning to look at the aftermath of the death-struggle. "He'll have a fit when he sees what happened to his beloved library."

CHAPTER FORTY

Eddie Strickland was aggravated. Aggravated and angry. He was in the middle of a tirade directed at the two couples and kept repeating the fact that he was very upset. "Y'know, you guys are really pissing me off! All of you! I got two people dead here in my backyard, two people dead up in D.C., your butler, lying there with a bullet in his neck and some yokel tried to kill the rest of you! And you characters insist on holding out information on me! What the hell is going on?"

Emily finally broke the uncomfortable silence when she said softly, "He's our cook."

"What?" shouted Eddie.

"Manfred," she corrected, "He's our cook, not our butler."

Eddie threw his hands in the air, "Cook, butler, what the hell's the difference? The point is, this is a police matter. Not something for a goddamned Boy Scout troop!"

Linc was sitting shirtless on the edge of a bed in the emergency room. He had already been seen a couple of times by the E.R. doctor. The first time to assess the injury and to send Linc down to radiology for x-rays. While Linc was downstairs having the pictures taken, Emily and Jennifer ran out to a local department store to purchase him a new shirt.

It turned out that the piece of metal had not lodged itself too deeply, and the doctor had no trouble removing it. He had cleaned out the wound, sewn in several stitches and re-dressed it. Now, Linc was waiting for the nurse to give him a tetanus shot.

Pitch and Jennifer were half-sitting on a railing that lined one wall of the cubicle. Emily stood close to Linc with her hand resting on his thigh.

"And you," said Eddie pointing directly at Pitch. "Lying right to my face in my own goddamned interrogation room!"

"I answered all your questions," said Pitch defensively.

"Yeah, you think so?" he replied leaning forward, trying to intimidate Pitch, "Well, you were pretty goddamned evasive about Lunderman, weren't you?"

"Eddie," said Linc with a firmness in his voice, "get off the kid. We've told you what we know. You've got a description of the guy. You've got his gun. You'll probably get his fingerprints. And if you send in the crime lab team, you'll be able to get his DNA. He cut himself on the broken lamp in the corner."

"Listen," said Eddie still irritated, "All of you. I've been here over an hour, and you've been feeding me the physical evidence. Fine. But you guys know what I'm talking about. I'm talking about the 'why' of what's going on. You guys know something, and you ain't telling me."

"Eddie," said Linc in a tone of resignation, "as soon as I find out something pertinent, you'll be the first to know."

Before he could reply, Emily interjected a question. "Eddie, were you able to contact Detective Laramie up in Memphis regarding the Blanchard killings?"

Emily's question had a calming effect on Eddie. He realized that she was being cooperative, at least on some level. "Yeah," he said, purposely avoiding saying "thank you." He added, "They're going to fax me the report on the Blanchard murders."

Emily nodded her head in approval.

"But don't think for a minute," said Eddie, his voice rising again, "that lets you guys off the hook. It don't. You guys better start coming clean or I'll throw all your asses in jail for obstruction." Eddie grabbed his notepad and the rest of his belongings and left.

With his cell phone battery depleted, Linc had attached his pager to his belt. The little unit had begun vibrating during Eddie's harangue. Fearing that Eddie would have become even more agitated, Linc had chosen not to check on who it was that might have called. Linc didn't want to add fuel to Eddie's fire. Now that Eddie had left, Linc checked the tiny display monitor. The call had come from Carmen. Since Linc spent so much time out of the office, he received her calls and pages on a regular basis. Together, they had devised a three digit number code that they used as a signal if Carmen had a situation that needed Linc's immediate attention. This particular call did not include the prearranged code, and was therefore, not an emergency. That meant that Linc could certainly wait to return it.

Moments after Eddie had left, Preston came charging through the door into the emergency room. He was shaken and confused. Having received Emily's telephone message, Preston had chosen not to return the call until after he arrived back home. Walking into the library, he became appalled at its condition. It had been destroyed. Seeing the large pool of nearly dried blood on the tile floor, Preston became frightened and panicked. He had run through the house, hollering Emily's name and calling for Manfred. Quite some time had elapsed before he had calmed himself enough to remember to return Emily's voice mail. When Preston finally spoke to his daughter, she was somewhat evasive, not wanting to go into too much detail over the phone. He kept interrupting with pointed questions about her well being as well as that of the others. Emily finally insisted that he come down to Good Samaritan Hospital and allow her to explain in person.

The moment Preston arrived at the hospital, Emily, Pitch and Jennifer began to tell him the story of what transpired that afternoon. They started by relating that Manfred had been shot and had undergone surgery. The surgeon had already come out and spoken to Emily, assuring her that Manfred was going to be all right. The doctor had said that Manfred's life had been saved for two reasons: the bullet had only partially severed the jugular vein, and someone had done a good job of keeping pressure on the wound, preventing Manfred from bleeding to death. When the surgeon made that comment, Pitch and Jennifer hugged each other. They felt like heroes.

Preston was deeply engrossed in hearing the dramatic events, when a nurse showed up to give Linc his tetanus injection and antibiotics. "All right, everybody," she announced in a drawl that smacked of Georgia Peach. "Y'all have to clear out right now. I have to give this poor man his shot."

Everyone stopped to look at the nurse. She was a pert and pretty woman with a small face and a slightly turned up nose. She was in her late thirties, dressed in standard white nurse's uniform with a little white ribbon that neatly fastened a pile of blonde hair into a bun. Her most outstanding feature was the tightness of her outfit. The uniform strained at her breasts but, fortunately, it was held together with a sturdy zipper. If the top-half of her uniform had sported buttons, they would have popped like champagne corks. Her white slacks were just as tight. They hugged her thighs, hips and cheeks of her buttocks like pantyhose two sizes too small. "C'mon now," she said to the visitors, as she began to pull the privacy curtain around Linc. "Out, out, out."

Preston backed out of the way of the closing curtain, while Jennifer guided Pitch to a safe distance. Emily stood her ground and said, "I thought you're only giving him a tetanus shot?"

"That's right, honey," the nurse said as she closed herself in with Linc, leaving only a narrow opening for Emily to exit. "Now, you go on and wait right over there with the others."

"Wait a minute," Emily insisted. "Why can't I wait right here while you give him his shot?"

"Honey," she said, her voice signaling that her patience was running thin, "I have to inject this medication directly into this poor man's tush. Now, do you know this man well enough to see him with his pants off?"

"Emily," said Linc, "why don't you wait with the others. I'll be right out."

Emily felt her cheeks get hot, as she walked over to where the others were standing. Preston broke her sullen mood by asking about the rest of the story. "So, if he wasn't an FBI agent," asked Preston, "who was he? How did my library end up looking like a war zone?" Pitch and Jennifer immediately resumed the tale from their own perspectives, while Emily just glared at the closing curtain. Soon, Emily had rejoined in the telling of the saga.

Moving up close to Linc, the nurse grabbed a handful of his belt and lightly shook it back and forth. "Now, you slip those trousers down, Lincoln," she said in a husky voice, "so I can . . . do my thing." She was looking into his eyes and smiling seductively.

Linc undid his belt and let his pants slip down. He was careful to allow only a little of his butt cheek to be exposed. Because he was shirtless in the first place, it meant that a lot of his bare skin was now exposed.

The nurse looked him over approvingly and told him that her name was Claire. She began making small talk by asking how he had been injured. Linc was momentarily taken by her name. It brought back memories of a long ago elevator accident. However, this Claire was a far cry from the Claire he remembered rescuing.

Linc answered her queries pleasantly, but did not offer too many details. He was just looking forward to re-joining Emily and the others.

Nurse Claire gave Linc his injection. Then, she took a large four-by-four gauze pad in her right hand and put some rubbing alcohol on it. With it, she swabbed the area of the injection. Her left hand came to rest lightly on his exposed stomach. She then surprised Linc by running her right hand over, under and around his butt, during which she loudly exclaimed, "Oh, Lincoln! My, oh my!"

He looked at her with a kind of half smile as he pulled up his pants and refastened his belt buckle.

"Now honey," said Claire as she boldly slipped a piece of paper into his pants pocket, "This stuff I gave you might make you a little woozy. So, if you should need me for anything . . . anything at all, just call me. Even if it's after eleven. That's when I get off."

Linc smiled a big smile and reached for the privacy curtain himself. He whipped it back, looked at his four friends and declared, "All set."

Emily came forward to help Linc put on his new shirt. She had overheard the seductive utterances while she was forced to stand with the others on the outside of the cubicle. The fact that this particular nurse had been alone with Linc bothered Emily immensely. She watched the woman pat Linc's rear end just before she walked away. Emily's mouth fell open. She stood and stared at the back of the nurse, her tight slacks emphasizing an exaggerated wiggle, as she walked down the hallway and disappeared around the corner. Emily was aware of a flood of emotions roiling inside of her. It had been a long time since she had experienced anything close to what was bothering her now. Was it loathing for this hussy posing as a nurse? Jealousy? Embarrassment at being shooed out of the cubicle? Perhaps all of them. Nonetheless, she was keenly aware of a feeling of possessiveness that she had never before felt.

Linc went about the business of checking himself out of the E.R. When that was done, Preston, who seemed very pensive, decided to take everyone out for dinner.

Once outside in the parking lot, Preston said, "Emily dear, why don't you take Pitch and Jennifer. Linc will ride with me. We're going to *Café L'Europe*. In case we get separated, it's in the three hundred block of South County Road."

Linc walked over to Emily's car. She rolled down the window to allow Linc to say something. Leaning in close, he said, "Don't drift back too far. Stay close to me."

She nodded.

Then, Linc said to Preston, "You get into the passenger seat. I'm going to drive."

Preston did not argue. The two car convoy left Good Samaritan Hospital and made their way across the bridge that went over the Intercoastal waterway. Back in Palm Beach, traffic was light as they drove down South County Road toward the restaurant. Linc kept a constant vigil on Emily's car, making sure it did not fall too far behind.

"Preston," said Linc as he made a sharp left turn, "we're in serious trouble."

"I realize that," said Preston. "We have to talk."

"You bet," he replied. "Now that the killer knows where Pitch is, we're going to have to hide him somewhere else."

"Oh? Oh. Right," said Preston obviously preoccupied. "Hide him somewhere else."

Linc looked over at Preston. "What's the matter with you? You okay?"

"Uh . . . yes," answered Preston, his mind distracted for an instant. "I'm fine. Fine."

"So, do you have any suggestions?" asked Linc.

"Suggestions? About what?"

Linc waited a long moment until he had Preston's full attention. "Preston, is there something you want to talk to me about?"

Preston blinked a couple of times. "No. I'm all right, Lincoln. Really. I just got sidetracked, that's all. You have my full attention now. Please go on with what you were saying."

"I was saying that if we don't hide Pitch somewhere else, we may not be as lucky next time."

"You think he might try again?" asked Preston.

Linc's pager went off. He double-checked the rearview mirror to make sure that Emily was following before he checked the pager. It was another call from Carmen, but since she still had not entered the pre-arranged emergency notation, his return call could wait.

"Preston, I have no doubt that this man will try again. He's a professional. He never panicked and he stayed focused. That makes him the most dangerous kind of killer. I'm sure he'll be back."

"So, the question is, what do we do with the kids?" Preston asked.

Linc offered a suggestion. "I was thinking about one of your apartments over in West Palm Beach."

Preston had vast real estate holdings that included large tracts of commercial properties and a sizeable number of residential rental units throughout South Florida. "Excellent idea," said Preston. "I should have thought of that."

"Can you think of any of your apartments that might be suitable?"

Preston pondered for just a second before saying, "I have a very nice furnished unit just off Dixie Highway that just became available. It's a two-bedroom, two-bath. Just a hundred yards off Dixie."

"Where on Dixie is it?" asked Linc.

"It's sort of right in the noise path of the airport," replied Preston, "but what the hell, it's free."

Café L'Europe was one of the finer restaurants on Palm Beach and was regularly frequented by the world's jet-setters.

Dinner could have been a sumptuous affair but, whereas the others only had appetites for salads and light fare, Pitch ordered like a man who hadn't eaten for a week. He was pumped. Besides having survived an assassination attempt, he felt like a stalwart for having helped save Manfred's life. Talking incessantly about the brawl in the library, Pitch replayed the moment when he pulled the chair out of Linc's path just in the nick of time. All during Pitch's re-telling of the saga, Jennifer hung onto his arm and his every word. Pitch was glowing.

The waitress refreshed the iced teas and brought coffee for Linc. He decided it was time to bring up the subject of moving Pitch and Jennifer to a safer location. Linc spoke at length about the probability of the killer returning and how their lives could be in jeopardy once again.

Pitch and Jennifer listened to Preston describe the apartment he had in mind. He sounded a little like a rental agent extolling the virtues of an apartment that had seen far too many tenants over the years.

Emily picked up on the suggestion, "We know it's not the Taj Mahal, but it'll be bright, clean and, most of all, safe."

"And it's only for a little while," added Linc. "Just until this thing blows over."

A quiet moment was followed by Pitch saying, "Jennifer, there's no reason for you to be in the middle of this danger. I want you to go home."

"What?" she said, not believing what she heard.

Pitch held both her hands and said, "You can go to your grandparents in Key West, or back to your folks up north . . ."

Linc interrupted, "We may be beyond that."

They all looked at him.

Linc explained, "The killer is a professional. He's efficient and competent. He had no compunction about killing Crystal and he won't think twice about hurting Jennifer. Especially if it means that you," Linc pointed directly at Pitch, "will give him what he wants."

"But how would he be able to find her," asked Pitch.

"A man like that doesn't come cheaply," clarified Linc. "Whoever he works for has a lot of money. That means he's well financed and has excellent sources. Finding Jennifer wouldn't be any trouble at all."

Jennifer asked, "So, if we move into this new place, we'll be safe, right? He won't be able to find us?"

"Nothing is a hundred percent, Jennifer," said Linc, "but you'll be safer there than at your grandparents. Now look. Preston here, has quite a few of these rental units . . ."

"Over a hundred just in Palm Beach County," qualified Preston.

"See?" said Linc. "With that many apartments, it would take someone a long time to discover your whereabouts."

"When do you think it would be prudent for us to move," asked Pitch.

Linc thought for a moment. "Tomorrow," he said. "After we come back from Crystal's funeral."

Jennifer hugged Pitch's arm tighter, "So, you don't think he'll come back tonight?" she asked nervously.

Linc smiled broadly, "What are you worried about, Jennifer? You'll be sleeping right next to Pitch, the man of the hour. Of course you'll be all right."

Preston gave Pitch a good-natured punch in the arm, and they all laughed. When the laughter subsided, Linc said, "I'll stand guard tonight in the living room just in case."

Arriving back at Preston's estate, they were greeted by Harold Bibbs. Mr. Bibbs, as he preferred to be known, was a regular part-time staff member who occasionally substituted for Louise or Manfred. He informed Preston that the police had left only an hour before. They gave instructions that they would be back tomorrow and that no one should disturb anything in the library. After Mr. Bibbs had gone home for the night, the five of them gathered at the entrance to the library to peer past the yellow police tape and into the semi darkness of the room.

Linc pulled Preston away from the others and whispered, "Remember that Smith and Wesson I gave you for your birthday a couple of years ago?"

When Preston nodded his head, Linc said, "Get it for me, please. I'll feel much better tonight with that .38 by my side."

Pitch and Jennifer didn't realize how exhausted they were until there was a lull in the conversation. Jennifer walked up to Linc, threw her arms around him and kissed his cheek. She thanked him sincerely for all that he had done, including saving their lives. Then, Pitch surprised Linc by stepping forward and hugging him as well. Bidding everyone a good night, Pitch and Jennifer retired to their upstairs bedroom.

Preston retrieved the pistol out of a locked drawer in his desk before putting in a call to Good Samaritan Hospital. He was assured that Manfred was resting comfortably and would be just fine. Preston came out of his study and joined the others in the living room. He handed the pistol to Linc and gave them both an update on Manfred's progress.

The living room was dominated by a long curving sectional in a heavy white on white fabric flecked with royal blue and persimmon. The huge unit made up two corners of a conversation pit. A matching two piece sectional and two chairs, one in royal blue and the other in persimmon, completed the grouping. In the center was a large contemporary coffee table of mostly glass, under which was a magnificent Persian rug that had splashes of all the colors in the furniture. The second half of the room was home to a grand piano that sat in front a series of bay windows, offering a panoramic view of the ocean.

Emily was sitting on one side of the two-piece sectional, with her shoes off and her feet tucked up underneath her. Linc was standing nearby.

Preston said, "Manfred's going to be all right. Thank God. He may never want to work for me again, but at least he's not dead."

"Daddy," said Emily, "right now I'm more worried about you. You look like you've been through the wringer."

Preston nodded. "It's just . . ." he started then hesitated. "After hearing what happened this afternoon . . . I mean, all your lives were in danger. I didn't realize the significance of . . ." Preston's voice trailed off.

"Preston," said Linc, "why don't you go get a good night's sleep. It'll be all right. I'll be standing watch here all night."

"It's not just that," Preston stammered, "It's the fact that I wasn't here. I was away . . . doing . . ."

Emily stood up and went to her father. "Daddy, you can't go around feeling guilty about not being here. You had no control over that. It just happened. Things happen and we never know when. I'm sure you wanted to be here, and I'm sure you're feeling terrible that you weren't. But try not to feel guilty about it. After all, things worked out all right, didn't they? We're all here and we're all fine."

Preston nodded his head.

"Now, Linc is right, Daddy. Try to get some sleep." Emily smiled warmly and continued. "You know what they say; things always look brighter in the morning."

Preston kissed Emily's cheek, nodded to Linc and went off to bed. Linc moved to the sectional and sat down. Emily sat right next to him and snuggled into his left side. He started to put his arm around her and winced when the stitches began to pull at the fresh wound. "Wait a minute, Emily. This is no good like this."

"Oh, my goodness," she cried. "I'm so sorry. I forgot about your stitches. Are you all right?"

"Sure," he said smiling through the pain. "I'm fine. We just need to switch sides."

As Emily and Linc stood up, his pager went off again. "Y'know," he said as he unhooked it from his belt and checked to see who was paging him at this late hour, "this thing has been non-stop tonight."

It was yet another page from Carmen. "Emily, it's Carmen again. This is about the fourth or fifth time she's paged me. Let me give her a call and see what's up."

Emily made herself comfortable while Linc walked into the Oak Room to make the phone call. She had no intention of going upstairs to sleep. Her plan was to stay here with Linc for the duration of the night. Emily played over the events of the day, focusing on the terrible battle that had raged in the library. She remembered being frozen in time. If it were not for Lincoln Bradshaw, she would be dead. It was amazing to see him fly across the room to save her life. Closing her eyes, Emily thought about how safe she felt whenever he was near. She daydreamed of being totally alone with him and basked in the warm feeling that came from the thought. Tonight, they could cuddle on the sofa and talk of intimate things. She sensed his interest and desire. When she kissed him at the office, she knew it was right and wondered what would have happened if Carmen had not barged in.

Remembering that Linc was still on the phone with Carmen, she stood and walked into the Oak Room.

"All right," Linc said into the receiver. There was a long pause as he listened to what Carmen had to say. "Yeah, sure. That's okay." Another long pause. He looked up at Emily while he listened to Carmen.

Emily noticed a different look in his eyes. She could not decipher its significance.

He said, "Well, keep in mind, Carmen, Emily and I will be going to that girl's funeral tomorrow, and then we have a couple of things to do. So, we probably won't see you until around noon time, maybe as late as one o'clock."

A short pause, then he said, "Thanks. You too," and hung up.

"What is it Linc?" Emily asked nervously. "What's wrong?"

After carefully replacing the telephone receiver, Linc said, "Carmen finished running that Comprehensive Report on Elaine Velachuk."

"And?" asked Emily.

"And she found out that Elaine Velachuk, a.k.a. Elana Velez, has been cohabiting with someone special."

"You're making me crazy, Linc. Just tell me what she said."

"It turns out," Linc said slowly, letting his words drift into the air, "that her 'live-in' boyfriend is none other than your ex-husband, Jubal Salaran."

CHAPTER
FORTY ONE

I t seemed as though the night would never end. The pain was just enough to keep Mendosa from falling into a deep sleep. He had tossed and turned all night, trying to find a comfortable place for himself, but to no avail. Time and again, he would come fully awake out of a nap-like state. It happened when a stabbing pain would shoot through his hand, or the wound on his thigh would begin throbbing.

After his struggle with the big man, Mendosa had stopped off at a large pharmacy and purchased the items necessary to treat his injuries. Once back at his motel room, he assessed the damage. The index finger on his right hand looked broken. It was considerably swollen at the base and bent backward at a punishing ninety-degree angle. The pain was excruciating and caused him to perspire profusely. There was no cut, no blood, and he could not see any sign of a protruding bone. Perhaps, he thought, it was only a dislocation. Preparing himself for what had to be done, Mendosa clenched his teeth and took a deep breath. Using his left hand, he grasped the errant finger tightly. Trying to reset it correctly, he yanked it in a mighty upward and away motion. Mendosa emitted a short throaty cry when the pain reached its apex. The agony was so severe that he thought he might black out. The process created an odd sound, as though someone were cracking his knuckles, and suddenly, Mendosa's finger popped back into place. Mendosa collapsed back onto the bed, his knees drawn up, as he rocked back and forth, gently caressing his right hand. After waiting a quarter-hour for the hot surging stabs to subside, he tested it. His distress level had diminished greatly, but he had almost no control with the injured finger. Besides having only partial mobility in his thumb, any motion of his middle or ring finger resurrected the pain.

Mendosa was now ready to minister to his leg wound. Crashing into that glass floor lamp had created a four-inch laceration on the outer side of his thigh. The incision had bled down his leg and into his sock and shoe. He removed two pieces of broken glass before using some antiseptic to clean out the gash. When he was satisfied, he used a couple of butterfly stitches to hold it together. He planned to leave it exposed to the air while he slept. He would wrap it tightly the following day in case any pressure had to be exerted.

It was now an hour before dawn, and Mendosa finally gave up trying to sleep. He went into the bathroom and ran the hot water for a minute. He filled a glass of the steaming liquid and sat gingerly in the chair next to the bed. In European fashion, he sipped his hot water while he replayed the events of yesterday and thought about his plan for getting the disc.

His first thoughts ran back to the fast pitched battle he had with that big man, the one whom the woman referred to as "Mr. Bradshaw." He was quick. Unpredictably quick. Mendosa figured him to be well over six-foot-two and broad enough to be into the two hundred-pound range. At that size, Bradshaw should not have been able to react as fast as he did. Mendosa had been startled to see him move. Another remarkable thing about his opponent was his extraordinary agility. Mendosa had tried several times to knock him off balance, but it was not until Bradshaw had become entangled in the ladder assembly that he finally went down.

As a youngster, Mendosa had learned the trick of ignoring pain. The mysticism of transcending it, came easily to Mendosa, giving him the ability to shut out pain for short periods of time. That endowment had proven itself invaluable when it came to his getting injured during a fight. Despite very few adversaries having that same ability, it was obvious that the man, Bradshaw, possessed it. Mendosa knew Bradshaw was hurt each time he was slammed into some solid object or heavy piece of furniture. Nevertheless, the man never showed the pain. As a matter of fact, Bradshaw's facial expression did not show any emotion at all during their struggle. Mendosa knew that his opponent was a force to be reckoned with, but he had neither the time nor the inclination to battle him again.

Mendosa was a pragmatist. He did not have an ego and never dwelt on the fates. He had some unfortunate luck yesterday when Bradshaw and that woman showed up, and more bad luck when that man-servant shouted something, allowing Bradshaw the time to react. But, those were things in the past. They were neither signs of doom nor bad omens. They were merely things that happened. Mendosa refocused on the task at hand. He had to find Pitch Pechowski.

Mendosa toyed with the idea that Pitch might still be holed up in that mansion, but the appearance of Bradshaw put another dimension into his thinking. Bradshaw was not an average citizen. He handled himself like a professional, and someone such as that would not allow that young, inexperienced Pechowski boy to stay in a place where he might be attacked again. Mendosa was certain that Bradshaw was in charge of Pitch's well being and would probably have him moved to a safer location.

Desperately wanting to control the technology of Pechowski's device, the assassin became obsessed with getting the disc. With it, he had omnipotence. He yearned for the wealth it could bring, but more than that, the wielding of its power was the one true aphrodisiac. He would direct his immediate energies into locating Pechowski.

The splinter division of the NSA run by Parlotti, had resources that seemed inexhaustible. Mendosa would have liked to use those connections to find Pitch, but he knew the door was closed and that Parlotti would no longer be cooperative. Mendosa understood that he was probably cut off from any contact with the division. On two separate occasions, he had ignored the ads in the newspaper that read, "The lass of Mont Valier, call home." Now, on his own, Mendosa needed a clear head in order to find this Pechowski person.

Once in his grasp, Mendosa needed only a few short minutes with the boy. Yesterday, Mendosa had tested Pitch for any weakness in his strength or resolve, using an old Roman Centurion technique of gripping the hand of your opponent and pulling them slightly off balance. He knew the young man would never be able to hold up under the pressure and pain that could be inflicted. Mendosa wanted what was inside Pitch's head. He had his target, now it was time to take aim.

*   *   *

The two vehicles traveled in tandem, only separated by a few car lengths. Pitch and Jennifer were in the lead car while Linc trailed at a safe distance. Feeling that his brightly colored Corvette would have been a red flag, Linc had chosen to drive Emily's car while she sat in the passenger seat. They were headed west on Forest Hill Boulevard into the town of Wellington to attend the funeral of Crystal Richards.

Crystal's family lived in Wellington. The area was fast becoming a bedroom community for the town of West Palm Beach. New homes were cropping up like dandelions in the spring. The quality of these homes was superior, attracting upper class and upper middle-class to the area. Wellington's fame and notoriety came from the internationally known *Palm Beach Polo Club,* which was the stage for some of the finest polo matches in the world. Prince Charles, himself, had been a frequent visitor and past participant of the tournaments. Even the late Princess Diana had made several appearances. Other well-known "Royals" were also often seen in the stands. Other attendees included some local resident luminaries from the entertainment industry such as the Gabor sisters and the Smothers brothers. Rush hour was becoming a nightmare.

The cemetery was located on the far west side of town. Pitch had directions in hand, and he seemed to be steering toward it without any mistakes. Following closely, Linc kept a watchful eye on everything around him.

The previous night, as Linc stood guard over the house, Emily had talked about her life with Jube Salaran. Although Linc knew most of the story, Emily wanted to fill in the gaps to which Preston may not have been privy. As more of her past unfolded, Linc became acutely aware of her character. Sensing her giving and honest nature, Linc became cognizant of how well she molded into his perception of perfect.

They had talked about the new revelation regarding Jube Salaran living with Elana Velez. Linc confessed to having had a dislike for "old Jubal baby," as he referred to him, and expressed his hope that the man was involved in the Sidney Aarons extortion case. Emily, on the other hand, had thought it was typical of Jube to get involved with a low-life person like Elaine Velachuk. Emily talked about her ex's constant scheming and conniving. She recalled how he was always conspiring with other shady characters in order to hatch some sort of devious money-making plot. Linc had found her storytelling fascinating, and the night had passed quickly, without incident.

As they drove along, following Pitch and Jennifer, Linc noted that Emily was still in a chatty mood. She was in the middle of telling a tale of her second date with Jube. It was an awful affair that involved a single slice of pizza, a couple bottles of beer and some terrible bites on her rump from sand fleas, when she halted in mid sentence and switched gears. Spinning in her seat in order to look him squarely into his eyes, she asked, "What happened between you and that nurse yesterday?"

Linc took his eyes off the road for several seconds to look at Emily. He was having trouble following the change in subject matter. "Nurse? What nurse?"

"You know perfectly well, what nurse."

"Emily, what are you talking about?" he said with a crooked smile. "You were just telling me about you and Jube on the beach with some beer and pizza."

"I'm talking about the nurse that practically threw me out of the cubicle so that she could have you alone with your pants down! What went on in there?"

Linc began a slow nod of his head. "Oh, right," he said as his crooked smile straightened into a grin. "Nurse Claire. With the needle."

"Well, Nurse Claire," said Emily emphasizing her name, "was moaning so loudly you could hear it all over the emergency room. What went on in there?"

At the tone of Emily's voice, Linc did a double-take. His smile broadened as he said, "She was fascinated with my butt and kept running her hands over it."

Emily waited for some kind of sign that Linc was joking. When none came, she asked, "And you allowed it?"

"Well," said Linc suppressing a chuckle, "to tell you the truth, Emily, her hands were as soft as fine deer-skin gloves, her long eyelashes were batting at me like hummingbirds, her lips . . ."

"Oh, shut up!" said Emily, reaching her hand over to cover his mouth.

When Linc at last felt Emily's grip relax, he held the palm of her hand to his lips and kissed it gently saying, "Frankly, Emily, I couldn't wait to get out of there. I'm glad you were there waiting for me."

The funeral service was a contrast to the overwhelming crowd that was in attendance at Scott's funeral. The family of Crystal Richards was small, and her parents did not have the circle of friends who had surrounded Sidney and Lenore Aarons. The biggest group of people was Crystal's classmates from her college. It seemed to Jennifer that the entire population of their dormitory was present. Pitch stood close to Jennifer as she went from one girl to the next, hugging each and sharing tears and grief.

Linc sat in the back of the chapel with Emily at his side. From this vantage-point, he could see the entry door as well as the backs of everyone in the room.

Emily noticed a man in a black suit standing just outside the chapel door. Although the leaves of a large silk plant hid the man's face, his height and build were similar to that of the FBI imposter. She whispered to Linc, "Look at that man standing just outside the entryway."

Linc turned to look, then whispered back, "It's okay. He's the funeral director."

Emily's breathing returned to normal.

When the procession relocated to the cemetery grounds, Linc went into high alert. Letting the crowd walk in front, he focused on the surrounding area. He studied every parked car and checked every group of trees and each clump of bushes that could have doubled as a hiding place. He watched each stranger intently, as his or her proximity to Pitch and Jennifer closed.

All during this time, Linc held Emily's hand. At one point, starting to walk away to offer condolences to Crystal's parents, Emily felt a firm tug on her hand. Looking up at Linc, she saw an almost imperceptible shake of his head. It was an unmistakable signal that he did not want her to leave his side. She continued holding his hand and stepped closer. Even with the possibility of an unknown danger lurking, she felt safe and secure standing next to him.

Before they left the graveside service, Linc met with Pitch and gave him detailed directions to the new apartment off Dixie Highway. Since it was very easy to find, Pitch said he didn't need the map.

"I want you to follow the exact route I've laid out," said Linc. "Don't deviate at all. Don't go through any red lights. As a matter of fact, don't go through any yellow lights either. I'll be right behind you, and I don't want to lose you."

"You think we might be followed?" Pitch asked.

"I just don't want to take any chances," said Linc. "This apartment is going to be your safe-house until we can catch this guy. Believe me, I know the route I've mapped out is a little convoluted, but if someone is following you, I'll be able to spot him. If you see me flash my lights, pull over and stop."

Pitch repeated the instructions. "Flashing lights, pull over and stop."

"And if you hear me blow my horn three times, take off."

"Take off?" questioned Pitch. "To where?"

"Anywhere," replied Linc. "Three beeps on my beeper, means you take off as fast as you can. Go somewhere crowded. We'll worry about catching up with one another at a later time."

"I'm nervous," stated Pitch.

"Relax," advised Linc. "This is all just a precaution."

The trip back to Pitch and Jennifer's new apartment was uneventful. With all the extra turns that Linc had routed, it took about forty minutes to complete. Vigilant for anything suspicious, he and Emily talked little during the drive. Finally, as they neared their destination, Linc broke a long silence when he picked up his cell phone and placed a call.

Emily never took her eyes off him. She watched as he surveyed the passing neighborhoods and constantly checked the rearview and side view mirrors, waiting for the phone connection to be made.

"This is Linc Bradshaw. Let me speak to Ferdie Dumay."

Emily remembered meeting Ferdie the previous day. He headed up one of the agencies that Linc used on occasion. Although the meeting was brief, Emily recalled that Ferdie seemed to be a person of high energy with eyes that darted and hands that were constantly in motion. Linc had explained that he used Ferdie Dumay's agency whenever he needed manpower.

"Ferdie? It's Linc. You got your people in place?"

Emily watched as Linc slowly nodded his head in response to whatever Ferdie was saying.

"Doors and windows too?"

Emily waited through another pause.

"Round the clock," stated Linc. "And they understand they're supposed to call my cell phone with a nine-one-one if anything pops, right?"

There was only a short pause before Linc said, "Okay," and disconnected.

Emily stated, "You hired protection for Pitch and Jennifer, didn't you?"

"Yes, I did."

"Is this costing a lot of money?" she queried.

"It's all right. Ferdie owes me a couple of favors, and I'm just calling them in."

Emily thought a moment before asking, "You think this is necessary?"

Stealing a moment from his ongoing surveillance, Linc said, "Better to be safe than sorry."

*   *   *

Vincent Parlotti turned to John Anderson, "I swear, all they do in this town is have meetings. Breakfast meetings, lunch meetings and dinner meetings. Then, there's cocktail meetings and all the freakin' meetings in between. Don't ever retire in Washington, D.C. You'll never have a moment to relax and enjoy yourself."

"To tell you the truth, Boss," said John Anderson, "I already got a place staked out in Arizona."

"Smart," stated Parlotti, unsmiling as he closed his briefcase. "I'm on my way over to the 'Hill.' I've got a twelve-thirty with Carrigan and he's just finishing up a meeting with Senator Boyd Williamson and his Appropriations Committee. When I get back, I'll let you know if we can still pay you a salary."

"No problem, Boss," said Anderson stone faced. "This job is so much fun, I'd do it for free."

Parlotti paused as he made his way towards the door. "What's happening with Gator and the Dutchman?" he asked. "Did you schedule their assignment?"

"I have them set to leave on Sunday," answered Anderson. "An evening flight direct into West Palm Beach."

"And they understand what it is they're supposed to do?"

"I've already briefed them on their assignment," replied Anderson. "They understand that Harpoon is their target. I made it perfectly clear that they are not to bring him in. Just leave him for the undertaker."

Parlotti nodded his approval and walked out the door.

CHAPTER FORTY TWO

It was eleven thirty-five in the morning when the four of them arrived at the new apartment. Linc and Emily decided to take some extra time to get Pitch and Jennifer settled into their new surroundings. The apartment itself was adequate, with two windows each in the living room and master bedroom that faced out toward the street. All the remaining windows faced the rear of the property. The back yard was terribly overgrown with thick trees and bushes that made it impossible to tell where one yard ended and the next one began. The apartment was part of an "eight-plex;" a building, shaped like a letter "H" laying on its side, that housed eight separate units. There was only one front entrance but two exits out the back of the building. Once a person climbed the three steps from the street and walked into the front vestibule, he had a choice of two staircases that led to the second floor. There were four apartments on each floor and a good-sized storage closet at the end of each hallway. The front and rear hallways, which extended the full width of the building, were connected by a perpendicular center hallway that ran from front to back. The design allowed for a breezeway effect as well as easy access and egress.

Emily had taken Jennifer out to pick up some sandwiches while Linc went over the security measures with Pitch. Linc explained that he had arranged for surveillance and would be notified if anything strange or suspicious occurred.

Linc's comment piqued Pitch's curiosity and he bent at the waist to look out the living room window. "Surveillance?" he asked. "You've arranged for surveillance out there? Even as we speak?"

Linc modified his statement by saying, "Actually, they're in the middle of setting up right about now."

Pitch took a step closer to the window and said, "Where are they going to be situated?"

"It doesn't matter," said Linc, drawing Pitch's attention away from the window. "It isn't necessary for you to know where they are. It's only important for them to know where you are."

Knowing that Preston had already made arrangements to have the new telephone installed, Linc picked up the phone and listened for a dial tone. Satisfied that it was working, he next made certain that his cell phone number was attached to the refrigerator and that Pitch understood how to use the three-digit emergency code.

Finishing lunch, Linc and Emily prepared to leave for the office. Before saying goodbye, Emily invited the couple to join her and Linc for dinner that evening. They agreed to meet at Preston's home at seven p.m.

Carmen was happy to see her colleagues. She was a very social person and preferred not to work alone. "*Buenas tardes,* people," she exclaimed as they came through the door. "I have tons of messages for everyone." She stood and handed Linc a small stack of messages and documents, but for Emily, she had only two pieces of paper. "This one," said Carmen pointing to the big sheet, "is a fax you got from Mr. Eddie. It's the report you were waiting for from the Memphis Police. And this one," she said handing her a small pink piece of paper, "is a message to call that same Mr. Eddie as soon as you get in."

Linc stopped what he was doing, put one hand in his pocket and said, "Jeez, Eddie doesn't want to talk to me anymore, huh?"

Carmen put both her hands on her hips. "He prefers to only talk to us," she said with a hand motion that encompassed both herself and Emily. "He doesn't think you have sensuous hips like we got."

Suppressing a wry smile, Linc said, "Listen, I'm going to be out of the office for a couple of hours. If either of you need me, buzz my phone."

"Where you heading?" asked Emily.

"I've got some, uh . . . field work to do."

Emily paused for a brief second before asking, "Okay if I come along?"

"No," said Linc. "You're not an agent or an operative. I hired you for your inside skills. You're a research analyst. And a damn good one, I might add."

Emily watched as Linc put the papers back on Carmen's desk and started towards the door. "You're going out to find Elaine Velachuk, aren't you?"

Linc straddled the threshold just long enough to smile at Emily and to give her a wink. Then, he was gone.

"Be careful," she whispered, even though she knew he could not hear the sentiment.

Emily took the Blanchard crime report into her office to study it while she placed a call to Eddie Strickland. There was one fact that instantly jumped out at her. It seemed that there were three murder victims mentioned in the Memphis report; Roger and Sandi Blanchard as well as Mary Franzheimer, their babysitter. However, the report also listed two survivors. They were the young Blanchard children, Adam, age ten and Sarah, an eight year-old little girl. Both were found bound with duct tape and lying in the same room as their murdered parents.

Emily's first thought was one of overwhelming compassion. The fact that two innocent children had been subjected to such a horrendous calamity was almost unthinkable. As she studied the report further, she wondered if the children might actually have been witnesses to the killings or if they had been carried there for some other reason. Her thoughts were interrupted by Carmen's voice when she announced that Eddie was on line two.

"Emily, you luscious hunk of woman!" began Eddie. "You want to come out and play?"

Ignoring his remark, Emily said, "thanks for faxing over that report on the Blanchard murders. I found it most interesting."

"I'm talking about a wild night of sex and you're talking about killings and carnage and chaos."

"Seriously, Eddie," said Emily, "did you get a chance to actually read it?"

"I glanced at it. What did you find so interesting?"

Emily spoke about the two Blanchard children being found alive. She proposed a couple of scenarios that could have accounted for them being found where they were. "You know," she said, "there's even the possibility that they were witnesses to the whole thing.

As Eddie mulled over her comment, Emily went on. "I need another favor, Eddie. Could you call that Detective Laramie up in Memphis again and ask . . ."

"Whoa! Hold up," interrupted Eddie. "That's one of the reasons I called you earlier. I spoke with Laramie and told him all about you. Y'know, what a 'looker' you are. Stuff like that. I also told him you were a consultant on this case. So anyways, now that he knows you're a professional, you can call him direct. He's expecting your call."

"Thank you, Eddie. You're a dream."

"Yeah, yeah, I know. Also, I wanted you to know that I had the crime lab boys do a rush job on the blood samples we got from that dude who bled all over your dad's library. Should have the results shortly. I'll fax 'em to you as soon as their ready along with any fingerprint information."

"That sounds wonderful, Eddie. Together, we're going to get this guy."

"Now hear me, Emily, and hear me good," said Eddie with a distinct change to his voice. "There's a price to pay for everything I'm doing."

"More sexual favors," said Emily trying to sound bored.

"I'm being serious," he said. "If you or Linc get any new information on this case . . . I'm talking about anything at all, you've got to feed it to me. Understood?"

"Yes, I understand," she said. "I'd like to make a suggestion."

"Shoot."

"Can you arrange for a sketch artist?" Emily asked. "There were five of us who got a good look at the imposter. Surely, one of your artists . . ."

Eddie interrupted. "I want you all down here at headquarters to go through the mug shots."

"I don't think we'll find him in the mug shots, Eddie," she said with a lilting tone.

"What makes you so sure?"

"I think he's a foreigner."

"Y'see!" shouted Eddie, exasperated. "This is the kind of bullshit I'm talking about! You're holding out on me!"

"No I'm not, Eddie," Emily said, surprised at his reaction.

Eddie felt frustrated. "Well, how the hell do you know he's a goddamned foreigner?"

"It's just a feeling," said Emily patiently. "That's all. It was something in the way he spoke, and the way he carried himself. Nothing specific. Just a feeling." Emily waited a beat and said, "Rest assured, Eddie, if I learn anything definite, I'll let you know immediately."

"Damn it!" Eddie said with waning frustration.

They were both silent for several seconds. "I'll see what I can do about a sketch artist," he said sullenly.

As soon as Emily hung up the phone, she placed a call to Detective Laramie of the Memphis P.D. She had to wait quite a while before he finally picked up his end of the call. When he did, there was that unmistakable southern drawl that poured out of his mouth like molasses. Laramie started with an apology. "Sorry about hanging up on you the other day, Missy. I thought you was some kind of reporter or kook or something."

Emily thanked him for the apology and went straight to the business of the Blanchard murders. She had many questions regarding the murder scene, including the weapons and the motive. Laramie was being very frank and direct. After about ten minutes of answering her questions, he said, "So, Detective Strickland tells me you're pretty close to solving this thing. Says you got a lead on who done it. Is that right, Missy?"

Emily was beginning to understand the cooperation she was receiving from Laramie. He was under the impression that she had the inside track. "The fact is, I'm working on it, Detective Laramie. Getting a little closer every day."

"Y'all can call me Emmett, Missy."

"All right, Emmett. One last question. When you spoke to the children, did they give any indication that they could identify the perpetrator?"

Laramie chuckled softly and repeated the last few words of her question. "' . . . Identify the perpetrator.' You're a mighty fine talker, Missy. But, y'see, the little girl was no help at all. Didn't even remember anything. The boy . . . his name is . . . uh, Adam, he gave a kind of description. Of sorts."

"You sound as though it didn't do you any good," said Emily.

"Hell, the tyke is only ten years old. Not much good at describing features. Not to mention he was in shock for a bit. We even tried a sketch artist, but to be honest with you, Missy, I'm afraid the whole thing is just too fuzzy, if you catch my drift."

Emily asked if it would be all right if they spoke again.

Laramie said, "Would it be all right? Hell yes! We're kind of in a box canyon if you know what I mean. Anything you can come up with, Missy, would be greatly appreciated. Besides, just hearing a pretty honey-suckle voice like yours makes me stand at attention like a hot firecracker, if you catch my drift."

Emily wasn't sure whether or not to thank Detective Laramie for his last remark.

*　　*　　*

Linc drove around the block several times. Next, he drove back and forth in front of the little house where he hoped to find Elaine Velachuk. There was no garage, only a carport that was open in the front and rear, but filled with enough junk to prevent any car from ever using it. And without any car in the driveway, it looked as though no one was home.

The neighborhood was a very poor development of tiny cracker box homes, located about a half dozen blocks off Military Trail. Neighbors here tended to keep to themselves and wanted others to do the same.

Linc parked the car in front of an empty lot about forty yards away and waited. Caution was his watchword for this day. After studying the house and the neighborhood, he began re-reading the Comp Report that Carmen had prepared. It included the address of the dirty little house that sat within Linc's view. Studying the outside dimensions and window configuration, Linc figured the house had two bedrooms and one bathroom. There would only be enough room for a small living room and a kitchen. Not a lot of places to hide. He double-checked the pistol that he had earlier placed in a holster and tucked into his waistband. He approached the house like he belonged, in case there might have been some neighbors watching, and walked directly around to the back door.

The foliage in the back yard was thick and wild. Nothing had been trimmed for months. With South Florida rains and humidity, a blatant disregard for pruning soon spells disaster for a homeowner.

Linc reached into his pocket and removed a tool that would allow him to pick the lock on the door. Even though it was broad daylight, he was secluded from any possible prying eyes. He knew there would be no alarm system and, in less than ten seconds, he was standing inside the kitchen.

He stood perfectly still and listened. There was no sound, other than the rustling of the leaves behind him. He made his way quickly through the house, hastily checking all the closets and ended in the master bedroom. It was the larger of the two bedrooms, but no bigger than twelve foot square. It had a queen-sized bed and two nightstands that practically took up the entire room. Each of the two small windows had cheap plastic mini blinds that had multiple bent slats, which had yellowed with age. There were also two dressers whose lower drawers bumped the bed when opened. The bed itself was unmade and the rest of the room was in general disarray. Linc looked inside the walk-in closet. It was jam packed with fine woman's clothing; designer labels that were stylish and expensive. Linc thought that if Jubal Salaran lived in this house as well, he must have been using a different closet. There wasn't any room in this one for any of his stuff. Linc realized that whatever money Elaine made went into shopping for her wardrobe. The contents of her closet made it obvious that clothes were a very important luxury. There was only one shelf that ran the perimeter of the closet and Linc checked it. There was nothing there that could be helpful.

Stepping out of the closet, Linc paused and rested his right elbow on the taller of the two dressers. He surveyed the room before glancing at the junk piled on top of the dresser. There, partially hidden by some magazines and hair curlers, was a single videotape. It had neither writing nor markings on it. Linc took it and held onto it as he continued his search. He went through every drawer in that bedroom until he was satisfied that there was nothing else of interest. The second bedroom was smaller and held a pull out sofa bed and one chair. There was an old unplugged computer that obviously had not been used for a long time. The closet of the second bedroom was smaller and had about one-third of it devoted to a man's wardrobe. The balance held more of Elaine Velachuk's clothing. The bulk of it seemed to be formal, even elegant, evening attire. There was nothing else of interest in the room.

Linc started to walk out, when a photograph in a small frame caught his eye. He picked it up and stared. It was a picture of two men standing side by side. One was smiling, and one was not. Linc recognized the smiling man to be Jube Salaran and thought he recognized the other one, but could not quite place his face. He studied it for a while before giving up his attempt to identify the stranger. Instead, he removed the photo, folding it once before putting it into his hip pocket.

Linc continued his search until he exhausted all the closets and drawers, even the ones in the kitchen cabinets. The living room was a sparse affair with only a small sofa and two chairs. The coffee table was a rickety pine thing that looked as though its collapse was imminent. Despite all that, there was a fairly new big screen TV and VCR.

Linc slipped the videotape he was holding into the VCR and started running it. After a short burst of static and a little snow, Sidney Aarons appeared in full view, with his hands full of Elaine Velachuk, a.k.a., Elana Velez.

As the tape ran, Linc thought about Elaine and Jube. He wondered just how stupid these two characters were. Could it be, he thought, that this was their only copy of the tape? Could it be that they made only one other copy to send to Sidney? He looked around the room. Linc realized that this was not the residence of some wildly successful blackmailers. These people were slobs. They lived sloppy and they probably thought sloppy. He wondered if it could be that simple.

Linc heard the car in the driveway. He had just enough time to eject the tape and take it with him as he hurried into the kitchen. Standing at a spot where he could not be seen by an entering person, Linc held perfectly still and listened to the sound of a key opening the front door. There was only one set of footsteps that faded away into the bedroom. Linc waited.

A few minutes went by, and Linc heard what sounded like bare feet going into the bathroom. Linc sat down on one of the two available barstools and relaxed. A short wait produced the flushing sound of a toilet followed by patting bare feet as they made their way toward the kitchen. Elaine Velachuk turned the corner and stopped dead in her tracks when she spotted Linc. Her hands flew up like she was warding off an evil demon. Startled, she called out, "Oh, shit!"

Naked except for thong panties, Elana looked even more stunning than she did in the video. Linc understood why Sidney had lost his self-control. This woman was gorgeous.

"Hello, Elaine," he said softly, hoping not to alarm her further, least she start screaming.

"Who the fuck are you? How did you get in here? I'm calling the cops!"

"I'll wait while you call them," said Linc, holding up the video for her to see. "Then, we can play this videotape for them. Have a little chat. Y'know, talk about blackmail and Sidney Aarons and other fun stuff."

Regaining her composure with amazing speed, she said, "You're a cop. Aren't you?"

Linc didn't move or answer. He made no gesture to give away his position.

"What do you want?" she asked relaxing enough to put her hands on her hips and to strike a sultry pose.

Linc rested the video in his lap. He took a moment to look her up and down and said, "I want you, Elaine . . . or Elana, or whatever your name is."

At that, she tilted her head back slightly and parted her lips. One hand stayed on her hip while the other moved downward, allowing her fingers to caress the inside of her thigh. She took a step toward Linc and sensuously licked her top lip before saying, "Ooo, good. And you'll be pleased to know I come with only a teeny, tiny price tag."

Linc got up off the barstool. He straightened his shoulders and stood to his full six feet, four inch height. Lowering his voice, he said menacingly, "You ain't gonna like it when the pain starts."

The effect was immediate. Elaine backed away and instinctively covered her bare breasts with her hands. "C'mon, now," she said through a nervous smile, "You don't have to do anything crazy. We can work something out, right?"

Linc moved toward her, backing her up until her buttocks bumped the corner of the countertop. "Like a trade, huh?" he said, continuing to sound threatening.

"Yeah, that's it," she said, still with a frightened edge to her voice. "Like a trade. Anything at all. You name it."

Linc held his ground for a long moment. Unmoving, unsmiling, he just glared down at her until she was thoroughly intimidated. Then, taking a half-step back, Linc gave her a little breathing room. "Yeah," he said as though the idea of a trade suddenly sounded good. "A trade. Tell you what. We'll trade for this videotape." Linc held it up just inches from her face. "I won't kick the shit out of you, or cut your face up, and in return I get to keep this videotape. You must have another one of these in a safe deposit box somewhere, right?"

Linc watched her face. He was waiting for the sign. Then it came; first, the hesitation. Then, the biting of her bottom lip, and the double blink.

"Sure," she said, "I got another one stashed away. I got a couple more stashed away," she corrected.

Linc had no doubt that she was lying. He now knew there was no other copy of the videotape. What a bunch of imbeciles, he thought. One lousy copy and they leave it lying around on top of a dresser. If Jube Salaran had anything to do with this caper, then Linc knew, for certain, he was dealing with one simpleton and one jerk.

"Good," said Linc. "I got my copy. I'll see you around."

He started to turn and was stopped by Elaine when she said, "Hey, wait a sec. That tape has been used over and over. Let me exchange it for a new one." She reached her hand out to take the video from Linc. His right hand, which was holding the tape moved away from her reach while his left hand shot out and grabbed her wrist. He applied pressure and twisted until her face contorted with the pain.

He leaned his face close to hers and said in a tone that spoke of peril, "Now, you listen to me. A trade is a trade. Your life for this videotape. Got it?"

Elaine just nodded.

"You following what I'm telling you?"

He was still squeezing her wrist, and she nodded more vigorously.

Linc said, "Now, I'm going out of town for a week. When I get back, I want you gone. Understand?"

Elaine Velachuk nodded.

"I'll be coming straight here to make sure you've vacated this joint. Understand?"

Elaine said, "Okay. Sure. I understand."

"And if I hear you have anything more to do with Sidney Aarons . . ." Linc squeezed her wrist until he heard her suck in a painful gasp, "you're toast. Understand?"

Elaine Velachuk, a.k.a. Elana Velez, understood perfectly.

Linc walked to his car and felt a slight breeze coming from the east. It made him aware that a pool of sweat had formed in the middle of his back. Relieved that the episode was over, he ran a hand over his glistening face, glanced skyward and muttered, "Whew!"

CHAPTER
FORTY THREE

Emily was still very pleased about how her day had progressed. She had been chattering away for the better part of the last hour, telling Linc all about her research and various telephone conversations. Now they were enjoying a quiet moment.

Emily and Linc were sitting out on the pool deck sipping drinks. They took quiet pleasure from the soft wisps of balmy air that rippled the water in the blue pool. The sun had set, but there was a lingering glow deep in the western sky. In the darkened palette above them, they could see big puffy cumulus shapes, like apparitions slowly drifting through the canopy. The stars would peek out briefly before being hidden by the passing of the next cloud.

Linc and Emily were sitting close together. Reaching out to touch Emily's hand, Linc paused when his cell phone rang. Checking the number, he said, "It's a call from Ferdie Dumay. It's not a 'nine-one-one', so don't be alarmed, but I've got to take the call."

"Sure," said Emily. "Go ahead."

Linc clicked it on. "Bradshaw."

The conversation was brief. Unable to discern the subject matter, Emily waited patiently for an explanation.

Disconnecting, Linc said, "Ferdie says his people are reporting that Pitch and Jennifer are doing some strange things."

"Strange things?" Emily queried. "Like what?"

"They keep looking out of their windows," Linc said with a puzzled look on his face. "Ferdie says they kept it up all afternoon, and it was making the surveillance teams very nervous."

"Do you think they're watching to see if . . . 'he' comes back again?"

"Who knows," said Linc. "But Ferdie says I should talk to them. Tell them to stay well inside, away from the windows."

Linc slowly shook his head and went on to express his frustration when it came to dealing with people who did not understand security. He added, "They might as well just paint a target on their forehead and be done with it."

Emily changed the subject and asked about Linc's adventures in field work. "How did it go this afternoon, Linc? Were you able to find Elaine?"

Linc told her the story of Elaine and the videotape. He related the account of what happened in a droll fashion, keeping the story uninspiring and matter-of-fact. Even with that, Emily was entranced by the tale. The thrill of field work excited her. During her years in Europe working for NATO Intelligence, she had begged to be allowed to accompany the agents during their assignments. Permission was always denied.

Relating the account, Linc purposely left out the incidents of his strong-arm tactics and Elaine's nakedness. Nevertheless, Emily had a nose for detail and asked questions about the smallest nuances. Linc had to stumble through a section or two of his story, but managed to satisfy her curiosity, circumvent the sordid details and still tell the truth.

"By the way," he said reaching into his hip pocket, "I found something in her house that you're going to find interesting." Linc took out the photograph that he had confiscated from the top of the dresser. Unfolding it, he handed it to Emily. Linc watched her reaction.

It was quite dark on the patio and Emily had to angle the photo so that the light from the living room would illuminate the details. "Oh, my!" she said. "Time has not been kind to my ex-husband. He looks like he's aged twenty years."

"I kind of thought so too," said Linc.

"Who's that standing next to Jubal?" asked Emily.

"I was hoping you could tell me," replied Linc. "He kinda looks familiar, but I can't quite place his face."

"If you should remember," said Emily as she smoothed out the crease and laid the photograph on the table, "let me know. I'm curious."

"Well," said Linc stretching his legs, "an old photo of your ex-husband isn't worth anything, but that videotape sure is."

"Sidney's going to be very relieved to hear you've got it," said Emily. "When are you going to tell him?"

"I was thinking about that," said Linc. "Being that he's Jewish, I don't want to intrude on his mourning period. I think it's supposed to last seven or eight days or something like that. Why don't you give Lenore a call tomorrow and see if you can determine their general mood. If you think things are all right, I'll let Sidney know sooner."

On their way home that afternoon, Linc and Emily had stopped off at the hospital to check on Manfred. He was coming back to his old self and had been perusing some new recipes when they came in to visit. He had told the pair that he was doing much better, and that the doctor planned to release him tomorrow.

Linc and Emily were in the middle of discussing Manfred's desire to return to work immediately, when Pitch and Jennifer arrived. Having been invited to dinner, they came out onto the patio to join Linc and Emily for cocktails.

The initial "how-do-you-do's" floated among the four of them. Pitch leaned forward, resting his elbows on the table and said, "Linc, you mentioned that there was going to be a couple of stake-out teams watching our apartment. When do they actually plan on arriving?"

Linc glanced at Emily and back to Pitch. "Why do you ask?"

"Jennifer and I have been on the lookout for them all day. They still weren't there when we left to come here."

Linc had his head cocked to one side as he asked, "So you guys probably checked everywhere, right? Looked out all the windows, doors, and checked the streets, stuff like that, right?"

Pitch and Jennifer both confirmed that they had indeed spent the day and early evening peering out all the windows in search of something they could not see.

Linc took a deep breath and started by telling them about Ferdie's phone call and the complaints from the surveillance team who was already in place. Linc went into a rather lengthy dissertation on the importance of tight security measures and how it was the safety of the two of them that had prompted this whole thing in the first place.

While Linc was expounding, Pitch absent-mindedly picked up the partially creased photograph that Emily had laid on the table.

Emily finally interrupted Linc's speech. "Lincoln, dear," she began, "I think they understand exactly what you mean, and they'll certainly try to be more careful." She turned to face the young couple. "Isn't that right?"

Pitch and Jennifer nodded affirmatively.

"Besides," continued Emily, "we're all getting a little hungry."

All at once, Linc realized that he had been going on too long and was pleased that Emily had such a gentle way of letting him know.

"All right," Linc said in summation, "At least now you know how I feel, and how I expect the both of you to behave. Any questions?"

"Yes," said Pitch, holding up the creased photograph. "Who is this fellow standing next to John Krum?"

Jennifer leaned in for a closer look. "John Krum, the rapist?" she asked.

Emily stood up quickly and looked over their shoulders, "John Krum? Are you sure?"

Pitch answered, "I don't know the identity of the gentleman on the right. However, the man on the left is definitely John Krum. I still have the newspaper with Scott's article. It has Krum's picture right on the front page."

They all turned their heads toward Linc. He had a strange smile on his face and was confidently nodding his head.

CHAPTER FORTY FOUR

I t was a bright, sunny morning and the roads were almost devoid of traffic. Saturday meant the working world would not be clogging the highways, and it was too early for the majority of the snowbirds and retirees to be up and about. Only Linc and the dedicated golfers were on the move.

Linc and Emily had decided they needed to go into the office to get some things done. He drove to Preston's to pick her up.

Upon Linc's arrival, Louise, who seemed to be in an oddly cheerful mood, greeted him. Before he could ask her if she had won the lottery, she surprised Linc by taking his hand in both of hers and thanking him for saving Manfred's life. Her expressions of gratitude went on for quite a while as she explained that she had a special bond with Manfred, and she wouldn't know what to do without him. She had pieced together the story of the incident in the library from Manfred, Preston, and the police. Her eyes welled, as she expressed her gratefulness for Linc's bravery.

Linc had never heard her talk this much and, after thanking her for all those wonderful sentiments, he came away wondering why he hadn't seen this part of her before. Striding across the living room towards the pool deck, Linc thought, 'How do you like that. Manfred and Louise. Son-of-a-gun!'

Preston and Emily were already sipping their second cups of coffee and looked up as Linc joined them.

"Good morning," they both said in unison, followed by Emily asking "Would you like some orange juice or tomato juice?"

"How about . . ." Linc pondered, "something sweeter. Like some tree ripened peach nectar with a dash of cinnamon and a small wedge of a Makasuto Plum?"

"Be serious," said Emily. "Orange or tomato?"

"Say," said Linc narrowing his eyes, "what kind of millionaires are you anyway? Denying me a simple request like that?"

"Here's your orange juice," said Emily, making the decision and handing him a glass. "And here's your sweetener," she added as she stood up and kissed his cheek.

Preston beamed. "It does my heart good to see you two like this." Then, just as quickly, a serious look appeared on his face as he said, "Listen, you two. There's something I need to talk with you about. I mean, to talk about with you," he stammered.

Before he could get his next words out, Emily's cell phone buzzed. She held up her hand and said, "Hold that thought, Daddy." Checking the display, she turned to Linc and announced, "It's Eddie. Doesn't he ever sleep?"

Activating the phone, she said, "Good morning, Eddie."

Her conversation had barely begun, when Linc's cell phone rang out. Looking at the display window, he saw that it was a call from Sidney Aarons. "Preston," he said, "I'm going to take this call inside."

Preston nodded with a mouthful of toasted bagel. He understood the need for privacy in Linc's line of business. As Linc walked back into the house, he said "How are you and Lenore holding up?"

With a trembling voice, Sidney recounted some of the details of the past several days. Then, he said, "Linc, I'm calling to find out if you've made any progress on . . . y'know . . . my little problem."

"Yes, Sidney," said Linc. "I've been able to make some progress." There was an audible sigh from Sidney, and Linc quickly added, "Now, don't start dancing the polka quite yet."

"Why? What's wrong?'

"There's nothing wrong, Sidney. I've been able to accomplish quite a bit, but you never know with these things."

"What do you mean, Linc?"

Linc filled Sidney in on some of the details. After talking about locating Elana Velez, Linc said that he felt fairly certain that he was now in possession of the only other copy of the videotape.

Sidney was overjoyed. "Then, that's it. I'm out of the woods."

"Sidney, I know you're happy right now, but listen to me. You can never tell with these things. She might have another copy of the tape or she might make a deal with the guy who videotaped you in the first place. Anything can happen. After all, you were cavorting with that sex-pot for quite a while. She might have something else on you."

Sidney was quiet for a moment. "Do you think so?" he asked.

"All I'm saying," said Linc patiently, "is that I want you to stay on the alert and be cautious. And for God's sake, be careful. I don't want to have to do this again."

Sidney still sounded elated. He asked Linc how much he owed him. Linc told him, "I'm not sure Sidney, but I guarantee it's a lot. I'll have Carmen send you a statement next week."

"Just make sure to send it to my office, not to my home. And mark it 'Personal and Confidential.' I don't want anybody else opening that particular piece of mail."

With the blackmail topic out of the way, Sidney asked if any new information had come to light on who murdered his son. Sidney went on to say that he was not too happy with what the local police were doing to solve the crime. He asked if Linc could lend his expertise in tracking down the killer.

"I'm working on it, Sidney," he said. "I'm already working on it."

Preston and Emily were chatting when Linc returned. Emily saw him coming and stirred up the pulp in his orange juice as she asked, "Who was that?"

"Just some client asking about the status of his case," replied Linc. "What did Eddie want?"

"Well," said Emily, enthusiastically, "yesterday I asked Eddie if he would send over a sketch artist so that we could all give him a description of our FBI Agent, Brant Sheffield. He just called to say that he arranged it."

Linc smiled at Emily. She was good. She was very good, and she didn't mind working independently. She was assertive without being abrasive and was comfortable making command decisions. He liked everything about her.

"Excellent," said Linc. "Now, the cops will have a working picture of our bad guy. You're doing a terrific job, Emily."

Emily beamed at the compliment.

Preston began motioning with his hand as he gulped his coffee, trying to wash down the last bite of a bagel so that he could say something. Linc and Emily looked at him.

"Why don't you just use the film from the cameras?" he finally asked.

"What cameras?" asked Emily. "What are you talking about?"

"The security cameras," Preston answered, wiping his chin with his napkin.

Linc and Emily were both staring at him.

"The security cameras in the house," Preston repeated. "I'm sure they filmed the whole incident."

"Preston," Linc reminded him, "You had those cameras dismantled several years ago."

"Yes I did," he said casually, "They buzzed and whirred and made a clicking sound that I found very annoying. But when Louise became aware that poor, sweet Jeanne Blakely and her two daughters had their house broken into and were murdered last year, she called the security company and had new, updated cameras reinstalled."

Emily scrambled for her telephone while the two men went into the house to check on the validity of Preston's statement. Eddie came on the line without much of a wait. "I've got some good news for you Eddie," Emily said gleefully.

She told Eddie about the cameras. She fully expected him to be excited or at least a little enthusiastic. Instead, he was very straightforward. He said he would come right out there with a couple of his technical support people in order to pull out some useful photos from the video. Then he said, "Now, I've got some good news for you. The preliminary DNA analysis on the blood samples from your library is almost complete. My computers are still working on it, but I'll bring you the report as it is right now."

It was late morning by the time Eddie and his team completed their work. He had arrived with two men who specialized in electronics. One man in his early forties, whom Eddie referred to as Gillie Bilder, and somebody who looked like a fifteen-year-old boy whom Eddie and Gil both referred to as "Sparky."

Sparky was a tall, gangly kid with a big mop of bright blond hair. When he walked, he tended to lope from place to place looking like "Goofy," the cartoon character. Despite the odd gait, Sparky was a whiz when it came to video technology. He had fast hands and never missed a beat. Preston was fascinated by this young man and kept up a steady barrage of questions about what he was doing and why. Sparky went about his business very quickly and efficiently and didn't seem to mind the intrusion. In fact, he kept up a running dialogue on everything he was doing, including the reasons why.

Just before Eddie departed, he gave Linc and Emily an update on whatever headway had been made in the investigation into finding Scott and Crystal's killer. It was precious little. It seemed to Emily and Linc that any progress in the case came from evidence and leads provided by the two of them.

However, Eddie was in a more expansive mood when he left that morning. He handed Emily the report on the DNA and fingerprint analysis that he had received as a result of the scuffle in the library.

Armed with that report and two excellent quality photographs of the man known as Agent Brant Sheffield, Emily and Linc headed for the office. Driving along North County Road, Linc said, "Emily, you'd better give Ferdie Dumay a call. Tell him to send someone over to our office to pick up a copy of these photos. This way he'll be able to distribute them to his people."

"The ones doing surveillance on Pitch and Jennifer." Emily phrased the question like a statement.

"Right," said Linc. "No sense having them work blind when we actually have a photograph. Now, they'll have a real face to look out for."

Emily asked Linc for Ferdie's number, just before she started to dial.

"By the way," said Linc. "I called Pitch and Jennifer earlier. Just wanted to check on how they were doing. Seems like they're feeling a little nervous being all alone."

"I know," said Emily, waiting for the call to connect. "I called too. I spoke with Jennifer and she told me you called. She said they had a lousy night and planned on taking a nap sometime during . . ." Emily's phone call connected to Ferdie Dumay's office, and she never completed her explanation of Pitch and Jennifer's nap time.

Carmen had already come and gone. She usually worked for half the day on Saturday and today had been no exception. The only difference was that today she left a half-hour earlier than usual to tend to some personal family matter. Even so, she managed to leave the mark of her presence in her wake. There was a full pot of coffee that had just finished brewing along with a stack of papers and messages waiting for Linc to peruse and sign.

Emily went into her own office and got to work. She compared the lab report, that referred to the incident in the library, to the one that dealt with the Blanchard killings in Memphis. Although she already knew the killer was the same person, she felt a satisfaction in seeing an initial DNA match. She wasn't as fortunate as far as the fingerprints were concerned. Eddie's boys were able to get a good set of prints off the pistol, but the Memphis team was not able to find any latent fingerprints in the Blanchard home.

Emily put in a call to Detective Emmett Laramie of the Memphis P.D. When he answered the phone he said, "Hey, little lady. You trying to make a pass at me or is this strictly business?"

"Emmett, does your wife know you flirt like this?" Emily asked smiling.

"Missy," Emmett replied with a hearty laugh, "I got five young children at home. All my wife knows about is head lice, talcum powder and diaper rash. Now what you got for me?"

"As soon as we hang up, Emmett, go check your computer. As we speak, I am uploading a couple of beautiful pictures of the killer. You'll be able to give them to the boy . . . Adam, along with some bogus pictures and see if he can make a positive identification."

Emmett whistled softly into the phone. "Detective Strickland said you were good. I guess he wasn't just a-whistlin' Dixie."

"Oh? Is that right. What else did Detective Strickland say about me?"

"He said you were prettier than a dance-hall girl. Hey, since you're uploading pictures, send me one of yourself. Maybe wearin' something flimsy and black."

Emily laughed and reminded Emmett about his commitment to his marriage. Then, she asked him not to forget to let her know the outcome of his session with little Adam Blanchard.

Emily was just hanging up the phone when Linc popped his head into her office. "I've got an idea," he said. "I'd like you to call Laura Parsons and have her meet us at my place tomorrow afternoon. Try to have her be there around two in the afternoon. I'm calling Eddie and doing the same with him."

"Are you trying your hand at matchmaking?" she asked with a smile.

"A matchmaker? Me? No way," he said. "But I've decided to feed them certain information about the people in your checkered past."

Emily cocked her head to one side in a curious gesture.

"Well," said Linc, "think about it. It turns out that you, Emily Collingsworth-Salaran, have been intimately involved with two of the most dastardly scoundrels in Palm Beach County. Namely, your old pal, Elaine Velachuk, and your old ex, Jube-the-boob."

"And you're going to tell Laura and Eddie about those two characters," she stated.

Linc squinted his eyes as he explained, "I'm going to save that part for Laura. I need to be real careful about preserving Sidney's identity and privacy, but I can definitely talk to her about the connection between Jube and Elaine Velachuk. The point is, Eddie is on the cusp of being demoted and Laura, God help her, is in danger of losing her job. Now we have a proof-positive connection between Jubal and that John Krum rapist guy. So, I give both of our guests copies of the photograph I heisted from Elaine's place and let them run with it. Even if nothing comes of it, the mere fact of the picture will get both of them some hearty back slaps from their bosses. And, if it does pan out, Eddie and Laura will both be heroes."

"I like that, Linc," said Emily, satisfied with his strategy. "And as for me, I finally get to see where you live. I like that too."

Having arranged the next day's meeting with Laura, Emily went to work on her present project. Her mission was to search the computer banks for a DNA match. Eddie had said that his computer division was already working on it, but she knew that her resources were much broader and deeper. She assumed that the Palm Beach County Sheriff's Department's search would take it through the local and state police files and probably into some of the files the FBI had set up for things like this. However, Emily felt she would have better luck searching the international files. It was a vague feeling, based on not much more than a hunch. Emily had spent most of the last decade in the European arena, working closely with people from every country on the continent. She was attuned to the nuances of European men, and she thought she had detected those subtleties in the man who called himself Special Agent Brant Sheffield.

Emily logged on to the Net and, using a series of passwords and secret code numbers, was able to generate several searches. She entered the DNA criteria from the lab report and included instructions on where the results were to be sent.

Concluding that the man did not originate from the Balkans or Scandinavian region, Emily concentrated her efforts in Western and Southern Europe. She activated searches in the files of Interpol and NATO. Once those were initiated, she did the same for the Top Secret Intelligence units in England, France, Spain, Portugal, Italy and two countries in North Africa; Libya and Tunisia. Doing searches in the two African nations was tricky. Libya and Tunisia did not normally cooperate with investigative teams outside of their own communities, but Emily knew of a couple of "back doors" that would allow her some limited access.

The process of launching these kinds of explorations was very time consuming. Seeing that Emily was reluctant to leave her workstation, Linc went out to pick up some hamburgers from a fast food chain. As the afternoon wore on, Linc made several more visits to Emily's office. On two of those occasions, she was so engrossed in her computer screen, she was not even aware of his presence.

It was some time after four p.m. when one of Ferdie Dumay's gophers stopped in to pick up the photograph of Agent Brant Sheffield. As the young man left, Emily entered Linc's office and plopped herself down in one of the chairs normally reserved for clients.

Linc put down his pen and leaned back before saying, "Y'know, you look beautiful when you're tired."

"Thank you, Lincoln. I needed that."

"Are you almost finished? It's getting kind of late."

"Not only am I finished," she said as she straightened herself up in the chair, "but I hit the jackpot."

"Tell me," Linc said with anticipation.

"I'm pretty sure the guy's name is Claude Mendosa. He was originally a Basque Separatist."

A big smile was spreading across Linc's face. "You're pretty good," he said. "How did you find out?"

"The DNA analysis," explained Emily, "along with a hunch. There was something about that man that made me focus my efforts in Western Europe. I had about eight searches going at the same time. The problem I ran into was, back in the seventies and eighties, the techniques for DNA imprinting weren't as sophisticated as they are today. So, I was only able to get partial matches. I came up with six possibles."

Linc leaned forward.

"But get this," she continued. "Two of the six matches are dead. One of them is in prison, one is a woman and the fifth one is a black mercenary from Uganda."

"None of which," joked Linc, "could have passed themselves off as Special Agent Brant Sheffield."

"Exactly," said Emily.

"Claude Mendosa, huh?" said Linc with a faraway look in his eyes.

Emily rested her arm on the desk and became very serious. "His dossier," she said with raised eyebrows, "reads like a Who's Who of International Terrorists. We were all very fortunate to have come away unscathed. This man, Mendosa, is a world class assassin."

*   *   *

For a Saturday night, the bar was not very crowded. Perhaps a dozen customers, all men except for one worn out woman hanging onto the arm of a skinny, middle-aged redneck. Even in the dim light, Mendosa could see that the woman wore too much makeup, and laughed too loudly each time the man spoke. Skinny man was wearing a baseball-type cap with a "Caterpillar" logo emblazoned across the front. Each time the woman tried to take it off, Skinny man would snap his head back and become more annoyed. Mendosa knew that, if the woman didn't change her tactic real quick, Mr. Caterpillar cap/ Skinny man would soon be leaving without her.

The rest of the men at the long bar mostly just stared into their drinks, waiting to take the next sip and start all over again.

There were about seven or eight tables separated from the bartender by two pool tables. Only one man was shooting pool, and he wasn't very good at it. The pool-shooter kept his highball glass on the green felt of the pool table and occasionally the bartender yelled, "Hey, Frankie! Get the goddamned glass off the table. You're gonna knock it over for sure." Frankie would remove his drink and place it on a nearby table where it stayed only until his next sip.

Three tables away from Mendosa sat two men having a serious discussion. Mendosa could not hear them, but neither man was smiling. Mendosa sat at his table with two other men. One was wearing a plaid shirt with its long sleeves rolled up. The other was wearing faded jeans and cowboy boots. His black shirt was unbuttoned half way down, exposing a gaudy tattoo of two crossed scabbards over skull and cross bones. Mendosa was speaking softly and had just finished giving them final instructions.

"Any questions?" asked Mendosa.

"How long is this gig gonna last," asked Plaid Shirt.

"Two, three days," answered Mendosa. "Four at the most."

"Tell me again 'bout how I get paid," said the tattooed man.

"Fifty bucks each tonight," explained Mendosa patiently. "A hundred bucks each at the end of tomorrow. A hundred-fifty for each of you by the end of the day on Monday. Then, we'll renegotiate if I need you longer than that."

Plaid Shirt nodded his head. "Sounds good."

Tattoo asked, "Any chance of getting an advance?"

Mendosa sat up straight and laid his palms flat on the table. He glared into the tattooed man's eyes for several seconds. "Don't . . . try my patience," he said coldly.

The tattooed man felt the icy chill from Mendosa's words. He slowly nodded his head and said, "No problem, partner. Count me in."

CHAPTER FORTY FIVE

The weather forecast had predicted scattered showers through out the day but, so far, the weatherman was dead wrong. A mass of beautiful, billowing, white clouds was gliding across a stark blue background, being pushed along by a stiff easterly breeze. For those people who did not take those things for granted and looked skyward occasionally, the contrast of colors was breathtaking.

Linc had arrived for what was becoming his ritual breakfast at the Collingsworth residence. It was Sunday, and Manfred had made the decision to come back to work the following day. Therefore, Louise had made arrangements with an agency, specializing in supplying competent domestic staff, to hire two cooks to run the kitchen. Because of the threat of showers, the table was set in the room Preston called "The Morning Atrium." Located just off the kitchen, it held a table large enough to seat six people very comfortably. The wood floors were a deep pecan color polished to a soft satin luster. The room's main characteristic was a wall of glass. The windows were quite wide and featured an angled section of windows above the vertical ones that offered a panorama of the world outside. The panes of glass faced northeast and welcomed just the right amount of sunshine. Outside, there were large schiflera trees and other broad-leaved plants that filtered the light. A typical sunny morning would cast a dappled, warm glow into the room. On this day, the breeze was causing a fluttering of shadows that seemed to play peek-a-boo across the two far walls.

The splendid weather, along with the anticipation of the day, kept a bounce in Linc's step. His spirits soared even more as he was ushered into the room and took a look at Emily.

She was wearing a white button-down shirt under a lime green blazer and matching short, pleated skirt. A pair of cufflinks and matching earrings both spotlighted dark green emeralds. Emily's hair was pulled back into a ponytail and held in place with a frilly green ribbon. The hairstyle gave her face the look of a petite ingénue.

Taken by the sight of Emily, Linc paused to admire her beauty. "If I knew how," he said, "I would write a poem about how beautiful you look."

Preston, who was enmeshed in a decision of choosing between an onion or pumpernickel bagel, suddenly shot a look at Linc. "Lincoln?" he roared, while sporting a broad smile, "That is so out of character for you to say!"

Emily did not take her eyes off Linc. "Don't you go picking on him, Daddy," she said dreamily. "I think he's doing just fine."

"Well," said Linc a little abashed at his exuberance, "It's just that you look so . . . I don't know. Nice."

"Thank you, Lincoln," said Emily, more than a little pleased at his compliment. "And a good morning to you, too."

The three of them ate breakfast, while chatting about current events. It was a slow news week, proven by Jay Leno's latest monologue which rehashed some of President Clinton's old foibles.

Preston had the Sunday Times open to the financial section, which prompted Emily to ask him a question about a particular group of stocks. Preston started to answer her by reading an excerpt from the newspaper, when suddenly he stopped reading and put the paper down. His action caused Linc and Emily to stop what they were doing and pay attention.

"There is something I need to talk about," said Preston. "To both of you."

Linc and Emily waited.

"I've been trying to tell you for the past few days, but somehow we keep being sidetracked."

Preston's face was visibly blanched causing Emily to say, "Daddy, are you sick or something?"

"No, no, dear," he said, calming her anxiety. "It's nothing like that. It has to do with that damn disc." As he spoke the words, Preston put the palm of his hand to his forehead.

Linc partially folded his napkin and placed it on the table. "You have the disc," Linc stated curtly. "Don't you?"

Emily shot a glance at Linc, flabbergasted that he would have said something so insulting and absurd. When she looked back at her father, she was astonished to see him nodding his head.

"I didn't fully realize the significance of the disc," Preston began. "The truth is, I didn't realize the danger that came with it. It wasn't until all of you were almost killed that the full impact of what I had done hit me right between the eyes."

Preston went on to tell how he happened to come into possession of the disc. Through his explanation and some questioning by both Emily and Linc, Preston spelled out the details.

He had spent a lot of time with Pitch, learning all about the device and how it worked. Preston stressed the sheer genius of Pitch Pechowski for having had the ingenuity and knowledge to invent it in the first place. Nevertheless, the real allure of the device was in its simplicity. "It is so basic," he said, "even a child could use it." Preston had immediately seen the possibilities of using it to make a fortune.

Preston started to explain the ins and outs of insider-trading, but was quickly cut off by the other two who understood why it was illegal. Weakly rationalizing his actions, Preston told them how temptation had gripped his entire being, even to the point of disrupting his concentration and sleep.

"All I could think about was that damn disc," said Preston in a trembling voice. "I'm embarrassed to say that my only focus was to use the bug to turn a healthy profit."

"So, what did you do?" asked Linc.

"When we went to the bank to get a safe deposit box, we dealt directly with the bank manager, Herb Marcus. Remember him? We've known each other for years. We sometimes go out for bagels and coffee. Anyway, it wasn't any problem at all for me to finagle a partnership in the safe deposit box. Pitch and Jennifer each had a key. And so did I."

Linc said, "I meant what did you do once you got the disc?"

"Oh," said Preston re-structuring his thoughts. "You see, there's this foreign company that has developed an anti-aging cream. It seems to work remarkably well. They've applied for U.S. Patents and are about to get them approved. As a company, they're woefully under-funded, and their stock is selling for a fraction of its potential."

Preston paused to take a sip of his coffee before continuing. "Now, I've been privy to some information. I know that Lansdorff Pharmaceuticals has expressed an interest in buying the start-up company, but hasn't made the decision yet. However, this past Thursday," said Preston emphasizing the day of the week, "there was a private board meeting at Lansdorff to decide whether or not to go ahead with the deal."

Preston just looked at the both of them.

"Go on," said Linc.

Preston hesitated. "Thursday," he re-emphasized, trying to impart the significance of the day. "This all happened on Thursday. The same day you children were almost killed!"

"We understand," said Emily reaching across the table to touch her father's hand. "What happened then?"

"There's not much to tell," said Preston quietly. "I used the device to tap into Lansdorff's secret board meeting. It's so easy. A couple of clicks and it was just like I was sitting in the room with them. Just like sitting right next to them and they never knew I was there. It was amazing!"

"So, what happened next?" asked Linc.

"Well, when I found out that they did, in fact, plan to purchase the technology, I bought all the stock I could in the new company."

They all fell silent, as one of the new staff members came into the room to clear away some dishes and to bring a fresh pot of coffee. When he departed, Emily said, "Daddy, how could you? Pitch trusted you. Think about what he might do when he finds out what you've done."

Linc said, "We're not going to tell him."

They both looked at Linc for an explanation.

"If he finds out what you've done," said Linc wagging a finger at Preston, "his faith in all of us will be shattered, and he might just take off. And that's going to leave both of them extremely vulnerable. I hate to say it, but they'll probably be dead within a week."

Preston started to apologize for his actions, saying something about his being as weak as Eve in the Garden of Eden, when Linc interrupted. "Preston, where is the disc, now?"

"In my wall safe in the Oak Room."

"Get it," Linc demanded in a tone that surprised Emily. "And give it to me."

Preston excused himself and left to retrieve the disc, returning in a few minutes.

Emily watched as Linc put the disc into his pocket. Turning to her father, she said, "Daddy, why don't you ask Louise to make arrangements for some food to be delivered to Pitch and Jennifer? They can't go out shopping and don't even have the basics to cook a meal."

It was a good idea. The act of kindness would benefit Pitch and Jennifer. It also served to break the tension that existed at the breakfast table.

*   *   *

Emily and Linc arrived at his apartment about half past one. They had told Eddie and Laura to meet them there at two o'clock. Linc's condominium was nestled on the fourth floor of a high-rise building in Palm Beach. It was a large six-room apartment with three separate bathrooms. Its most dramatic feature was the huge wrap-around terrace that overlooked the Atlantic Ocean.

Linc started the excursion by opening the wide bank of sliding glass doors that led to the terrace. They were "pocket-sliders" and disappeared into the wall, allowing an unobstructed twelve-foot view. The brisk breeze churned up the surf, as the muted roar of the ocean came drifting into the apartment. Emily commented on its spaciousness and tasteful decor. It wasn't something she would have expected from a bachelor.

Linc admitted to having had a professional decorator help with the color selection and choice of furniture, but prided himself on having made the final decisions. When Emily praised how nicely he kept his home, Linc sheepishly confessed to having a weekly cleaning service that he depended on to do laundry, dusting and other things that ultimately "saved his life."

Making herself at home, Emily took off her shoes and searched around the kitchen until she found the coffee-making essentials. She had just managed to start the coffee brewing when the phone rang and the doorman announced the arrival of Laura Parsons.

Laura was her usual caustic self, but Linc remained gracious, as he welcomed her to his home. Emily did the honors of showing Laura around. Before the tour was over, the doorman repeated his call. This time, he proclaimed the arrival of Mr. Eddie Strickland.

Emily started to make the introductions, but it turned out that they already knew each other, having met professionally on several occasions. As an Assistant District Attorney, Laura worked closely with a lot of the police officers in the county.

Emily and Laura served the refreshments and settled in to hear what Linc had to say. Linc and Emily were sitting side by side on one of the two sofas. Laura sat by herself on the other sofa while Eddie chose to stand, saying, "What can I tell you. I think better on my feet."

Laura looked down and remarked, "And big feet they are! They look like friggin' snow-shoes."

Eddie flicked his eyebrows in classic Groucho Marx style and said, "Hey, y'know what they say about big feet."

"Dream on." said Laura with a wave of her hand and a big smile on her face.

Linc hushed the two of them up and began explaining why they were invited. He initiated the meeting by reminding both Eddie and Laura about the pressure each was under because of the John Krum rape case. Careful not to divulge any information that would be embarrassing to either of them, Linc still managed to make the point of letting them know that they were, kind of, in the same boat. There wasn't any need to tell Eddie about Laura almost getting fired. Nor was there any reason to tell Laura about the new Chief of Police and his dislike of Eddie.

However, Linc did stress that both of their lives were pivoting around John Krum. "I have a lead," said Linc. "For both of you." Reaching under a pile of magazines on the coffee table, he pulled out two copies of the photograph he had taken from Elaine Velachuk's bedroom. He handed them to Laura and Eddie.

"Who's the guy standing with Krum?" asked Eddie.

"Holy shit!" cried Laura. "It's your ex-husband, Jubal Salaran."

From that point forward, the conversation among the four of them became very spirited. Linc told the pair his theory. Besides the photograph, he felt there was an additional connection between Krum and Salaran. Linc suggested that since John Krum had been bragging that he had information about the murders of Jeanne Blakely and her daughters, Jubal Salaran might also have that same information. "After all," said Linc, "Jubal made his living squeezing money out of all the Palm Beachers."

Laura and Eddie were getting into it. They began throwing out ideas on how best to follow up on these new details. Laura asked several questions about Elaine Velachuk's connection. Linc was able to dodge all of them, thereby managing to protect Sidney Aarons' secret affair as well as his reputation.

Eddie was pacing back and forth and continually running his hand through his hair. Exasperated, Laura finally slapped the arm of the sofa and said, "Eddie, would you please stop pacing like a caged animal?" Everyone looked at Laura as Eddie said, "What's the matter with you?"

Laura cocked her head to one side. "You're making me nervous," she declared. "C'mon and sit down," she said as she patted the cushion next to her.

Eddie stepped to the sofa. Hesitating before sitting down, he asked, "You ain't gonna bite, are ya?"

A wicked smile crept across Laura's face. "Only the parts you want me to."

Eddie sat down, as Linc brought out the original photograph he had taken from Elaine's house. Smoothing out the crease, he said, "As for you, Miss Parsons, you're going to love this part."

Linc handed the beat up picture to Laura. "There's a strong possibility," said Linc, "that your old high school nemesis, Elaine Velachuk, is also somehow involved with Krum. And something tells me you'd like to sink your teeth into that idea."

Laura started getting excited. Eddie interrupted by asking, "Who's Elaine Velachuk?" Laura and Emily started a rapid-fire explanation of the bimbo's role in the unfolding tale of events, stressing the fact that she was a former high school classmate.

Linc noticed that during the animated discussion, Laura had scooted herself across the sofa and was now sitting very close to Eddie.

The meeting had been going on for more than two hours when Eddie stretched and said, "All right. I've had enough, already. I'll look into this tomorrow."

"You mean, *we'll* look into this," corrected Laura.

Eddie studied Laura's face for a moment before saying, "What do ya say, you and me get outta here. Maybe go grab a cup of coffee or something."

Laura had a little smile when she asked, "What makes you think I want to have a cup of coffee with you?"

"What, are you kidding?" said Eddie. "I've been watching you. You've been undressing me with your eyes all afternoon."

"Hey, you pork chop!" shouted Laura indignantly. "That's my line!"

"Besides," said Eddie, "I like your style."

"Well, since you put it that way. Okay, but remember, I'm not one of those blow-up dolls you're used to being with."

Eddie tried to stifle a laugh, but was unsuccessful. It came snorting out through his nose. "Hey Linc," Eddie smirked, "you didn't tell me what kind of sharp tongue she had. Do you think I'll ever be able to get to first base?"

Laura stood up. She reached out and grabbed a handful of Eddie's shirt. With a fistful of fabric, she gave him a strong tug up and off the couch and pulled him toward the front door. "C'mon already," she said in mock exasperation. "Enough with this male-bonding shit. Let's get outta here."

Emily played the role of hostess and showed the two of them to the door. Saying goodbye, to the couple, she returned and sat next to Linc. "Well, maybe you didn't mean to be a matchmaker," she said, "but something seemed to click with those two characters."

"Characters, is right," he said. "Say, did you remember to lock the door?"

"Yes," she said as she snuggled next to him. "Does this mean we're finally alone?"

"I hope so," he said softly.

Emily turned her head to look into his eyes. "So, what would you like to do now?" she asked.

"I don't know," he said. "Are you getting hungry?"

Lifting her chin slightly until her lips were next to his ear, she whispered, "Not for food."

CHAPTER FORTY SIX

All during Monday morning, Carmen kept looking, squinty-eyed, at Emily. Emily would just smile whenever she realized that she was being scrutinized. Emily just felt like smiling today. The world seemed like such a pleasant place. Colors appeared brighter, aromas were more pleasing and songs on the radio all sounded like a symphony. Everything seemed to be in sharp focus.

Around mid morning, Carmen brought a fresh cup of coffee into Emily's office and unceremoniously plopped herself down into one of the empty chairs. "I have been thinking," Carmen said in her lilting Cuban accent, "I remember you said that Mr. Linc and you had to go to the cemetery on Friday. But you know what?" she asked narrowing her gaze.

"What?" asked Emily, trying to carefully take a sip of the steaming brew.

"You don't look like a woman who's just been to a funeral. There is something twinkling in your eye."

Before Emily had a chance to respond to Carmen's perception, Linc appeared in the doorway. "Carmen, where is the 'Kennedy file'? It was supposed to be on my desk."

"It is on your desk," Carmen explained. "I put it there even before you two showed up this morning. Late, I might add."

"Come show me," said Linc, as he turned and left to go back and search.

Emily went back to work. She most certainly was feeling different this morning. Everything was different. Sipping her coffee, Emily marveled at how much better it tasted. Her mind drifted back to yesterday.

Their lovemaking began in a torrent of anticipation. With the roar of the ocean waves coming in through the open doors and mixing with the sounds of desire, Emily had felt her passion rise quickly to a crescendo and sustain itself through a series of long, trembling climaxes. Emily and Linc had kept the fires burning long into the night. Through their moments of pleasure, she experienced fervor that rose through sharp, jagged peaks of intense heat before receding into warm glowing embers. She basked in knowing that everything was right. Emily had fallen in love.

It was difficult focusing on the tasks at hand when such experiences kept flooding her mind. Nevertheless, Emily knew there was a job to be done and only she had the know-how to do it.

Now that Emily had discovered the identity of the killer, she zeroed in on finding out all she could about the man. The name, Claude Mendosa, appeared on the 'wanted list' of eleven different organizations in five different countries. It seemed as though there were many people who each knew a little something about him, but nobody had it all. From what Emily could gather, she was the first to obtain an actual photograph of the assassin. It would be highly prized by those various police organizations and Emily intended to use it as a bargaining chip to get deeper into the man's life. She was looking for something, anything, to give her some hint as to his whereabouts.

The dossier she was creating grew thicker by the hour until she came across an interesting tidbit. One of the searches Emily had initiated, was into the data banks of CESID, *Centro Superior de Informacion de la Defensa,* Spain's version of the CIA. During an interview with a former ETA Separatist, information was gathered on Claude Mendosa. As a young terrorist growing up in the Basque region of Spain, close to the French border, he had been given two nicknames; "*Tueur au sang-froid*" and "*L'assassin du Mont Valier.*" Emily's fluency in French allowed her to translate them into "cold-blooded killer" and "The Assassin of Mount Valier," neither of which lessened her fear or gave her any comfort.

Emily was juggling a lot of Internet access codes, as she combed the Web for information. Although she had four different searches, all going on at the same time, she decided to initiate a fifth. The CIA had a monitoring division whose job it was to look and listen for key words that might spell trouble. Communication satellites and banks of computers randomly examined various forms of verbal and written transmissions, looking for keywords like "bomb," "terrorist" and "hostage." When they uncovered such words or phrases, the alert button would flash and signal the need for further investigation.

Interpol and NATO Intelligence had similar systems. Not quite as comprehensive or sophisticated as the CIA's, but very efficient nevertheless. Emily's realm of expertise was, in fact, Interpol and NATO. There, she could not only hack into the monitoring stations, but she also had a semblance of control.

Emily plugged into each of the European based organizations and, one by one, changed the parameters of their search engines to include the two nicknames that belonged to Claude Mendosa. Then, she instructed the system to also include any derivatives of the names.

Emily hit paydirt. Within thirty minutes of activation, she was notified that the phrase "The Lass of Mont Valier" had appeared in the Personal Ads in *Le Monde,* one of the daily newspapers in Paris. Emily contacted her old boss in Germany, Gunnar Hansen and asked him to use his authority and/or influence to get the American monitoring stations to search the major newspapers in the U.S. for similar phrases.

By noontime, Colonel Hansen had forwarded the answer to Emily. The same ads had appeared in *The Washington Post* on twenty-one separate occasions over the past eighteen months. Emily put in a call to Eddie Strickland with a message that he should return her call after lunch.

During their lunch, Linc listened as Emily brought him up to date with all that she had uncovered up to this point. He was more than impressed and told her so. He also complimented her eyes, making it very difficult for Emily to remember exactly what she had been saying. Linc was holding her hand and noticed the glow on her face.

As lunch was coming to an end, Linc said that he had called Pitch and Jennifer to check on them. It turned out that Preston had arranged for a steady stream of catering vans to deliver all sorts of foods and delicacies. A sizeable portion of Preston's selection included smoked salmon, whitefish and sturgeon. Laughter ensued as Linc retold the story he heard from Pitch. Jennifer thought that Preston's generosity was wonderful and had told Pitch that he'd better pay attention to what was happening because she would expect this kind of service for the remainder of her life.

Emily began to chuckle. "Well, obviously," she said, "Daddy is feeling a little guilty about swiping Pitch's disc."

"Good," stated Linc. "Hopefully, your father has learned his lesson."

Within minutes of arriving at the office, Eddie returned Emily's phone call. She filled him in on the crux of her findings and told him about the Personal Ads that were showing up in the newspapers.

"Eddie," she said, "we need to find out who's placing those ads. Someone's been sending messages to this Claude Mendosa person. If we can find out who it is, then we'll discover his contact."

Eddie asked for all the pertinent details and said he would get right on it. "When I was up in Washington," said Eddie, "I met this cop. We've gotten to be pretty friendly. I'll give him a call and put him to work on it."

"Do you think he'll be willing to help us out?" she asked.

"I think so," Eddie replied. "This is the same cop I worked with on that Lunderman murder. The case is still open on his blotter, so I know he'll help us out. I'll send him the photo of this Mendosa guy. That'll wet his whistle."

"Why not just tease him with that picture, Eddie?"

Eddie hesitated before asking, "Tease him? What are you talking about?"

"Tell him you'll be getting some photos of the killer, but first ask him to go to the 'Post' and find out who placed the ads. When he sends that information to you, *then* send him the pictures."

There was a pause before Eddie replied. "You sure you never sold used cars?" Then, he hung up before Emily could respond.

At four o'clock in the afternoon, Eddie called back. He was trying to be cool, but Emily detected an unmistakable excitement in his voice. Eddie related what his friend, in Washington, D.C., had uncovered. "So after all of that," said Eddie, "the ads are being placed by this outfit called 'T.C.H. International' and signed for by some yokel named John Anderson."

Emily was about to ask a question when Eddie continued. "Now, when my buddy, Chris, was investigating the Lunderman murder, there was another dead body in the same room; a guy named Walter Mahler. Some kind of low-level government employee. And when Chris tried to follow up on Mahler by checking his personal phone logs, guess what?"

"Who's Chris again?"

"Chris Belcher. He's the Detective up in D.C. I've become friendly with. He's a good guy."

"Okay. So what did he find?" asked Emily, intrigued by the direction this was going.

"This Mahler dude had placed several calls to this outfit called 'T.C.H. International.' It's obviously some kind of front for who-knows-what."

"Why do you say that?" asked Emily.

"Because when my buddy called this 'T.C . . . . ' whatever, he got someone who told him it was an import, export company."

"So?"

"So," explained Eddie, "the next thing you know, Chris and his partner get a call from a couple of heavies from the NSA, who tell 'em to lay off. Remember I was telling you and Linc about that, and I didn't know what NSA stood for?"

Emily did recall the conversation. "So, you think T.C.H. is a front of some sort?"

"Hey, c'mon Emily," said Eddie surprised at her naiveté. "I mean, it's like an awful big coincidence, don't you think? T.C.H. talking to your killer through newspaper ads, T.C.H. involved in the murder of Walter Mahler . . . I'm talking, big coincidence. Moon and stars coincidence. This is like the Captain Kirk of coincidences. Know what I mean?"

"So, you're saying that the government might be involved in some way, right?"

"Hey. I'm not sure what to think," replied Eddie. "At this point, all I can tell you is the whole thing stinks."

Eddie and Emily continued to talk a while longer before hanging up. Emily turned to her computer and initiated two separate searches. The first was for a list of all U.S. Government employees with the name, "John Anderson," and the second was for any company or corporation with the name or initials, "T.C.H. International."

Linc came into her office at about a quarter to five and sat in a chair next to her workstation. "How are you doing?" he asked.

"I'm working on a list of names of government employees," she said, "one of whom might be Mendosa's contact." She paused in her typing to hand Linc a stack of papers that had been freshly printed by her new laser printer. "Better read this," she said. "It'll give you some good background on Mendosa."

The list streaming across her screen seemed endless. There were ninety-two "John Andersons," employed as civil servants in one capacity or another. Emily began the tedious process of elimination. She crossed off government agencies like the Department of Education, Department of Transportation and the Agriculture Department. She circled the name "Anderson" when it was connected to agencies such as the FBI or Bureau of Alcohol, Tobacco and Firearms.

Emily was nearing the end of the list when she came across a "John Anderson" who was employed by the National Security Agency, The NSA. "I may have found him," she said quietly.

Linc stopped reading and looked at her computer screen.

"The personal ads that have been placed in *The Washington Post* and *Le Monde*," said Emily, "are being signed for by a 'John Anderson' who works for some outfit called T.C.H. International. Eddie and I both think it's a bogus company. Some kind of front, maybe for the NSA."

As she spoke, she clicked on several "hyperlinks" which appeared on her monitor and they, in turn, brought her through a series of subwindows. Suddenly, the words, "John Anderson/NSA-TCH," were highlighted and flashing on her computer screen.

"What does 'TCH' stand for?" Linc asked.

"I don't know," replied Emily shaking her head. "But let's find out."

Emily entered another series of passwords and got into the data bank of the NSA. When she queried the system as to the meaning of "TCH," her screen flashed the words: "Access Denied—Confidential." Underneath that was written the request: "Enter Password."

Emily tried several passwords, all with the same result. Her access was denied. She removed her codebook from her purse and looked up a couple of passwords that she had forgotten. She tried three different ones and still ended by hitting the same wall. She could not get into that particular file.

Emily sent off an urgent e-mail to Colonel Hansen asking him if he knew the derivation of "TCH," or if he had an updated password that would allow her access. While waiting, she continued her search for information on "T.C.H. International."

Linc had been reading all about this Claude Mendosa fellow. The more Linc read, the more impressed he was by the killer's deeds. It seemed there were a lot of very heinous crimes attributed to Mendosa. According to some of these reports, he was a top-notch assassin, responsible for killing over three dozen people, including at least two Heads of State. Mendosa was an accomplished sniper and bomb maker. Besides being adept with a garrote, the Spanish weapon for strangulation, he was also accomplished with a knife, a sword and a pistol. Linc could personally attest to that last weapon.

"You were right, Emily," said Linc looking up from his reading.

"About what?"

"That we were all very lucky to have come away without being killed."

Before she could comment, a tone sounded from the computer signaling an incoming e-mail. Emily opened it. It was the response she was waiting for from Gunnar Hansen. Hansen wrote that he did not know the meaning of "TCH," but did give her the latest updated password for entry into NSA files.

Linc leaned forward to get a better view of her screen.

Emily entered the password and waited. The screen went blank momentarily. All at once, it lit up with the bold initials, N S A, emblazoned across the top. She was in.

She scrolled down to one of the search engines, typed in "TCH," and waited. The screen blinked off and on and there it was. "TCH" stood for "The Clearing House," a top-secret division of the NSA that dealt with problems needing extreme solutions. Included in the data were lists of employees and "outside contractors." They also contained their code names; obscure and clandestine aliases such as, "Shadow," "Bullet" and "Miasma."

Emily also found "John Anderson," listed along with his codename. "This is the 'John Anderson' I've been looking for," she said.

"How can you be sure?" asked Linc.

"His codename is, 'Tiger.' That's the name that has appeared in all of the personal ads."

Before elaborating further, Emily spotted the name Walter Mahler on the list, codenamed "Weasel." Mahler's name had a notation after it stating: "deceased," and the date of his death. Emily noticed that not all of the listed employees had codenames. She guessed those were reserved for the field operatives. Emily and Linc both looked for the name Claude Mendosa. It wasn't there. However, next to the code name, "Harpoon," was another notation reading, "The Lass of Mont Valier."

"That's him!" she shouted, pointing to the name.

"Who?" asked Linc leaning forward to get a better look.

"Claude Mendosa," she said with a squeal.

"Where?" asked Linc squinting his eyes. "Which one?"

"Here," she said excitedly and pointed to a particular spot on the screen. "Code name 'Harpoon.' That's 'The Lass of Mont Valier,' the name in all the personal ads."

"The Lass of Mont Valier," repeated Linc. "Sounds like a woman."

"It's a contraction," Emily said excitedly. His old nickname in French was *L'assassin du Mont Valier*, which translates to, 'The Assassin of Mount Valier. He just shortened it to 'the lass of Mont Valier. It's him!"

Emily could no longer contain her excitement. She jumped off the chair and hugged Linc around the neck. That only lasted a second before she let go and sat back down in her chair. "What should we do now, Linc?" she asked like a little girl in a candy store.

Linc took a moment to study the information on the screen before pointing to a particular name and saying, "We contact this guy."

"Okay," she agreed nodding her head. "Then, what?"

"Then we get him to call off his attack dog."

Emily studied the name of the person Linc was pointing to. The information on the monitor stated that the man was in charge of The Clearing House. Emily softly pronounced his name, "Vincent Parlotti."

*   *   *

Manfred had excused himself for the evening. It was his first day back to work since having been shot, and he announced that he was far more exhausted than he would have imagined. Bidding Manfred a good night, Preston, Linc and Emily retired to the Oak Room.

While Preston poured three glasses of Chardonnay, Linc and Emily told him all about Emily's search for the killer. As the story unfolded, Preston became mesmerized. When they reached the part about the NSA, Preston appeared eager to interrupt the tale. He waited for an opening and said, "Are either of you aware that I have contacts that deal with the NSA? High level contacts?"

Linc and Emily looked at each other. "Preston," said Linc nodding his head, "Emily and I have already discussed this. Both of us are fully aware of all the influential people you know in Washington. One of the reasons we're telling you all this is so that you can help us."

Preston had never been an actual part of any of Linc's investigations, but the thought had always intrigued him. The idea that he would now be involved excited him. He rubbed his hands together gleefully. "What would you like me to do?" he asked.

They told Preston what Emily had discovered about the imposter, Special Agent Brant Sheffield, and the fact that he was the man who had killed Scott, Crystal and Professor Lunderman. Emily went on to say that his real name was Claude Mendosa and that he was a contract assassin for a division of the NSA known as "The Clearing House."

"The Clearing House?" asked Preston. "I've never heard of them."

"It's very hush-hush," said Emily.

"Top Secret," added Linc. "People like you and me are never supposed to know about it."

"Now this is important, Daddy," said Emily. "This Claude Mendosa character goes by the code name, 'Harpoon.' I don't think they know his real name. Probably just one of his aliases."

"Right!" said Preston thrilled at the intrigue. "One of his aliases. What was the name he used when he came here?"

"Brant Sheffield," repeated Linc.

"Right," said Preston, starting to fidget and nervously tap his foot. "Brant Sheffield."

"But remember, Daddy," said Emily trying to speak slowly in order to calm her father's excitement, "they may not know him by that name. They will, however, know him by the name, 'Harpoon.'"

"Harpoon," said Preston, getting even more excited. "He really has the code name, Harpoon?"

Emily just nodded her head.

"Harpoon," Preston said with a mixture of anxiety and reverence. Then, he suddenly brightened and said, "Secret code names, top-secret organizations, government assassins, this is like a bloody James Bond film!"

Linc could not help smiling at Preston's childlike enthusiasm. "Listen to me," Linc said, trying to bring the seriousness of the situation back into focus, "the name of the man who directs The Clearing House is Vincent Parlotti. He's the key to all of this. You've got to get hold of this guy and get him to call off Mendosa. Ultimately, that's what's going to save the lives of Pitch and Jennifer."

Up until the moment that Linc suggested the possibility of Pitch and Jennifer both being murdered, Preston felt as though he were part of a play, a fantasy. It hadn't been quite real. Suddenly, his demeanor changed. It was obvious that he abruptly became fearful of the possible consequences.

Preston began asking a lot of questions. Linc and Emily didn't have all the answers, but they responded to his inquiries as best they could. Getting a pen and paper, he jotted down some of the key words, names and phrases. When Preston was satisfied that he had all the information he needed, he placed a phone call. Linc and Emily listened as Preston asked to speak to Senator Boyd Williamson. The silence lasted less that a minute followed by Preston ending with, "Tell Boyd that this is Preston Collingsworth. Oh, and tell him . . . it is imperative that he return my call immediately. Better yet, tell him it is a matter of life and death."

CHAPTER FORTY SEVEN

"**I**t was really nice of you folks to stop over like this," said Jennifer as she stood up to say good-bye. "Peter and I have been feeling a little alone through all of this."

Emily stepped toward Jennifer and hugged her. "I'm just sorry that we haven't been more visible up until now," she said as they embraced. "But from now on, we'll make an extra effort. Won't we, Linc?"

After having left Preston waiting for his return phone call from the Senator, Linc and Emily had gone out to get something to eat. During dinner they decided to drop in to visit with Pitch and Jennifer. On the drive over, Linc and Emily discussed how the conversation should proceed and decided not to alarm the young couple any more than necessary. Linc and Emily purposely chose not to tell Pitch and Jennifer anything about Claude Mendosa, not even his name. Linc had surmised that, if the couple knew of all the terrible crimes the assassin had committed, it would have only served to frighten them further.

Emily agreed.

It was almost eleven p.m. and the visit had gone smoothly. Jennifer had been the consummate hostess. Since Preston had arranged to have a parade of catering vans deliver everything from breakfast to late night nibbles, Jennifer was able to offer an array of delicacies, including cheeses, desserts and wine.

Jennifer came over to where Linc was standing. She reached her arms up and hugged him, holding the embrace for several seconds. "I just don't know how to thank you," she said unlocking her arms from around his neck. "I've never been this . . . I don't know how to say it. It's just that Peter and I don't seem to have any control over our lives right now. And you've been kind enough to take over. When a person is lucky enough to find someone like you, someone we can trust, someone who is so concerned about our protection . . ."

Linc interrupted when he noticed her eyes welling up. "You don't have to thank me, Jennifer," he said, trying to lighten the moment. "You two are a terrific couple, and I'm sure anybody would do the same."

Then, without waiting for Jennifer to respond, Linc turned to Emily, "Are you about ready, Emily?"

Emily went to give Pitch a hug. "I'll tell you, what," said Pitch taking Emily's arm and guiding her to the door, "I'll walk you people downstairs and see you to your car."

"That's not necessary," said Emily. "We can see ourselves out."

"Don't be silly," said Pitch holding the door open for Linc and Emily. "Jennifer? I'll be right back."

The three of them walked downstairs and out the entrance to the street. Linc had parked his car directly in front of the apartment building. While he and Emily were upstairs visiting, someone had moved a couple of big garbage cans and lined them up close to his bright red Corvette. Moving one of the cans away from his front fender, Linc unlocked the car door and opened it for Emily.

"There's something I need to ask you, Linc," Pitch said hesitantly.

Linc stopped what he was doing. "What is it, Pitch?"

"Isn't there any way we can get Jennifer out of here? Out of harm's way?"

Emily touched his arm. "What's going on, Pitch?" she asked.

Pitch hung his head down. "It's just that she's so afraid," he lamented. "All the time. I just can't tell you how fearful she's become since we moved into this place."

Linc sympathized. "I'm not sure what we can do about it this late in the game," he said.

"She was much better when we were staying at your place," Pitch said to Emily. "Her emotional stability slid downhill right after Crystal's funeral. I think that had a lot to do with it."

Emily asked, "Linc, couldn't we bring them back over to my home and maybe arrange to have the surveillance teams cover the grounds?"

"Are you kidding?" replied Linc. "Your place is so big it would take an army of security men to cover it around the clock. Two-dozen men for sure. Maybe more."

"So?" responded Emily. "Daddy will pay for it."

"He will?" asked Linc with one raised eyebrow.

"Sure," she said with a big smile. "I'll just remind him of all the money he'll save by not having to send over truckloads of expensive food."

When the snickering subsided, Linc said, "All right, Pitch. We'll try to make the arrangements and get you guys moved out of here sometime tomorrow. Wednesday at the latest."

After the three of them bid their goodnights, Pitch ran upstairs, eager to tell Jennifer the good news.

*   *   *

The car, an old Chevy Camaro, was parked about forty feet away. It was dark blue, except for the passenger side fender, which was painted in red primer. At that time of night, it was not surprising that everyone missed the fact that the Camaro was there. Sitting behind the wheel, the man with the tattoo slumped down low so that only the very top of his head was visible from the street. It had been his turn to follow the red Corvette and now, he knew that he had hit pay dirt. He slid down in the bucket seat, completely out of sight, as Linc and Emily drove past him and down the street. The tattooed man looked up just in time to see Pitch disappearing through the big columns that framed the entrance into the apartment building. Although the tattooed man needed to get to a phone, he nervously waited a full five minutes, making sure that the red Corvette would not be doubling back. Then, driving the Camaro to a *Circle K* convenience store on Dixie Highway, he made the call.

Mendosa had been cleaning his pistol. He had partially loaded the clip with only six bullets when the telephone rang. Mendosa snatched up the receiver even before the first ring had ended. "Yes," he said curtly.

"Mr. Nelson?" said the tattooed man. "This is Lou. I found him!"

Mendosa stood upon hearing the news. "Where?" he demanded. "And where are you?"

The tattooed man, named Lou, gave Mendosa the details. He spoke excitedly, sounding like a little boy who was the first to find the hidden Easter egg.

"You wait right there at the convenience store," ordered Mendosa holstering his pistol. "And don't go back to the apartment building, you understand?"

"Sure, Mr. Nelson," said tattooed Lou. "I'll wait right here. I did good, huh?"

CHAPTER
FORTY EIGHT

L inc was stopped at a red light just a quarter mile from where he lived. Emily was relaxed in the passenger seat. She had her left wrist on Linc's shoulder and was dreamily playing with a lock of his hair that had shagged down over his collar. "It's almost time for you to get a haircut," she said softly.

"Then you won't have anything to grab onto during our passionate moments," he said with a smile.

Emily leaned her head back in her seat. A smile came to her lips, as she turned to look out at the stars in the night sky. It was just before midnight and they were driving back to Linc's apartment to spend the night.

Before Linc and Emily had left for dinner, she had exchanged her pocketbook for one that was considerably larger. It was an oversized affair in which she packed her toothbrush, hairbrush and makeup kit. Next, she stuffed in a change of underwear and a pastel, peek-a-boo nightie with spaghetti straps. Finally, she managed to cram in a casual outfit, consisting of a skirt and shirt that she planned to wear the following day. Emily had recited a little prayer to the laundry gods, asking for their help in getting the wrinkles out in the morning. After packing, Emily realized that her cell phone was somewhere on the bottom of the pile. She hoped she would not be receiving any phone calls.

Linc had managed to get Mendosa out of his mind, as he and Emily drove to his condo on the beach. Waiting for the light to change to green, he glanced over at Emily, studying her profile. Thoughts of what he was getting himself into scurried through his head. There was no doubt that Emily was beautiful. Lithe and supple, she moved like a dancer. Her laughter was fresh and pure, reminiscent of a child chasing a butterfly. Yet, her smile could be disarming. And when she lifted her chin to look into his eyes, she exuded seductiveness.

Emily had the qualities Linc had hoped, one day, to find. Rather that just paying lip service, she never hesitated to get involved. Not only was she understanding and sympathetic, Emily was also a good listener. But one of her best qualities was her willingness to put her heart and soul into everything she did. From her research at the office to her passionate and inventive lovemaking, Emily extended herself to the fullest.

Linc knew exactly what he was getting himself into. The grief he felt from having lost a woman he loved to a drunk driver was fading. And unlike the infidelity of his fiancé, Lisa Decker, Linc knew that Emily would never betray the bond of trust that had developed between them. Linc chose to allow his feelings to grow.

The light turned green, and Linc's cell phone began to ring. It brought both of them to attention.

"Kind of late to be getting a call, isn't it?" asked Emily.

"It's probably your father," said Linc fumbling for the phone. "He said he would call as soon as he heard from Boyd Williamson."

Emily watched as Linc clicked the phone to the "on" position and said, "Bradshaw."

Two seconds later he said, "Hey, Ferdie. What's going on?"

Emily wondered why Ferdie Dumay would be calling this late at night. Then, she had a sudden moment of panic, as she surmised that Pitch and Jennifer were in some sort of trouble. Emily sat up straight in her seat and tapped Linc's arm. "Pitch and Jennifer?" she said, alarmed. "Are they all right?"

"Hold on a moment, Ferdie," said Linc. Turning to face Emily, Linc said reassuringly, "They're fine, Emily. No problem at all. It's just that Ferdie can't get hold of one of his guys."

As Emily was taking a deep breath of relief, she heard a muffled ring. It was her own cell phone ringing in the bottom of her pocketbook. Emily frantically reached her hand down inside, searching for the receiver. After the fifth ring, she pulled it out and spun it right side up just in time to say, "Hello?"

It was Preston. "Hi, Daddy. Is everything all right?"

"Yes, yes," said Preston still keyed up from earlier in the evening. "Is Linc with you?"

"Yes. He's right next to me. He's on the other phone."

"Oh, of course," said Preston. "I tried calling, but his line was busy. So, I dialed your number. I hope you don't mind."

Before she could answer, Preston went on. "I just got off the phone with Senator Boyd Williamson. I brought him up to date with what's going on, and filled him in on what we need him to do."

"And what did he say?" asked Emily.

"Very interesting," replied Preston. "He wanted to know how I could have possibly come across the name of Vincent Parlotti. Boyd went on and on about it. He talked about it being a name that only a handful of people in the whole world should know."

As Emily continued to talk to her father, she noticed that Linc had made a U-turn and was heading the car back in the direction from where they had just come. She refocused her attention on the conversation with her father. "Will the Senator honor your request and try to make contact with that Vincent Parlotti fellow?"

"Yes, yes," said Preston. "He won't waste any time. He'll try getting hold of him right away."

"Excellent, Daddy. Good work."

Emily went on to tell her father about the new plans to bring Pitch and Jennifer back to the house. After explaining the reason for the move, she talked about the expense of fielding twenty or so agents for round-the-clock protection.

Preston did not seem to mind at all. On the contrary, he was pleased at the prospect of having Pitch and Jennifer back in his home for a while. Besides being good company, a bond had begun to grow between Pitch and himself. "When will you bring them back?" he asked.

"As soon as Linc can make the arrangements," she said. "As a matter of fact, he's on the other phone talking about that right now."

"First-rate," exclaimed Preston. "I think it's a prudent idea." Switching subjects, Preston asked, "What time will you be coming home?"

Emily skipped two beats before answering. "I won't be coming home tonight, Daddy. I'll see you tomorrow."

"Won't be coming home? Why . . ." Preston stopped in mid sentence. There was an awkward pause before he continued. "Oh. Okay. Certainly. Well, good night, Emily."

Emily disconnected and placed her phone back into her pocketbook. She listened as Linc was saying goodbye to Ferdie.

While Linc clicked off his phone, Emily said, "I was just talking to Daddy. I'll tell you all about it, but first, tell me where we're heading."

"I'm just going back to where the surveillance team is," said Linc, "so I can do Ferdie a favor. What did your father have to say?"

"He finally spoke to Boyd Williamson," said Emily. "But wait a sec. What kind of favor does Ferdie want at this time of night?"

"One of the guys on the stake-out is a fellow by the name of Johnnie Capella. We call him 'Cappy.' I used to work with him. Anyway, his wife was in a car accident tonight and Ferdie's been trying to get hold of him. There must be something wrong with the lines. Neither Cappy nor O'Brien are answering their phones. Did your father ask the Senator to get hold of Parlotti?"

"Yes," said Emily. "Daddy said the Senator will make it a priority issue." Emily hesitated before asking, "Linc, do you think Jennifer and Pitch are all right?"

"I'm sure they're fine," answered Linc reassuringly. I talked to Ferdie about increasing the scope of the surveillance and moving it to your place. He's figuring on twenty two agents and he'll be able to have it all in place by Wednesday morning. What else did Preston say?"

"He said that Senator Williamson is going to try to get hold of Vincent Parlotti tonight." Then, lightly touching Linc's arm, she asked, "Linc, isn't it a bit unusual for the surveillance team not to be answering their phones? I mean, don't they have cell phones or something?"

CHAPTER FORTY NINE

Holding a wad of money in his hand. Mendosa counted off three one hundred dollar bills and handed them to Tattooed Lou. "Tell your friend I won't be needing him any longer either."

"So, that's it?" said the tattooed man, upset that his employment had been terminated. "I manage to spot the guy you're lookin' for, and that's it? Case closed?"

"I told you at the outset," said Mendosa, staring intently into the man's eyes, "this was just a temporary assignment. Now, you did a good job, and I gave you your money. That's it."

"Hey, look, Mr. Nelson," said Lou pleading his case, "This is the kind of stuff I'm good at. You could use a guy like me. You oughta keep me on the payroll, maybe a couple more days. I could really help you out, know what I mean?"

They stared at each other in silence. Mendosa was anxious to get going, and he needed to end this quickly. "Look," said Mendosa patiently, "if I need you for something else, I'll get in touch with you. But for right now . . . go home."

Lou glanced down at the money in his hand. Mendosa knew that depending on what the tattooed man said next could determine whether he lived or died.

"Okay," said Lou sullenly.

Mendosa turned and walked down the street. There was no wind. Not even a breeze. In just the past several hours, the night air had become heavy with humidity and hung like a coffin cover over the area. The Tequesta Indians of South Florida had a saying: "When the good wind stops, the bad smell begins."

Mendosa had assumed that there would be some kind of security arrangements in place as protection for Pitch Pechowski. Keeping to the night shadows, Mendosa slowly walked the side street looking for where a security team might be concealed.

Discovering the surveillance window in just a matter of minutes, Mendosa sneered at the amateurish attempt to camouflage the team's hiding place. Approaching through a darkened alley, the assassin stealthily climbed the stairs. Removing his stiletto, Mendosa silently released its blade.

* * *

Pitch and Jennifer were locked in an embrace. She had just been crying great heaving sobs while tears had run down her face and pooled on the front of Pitch's shirt. She was calming a bit as Pitch held her tightly and spoke soothingly. "Are you going to be all right, Jennifer?" he asked, as he stroked her hair.

"Uh-huh," she said between sniffles and erratic gulps of air. "I'll be okay." Jennifer swallowed several times, trying to catch her breath. Relieved, she managed to take a deep ragged breath and smile.

"I didn't expect that reaction," said Pitch as he wiped the tears from her face with his fingers.

"It's just that I've been so nervous," she said as explanation. "Ever since Crystal's funeral, I've felt like we've been targets. Like it's only a matter of time before that . . . that man finds us, too."

"I know," Pitch said reassuringly, as he wrapped her in his arms again. "I know."

"So, when you told me that Linc and Emily were going to bring us back to her place and arrange for an army of protection, I just couldn't contain myself. I feel so relieved. I'm sorry for being such a baby."

Pitch and Jennifer spent the next fifteen minutes talking about how things were going to be all right once they returned to Preston's estate. They touched, kissed and held each other. Their relationship had been growing stronger, even before this calamity had begun. Now, each of them was sure that they belonged together. They felt comfortable and complete when they were near one another.

"Come on," said Pitch as he stood up. "You've been through a cataclysm of emotions. Let's get you ready for bed."

Jennifer stood up and looked around the apartment. "Peter," she said pleadingly, "could you first give me a hand cleaning up?"

"Of course," he said enthusiastically. "We'll get this place ship-shape in a quark-flash."

"All right," she said, smiling. Jennifer was glad to hear Pitch returning to his old self. She enjoyed the way he used scientific references in his speech, and felt that some stability was about to return to their lives. "Tell you what," she said with renewed vigor, "I'll do the dishes and you take out the garbage. All that smoked fish and those cheeses are starting to smell."

"Good idea," said Pitch, taking out a fresh plastic bag for the refuse. "I noticed they've already put out the garbage cans. So, I guess tomorrow is pick-up day."

Pitch went about his business efficiently. Clearing off the leftovers from the little kitchen table, he put them in the bag and tied the top with a knot. Next, he took the trash can from under the sink, removed the plastic insert and tied that as well. Armed with two full bags of garbage, he walked out, leaving the door open. He called out over his shoulder, "I'll be right back. Don't get started in the shower without me!"

Jennifer giggled as she listened to Pitch's footsteps going down the stairs.

Pitch tried to be quiet about lifting the lids off the big garbage cans that were lined up by the curb. It was approaching midnight, and he did not want to disturb the neighborhood. Closing the top lid, he stretched his back and slowly became aware of the night's stillness. Pitch took a moment to glance up and down the sidewalks. There were no cars moving on his little street. Standing some one-hundred yards west of Dixie Highway, he caught sight of an occasional car speeding past, heading north or south. Unlike the quiet, residential street on which Pitch was standing, Dixie Highway was well lit. There was one street light further down the block, which did not do much to illuminate the entryway to his building. Only the residual light from Dixie Highway, casting a meager glow in his direction, gave some semblance of luminescence.

Pitch swept his eyes past the row of houses on the opposite side of the street and caught a glimpse of something moving in the alley that lay between two buildings. Despite being too dark to identify, Pitch took an instinctive step backward into the shadows.

Pitch squinted and perceived that whatever it was seemed to be moving toward him. The object loomed out of the murkiness of the alleyway and Pitch could see clearly that it was a man.

Odd, he thought, that someone would be walking the alleys at this time of night. The person was still moving forward, and Pitch could now see the left side of the stranger's face, as it came into the glow of lights emanating from Dixie Highway. The man took several more steps when suddenly, a car horn pierced the silence. Some unknown driver at the corner, annoyed at nothing in particular, was laying on his horn.

Pitch was about to turn his head to look and see if he could ascertain the reason for the commotion, but something made him stop. The man across the street turned his head in the direction of the noise, and his face became illuminated. Pitch went cold. It was Special Agent Brant Sheffield, the man who had tried to kill them all in Preston's library.

Pitch was momentarily frozen in his tracks. Ceasing all motion, he held his breath and silently prayed that he was hidden from view. His heart was beating like a drum and a cold, clammy feeling encapsulated his entire body. The horn sound stopped and Agent Sheffield faced forward and resumed his stride.

Pitch's mind was a blank. Fear was his only emotion. Statue-like, he stood there, unable to inhale, exhale or blink. Like a man with his head in a guillotine, Pitch waited for the inevitable downward swooshing of the blade.

The sound came from behind and above him. "Peter?"

It didn't register in Pitch's brain.

Jennifer called out again. "Peter? Are you all right?"

At that, Pitch spun like a top on his heel, and charged up the stairs as fast as his legs could churn, yelling at the top of his lungs, "Jennifer! Oh, my God! Jennifer!"

Pitch screamed his warning as Mendosa stepped into the street and stopped. He stood his ground for a couple of seconds, determining if any real threat existed. After glancing up at the lighted windows of Pitch's apartment, he resumed his relentless march.

*   *   *

Preston was standing next to his desk in the Oak Room. He held the telephone receiver to his ear while he waited on hold. Senator Boyd Williamson had called and told Preston that a conference call had been arranged with Vincent Parlotti. Preston was waiting for the conference connections to be made.

Boyd Williamson came back on the line. "Preston," said Williamson, "I have Vincent Parlotti on the other end."

"Hello, Mr. Collingsworth," said Parlotti.

"Good evening, Mr. Parlotti," replied Preston.

"Preston," interjected the Senator, "I've given Mr. Parlotti some background on who you are and the important role you've played here on 'The Hill.' He has some questions for you."

"And I have some questions for you, Mr. Parlotti," said Preston.

"Tit for tat, eh?" asked Parlotti.

"Quid pro quo," answered Preston.

These two powerful men were about to have a first time conversation, one that was vitally important to the well being of others. This call was going to deal with people's lives. Each man had a strong personality. They instinctively tried to achieve the upper hand through various tactics such as intimidation, one-upmanship or knowing something the other did not.

"Suppose we get right to it, Collingsworth," said Parlotti, purposely dropping the 'Mister' title. "How did you come across the code name of 'Harpoon?'"

"How that occurred is not important," stated Preston. "What is important, is that you've sent him on a mission, and that mission must be terminated."

"Not important?" repeated Parlotti, with an edge to his voice. "Do you have any concept of the term, 'National Security?' Do you understand the meaning of that phrase?"

"Don't patronize me, Parlotti. Let me tell you what is important. There are innocent lives at stake here. Many of them. A multiple murder almost took place in my own home. Do you understand that phrase?"

Parlotti started to raise his voice. "Senator Williamson has told me you're supposedly a heavyweight when it comes to Washington politics, so don't play the role of an innocent. I know you understand what it means when it comes to matters of national security."

Preston hesitated.

Parlotti continued, his voice barking into the phone, "No one, outside of a handful of people with the most stringent security clearance, is supposed to know that code name. Now, tell me how you came to have that information."

Preston lost his patience. "The only question to be answered during this conversation is whether or not you will prevent this man from killing any more innocent civilians. Perhaps I should begin by asking, are you capable of stopping this man?"

Boyd Williamson interrupted. "Gentlemen, gentlemen," he mediated. "Adversarial people cannot accomplish what needs to be. I would like both of you to take a moment and re-group. Let's try this again."

Parlotti spoke first. "Collingsworth, do you know where 'Harpoon' is right now?"

"No, I do not," answered Preston. "But it's only a matter of time before he strikes again. And maybe we shouldn't be using his code name like this over the phone. Is it all right to call him Mendosa?"

There was a pronounced silence on the other end of the phone before Parlotti spoke. "Mendosa?" he asked curiously.

"Yes," said Preston sensing a return to the upper hand. "His real name is Claude Mendosa. I was told that you might not be aware of his real name. I'm beginning to wonder, since you have such obvious limitations, if you really can be of assistance. Tell me, Mr. Parlotti, can you really help us?"

"Perhaps," conceded Parlotti. "Since you don't know where this Claude Mendosa is, then tell me, where is Pitch Pechowski?"

"Pitch is safe," said Preston, annoyed that Parlotti was switching gears. "We have him tucked away in one of my apar . . ." Preston stopped in mid sentence when he realized Parlotti's depth of knowledge. Preston suddenly understood that he was not approaching this subject from the same perspective as Parlotti. Preston started again. "So, you do know about Pitch Pechowski," he said. "Well, I have no intention of telling you where he is."

Parlotti quickly asked his next question. "Then tell me this, which one of you is in possession of the disc?"

Preston was stunned. This man Parlotti seemed to know so much. When Linc and Emily had asked for help in contacting Parlotti, Preston thought of it as an adventure, an exciting Hollywood script filled with code names, passwords and cloak and dagger. Approaching this phone call with the smugness of someone who thought he had the upper hand, he never anticipated that Parlotti would always be at least one step ahead. Preston was out of his element and losing control. Without knowing what other secrets Parlotti might possess, Preston decided to focus on to the original purpose of the call. "Mr. Parlotti," began Preston, "There are many things we need to discuss and should discuss, but we don't have a lot of time. For this moment, the only question that needs answering is can you do anything to stop this man?"

"I can do many things, Mr. Collingsworth," said Parlotti in a godlike tone, "and I will try and help you. But first, I need you to cooperate with me. Tell me what you know and how you know it. After that, I'll put some things into motion. Those are my terms."

Preston was not sure what to do. He didn't know this man Parlotti and therefore had no reason to trust or confide in him. Furthermore, Parlotti might even be the one behind all the murders that had been occurring. On the other hand, Linc, Emily and Boyd Williamson all seemed to think that Parlotti was the man in control.

Preston needed to talk to Linc. He was not sure just how much trust to put in Parlotti and wanted Linc to make that decision. "I'm going to have to get back to you," said Preston.

CHAPTER FIFTY

After making the turn off Dixie Highway, Linc drove down the short length of street. He slowed his Corvette to a crawl and peered out the windows into the night.

"What are we looking for?" whispered Emily, suddenly apprehensive.

Looking out the passenger side window, Linc leaned across Emily and said, "I'm trying to see if there's any sign of Cappy and O'Brien. They're squirreled away on the second floor of that house back over there," he gestured in that direction with a nod of his chin.

Linc's car was barely moving as it came even with the entrance to Pitch and Jennifer's building. Rolling down his own window, Linc craned his neck to look up toward Pitch's apartment.

"What do you see?" asked Emily in a hushed tone, as she also bent forward to look up and out the front windshield.

"Just seeing if there's any light coming from . . ." Linc paused as his words were interrupted by a loud muffler and the high beam of a single headlight. They belonged to a car approaching from the rear. Linc pulled his car closer to the curb, allowing some room for the noisy car to pass. He noticed that it was moving very slowly.

As the single-beamed car pulled up alongside Linc's automobile, Tattooed Lou suddenly realized that it was the same red Corvette he had spotted earlier. He glanced out the window of his Camaro and saw Linc. Their eyes met for only a split second.

Tattooed Lou had been reluctant to leave this job. The money was great, and he was excited to be a part of something. Lou had hoped to accomplish something impressive. By demonstrating how valuable he was, perhaps Mr. Nelson would ask him to stay on the job. But the last thing Lou anticipated was seeing the red Corvette again.

Lou knew immediately that he had made a mistake. If he hung around for another second, he would be in serious trouble. In the next instant, Lou accelerated his Camaro, spinning its wheels in an effort to move out as quickly as possible.

The night air was shattered with the roar of the muffler and the sound of squealing tires. Emily jumped and sucked in a gasp, as the Camaro screamed its getaway and fishtailed down the street. Quickly flipping open the glove compartment, Linc removed his pistol. "Emily, stay in the car! Call Eddie! Have him get down here with back-up!" He had opened the car door and was moving out, as he hollered over his shoulder, "Roll up, lock up and drive out of here!"

Linc ran across the street and ducked in behind one of the big entry columns. He leaned against it looking in all directions, as he undid the safety on the .38 caliber Police Special. The only sound he heard was the engine of his own automobile as it sped down the block. That sound diminished and silence overtook the night.

Linc darted to the base of the stairs and pressed himself against the wall. He could not see any movement or hear anything unusual. Holding his pistol in his right hand, he cautiously moved up the stairs. An adrenaline rush was making his fingers tingle and his mouth dry. Two steps from the top landing, he pulled up short when heard a loud crash followed by the sound of splintering wood. It was coming from the direction of Pitch's apartment. It sounded as though the door had just been hit with a battering ram. Linc sprang up the last two steps. Pitch's front door was not visible from this vantage-point. From where Linc stood, there was a distance of eight feet to a left turn that led directly to the apartment. Linc heard a loud "thump," followed by the distinctive sound of two shots being fired through a silencer. The two pops were followed by the thud-like sounds of bodies hitting the floor. Linc hollered at the top of his lungs, "Men-do-saa!"

*   *   *

Jimmy Dalton had just informed Eddie about Emily's call for back-up. There was a mad scramble, as they gathered their weapons and Kevlar vests and rushed out the door. The S.W.A.T. Team was already on its way, along with about a dozen other available cops. Knowing that it was Linc who had called for immediate back-up, the two cops ran for their car. Dalton, who was overweight and out of shape and already gulping air from the exertion, huffed, "What do you think it is, Eddie?"

"Don't know Jimmy," said Eddie as he slid behind the wheel, "but if Linc called for back-up, it probably ain't no drill."

*   *   *

Linc had no doubt that it was Mendosa who was only eight feet away and right around the blind corner. Knowing also that Mendosa was armed, Linc paused. He saw a shaft of light coming from Pitch's kitchen. Determining through the pattern of light and shadows that the door to the apartment was partially off its hinges, Linc still had no way of knowing whether the entrance was accessible. If Mendosa had been able to force it open wide enough to get inside, then Pitch and Jennifer were probably dead and Mendosa had already escaped out the back door. On the other hand, if there weren't enough room to get through the front door, it meant that Mendosa was still trapped in the tiny hallway just ahead.

Linc tensed, as he heard a shuffling movement coming from the hidden vestibule. To his left, Linc could see a long hallway that ran through the building, front to back, and led to an open railed veranda. Coiled for action, Linc tightened his finger on the trigger while leveling the pistol.

The next fraction of a second was nothing but a blur. Linc saw the long silencer poke its snout out from behind the corner. He dove for the protection of the hallway and landed flat on his stomach. Two shots rang out. Scampering to his knees, he spun around, positioning himself to return fire. Linc started to peek around the corner. Another shot spit from the assailant's pistol, shattering the wood molding right in front of Linc's face. Splinters of wood exploded in front of him, showering his hair. A particle of debris lodged in Linc's eye. He blinked furiously as tears formed in his eye and ran down his face. From a kneeling position, Linc reached his hand around the corner and blindly fired three shots in the direction of Mendosa. Linc brusquely swiped at his eye, hoping to dislodge the annoying wood chip. In the distance, he could hear the sounds of multiple sirens.

This was not a good situation. It was Linc's right eye that was watering and obstructing his vision. He had to lean to his right in order to see what was happening around the corner, and the blurred vision in his right eye meant that he was forced to lean farther out than he should have. But the moment was critical and desperate, and he had no choice. He shifted his body to look around the corner.

Trying to stay balanced and ready, he leaned far to his right. Linc heard the shot as it came from the silencer and felt it tear into his right arm just above the elbow. There was an instant of searing heat as his hand went numb and the pistol fell from his grasp. But in that same moment, he also heard the unmistakable sound of a hammer hitting a firing pin on an empty chamber. Either Mendosa's gun had misfired or was out of bullets. Ignoring the pain, Linc sprang forward like a leopard.

Mendosa was out of ammunition. Reaching into his pocket to whip out the long bladed stiletto, Mendosa prepared to slash and slice his opponent to ribbons in the blink of an eye. Almost too late, he realized that the big man was coming at him at blinding speed. The long handle of the knife had not quite cleared the confines of his pocket, and there wasn't even time to press the release button that would allow the blade to come to life. Mendosa barely had time to lean forward to counter the body blow. The two men charged each other like Sumo wrestlers in a death match. The impact was an explosive collision that caused Mendosa's knife to fly out of his hand and skitter the length of the hallway, disappearing under the door to one of the storage bins.

Having the momentary advantage, Linc bulldozed Mendosa into the wall, hearing him grunt on impact. But Mendosa was wiry and fast.

Like a slithering snake, he twisted and slipped out of Linc's grasp. Mendosa threw two blindingly quick punches, but Linc's reflexes were instantaneous, enabling him to block them both. At the same time Linc cocked his left arm and fired off a jack-hammer blow that caught the assassin high in the rib cage. Mendosa was hurt and took two quick steps backward. The wailing of the police sirens grew to a crescendo.

Then, Linc saw it. His .38 was lying on the floor just a few feet away and close to the head of the staircase. Mendosa saw the pistol as well, and dove for it. Linc dove for Mendosa. Hitting the floor simultaneously, Mendosa reached for the weapon just as Linc got his left hand in the way, preventing the killer from getting a grip on its handle. Linc put his right arm under Mendosa's neck and rolled to the left. The action pulled Mendosa over the top of Linc and away from the pistol. Linc's greater strength and momentum snapped Mendosa head over heels. Slipping out of the head lock, Mendosa arched into a kind of back flip. In the melee of arms and legs, somebody's foot kicked the gun and it tumbled harmlessly down the stairs.

Mendosa managed to get to his feet just a heartbeat before Linc. Jumping up to square off with his adversary, Linc was surprised to see Mendosa turn and run down the hallway toward the railing at the rear veranda. As he bolted after him, Linc could hear several cops shouting from the first floor.

Mendosa glanced over his shoulder at the sound of Linc's footsteps, and was amazed at the big man's unpredictable speed. Knowing that he would not be able to outrun him, Mendosa stopped short, turned and braced himself for the force of Linc's shoulder blow. At the last possible moment, Mendosa bent low and managed to plant his shoulder just below Linc's center of gravity.

Linc knew instantly that he was in trouble. It had happened on the football field a number of times. If you over-commit when charging an opponent, you leave yourself vulnerable to getting flipped over his back. Mendosa had position, and Linc was left powerless. He tried desperately to grab hold of Mendosa, but was unable to get a solid grip. Linc felt himself being lifted up and over the railing.

Linc heard the shouts of a cop as he yelled, "Freeze!" But Linc was already in mid air, trying to reach out and latch onto the railing. Out of the corner of his eye, he saw Mendosa running down the rear hallway. Linc fell sixteen feet into the back yard.

Captain Baumgarten was hollering orders to the rest of the police squad. Demanding that the area be cordoned off, members of the S.W.A.T. Team ran to their positions atop the adjoining and adjacent buildings. Three cops had already entered the street-level lobby. Two more were on their way around back in order to come in from the rear.

Eddie Strickland pointed to the left side of the building and said, "Jimmy, go down the alley! I'm going in the front!"

With his service revolver drawn, Jimmy Dalton moved carefully down the alley. Eddie followed the three cops who had preceded him into the building.

Shouts of, "Clear," were called out each time a cop felt that he had reached a point of advance and was sure there was no danger behind him. The word, "Clear" was being called out from various sectors. The cadence of that cry was finally interrupted by the shout of "Man down!" The call came from the cop on the second floor who witnessed Linc getting tossed over the side.

The two policemen who first got to Linc, saw that he was barely conscious and having trouble breathings. He had some deep cuts that were bleeding profusely. One of the cops was on his radio reporting the injuries to the E.M.S. personnel, while the other asked Linc how he was doing. Linc grimaced as he fought to stay aware, "Pitch and Jennifer," he gasped. " . . . apartment two-oh-six. Send someone . . . check on them."

Linc had trouble hearing the words as the cop called into his radio, "Suspect may be in unit number two-oh-six, second floor. Proceed with caution."

Linc looked at the cop who was kneeling in front of him. The man was speaking, but seemed to be out of focus. Linc was vaguely aware that he was having trouble comprehending. The curious cacophony of sounds that surrounded him slowly faded to nothing.

CHAPTER FIFTY ONE

Emily didn't know what to do with her hands. She folded, then unfolded her arms before absent-mindedly twirling the straps of her pocketbook. Anxiously watching as one of the paramedics secured Linc to the stretcher, she bit her bottom lip while the other set the I.V. line. Emily shuddered at the thought that Linc was close to death. This was the second time within a week that he was going to a hospital; only this time there was, unquestionably, no resistance.

Ten minutes earlier, the police had cordoned off the area and refused to let Emily through. Even though she kept insisting that she knew Lincoln Bradshaw, it didn't do any good. In desperation, she decided to ignore the regulations and break through the barricades. She managed to go only a few feet before she was physically stopped by a cop who escorted her back to the other side of the line. Emily picked up smatterings of conversation from the nearby cops. Two of them were discussing the description of the perpetrator and it confirmed her worst fears. Mendosa had been there.

Emily spotted Eddie Strickland and called out his name. In a few minutes, Eddie stood by her side, as she begged the E.M.S. squad to tell her something of Linc's condition. They would only confirm that Linc had been shot and was unconscious. Adding that they needed to transport him to the hospital as quickly as possible, the emergency medical team went about their work with unqualified efficiency. To Emily's eyes, it all looked very serious and somber.

A light breeze fluttered by causing Emily to feel a chill. "Where do you have Mendosa?" she asked Eddie, without taking her eyes off the ambulance. "Is he alive?"

"They think he got away," Eddie said, running a hand through his hair.

Emily spun around to face him. "What do you mean 'got away?' How could he possibly get away?"

"I don't know," Eddie said, as he looked around at all the police milling about. "We sure had a lot of these boys in blue here. But somehow he slipped past us."

Emily felt angry. The love of her life was gravely injured and might even die, while his killer, this aberration in her world named Claude Mendosa, was still at large. It wasn't fair.

Eddie continued. "We can't find the Pechowski kid either."

Emily put a hand to her mouth. "Pitch? Oh, no!" she uttered. "What about Jennifer?"

Eddie was momentarily distracted by the unexpected wail of a siren. "We can't find either one," he said.

Emily clutched her pocketbook. "Are they . . . are they dead?"

"It doesn't look good," said Eddie slowly shaking his head. "But I'll let you know as soon as I know something."

Emily experienced a sinking feeling of dread. With the world seemingly caving in, her eyes filled with tears, as the grief of losing loved ones swept over her. Then, her cell phone began ringing.

Emily was wiping away her tears, while she fumbled in her pocketbook trying to get at her phone. Giving her some privacy, Eddie walked away. She hit the button that activated the unit and weakly said, "Hello?"

"Emily?" said a female voice obviously distraught with emotion.

Emily was momentarily confused. The voice sounded vaguely familiar, but for some reason she was having trouble putting a face with it. "Yes?" she asked hesitantly.

"Emily . . . it's me . . . Jennifer!"

*   *   *

Pitch and Jennifer had long since escaped out their back door. Upon recognizing FBI Agent Brant Sheffield and hearing Jennifer's call, Pitch had wasted no time. He practically flew into the apartment, grabbed Jennifer by the wrist and without explanation or hesitation, ran down the back staircase. Holding hands, they stayed low and weaved their way out through the back yard. Jumping several fences and dodging a barking dog that almost gave them a heart attack, they finally emerged two blocks south of their apartment building. Staying close to the shadows, they held hands and walked quickly along Palmetto Street. Fear was their predominant emotion. Jennifer jumped at any sound that could have been mistaken for footsteps, while Pitch kept snapping his head around making certain they were not being followed. At one point, they both froze in their tracks at the sound of palm fronds rustling in a little gust of wind. Their nerves were as taut as piano wire and it took an effort to calm themselves.

After about a mile, they made their way east to Dixie Highway, searching for a public telephone. Pitch stood guard outside the booth, while Jennifer stepped in to dial Linc's cell phone. Only able to get his voice mail, Jennifer hung up and dialed Emily's number.

"Where are you?" asked Emily in a rush of words.

Jennifer began to cry. She could not control the opening of the floodgates that had held back her tears. Try as she might, Jennifer was unable to get a coherent word out of her mouth.

Emily was becoming frantic and she kept repeating, "Are you hurt? Where are you?"

Jennifer gave up and handed the phone to Pitch. He maneuvered himself into the tiny phone booth alongside of Jennifer and said, "Emily? It's me, Pitch."

Emily felt a wave of relief wash over her as Pitch began to speak.

"Emily," he said with nervous anxiety, "we were attacked. Attacked. That FBI agent . . . Sheffield . . . Brant Sheffield; he came after us. He tried to . . ."

Emily interrupted and told him she knew all about that. "Where are you now?" she asked in a hushed tone.

Pitch told her where they were, and that they were all right for the moment.

Emily instructed them to stay put. "Try to stay out of sight,' she said, "but keep a lookout for Daddy's car. It's the dark blue Bentley." After disconnecting with Pitch, Emily called her father and told him what needed to be done. Preston assured her that he was on his way to pick up the young couple as soon as he hung up. Emily placed her next call to Ferdie Dumay, after which she got into Linc's Corvette and followed the ambulance to the hospital.

* * *

John Anderson was trying to come fully awake. It was one-thirty in the morning, and he was sitting on the edge of the bed, rubbing his face with one hand while holding the phone in the other. Vincent Parlotti had just finished talking about what transpired during his conference call with Senator Boyd Williamson and Preston Collingsworth.

Anderson took a huge step towards wakefulness when Parlotti informed him that Preston had discovered Harpoon's real name.

"This man, Collingsworth," explained Parlotti, "is a friend of Senator Williamson. And I'll tell you something else, I think he might actually have the disc, or at least he knows where it is. Collingsworth also knows where this Pitch Pechowski can be found. I'm sure of it."

It was not often that Parlotti called Anderson at home, especially at this hour. "What do you want me to do?" asked Anderson.

"I want you to get me down to Palm Beach tomorrow," commanded Parlotti. "I have a briefing with Carrigan at ten-thirty. So, get me a flight sometime after that. On second thought, I want you with me. And another thing . . ."

"Hold on," said Anderson. "Let me just jot down some notes."

When Anderson was ready, Parlotti continued. He rattled off a laundry list of instructions, finishing with, "Contact Gator and the Dutchman. I want them available and at my side while I'm meeting with Collingsworth. I'll call Boyd Williamson. I'm going to need him there to assure that Collingsworth will cooperate."

"What's your plan once we get down there?" asked Anderson.

Parlotti took a moment to contemplate his answer. "Y'know," he said nostalgically, "once, about twenty years ago, when I was a fresh faced government employee, they sent me to a three week course in the use of diplomacy. I thought they might have been grooming me for a slot in the State Department. Anyway, I think it's about time I put my schooling to use."

"No disrespect, Boss," replied Anderson, "but I've never known you to be real diplomatic."

"That's precisely why I want you to have Gator and The Dutchman close by. I want to be sure they can hear the snap of my fingers."

*　　*　　*

The big round clock stood like a sentry over the door and silently announced that it was ten minutes before five a.m. Emily was sitting alone in a vinyl settee meant for two, watching the second hand make yet another sweep of its circumference.

The doctors and nurses sped Linc through the ballyhoo of confusion that was the emergency room and up into surgery in record time. Now, Emily just waited for someone to give her some news. Although most of the time, she was too numb to focus on any particular thought, once or twice, she found herself praying silently. Occasionally, a nurse would stop by between rounds with a simple, "How are you doing?" On one of those mini-visits, Emily was handed a hot cup of coffee. She was grateful.

Linc had been in surgery for better than three hours, and Emily did not know whether that was a good sign or a bad one. The only thing she was sure of was that his life was in jeopardy and by extension, hers as well.

Eddie Strickland walked through the door to the waiting room. Without breaking stride, he came right over to Emily, slid into the seat next to her and put his arm around her. "Hi, kiddo," he said. "Sorry it took so long to get here."

Emily didn't speak. She laid her head in the crook of Eddie's arm and closed her eyes.

"What's the latest word?" he asked.

Emily just shook her head slowly from side to side.

"Linc still in surgery?" Eddie asked.

"Yes," stated Emily. "It's been almost three and a half hours. I'm just hoping to hear something . . . anything."

"Anything I can do for you?" he inquired.

"You could catch that . . . bastard, Claude Mendosa, and put him behind bars forever. That would be nice."

"Well," said Eddie running his free hand through his hair, "you ain't gonna like what I got to tell you about that."

Emily sat up and turned to look at him.

"They found one of the cops who was on the S.W.A.T. Team up on the roof of the building next door." Eddie looked down as he continued. "His neck was broken . . . and his uniform was missing."

The color drained from her face. "What now?" she lamented, her fingers tightly interwoven in her lap.

Before Eddie could answer, a doctor came into the waiting room. "Mrs. Bradshaw?" he asked looking at Emily. "I'm Doctor Charles."

"Please," she responded as she stood up, "call me Emily."

Dr. Charles was a handsome young man in his middle thirties with thick eyebrows and kind eyes. Dressed in his surgical garb, the doctor still had his mask hanging around his neck and one of its ties looped around one ear. Emily eagerly waited to hear what he had to say.

He motioned her back to her seat. "Please sit down, Emily. Let me start off by saying that your husband is going to be all right."

Emily put both hands to her mouth, as she felt the first twinges in her nose that usually preceded a rush of tears.

"I was part of the team who helped put Humpty-Dumpty back together again," he said as he pulled off his surgical mask. "It required a lot of specialists. So, let me fill you in."

Doctor Charles told Emily and Eddie all about Linc's injuries as well as his present condition. Linc had taken an awful tumble when he was thrown off the veranda. As a result of the fall, he had suffered a separated shoulder and a major laceration near his left armpit that required over forty stitches. Dr. Charles took a deep breath. "Your husband also has three broken ribs that he probably sustained in the fall." The doctor continued by explaining that two of the cracked ribs had caused a collapsed lung, but the worst part was that a fracture of the third rib caused some additional internal damage. He told Emily that Linc's spleen had been pierced and surgery was required to remove it. The doctor offered some good news when he told her that Linc's liver had not been damaged, as was so often the case.

The doctor went on to say that Linc had also sustained a concussion and that Emily would notice a big knot behind his left ear. Trying to assuage her concerns, the doctor said that the radiological exams revealed that there was no active bleeding or blood clots in Linc's head. Dr. Charles explained that the least of the patient's problems was the gunshot wound he had suffered. The bullet had entered the outside of his right bicep area and exited cleanly. Besides all that, the rest were just cuts and bruises that a few stitches and bandages would solve.

Both Emily and Eddie had some questions for Dr. Charles. Showing great patience, he talked about the healing process and answered their questions. He was relaxed and chatty and his bedside manner put Emily at ease. The doctor finished by saying, "He'll be in recovery for about another hour. Then, we'll move him to I.C.U. Just a standard precaution, you understand. Prepare yourself before you go to him. It can be a little frightening to see someone right after all that surgery. But I want you to know that he's a strong, healthy strapper, and you'll be noticing that he'll come around very quickly."

"When can I see him?" asked Emily.

"As soon as he's settled into I.C.U." The doctor patted her hand and said, "Tell you what. You relax right here, and I'll make all the arrangements. I'll have the nurse bring you in when he's ready."

CHAPTER
FIFTY TWO

John Anderson had been able to make all the arrangements. Even though the list of things to do seemed endless, he managed to fight his way through the briar patch and still be on time. The snag came when Vincent Parlotti was notified that Senator Boyd Williamson would not be able to leave for Palm Beach until four p.m.

Parlotti was furious. He contemplated going alone, but he needed the Senator with him on this trip. It was Boyd Williamson who knew Collingsworth, and without Williamson to buffer the trust factor, Parlotti didn't have a chance. If he were going to get the disc, he needed the negotiations to go smoothly. And in order to ensure that, he required Senator Williamson's presence.

Parlotti paced around his office like a caged animal, cursing anything and everybody who crossed his path. He had been ready to leave for Florida several hours before. Now, all he could do was sit on his hands. Parlotti felt as though he were bound and gagged while having to wait for Senator Williamson.

Over the years, Anderson had learned how to busy himself and to stay out target range. He waited while his boss vented.

At one point, Parlotti climbed onto his soapbox and ranted, "National security doesn't get the kind of respect it used to." He went on to say, " . . . how shameful it is that Senator Williamson doesn't fully grasp the implications of what we're about to do." And, " . . . the Senator is setting a pretty piss-poor example for his colleagues."

The time for leaving drew near, and Parlotti had spent most of his anger. Anderson had originally tried to wrangle the use of a government airplane for this trip, but was unsuccessful. Instead, he scheduled their flight on a commercial airline. It meant that their schedule was much more restricted and that they had to leave the office at a pre-set time. The hour was at hand as they gathered their things and headed out the door.

Parlotti shot Anderson a glance. "Did you reconfirm with Boyd Williamson?" he grumbled.

Anderson could tell by Parlotti's tone that he was at last, calming down. The worst of his temper storm was over. "Sure did," said Anderson choosing to still keep his answer short.

"Well," asked Parlotti letting off the last of his steam, "is that liberal little prick finally going to meet us at the airport?"

"Y'know, Boss," said Anderson holding the door open for Parlotti, "it's a good thing you never worked for the Diplomatic Corps."

"Oh yeah? Why?"

"You never would have amounted to shit."

Parlotti stopped in mid exit. He glared at Anderson before giving him a wry smile.

*   *   *

Linc was doing better. By noontime they had moved him out of I.C.U. and into room four-sixteen, a rather large semi-private room where he happened to be the only patient. Not only was he was fully conscious, but the worst of the pain was now under control. He had also regained some of his sense of humor. Linc was hooked up to an I.V. that fed him a few nutrients, along with some new "designer" pain medication. Considering what he had been through, he was feeling pretty good.

Emily had not left Linc's side. His recovery and well being were now her priority. Working along with the other nurses, Emily did whatever she could to make their jobs easier and Linc more comfortable. She would stop every few minutes to touch his hand or kiss his face. She could not remember ever feeling more needed.

Emily had made several phone calls and as a result, there was a small parade of visitors who came by. One of the bright spots came when Carmen arrived. She brought along a home cooked "flan," a dessert dish she referred to as her Cuban custard, complete with a caramelized topping. She was in rare form, as she kept up a steady stream of funny one-liners. Linc was trying not to laugh because of the pain, but was unsuccessful most of the time. Carmen told the couple not to worry about the workload at the office, assuring both of them that she would handle everything.

Carmen left after giving hugs and kisses. Linc and Emily could hear the woman singing as she went down the hall, " . . . now direct your feet, to the sunny side of the street . . ."

During their time alone, Emily brought Linc up to date. She told him that Pitch and Jennifer were at home, and that she had made arrangements with Ferdie Dumay to have that army of agents sent over to her father's estate. She also informed Linc that Mendosa had escaped.

Linc's shallow breathing was making speech a little difficult. Mostly, he just shook or nodded his head as required. When he did talk, it was slow and deliberate. "What about Cappy and O'Brien?" he asked. "What happened to them?"

Emily touched his hand. "They didn't make it, Linc. The police found them . . ." Her voice trailed off. "Mendosa had already gotten to them."

Linc closed his eyes and nodded his understanding.

Preston had called a half-dozen times and would have been there if it weren't for his conscientious duty to stay with Pitch and Jennifer. From their perspective, they felt somewhat responsible for Linc's condition, and they called several times to check on his progress.

The hospital room was becoming more cheerful as the winter sun dipped toward the horizon, bathing the far wall in sunlight. Twelve hours had passed since the surgery and Linc was definitely feeling stronger.

Emily was in the middle of selecting the following day's choices from the menu when Preston called with some news. He told Emily that Vincent Parlotti and Senator Boyd Williamson were on their way to Palm Beach. They had called Preston to arrange a meeting. "They think I'm the key to this whole sordid affair," said Preston. "I think they're expecting to learn the secret to Pitch's device. At the very least, they're going to want me to hand over the disc. And Boyd made a reference to having me divulge my sources about this Harpoon/ Mendosa character."

Emily understood. "I hate to say it, Daddy, but what their hoping to accomplish, makes sense. I'd be looking for the same thing if I were in their shoes."

"I suggest," said Preston, "that you talk it over with Linc and decide exactly how you want me to handle it."

Saying good-bye to her father, Emily relayed his message to Linc. She and Linc discussed the problem for a while, trying to formulate a strategy. Within fifteen minutes, Emily called her father back to let him know the details of the newly devised plan, including what they needed Preston to do in preparation. Then, before Emily left for Linc's condo on the beach, she called Ferdie Dumay to make additional arrangements. The round trip took her only forty-five minutes.

*   *   *

It was seven-thirty in the evening by the time they deplaned and rented their car. Parlotti, Anderson and Senator Williamson were on their way to the Palm Beach estate of Preston Collingsworth. Gator and the Dutchman had met the party at the airport and were in a separate car close behind. As they drove towards the ocean on Southern Boulevard, Anderson called ahead to make sure that everything was in order and that Preston Collingsworth understood that their arrival was imminent.

Louise answered the phone call. She informed Mr. Anderson that there had been a change in plans. "Mr. Collingsworth," she stated succinctly, "is waiting for you at Good Samaritan Hospital. He's on the fourth floor, room four-sixteen."

"Hospital?" asked Anderson, incredulously. "I just spoke to him a couple of hours ago. What happened to him?"

"Mr. Collingsworth is in perfect health," said Louise with just the right touch of annoyance in her voice. "He asked me to inform you that room four-sixteen at Good Sam Hospital is to be the designated meeting place."

A thought flashed through Anderson's mind. 'It's always something weird when you have to deal with eccentric billionaires.'

Louise gave him the directions.

Anderson gave the new instructions to the driver before relaying Louise's message to Parlotti and Senator Williamson. The three of them started an animated discussion as to why Preston would seek to have this meeting in a hospital room. Anderson chalked it up to the eccentricities of a rich man. Parlotti had a different viewpoint and asked the Senator if Preston Collingsworth was the sort of man to set some kind of trap?

Williamson shook his head. "No. Not at all," he replied. "That would be completely out of character for Collingsworth. I think the problem is that he doesn't trust you. I think he's chosen to have this meeting in a very public place so that he can feel less vulnerable."

At eight-eleven p.m. the five of them were walking down the fourth floor corridor of the hospital, checking the numbers for room four-sixteen. Anderson led the way with Parlotti and Williamson close behind. Gator and the Dutchman brought up the rear.

Two men stood guard outside room four-sixteen. One was a clean-cut, ivy-league looking man wearing a dark gray business suit. The other was a giant. Six-foot, ten inches tall and broad as a wall, he sported a crew-cut and a goatee. Emily had prearranged their presence when she had called Ferdie Dumay. The two men were armed agents whose sole responsibility was to make sure that things did not get out of control. Their job would be to check ID's and only allow Parlotti and Williamson into the room. Once inside, the sentries were to make sure that the participants were given complete privacy.

The two guards stood shoulder to shoulder at the open doorway. Ivy-league directed his comment to the approaching group. "Gentlemen," he said in a firm, business-like tone, "if two of you plan on going into this room, I'll need to see some sort of ID."

Preston and Emily were standing on each side of Linc's bed when they heard the conversation at the door. Preston turned around and peered between the two guards to see who the visitors were. He spotted Boyd Williamson. "Boyd!" called Preston, gesturing with his hand. "Boyd, get in here,"

There was immediate and audible confusion at the door. Senator Williamson started to take steps towards the room and Parlotti, Anderson, Gator and the Dutchman all fell into step behind him. Their path was quickly blocked by Ivy-League and the Giant, who put their hands up to physically prevent the group's entry. Feet were shuffling, as the small crowd of people at the door began to jostle each other. A moment of extreme tension and trepidation sparked through the air.

Linc gathered his strength and shouted from his reclining position on the bed. "Preston! Sit down!"

Even before Linc had bellowed his name, Preston realized that he had done something stupid. This was a tricky situation, one that had explosive potential and needed to be handled with great care and caution. He sat down in the closest available chair and pursed his lips.

Linc called out again. "Okay, Moose! Take it easy." Then, turning to Preston, he said, "Preston, why don't you point out to Moose which one of those gentlemen is Senator Boyd Williamson and bring him in here. Alone."

Preston sheepishly walked to the door. Moose and Ivy-League parted slightly. Preston offered his hand to Williamson. The Senator was about to take it and enter the room, when Gator and the Dutchman stepped forward.

"Hold it!" ordered Gator. "Nobody's going in there until me and my partner check out the room."

Moose and Ivy-League came together again, closing the portal. All other eyes focused on Linc.

Ignoring the pain of surgery and stitches, Linc lifted himself up on his left elbow and slipped his right hand under his pillow. He spoke in a voice so harsh that it startled Emily, "If you or your partner step one foot into this room, neither of you clowns will be walking out!"

A thick silence hung in the air. Hostility was palpable as everyone stood motionless and tension filled the room. Fear gripped Emily, Preston and the Senator. Linc watched as Parlotti put his hand on Gator's shoulder. Glancing at Parlotti, Gator slowly pulled his hand away from the lapel of his suit jacket and took a half step backward. Moose let out an audible sigh of relief.

Linc shifted his gaze to Williamson. "Senator Williamson," acknowledged Linc, easing the tautness out of his voice. "Good to see you again. Come on in. Please."

Williamson stepped into the room and pumped Preston's hand. The Senator was noticeably relieved that a dangerous moment had passed uneventfully. He walked over to Linc's bedside and said, "Lincoln, what happened to you?"

"One of Parlotti's boys," Linc said as explanation. Then, he shot a glance at the doorway and back to Williamson. "Is that Parlotti standing out there?"

Williamson half turned. "Yes. That's him. Is it okay if we bring him into the room?"

Grimacing as his stitches pulled at his left side, Linc eased his body back down on the bed. He turned to Emily who had been standing still the whole time and said, "Emily, go let Parlotti in. And make sure the boys keep everyone else outside."

As Emily walked to the door to greet Parlotti, Linc said, "And have them close the door."

Parlotti walked into the room and the door closed behind him. They could all hear John Anderson's muffled complaint, "I'm not happy about this!" he shouted as the door swung shut.

CHAPTER FIFTY THREE

Introductions were made, and the conversation moved directly to the problems at hand. Parlotti sat in a chair on the left side of Linc's bed while Emily stood on the opposite side holding Linc's hand. Preston and Senator Boyd Williamson were both seated at the foot of the bed. Linc had his bed propped up, making it easy for him to converse with everybody in the room.

During the brief preliminary discussion, Parlotti sensed that the pivotal person in all of this was going to be Lincoln Bradshaw, not Preston Collingsworth as Parlotti had first assumed. Once all the participants took their positions in the room, Parlotti could see that Linc, even from a reclining position on a hospital bed, commanded the events around him. Parlotti directed his first comments to Linc. "Senator Williamson has briefed me, Linc. He's told me all about you. He's assured me that you're a very capable young man. Even though right now it looks like you've had the crap kicked out of you, you've managed to uncover some things that we thought would have been impossible. You kinda put a gaping hole in our lock-tight security door. As a result, I have a lot of questions I need to have answered. But for now, one answer will do. Where is the disc?"

"We're going to get to that shortly," said Linc straight-faced. "However, I want you to know that I have a lot of questions myself. But, seeing as you're the NSA and all, I have a feeling that you and I are going to be dancing around a couple of the same question marks. So, before we get to the matter of the disc, let's talk about one of my priorities. Let's talk about Claude Mendosa, the man you call 'Harpoon.'"

"All right," said Parlotti, crossing his legs. "Let's talk about him. How did you manage to uncover his identity? That happens to be a very well guarded secret."

Linc just smiled faintly. It was too soon in this discussion to be giving up that information. Linc intended to divulge that only if he had to. Perhaps as a bargaining chip later on.

When Linc did not answer, Parlotti spun in his chair to look directly at Preston. Turning forward again, Parlotti's eyes darted back and forth between Emily and Linc. They came to rest on Emily. When their eyes met, he held her gaze for several seconds before turning back to Linc. Parlotti proved to be intuitive. "It's nice when you have a capable staff," he said cryptically.

Linc was impressed. This man Parlotti didn't let anything get past him. "Let's get back to Mendosa," said Linc, adjusting his perception of Parlotti's ability. "He's killed ten people so far. That we know of. Seven of them are dead as a direct result of that disc. Now, since he works for you, I want you to call him off."

Parlotti denied the charge. "He does not work for me," he said emphatically. "The truth is, he used to work for us as an independent. That was quite some time ago. Then, he went bad. We've been trying to rein him in ever since."

"So, you're telling me he's just going to keep on coming, like a rabid dog?"

"This business with the disc . . ." said Parlotti, shaking his head. "It's gotten into his brain. We think it's making him greedy. Greedy and unreliable. Now, he's following his own agenda. He used to be a very competent operative . . ."

"I'll bet," interjected Linc.

"He was dependable and stable," said Parlotti, ignoring the dig. "Then, he turned into a rogue. He wouldn't respond to any of our commands."

Linc tried to find a comfortable position, "Well," he said, "here's my problem . . ."

Before Linc could continue, Parlotti jumped in. "You want to know what I might be able to do to protect Pitch Pechowski from getting his head blown off. Right?"

"Exactly," answered Linc, wincing in some pain. "Since Mendosa, like you say, doesn't follow orders, then what's to prevent him from going after Pitch? He isn't going to listen to you."

Parlotti emitted a ominous, deep-throated chuckle. "There is a way," said Parlotti, inferring an ability to wield some mysterious power. "But first, let me ask you a question . . ."

It was Linc's turn to finish Parlotti's thought. "You're going to want to know, if you can promise protection for Pitch Pechowski, will I turn over the disc to you?"

"You do realize," said Parlotti, "that the disc isn't all that important."

"Oh, really?" said Linc unimpressed with the man's comment.

"I'm more interested in protecting the national security of this country," said Parlotti. "I want to be sure that Pitch, or you, or anybody doesn't use the knowledge that's on the disc to undermine the safety and security of the United States."

"That's very altruistic," said Linc, "but . . ."

Parlotti interrupted. "Did you know," he said, "that the telephone company already has that technology in place?"

"Is that so?" said Linc with an edge of sarcasm.

"Sure," said Parlotti. "It's old hat. The phone company has had the ability to duplicate that trick for years."

Emily spoke for the first time. "I'm relieved to hear that, Mr. Parlotti," she said with exaggerated deference. "Now, we know that it's perfectly all right for us to destroy the disc."

Everybody's eyes, which were focused on Emily, shifted to Parlotti. He paused before answering. "The purpose of our wanting the disc," he said, choosing his words, "is so that we can have our scientists determine the direction that Pitch took when he developed it. We don't want other people doing the same thing."

"Oh, I see," said Emily, her eyebrows raised in mock surprise. "It wouldn't have anything to do with our government wanting the disc so they could spy on its citizens, would it?"

Parlotti hardened his countenance. He bit off his words as he said, "You've been reading too many conspiracy theories, young lady."

Boyd Williamson chimed in. "Emily," he said condescendingly, "you know me. You've met me on a number of occasions in the past. Your father here, knows me, and trusts me, I might add. So, believe me when I tell you; our country does not work that way. The days of 'Herbert Hoover' are gone. We work in legitimate ways, straight on the up and up. If a matter of national security arises that warrants us to intervene, we go directly to the Justice Department in order to authorize a wire-tap. And even then, only under dire circumstances."

Linc held up his hand preventing further discussion. "We're getting out into left field here. I want to talk about the safety of Pitch Pechowski. I want to know what you can do to make sure he stays happy and healthy."

"Look," said Parlotti, turning to look at Preston, then Emily and finally Linc, "I'm not an unreasonable man. I've done my homework and learned a lot about this young man named Pitch. Not only do I fully understand the implications of what he's done, but I'm also fully aware of his capacity to do other great things. I know all about his past, his previous inventions and . . . and pranks. I also know, if his genius can be harnessed, or at least channeled in a particular direction, that he could probably accomplish some pretty amazing things."

"What are you suggesting?" asked Linc.

"Just what we talked about earlier," said Parlotti. "A trade. I'll put some things into motion that will ensure that Harp . . . that Mendosa won't bother young Pechowski anymore. In return, you give me the disc and let me talk to Pitch." There was a moment of silence as everybody mulled over Parlotti's suggestion and waited for Linc to make a decision. Parlotti broke the silence himself by sweetening the deal and adding, "You people can be present while we're talking. How does that sound?"

"What assurances do I have," said Linc, "that you can hold up your end of the bargain?"

"The answer to that is two-fold," said Parlotti coming up out of his chair to stand next to Linc's bed. "First, think about this; what assurances do I have that you don't have a duplicate copy of the disc? How can I be sure you won't use it anyway?" Parlotti paused a few seconds before answering his own rhetorical question. "The answer is trust and faith. I'm willing to extend that if you're willing to do the same."

There was a moment of anticipatory silence.

"Secondly," he continued, "I think this Pitch fellow has so much potential, I'd be willing to offer him a job. Y'know, get him a high paying slot in one of our think tanks. Then, he could rub shoulders with the rest of the egg-heads. He'd be as safe as a dollar in Fort Knox."

"Okay . . ." said Linc slowly nodding his head. "I'd be willing to give 'trust and faith' a chance. But first, tell me how you plan to call off Mendosa."

"Look," said Parlotti with a slight tone of exasperation, "I'm really walking a thin line here. This whole conversation is already skirting the edge of some very top-secret stuff. Let's just say, we do have a way of getting a message to him."

Emily spoke up. "Like your ads in the personal columns?" she asked. The ones that always start with 'The lass of Mont Valier?'"

Parlotti stared at Emily. A very thin smile came to his lips. "So much for top-secret stuff," he muttered.

"Well?" prodded Linc.

"Okay," he acknowledged. "We put ads in a bunch of newspapers letting Mendosa know that we have the disc, that the disc is off the market. Once he learns that fact, there won't be any need for him to go after anybody. His motivation will have been taken away. He'll have been defused."

Preston spoke for the first time. "I'd prefer to see him behind bars. Locked away for eternity."

Parlotti never turned to look at Preston. His tone was ice cold when he said to Linc, "We're working on that."

Linc looked deep into Parlotti's eyes and understood the implications of his last remark. "All right," said Linc, making up his mind. "Let's get this show on the road." He nodded his head to Emily who walked around the bed and over to the bathroom. All eyes followed her.

As she opened the bathroom door, Linc said, "Vincent Parlotti, let me introduce you to Pitch Pechowski and Jennifer Morano."

Pitch stepped into the room with Jennifer very close behind him.

"Well, Pitch?" asked Linc "Were you able to hear the whole discussion?"

"Yes," he replied. "Indeed, I was. Even the part when Mr. Parlotti, here, referred to me as an egg-head."

Pitch's comment had the instantaneous effect of reducing the tension in the room. Preston and Williamson both snickered. Linc chuckled and Emily smothered a laugh with a hand to her mouth.

"An unfortunate phrase," began Parlotti. "Pitch," he continued as he extended his hand, "you may not believe this, but I am very happy to finally make your acquaintance."

After Parlotti and the Senator had been introduced to the couple, Parlotti did not waste any time in asking for the disc. Pitch casually removed it from the breast pocket of his shirt and handed it over.

Parlotti studied the disc briefly before putting it into his own breast pocket. Then, he asked a series of questions relating to the capabilities of the device. Several of Parlotti's queries dealt with whether it had been tested on any long distance phone calls, but Parlotti's main interest was whether the device worked equally well on cell phones. Finally, he asked if the disc contained instructions on how to use it.

Pitch tried to keep his answers brief, letting Parlotti know that it seemed to work perfectly well on the few long distance calls he had made. He went on to answer the problem of cell phone application by stating that the system had to be re-programmed one way for digital phones and another way for the older analog models. He also told Parlotti that the disc did contain a full set of instructions.

Pitch was very forthright in his answers and seemed somewhat relieved to be rid of the responsibility that came with possessing such an insidious instrument of intrusion.

Parlotti finished up by stating that he was going to arrange to have two of his best scientific minds come here to Florida and debrief Pitch on the technical details of the device.

Linc asked Parlotti a couple of his own questions relating to the security issues that would be presented by the arrival of two strangers. Parlotti quickly came up with a suggestion that satisfied everybody's concerns. It involved sending the scientists down with his assistant, John Anderson, or Senator Williamson.

The Senator expressed his willingness to accommodate Parlotti's suggestion. Linc was satisfied.

The meeting was obviously drawing to a close. Linc asked, "Anybody have any questions before we wrap this up?"

Emily half-raised her hand. "Mr. Parlotti," she asked, "what's going to happen to the disc?"

Parlotti paused at the question. He had hoped that this part of the discussion was over. "We're going to make sure that it won't do any harm to the security of our nation."

"Will you destroy it?" Emily asked.

"First, we'll decipher it," answered Parlotti. "With Pitch's help, we'll look for a way to prevent it from doing any harm."

Emily wasn't satisfied. "Look," she said, "Twenty years from now you'll be retired. The NSA will have a new chief and someone else will be in command of your Clearing House. We'll even have a new President. So, what's to prevent anyone of them from resurrecting this disc and using it to trespass and violate anyone's right to privacy?"

Parlotti momentarily put his head down and gathered his thoughts. "Look," he began, "your government has been responsible for a million different secrets over the time of its history. This is just one more that we'll be responsible for safeguarding. Have some faith. After all, it's your government."

Emily was about to say something else, then thought better of it.

Parlotti turned his attention back to Pitch. He extended his hand and said, "Thank you, Pitch. I appreciate your honesty and your willingness to be helpful. I'm pleased to tell you, you're much more than I expected." Then, Parlotti turned back to Linc. "You do realize, it'll take a bit of time to put these things we've discussed into motion?"

"I don't expect you to drag your feet on this," stated Linc.

"Not at all," replied Parlotti. "I want you to keep these two young people under tight protection for another week. In the meantime, I'll also make arrangements to have some of my own people help in the security coverage, if that's all right with you. It shouldn't be more than a week. Mendosa checks the personal ads every day."

Parlotti turned back to Pitch. "I was serious when I said we want you on our side. I'm prepared to offer you a job with a GS-12 rating."

"What's a GS-12 rating?" asked Pitch.

"It'll be a government job that starts you off around seventy-five thousand a year."

Pitch gave Jennifer a big smile. It quickly faded as he turned back to Parlotti. "Mr. Parlotti," he said with his head down, "I have to be honest with you."

Everyone waited for Pitch to finish responding.

Pitch looked directly at Parlotti and said, "This whole episode has made me very nervous. And fearful. Jennifer's life, as well as my own, has been placed in jeopardy, and we almost got killed on two separate occasions. No offense, but I think I'd be afraid to work for you."

"You wouldn't be working for me, Pitch," explained Parlotti, "I would arrange to have you placed in the middle of the scientific community. Y'know, working with other scientists. Your peers."

"Believe me, Mr. Parlotti," said Pitch, "it sounds quite inviting, but it's something I'll have to think about."

"Of course," said Parlotti as he jotted something down on a small notepad. "I understand. I'd expect you to take your time with this kind of decision. Have you ever heard of Dr. Leonid Bialikoff?"

"Certainly," said Pitch. "He's a giant in the world of science and engineering. Dr. Bialikoff is with the California Institute of Technology in Pasadena. He's developing the next generation of lasers."

"Pretty good," said Parlotti, "but last week he took a position with NASA in Houston. He's part of a long-range think tank developing ideas for our future space program. I know him quite well, and he's told me he's looking for a few bright people to help round out his staff. Would you consider checking out that possibility?"

Pitch was dumfounded by the suggestion. It sounded like a dream come true. He wasn't sure how to respond. He glanced at Linc and Emily, as if they might suddenly have been transformed into Alex Trebek, the man with all the answers.

Jennifer spoke for the first time. "What would you be expecting Peter to do for you in return?" she asked suspiciously.

Parlotti stared at Jennifer and Pitch for a long time. He saw two young people who were stressed from a nightmare of running and hiding. Fear had been their constant companion for the past week. Despite that, Jennifer's question was based on something more than just her trepidation. Jennifer and Pitch were not only suspect and dubious, but also wracked with cynicism. They simply did not trust Parlotti.

Without answering Jennifer's question, Parlotti turned away from the couple, as his eyes swept the rest of the room. He held each one's gaze for just a brief instant before saying, "You know what, people? I'm going to leave it up to all of you to convince these young folks that I'm really a nice man, and that my motives are only based on what's best for the United States of America."

Parlotti turned to Senator Williamson. "Are you ready to go?" he asked abruptly.

Williamson replied, "You go ahead. I'll catch up with you in the lobby."

Parlotti left the room and met up with John Anderson, Gator and the Dutchman. Anderson had been pacing the corridor in frustration during the entire meeting. The two men walked towards the elevator with Gator and Dutch right behind them. Anderson said, "What the hell went on in there, Boss? Where's the Senator?"

Parlotti only answered the second question. "Williamson is just saying his good-byes," replied Parlotti. "He'll meet us in the lobby."

"Okay. So, what went on in there?" Anderson asked again.

Parlotti continued to ignore the question. Instead, he said, "I want you to do two things. First, put a series of ads in the Post, letting Harpoon know that the disc is off the market. Run the ads every day for a week. That should keep him away from Pechowski. Also, remind me to send off a letter to Dr. Bialikoff. I need to let him know about this Pechowski kid. Y'know, the kind of smarts he has. See if Bialikoff can arrange a job for him."

Frustration was building in Anderson. "What the hell happened in there?" he asked a third time, irritated at the lack of response. "You get turned into some kind of boy scout, or what?"

Parlotti had pushed the button for the elevator. He looked at

Anderson and realized he had not told him everything. "Not hardly," he said, biting off his words. "I made a deal. Now, I've got the disc in my pocket. We call off Harpoon, and for that I get to keep the disc and also keep an eye on whatever else the kid comes up with next."

"And that's it?" asked Anderson.

Parlotti looked at Anderson and held his gaze for several seconds. He didn't understand Anderson's question. "You make it sound like we lost," said Parlotti, narrowing his eyes. "Let me tell you something," he continued, as a sneer crept across his face, "this disc I'm holding is going to change the way we've been doing business."

"What do you mean, 'the way we're doing business?'"

A thin smile came to Parlotti's lips. "It's all about having access," he said, tapping his breast pocket. "With this little device, we have it. We can open any door we want. Any door. Any home, any business, any secret hide-a-way. Hell, I'll be able to open the door to the goddamned Oval Office. And no one will even know we're there in the room."

Anderson nodded his approval as he said, "I guess that means we can burn the Boy Scout flag."

"Right," answered Parlotti. "And dance around the goddammed flames."

CHAPTER
FIFTY FOUR

The long hot days of summer were in full bloom. The thermometer sat at ninety-two degrees during the day, along with a humidity level that made sunglasses fog up as soon as one walked out of an air conditioned room. The snow-birds and the tourists had gone home to the north, vowing not to return again until the first signs of frost. The roadways had less traffic and the restaurant lines were not as long. For Floridians, it was a time of tranquility, a respite from the winter's hustle and bustle. The change was nice.

Despite all that, some things did not change. Life went on for most of the local folks in much the same way, regardless of the season. Linc continued to run his agency and Preston continued to throw his parties.

It was Saturday and Linc and Emily were finishing some loose ends at the office. They had new cases to work on and new mysteries to solve. Emily had proven to be a very valuable asset to the business. Not only did she possess an expertise for doing research, but also showed a unique ability to help make the business grow. A dramatic increase in the number of active accounts had required Linc to hire additional help. There was now one more field agent who spent the majority of his time conducting interviews and working undercover. In addition, Linc had hired a "gopher" who was primarily Carmen's assistant.

The others had left the office for the weekend, and Linc and

Emily were preparing to do the same. Emily stopped what she was doing. "Linc," she began, "there's something that's been on my mind, and I'd like to take a moment to talk about it."

"Sure," Linc replied. "What's up?"

"During the time you were recuperating from that Mendosa business, wouldn't you say that I kind of ran the agency?"

Linc paused in the middle of putting some papers in his briefcase and leaned against his desk. "Yeah," he said slowly, not quite sure what was coming next. "Kind of."

"And you even told me," said Emily, "that I did an exemplary job."

"Go on," said Linc, nodding his head.

"You've mentioned on several occasions, that you're very pleased with all the new accounts I've brought into the agency."

"What are you driving at, Emily?"

"I'm trying to express how I feel," said Emily. "You see, when we first talked about me becoming part of your agency, I wasn't referring to being an employee."

"Oh?" questioned Linc.

"My thought was to become an integral part of it. You know what I mean? A piece of the action. I was hoping to have some sort of partnership." Emily pursed her lips and studied Linc's reaction, looking for any sign that might suggest a response; approval, denial, anger, anything that might give her a sign that he understood.

Linc lowered his voice a notch and said sternly, "Emily, I do not want to discuss this matter at this time."

Emily was baffled. She did not expect that response at all. She tried to ask why he felt that way, but he again insisted that the matter was not open for discussion. Emily tried to coax him into an explanation, but to no avail. Linc was adamant. Emily resigned herself to the fact that it was a topic that would have to wait. She had patience. When Linc had left the hospital after his surgery, Emily moved into his place under the thinly veiled guise of his needing her help during his recovery. She never left. Emily realized that their living arrangements left plenty of opportunities to present her views again.

They locked up the office and walked to the parking garage. They talked about the upcoming party that was being given by Preston that night. The theme for the soiree was to congratulate and honor Pitch Pechowski on his achievements at NASA under the tutelage of Dr. Leonid Bialikoff. Pitch had been instrumental in engineering a unique system designed to protect and repair the immense solar panels that were planned to be used in the future of space exploration. His invention consisted of a form of liquid polymer shielding that prevented dust particles and tiny meteorites from tearing the solar panels to shreds. It worked by virtue of the polymer's "oozing" effect, a sort of self-healing process. An exciting by-product was that engineers from different fields were discovering other applications for Pitch's invention. One of its uses was in the field of medical prosthetics. Preston managed to get in on the ground floor of a new company that would be licensed to manufacture the devices. For Preston's finances, it promised to be exceptionally rewarding.

Preston had invited Pitch and Jennifer to be weekend guests at his estate. They were flying in to Palm Beach International Airport that same afternoon. Emily had told her father that she and Linc would pick up the guest of honor. Then, the two couples would arrive at Preston's house in time to have a bite to eat and to change clothes for the party. Pitch and Jennifer would not be returning to Houston until Monday afternoon.

Linc handed his parking pass to the garage attendant and then steered the Corvette towards the airport. At the first red light, Linc said, "Preston told me something about inviting Vincent Parlotti along with Senator Boyd Williamson. Have you heard whether or not they're coming?"

"The last I heard," answered Emily, "was that Boyd Williamson will attend, but not Mr. Parlotti. Something about him never attending social functions."

"I can understand that," said Linc sarcastically. "It isn't considered well-mannered to have a man like that at your party. After all, he might decide to arrange the assassination of your other guests."

Emily giggled.

"Who else is going to be at this party tonight?" asked Linc.

"Several congressmen who are responsible for overseeing the science wing of our government, along with a couple of high ranking officials from NASA. Oh, and let's not forget the usual Palm Beach riff raff, including Countess Erika and her husband, Alexander the Great."

Linc wrinkled his nose at the memory of the Countess Erika squeezing the cheek of his butt. "I'll have to remember not to turn my back on that woman," he joked.

It had been more than three months since Emily and Linc had seen Pitch and Jennifer. When they arrived, it was a warm and wonderful reunion. Linc could not remember seeing either of them so relaxed and confident. Happy to see their friends, Pitch and Jennifer spoke over top of one another, as they related the highlights of their lives since they last saw Linc and Emily.

Jennifer had transferred to Texas Southern University in Houston and was finishing her degree. As for Pitch, he seemed to have found the mystical Shangri-La. Life was good. He loved his job and the environment of working with some of the greatest scientific minds in the world. He told Linc and Emily about a few of the projects he was involved in and about how supportive all of his supervisors and co-workers had been.

Linc said, "You're making us proud, Pitch. We enjoy reading about your accomplishments."

"Thank you," said Pitch.

Jennifer added, "Peter isn't about to tell you this, so I will. Dr. Bialikoff said that if Peter keeps up this level of accomplishment for a few years, his name will be entered into candidacy for the Nobel Prize."

That night the party at Preston's went extraordinarily well. Preston had invited more than seventy people, and everybody had a marvelous time. A five-string ensemble, who kept the mood at a sedate level, provided the music for the first two hours of the party. Then, a giant gong sounded. The guests turned their attention to the center of the room. Preston had gone the extra mile for this particular party and had arranged for a team of professional magicians to perform a special act. The theme of the magic show was physics and rocketry. The performance lasted almost half an hour and everyone found it fascinating, amusing and entertaining. The production received numerous rounds of spontaneous applause and sparked some animated discussions. From that point forward, the music changed. A piano player, who knew how to get everyone's toe tapping, was the center of a four piece jazz combo.

Due to a previous engagement, Sidney Aarons and his wife, Lenore, were not able to attend. However, the Countess Erika and her prissy husband, Alex, were present. Emily worked diligently at steering Linc away from the woman's grappling fingers.

At one point, Senator Boyd Williamson took Linc aside. "Lincoln," he pontificated, "I have a two-part message for you. First, Vincent Parlotti sends his best and says he apologizes for not being able to make it to this gathering. The second part is . . ." at this point Williamson leaned in close and spoke in a conspiratorial whisper, "he wants you to give him a call on Monday morning at precisely ten-twenty-two a.m."

Linc asked Williamson what it was that Parlotti wanted to discuss, but the Senator claimed not to know.

At eleven p.m., the band played a short fanfare, and the lights were lowered. Manfred wheeled out a rolling cart with two gigantic cakes. Each was multi-tiered and had sparklers showering the air with pin points of glee. Big bouquets of buttercream flowers cascaded down the sides of the luscious desserts. Gathering around to read the inscriptions, everyone saw that one cake said: "To Pitch, our Future Nobel Laureate." The second cake was inscribed: "To Emily, Congratulations on your Partnership."

The crowd broke into applause. Looking to her father for an explanation, Preston pointed to where Linc was standing. Emily turned and, with a look of confusion, asked, ""What's this all about, Linc?"

"It's about you becoming Vice President of the Bradshaw Agency," he said with a warm smile. "It comes with a full partnership and a paid membership to the Palm Beach Country Club."

"Oh, my God!" she squealed as she threw her arms around him.

Reminding Emily of her earlier request, he said, "You almost made me spill the beans this afternoon."

After cutting her cake, Emily turned to thank Linc once again, only to find him talking on his cell phone. Eleven o'clock on a Saturday night seemed to be a strange hour to be getting a phone call. The guests surrounding the ceremony broke into laughter as Pitch fed a dollop of icing to Jennifer.

The party crowd began filtering out about half-past midnight, and by one-thirty in the morning only Linc, Emily, Pitch, Jennifer and Preston were left. They were sitting on the curved sectional in the living room and savoring the memories of a grand celebration. Jennifer was humming the last strains of "Take the A-Train" when Pitch asked, "Any word on Mendosa?"

"He seems to have disappeared," answered Linc. "Absolutely no sign of him in the States. The last word I got from the NSA was that one of their people thought they spotted him in Belize. There's a large Asian contingent which has moved into that country, and Washington thinks that he might somehow be connected with that group."

At the same time, Pitch and Jennifer reached out to hold each other's hand. "By the way," said Pitch getting comfortable by slumping down in the seat, "how's your friend Eddie Strickland? Is he still on the police force?"

Linc told Pitch about Eddie. Not only was he still with the Sheriff's Department, but he was doing rather well. It turned out that his nemesis, Captain Baumgarten, had taken a position with another police department somewhere out west. Linc thought it might have been Denver. Linc went on to say that Eddie had been working on the John Krum rape case and had had some success.

Emily chimed in to say that Eddie and Laura Parsons had become quite the couple and seemed to be like two peas in a pod.

Pitch sat up and leaned forward. "The John Krum rape case," he said pensively. "That was the last thing Scott wrote about, remember? That villainous Krum and his lawyer were trying to negotiate a deal for some kind of immunity. What was the outcome of that farce?"

"There was no deal," replied Linc, shaking his head as he spoke. "The D.A. was able to uncover the truth without Krum's help. The trial went quickly, and Krum was sentenced to die."

Emily picked up the story. "Of course, we expect to see the appeals process kick in. So, it will probably be years before he . . ."

Jennifer interrupted, "I thought for sure he was going to get off. What happened?"

Linc and Emily looked at each other. Emily decided to answer the question. "If you recall," she said, "Krum had claimed to have information about the Blakely murders. You know, the murder of the widow Jeanne Blakely and her two teenage daughters?"

Pitch and Jennifer both nodded.

"Well," continued Emily, "Laura and Eddie teamed up in order to put pressure on Krum. After all, he was bragging that he had information about the killer. If you remember, everyone was prepared to give Krum a deal on his rape charge in return for that information."

"Yes," said Jennifer somberly, "we remember."

"Well," said Emily, "Krum told everyone that the Blakely murder was committed by none other than my ex-husband, Jubal Salaran!"

"Are you joking?" asked Jennifer.

Preston interjected, "I knew he was bad all along, but I honestly didn't think he would go that far."

"Hold on a moment," said Pitch, holding one finger in the air. "If your ex-husband was the killer . . . how come John Krum got sentenced to death?"

Linc took over the telling of the story. "Once everyone became aware that Jube was the killer, they came down on him like a sledgehammer. But, guess what? He had a different story to tell."

Preston added, "He was always good at weaseling his way out of tight spots."

Emily ignored her father's comment and said, "It turns out that John Krum and my ex-husband were buddy-buddy. They had this scam going. You see, Jubal was a tennis instructor, and he and Krum worked together. While Jubal was teaching the residents of the estate how to hit top-spin, Krum was upstairs pilfering the family jewels."

Emily paused to let the drama of her statement sink in.

Linc picked up the tale. "It seems that Jube used to teach tennis to one of the Blakely girls. She probably became infatuated with him and, well . . . one thing led to another." Linc stopped himself from going into any sordid details. "Anyway, he confessed to having sex with the girl. Now, while that was going on in one bedroom, Krum was down the hall, in a different bedroom, heisting some gold necklaces. Pretty soon, he comes waltzing in, sees what's going on and wants his turn with the teenager. In the middle of all this, the Blakeley woman and her other daughter came home and found them. That's when Krum killed them all."

Preston added, "They were good people."

Jennifer directed her next question to Emily. "What happened to your ex-husband?"

Before Emily could reply, Preston answered with a smile, "Twenty years to life."

"So," said Pitch, "John Krum was just trying to point the finger of guilt at your ex-husband even though he, himself, was the murderer."

"Correct," said Emily. "Not only was it designed to divert attention away from himself for the murder, but also to get him off of the charge of raping that little eleven year old."

Preston said, "At least now, he'll fry in Florida's notorious electric chair."

Unable to keep from expressing her view, Jennifer said, "I wish they would stop all capital punishment, especially the electric chair. It's so barbaric."

"I have this idea," said Pitch, "for a different type of electric chair. This one would work on an entirely new principal . . ."

Preston interrupted. "I'd like to hear more about this liquid polymer you've invented," he said rubbing his hands together. "Are you going to be coming up with any new products as a result of your research?"

"Wait, wait, wait," said Jennifer holding up her hands as though she were directing traffic. "This is supposed to be a social evening, not a scientific symposium. We're here to enjoy the camaraderie and affection of good friends. Not to discuss your inventions."

Linc looked at Preston and began to chuckle at the man's expression of rejection. Like a little boy who had just been told that he could not have a lollipop, Preston slumped into his seat with the look of defeat etched into his face.

"Now, Preston," Linc said with a big smile, "don't be so

disappointed. After all, wasn't it one of Pitch's inventions that started all that trouble in the first place?"

Pitch added, "A better way of putting that would be that it almost cost all of us an early demise."

Trying to remember and elusive thought, Linc asked, "Didn't you have some kind of name for that little device of yours?"

Pitch nodded his head and sheepishly said, "During an errant moment of grandeur, I named it The Ultimate Bug."

There was something about the utterance of that name that cast a reflective mood over the five of them.

Emily was first to break the momentary silence. "Pitch," she said with conviction, "you should have called it The Ultimate Corrupter. That would have been more appropriate."

"I don't know about that," said Jennifer in preparation for her version. "Everything about that device smacked so much of 'Big Brother,' it should have been called The Ultimate Intruder."

Holding up a hand from his slumped position, Preston ventured, "I vote for The Ultimate Moneymaker."

All eyes turned to Linc for his recommendation. He looked at each of the people he had come to know so well and just smiled.

It was getting late and time for everyone to turn in for the night. They said their good-byes and ended with the promise of seeing each other the next day. Linc and Emily saw themselves out.

Hesitating before sliding into the Corvette's passenger seat, Emily said, "When I was cutting my cake this evening, you were on your cell phone. Who was calling so late on a Saturday night?"

"It was Demetrius Kaltarakis, said Linc.

"Demetrius?" exclaimed Emily, recalling the day Linc took her around and introduced some of the people he worked with. "He's the Greek gentleman who deals with international shipping, right?"

"That's right," replied Linc. "He sends his best to you."

"That's all well and good," said Emily, smiling with the recollection of Mr. Kaltarakis kissing her hand during their meeting, "but I'm sure that isn't why he called so late on a Saturday night."

"You're right," said Linc.

"Then, what was the urgency?"

"He needs our help," stated Linc. "We're going to be taking off for your old European stomping grounds. You'd better brush up on all those covert code names and passwords you learned from NATO."

ACKNOWLEDGEMENTS

Helen Stillman, for her unfailing belief in my ability and her gentle push to start me on this project. Her help in dressing the characters and in decorating the scenes was wonderful. Her talent will be sorely and forever missed.

Dr. Charles Stillman, for his medical expertise, his capacity for logic and, of course, his sharp sense of humor, sharpened by his reading of the first draft. Mostly, I want to acknowledge the unique way in which he was able to thrust his finger into my gray matter and bring me wide awake.

Ilisa Stillman, for her enthusiasm, energy and overall excitement about this project. Her work experience in NATO's environment proved to be invaluable. I also thank her for helping me understand the convolutions of undercover, investigative work.

Michelle Stillman, for her patience in schooling me in the intricacies of Microsoft Word. Her editorial comments made key paragraphs more realistic. I am also indebted to the timeliness of her jokes.

Pearl Davidow, Queen of the Crosswords, for her inexhaustible cistern of facts, both significant and insignificant.

Pasco County Sheriff's Deputy, James Fiedler, for his clear-cut verbal pictures of what police work is all about.

Daniel Davidow, for a lifetime of original quotes that are sometimes funny, sometimes biting and sometimes poignant, but always hit the mark.

Dr. Rosalyn Secor, for her multi-lingual expertise and her skill at getting me to think like a Frenchman and a Spaniard. Her tireless dedication to editing the book gave the story a flow it desperately needed.

A special thank you to Dan Hamlin, Edith Krum, Angelo DiVita, Merriam Fredd and Roland Reigel for recognizing my potential. An additional heap of gratitude to Howie Pomerantz, Bill Bendell, Marge Friedman, Jean Chipp, Bill Smith, Sue Sellack, Doug Dymond, Gail Christiana, Sandi Schonger, Diane Doyle, Frank Spada, Liz Crossman, Bob Misner, Bill Stone and all the rest of my teachers and fellow students who helped me spend an idyllic youth hidden away in the mists of the Rondout Valley.

And finally, I wish to acknowledge my friend, my dear friend, Bob Maher, whose well-spring of knowledge rivaled that of an encyclopedia. His theories on politics, economics and social science were fascinating and stimulating. But his charm was in the fact that his ideas were always presented with the enthusiasm of a little boy on a carousel.